WAGE$
OF
GREED

STEVEN J. CLARK

ISBN:978-0-9914869-7-7

In memoriam:

Anthony G. "Tony" Hillerman

1925 – 2008

You created the genre and became its master.

Bon voyage dear friend. We miss you more than

words can say.

DEDICATED TO MY DEAR WIFE, LAURI.

Thanks for your endless patience, unrelenting support, and your belief in me as a writer.

ACKNOWLEDGMENTS

Special thanks to my editors, Tristi Pinkston, Shirley & Bob Bahlmann, Amy Jones, and Sue Player for their expertise and extraordinary attention to detail. To Terry and Suzie Eustice, you were there at the beginning and loved me enough to believe this could happen. To Dennis and Kathy Phipps, you opened your hearts and your home, I love you and think of you every day. To my dear friend, Pamela Keen, you kept this going and kept me sane. To my beta-readers, Laci Warby, Shar Hess, Dr. David Rosier, Lynne Harris, Gayla Eakins, Leslie Christofferson, Laura Christensen, Ellen Lee, Patricia Contreras, Karen Schowalter, Patty Delight, Susan Riva Miller, and Natalie Zabriskie, thanks for your sharp eyes.

And finally to Nicki, who came home one cold and rainy day in 1979, when I was a lowly electrical contractor, and found me hunched over a typewriter (remember those) tapping out the first few paragraphs of this book. She asked me what I was doing and I told her, "I'm writing a book." Her incredulity and skepticism were priceless. God love you, Nicki, yes, I really could do this. I pray you are well.

For my children, Rebecca, Carrie, Darren, Ryan, Laci, Morgan, Erika, Lane, Holly and Michael. I love you all

Glossary of Navajo Terms

Atse': Meat from a sheep, usually a lamb or ewe, which is a staple of the Navajo diet.

BIA: Acronym for the Bureau of Indian Affairs.

Bilagaana: The name the Diné call the white man.

BLM: Acronym for the Bureau of Land Management

Chindi: The ghost of a recently departed Diné. Chindi may be benevolent or hostile. It is believed that someone's Chindi remains close for some time after death and that mentioning the name of the dead person or remaining close to their burial place can lead to a person being haunted by the Chindi.

Diné (The People): The actual name of the people known to the world as the Navajo. The word 'Navajo' is derived from the Spanish phrase *Apachu de Nabajo,* an adaption of the Tewa, *navahū* meaning, "fields near the ravine."

Dinétah: The land claimed as the ancestral home of the Diné. It is the land that lies between the four sacred mountains which are:

> *Tsisnaasjini* Mount Blanca (sacred mountain of the east) near Alamosa, CO
>
> *Tsoodzil* Mount Taylor (sacred mountain of the south) near Grants, NM
>
> *Doko'oosliid* San Francisco Peaks (sacred mountain of the west) near Flagstaff, AZ
>
> *Dibé Nitsaa* Mount Hesperus (sacred mountain of the north) near Durango, CO

Hooghan: Known in English as a hogan. Until the wide-scale introduction of modern U.S. housing to the reservation, families typically resided in a hooghan. It is a six or eight-sided structure traditionally constructed of juniper or pinion' uprights at each corner. Sticks were latticed between the uprights and the sidewalls plastered with mud. The roof was constructed in the same manner. Hooghans have one door, always facing east toward the rising sun. If someone dies in a hooghan, the north wall is destroyed and no one lives in the structure thereafter out of fear the Chindi of the dead person will haunt them.

Hozho: Harmony. Restoring a person's harmony is frequently the object of 'sings,' ceremonies intended to heal a person's damaged or haunted spirit.

Ma'ii: Coyote. Also known as the 'Trickster.' Coyotes are regarded as being very intelligent and capricious. They are held in high regard by the Diné.

NALM: An acronym for <u>N</u>ative <u>A</u>merican <u>L</u>iberation <u>M</u>ovement, a fictional paramilitary group created by the author for the purposes of this book.

Reservation: Its slang term is 'rez'. At nearly 14 million acres, the Navajo reservation is the largest in the country. Roughly the size of West Virginia, it covers nearly all of northeastern Arizona, southeastern Utah south of the San Juan River, and a sizable chunk of northwestern New Mexico. Indian reservations are considered sovereign nations by the federal government, but are administered as a federal protectorate. They have many of the same rights as states do.

Navajo Names: Modern Diné have their own native name and an adopted American name. I have used the American name adaptation for characters in this book.

INTRODUCTION

Though this book is a work of fiction, history, ironically, has made it more a book of prophesy than just the fanciful musings of its author. I have a great love for the Navajo people. From the mid-nineteen fifties through the early sixties I spent my summers working for my grandfather, Fred Mecham, on his farm in Genola, Utah. Each year the Sam Johnson family, cousins and uncles included, would come from the Navajo reservation to thin our sugar beets. I became great friends with their son, Bobby, and at age 15, developed quite a crush on their daughter, Lena. I wish I knew where Bobby and Lena were today.

Like many my age, as a child, I played endless games of cowboys and Indians. In my games, the Indians always lost. Later I learned that the truth about American Indians was not what was depicted in the heroic images displayed on the silver screen. Rather, it was a story of serial mendacity, exploitation, and betrayal, perpetrated by the very people whose duty it was, (and is,) to preserve and protect their interests.

In 1975, I conceived the storyline for this book out of thin air while driving between Durango, Colorado and Farmington, New Mexico. In 1978, I was again driving, this time in California, when I heard a news broadcast telling of a settlement the Navajo Nation had made with Mobile Oil and others over unpaid royalties. The broadcast sounded as if it had come straight from my story.

Life happened and the book languished unfinished for years. Fast forward to 2014. After publishing my debut novel *(All The Pretty Dresses)* in early February, my thoughts turned once again to the book I had started so many years ago. I (figuratively) dusted off my manuscript file with the determination that this would become my second published book. As I updated it from its 1979 version, I was concerned that the story might be out-of-date. But in September, just as I was writing the final words, imagine my surprise when I heard yet another radio broadcast that told me *Wages of Greed* was perhaps more timely and relevant than it had been in 1979. The newscast cited a press release, dated September 14th, 2014, saying that the Navajo Nation had just reached a $554 million dollar settlement for, among other things, the non-payment of oil and gas royalties to the tribe.

So, dear reader, as you turn the pages of Wages of Greed, understand that while the characters are fictitious, and many of the details are the product of literary artistic license, the underlying story behind *Wages of Greed* has almost entirely come true. For more details, see my Author's Comments at the end of the book.

STEVEN J. CLARK

Chapter 1

"BOOM!"

Ear-splitting sound waves reverberated off the sheer, thirty-foot walls of the isolated wash fifteen miles southwest of Shiprock, New Mexico. Though the sound was confined to the immediate area, there was no hiding the cloud of fire and smoke that curled hundreds of feet into the air.

"It works!" Eddie Nez exclaimed as he sprinted from behind the bend in the wash where he, Albert Horseman, and David Nakai had found protection from the blast.

"Aieeeee. There's nothing left," Albert shouted as the trio skidded to a halt at the edge of the ten-foot-wide crater.

"Where'd the pipe go?" David asked.

Earlier, while Eddie had attached the detonator to the three explosive-filled fuel cans, David and Albert cobbled together a collection of rusty pipes into something that approximated a natural gas wellhead. That was the structure to which the bomb was attached. Now all that was left was a crater where the pipe had been.

Their first full-scale test came off perfectly. Eddie nodded his head in satisfaction, remembering the hours he'd spent on the Internet, researching bomb-making techniques. A stack of discarded timers on his back porch told the story of the difficulty of finding just the right one he could modify into a safe and reliable detonator. In the end, it was the simplest and cheapest wind-up kitchen timer from Walmart that did the trick. The only metal parts were the timing spring, the bell and the clapper. With a wire soldered to the clapper and another to the bell, when the timer reached zero the clapper struck the bell and the electrical circuit was complete. But that had to happen only when they wanted it to. If there was the slightest contact between the bell and the clapper at the wrong time, Eddy and everyone around him would be dead in an instant.

Then there was getting the mix of fertilizer and diesel fuel just right. Eddie's first test was with a quarter cup of each mixed in a frying pan on his kitchen stove. He ignited the concoction with the bare ends of an extension cord. The *whoosh* that resulted wasn't so much an explosion as a ball of fire that boiled up and rolled across the ceiling. With singed hair and eyebrows, Nez found himself beating out a half-dozen tiny fires that threatened to burn his trailer to the ground. It was the last experiment he conducted indoors.

Their largest previous test was conducted in a hole in the sand on the bank of the San Juan River a couple of miles out of town. It used three plastic peanut butter jars to simulate the fuel cans. It was loud enough to make their ears ring and had told them that their detonator and pasty explosive concoction worked.

"What a difference," Eddie said, staring into the still smoking crater.

"Like dynamite compared to a fire cracker," Albert agreed.

"Where's the pipe?" David asked again.

"Let's go find it!" Eddie said. "Albert, you and I will head south. David, you go north."

The banks on both sides of the arroyo near the blast were cratered by shrapnel. They searched for some distance before finding anything recognizable.

Ninety feet from the crater, Albert said, "Got something." He pointed at a mangled piece of pipe sticking out of the dirt wall about ten feet up.

"Right here," Eddie heard David shout from the other direction. He was nearly a hundred yards on the other side of the crater, pointing at the floor of the wash.

There should have been more. Apparently the main body of pipework had been blown over the sides of the wash and now lay scattered on the desert floor above.

"Man, that was huge," David exulted when they gathered back at the crater. "I say we do it now — tonight!"

"No." Eddie said. "We all agreed this would be strictly a last resort. We wait until after the next NALM meeting. If we don't hear what needs to be said there, then we go."

"I don't understand you," Horseman replied. "You just buried your grandfather and yet you want everybody to sit back and keep taking it?"

The question brought Eddie an all-too-familiar stab of pain and anger. Five years ago, when Gannon Oil had drilled the gas well on his grandfather's land allotment, the well money transformed Grandfather's life. He and Grandmother moved out of the old family *Hooghan* into one of those new pre-fab houses the government provided that had indoor plumbing and electricity. Instead of a fireplace, he could heat the house simply by adjusting the thermostat on a propane furnace.

There was enough money for a pickup truck and for food bought from the store in Shiprock. Grandfather sold off his flock of sheep, but kept a few chickens around, because Grandfather liked chickens.

But two years ago, everything changed. The oil company turned off the well and the flow of money ceased. His grandparents went from riches to rags in a matter of weeks. When the money ran out, so did the propane, and there was no fireplace. When the truck ran out of gas, there was no way into town to purchase the store-bought food for which there was no money anyway. When the last of the chickens ran out, Grandfather was reduced to hunting jackrabbits to feed himself and Grandmother. But Grandfather was silent about all of this, and Eddie didn't discover it until it was too late.

In January, the moon of crusted snow, Eddie discovered the depths of his grandparents' misery. Visiting their place for the first time in more than a month, he was concerned when Grandfather failed to answer the door. Breaking Navajo courtesy that respected privacy, he opened the door and called in, "Grandfather, it's Eddie. Are you here?" He stepped in and closed the door against the cold, bracing wind. But closing the door did nothing to take away the chill.

This house is too cold. Then he realized it was also dark. The sun had set more than a half hour before, but not a light burned anywhere inside. *What's happened to the electricity? This is definitely not right.* He called out again, louder this time. "Grandfather, it's Eddie. Are you home?"

Silence.

Someone must have come by and picked them up. He turned to leave, then he thought he heard something. Was it his grandparents or had some evil spirit, somehow gotten into the house? Hesitant and watchful, he walked toward the sound. He found his grandparents lying in their bed, covered with blankets. His Grandfather recognized him, but the man was so weak from thirst, hunger and cold that he could barely raise his arm to gesture for Eddie to come in. Tears flowed from the old man's eyes. "Your grandmother," he whispered. "I think she is dead." Indeed she was.

After a week in the BIA hospital in Farmington, Eddie's grandfather ended up in the nursing home in Shiprock, but only for a few months. He never fully recovered. He missed his wife of more than fifty years. On the last day of his life he told Eddie how he wished he had never allowed the *Bilagaana* to drill the gas well on his land. He grasped Eddie's hand and told him in a tortured whisper, "The well is cursed with an evil spirit. Before you sing me onto the Shining Path, promise me that you will get rid of the *Bilagaana* well before anyone else tries to live on my land."

Eddie leaned over and whispered the great secret he carried, of his plan to get rid of not just that well, but all the others if the oil company wouldn't turn them back on. The old man's grip tightened. His eyes lit up for the first time in months. Grandfather and grandson sang the warrior's battle song so loud and long that a nurse finally came and shushed them.

The next morning, Grandfather was dead. As far as Eddie was concerned, Gannon Oil had killed his grandparents as surely as if they had held a gun to their heads and pulled the trigger.

Eddie ached for revenge. But the warrior in him knew he had to act smart, like *Ma'ii*, the coyote. "Don't worry, Albert," Eddie said to his companion. We will listen carefully at the next NALM meeting. Then we will decide whether to use what we have learned to make the well on my grandfather's land disappear. We will burn this desert down around Gannon Oil's ears if we have to! But for now, let's get out of here before someone comes around to investigate that smoke cloud.

Chapter 2
One year earlier

All morning long he'd tried for a different result. But no matter how many times Danny re-calculated the numbers, they always came out the same. He was one hundred and twenty-two dollars shy of being able to make Kathy's full paycheck. It was the third week in a row she'd end up short.

He sighed. *Maybe the public defender fees will show up.* Not likely. That check hadn't been on time in years.

Danny usually heard everything going on out in the reception area of his small, two-room office on the second floor of a rundown building in a seedy Farmington commercial district. But his concentration on the money problem was so intense that he was taken by surprise when Kathy escorted an older Navajo couple into his office.

"Danny, this is Mr. Robert Begay and his wife, Lena," Kathy said. "Mr. and Mrs. Begay, this is my boss, Danny Whitehorse."

Danny scrambled to gather the papers spread across his desk into something resembling order as he rose to greet the couple.

"*Hosteen* Begay." Danny used the honorific showing the respect due an elder of the tribe. "Welcome to my office. Please sit down." He indicated the two worn wingback chairs against the wall in front of his desk.

There was no handshake. That was a white man's custom. Robert wore a long-sleeved flannel shirt tucked into worn blue jeans and a pair of ancient-looking leather cowboy boots. He nervously turned a black, broad-brimmed hat in his ham-sized hands. He held his eyes turned just slightly away from Danny's feet, as Navajo greeting tradition demanded.

Lena was probably of an age with Robert, but her wrinkled face and toothless smile made her appear older. She wore a long-sleeved, cream-colored shirt, and an ankle-length, gold-velvet skirt that had seen far too many years. Her hammered silver Concho belt and turquoise squash-blossom necklace were likely her richest possessions.

Robert's eyes darted warily about, as if he had no idea what to do in such a foreign place. The couple reminded Danny of his Aunt Ona and Uncle Samuel who still lived in the traditional Navajo *hooghan* where Danny had been raised, forty-five miles southeast of Farmington near the reservation village of Nageezi.

After exchanging the respectful courtesies and family information called for in the greeting formalities of the *Diné*, Danny asked, "How may I help you Mr. Begay?"

The man reached into a shirt pocket and withdrew two crumpled envelopes. He unfolded them then hesitantly handed one to Danny. Speaking in the clipped accent of older generation Navajos, he quietly said, "A man, a *Bilagaana*, come to my home and give me this paper. He say paper makes it so he can take my pickup truck away. I need my truck to find work, so I chased him away. But he say he will come back. I do not read the *Bilagaana* words, so my son, Nathan, he read this for me. Nathan says it lets the man take away my truck. My brother told me what you do for work and that you can help us, so I come to tell you about this."

Danny opened the envelope to find a writ of repossession issued by a local court in favor of Farmington's Chevrolet dealership. He was moderately surprised to see that it was for a newer model truck. Few older generation *Diné* had vehicles that cost this much. "When did you buy this truck?" he asked.

"I have this truck almost one and a half years."

"And you are behind on your payments. Is that correct?"

Begay's head lowered. "Yes," he whispered.

Danny knew the confession was costing the man an enormous emotional price. Debt was a rare thing among the reservation's older generations. The ability to honor debts was one of the basic elements of a man's pride. Robert Begay was clearly being crushed under his own sense of dishonor and shame.

Danny spoke in Navajo to make the man more comfortable. Lifting the paper in his hand he said, "Obviously this rude *Bilagaana* does not know you, Grandfather. If he did, he would know that you would give honor to this debt."

The man looked up sharply, surprised at the unexpected praise. "I have always given honor to my debts," he said, "and I shall give honor to this one. But the company stopped sending us money before I finish paying for my truck. To earn money I need a job. A job is very hard to find for *Diné*, especially one as old as I am."

"Company? What company is that, Grandfather? Did you lose your job?"

"Gannon Oil Company," Robert replied. "I do not work for them. They drilled a gas well on my land and send me money every month. Three months ago, we get no money. They have sent no money since, so I cannot send money for our truck. It is very bad." The man's shoulders drooped again. His wife dabbed at tears with the corner of her shawl.

"So they pay you royalties. Is that right?"

"Yes. Royalty is the right word."

"Did they tell you this was going to happen?"

"No! In moon of crusted snow, the one the Bilagaana call January, a man from company come to our house and say they need to work on our well. Soon many men come with big machines. They dig all around and put a new pipe into the ground. Then they try to make everything look like it was before.

"In the moon of squeaky voice, we wait for money but it doesn't come. We get this instead." Robert handed Danny the other crumpled envelope.

The envelope contained a one-page letter dated March 1st. Across the top it said, "NOTICE OF CESSATION OF PRODUCTION." It stated that due to "depletion of gas production capacity," the Gannon Oil Company was exercising its option to cease production from the well located on the Begay property. It cited several paragraphs in the lease terms as their authority to do so.

"I'm afraid it's not good news, Mr. Begay. Gannon Oil has turned off the well on your land."

"Why? We did not tell them they can turn off our well."

"They think there's not enough gas left in the well to continue using it. Do you have your lease documents with you?"

"What is this thing you call 'lease'?"

"The *Bilagaana* should have given you papers to sign that gave the oil company permission to drill on your property."

"Yes. They give me some papers. I wrote my mark on them but I do not know what they say. I wrapped them up and put them in a box. I will bring them to you tomorrow."

"Good. I'll look at them and call the oil company to see what I can learn. I can't make you any promises, but regardless of what the oil company says, I can keep the car company from taking your truck—at least for a while. You did the right thing by coming to me."

The man stood. "You are a good man, Danny Whitehorse. I know your Uncle Samuel. He raised you well." He paused a moment and shook his head. "These *Bilagaana* are very strange. They send many people and big machines to work on a well that they are going to turn off. Why not just turn it off and not spend so much money?"

"I don't have an answer, Mr. Begay. But I'll try to find out."

"Have the others come to talk to you?"

"Others?"

"Others have had the same thing happen. It is very bad."

"How many others?"

Robert shook his head sadly. "Many," he said. "Very many."

Chapter 3

Danny was puzzled. Why did Gannon pay the Begays in the first place? Land on the reservation belonged to the tribe, not to individual tribe members. The tribe made land allotments to individual families or, in the cases of cities, to larger groups. The allotments worked like a lease. Individuals or families could live on the land allotment, but they did not own the land.

A little research explained the mystery. In 1978, a near rebellion by tribal members living in the north on Utah's Aneth oil field, forced a policy change. Thereafter, allotment holders were included in oil leases and pipeline rights-of-ways.

As Danny read the lease papers Robert delivered, he discovered that Gannon Oil agreed to pay the allotment holders a 3% premium over and above the normal 70/30 split of royalties between the tribe and the allotment holders.

Gannon must have wanted these leases in a hurry. Having the allotment holder on Gannon's side would have made the tribe's normally glacially slow approval process move a little faster.

Then Danny's heart sank as he read the language that stopped everything cold. It said that Gannon Oil could ". . . terminate or cease production solely at the Company's discretion." It was unambiguous and unassailable. If Gannon decided to turn off a well, neither the tribe nor the allotment holder had any say in the matter.

Maybe there was a loophole. He called tribal headquarters in

Window Rock, Arizona, a hundred and twenty-five miles southwest of Farmington. The call was forwarded three times before he finally spoke with an official from the Office of Tribal Natural Resources. "Yes, Mr. Whitehorse," the man responded politely, "those well shut-offs are not just at Eagle Dome but on Tabletop Mesa too. It's costing the tribe millions in lost revenues."

"Has anyone investigated this?" Danny asked.

"I'm just as concerned as you are, but the tribe doesn't have money for such an investigation—and we wouldn't know where to start if we did. That gas royalty money pays my salary. I'm not sure I'll even have a job next year."

Danny thanked the man for his time. *Might as well go straight to the source.* He dialed Gannon Oil. His call was forwarded to someone named Lucas Blackthorn who introduced himself as Gannon's Chief of Security. *Why are they sending me to a security officer rather than a production or accounting person?*

"Mr. Whitehorse, those fields have simply been over-pumped and need to regenerate," Blackthorn said. "A few years from now we may be able to frack some of them to get more production, but for now there's just not enough gas left in those wells to justify their continued operation."

"How long do you expect the wells to be off?"

"If we let that field lay fallow for ten or fifteen years, we may eventually get some production capacity back, but until then, all bets are off."

Danny gasped. "Ten or fifteen years? Those people have to wait that long?"

"I'm afraid so. Unfortunately geology is on a much slower timetable than you or I."

Danny didn't like it, but had to accept the explanation. The next day he prevailed upon a local rancher to take Robert Begay on as a ranch hand. To stave off creditors, he filed a Chapter 13 bankruptcy petition in behalf of the Begays and took the fees out of his own nearly empty pocket. He had saved the Begays' truck, at least for now. Danny knew the humble man and his quiet wife would eventually pay him back.

Chapter 4

Lucas Blackthorn hung up the phone, swiveled one-hundred-eighty-degrees in his office chair and looked out on the city through the floor-to-ceiling smoked-glass windows that comprised the back wall of his sixth-floor office.

Perched on edge of the river bluff, the oval-shaped, black glass structure as long as a football field dominated the Farmington skyline. The edifice sat by itself between the bluff and Airport Boulevard. Red Gannon, an avid flyer even at his advanced age of eighty-one years, made sure the building had its own private taxiway from the airport side to accommodate his two personal jets.

Ever since the day he and Red Gannon kicked off the Cayman project, Blackthorn had expected such a phone call, but he was surprised that the tribe wasn't the first to complain. While individual families were losing a few thousand each, the tribe was losing millions. He smiled. *Those idiots just roll over and let us do anything we want.*

He couldn't help but think how much better his life had been ever since meeting Red Gannon in 1977. Gannon already had a twenty-year reputation as one of the Texas Panhandle's most ruthless wildcatters. When things got too hot for him there, he cast his eye on New Mexico. Natural gas reserves had been known about for years east of Farmington, but playing a hunch, he drilled his first well on the reservation eighteen miles southwest of town, where prying eyes couldn't see. His well, Eagle Dome #1, revealed a vast new gas field across the Navajo reservation boundary, where none was thought to be.

Marion Lucas Blackthorn, grew up poor in Goodland, Kansas. His first name subjected him to endless teasing, causing too many fights to remember in grade school. He was constantly in trouble with teachers and administrators, but he earned an early reputation on the playground as a hard-knuckled scrapper.

He insisted that everyone call him Lucas instead of that other sissy name. He grew up big, lean, and quick-tempered. Kids learned by hard experience that Lucas Blackthorn was not someone you messed with — nor ever called Marion.

His dad was a hopeless, abusive alcoholic who couldn't hold a job, and took his failures out on Lucas and his mother. He was sixteen when his mother died. A week later, when his drunken father tried to take after him with a tire iron, Lucas left him crumpled and bloody in the front yard. It was the first time he had ever stood up to the man.

He quit school and left home, making his way from job to job until he ended up in Farmington, New Mexico, a big, brash eighteen-year-old with a chip on his shoulder and a short fuse. He hired on as a roughneck on Red Gannon's Eagle Dome #1. When Gannon let out word that he needed some muscle to help keep the workers' mouths shut about his new strike, Lucas was more than happy to oblige.

Rumor had it that one of the men was trying to peddle his knowledge of the discovery. When the man failed to show up for work three days in a row, Gannon asked Blackthorn about it. "You don't want to know," was Lucas' curt reply. Two days later the man's badly beaten body was discovered on the banks of the San Juan River two miles west of Farmington. The message to everyone was clear.

Gannon tried to keep his discovery secret while he bought up all the leases he could, including signing a contract with the tribe that gave him exclusive natural gas leasing rights on the reservation between Farmington and the Arizona border.

As Gannon punched in more wells, he began searching the reservation for more gas — this time up on Tabletop Mesa, north of Shiprock. The man's luck was uncanny. The gas reserves there proved even larger than at Eagle Dome.

When the inevitable news of the vast strike leaked out, companies like Chevron, Tenneco and Shell all showed up. But Gannon had his leases, and his agreement with the tribe, which meant he had the reservation all to himself.

Blackthorn's job as chief head-knocker pretty much ended once word of the strike got out, but Gannon didn't want to let such a useful kid go. "Lucas," he said, "I'm sending you to school." It was one of Gannon's more profitable investments—for both men. Today his official title was vice-president in charge of security. But in fact, he was Gannon's second in command, ahead even of Gannon Oil's figurehead president, Jim Parker.

Blackthorn smiled to himself. *Not bad for a kid whose only beginning assets were a hard head and two fists.*

The attorney's call hardly qualified as a threat. Just the same, Blackthorn picked up his phone and dialed Ben Whittington, the head of Gannon's legal department. "Whittington," he barked, "tell me what you know about a local attorney by the name of Danny Whitehorse."

"Can't say I've ever heard of him. Why?"

"Nothing important. He called and asked me about one of our wells out on the rez."

"Is there a problem I should know about?"

Whittington knew nothing of the Cayman project. "No, no. I'm just curious. Find out what you can about him and have a report on my desk by noon tomorrow."

I'd better mention this at the next Cayman meeting. He unlocked the one drawer in his desk that he kept locked and withdrew a file, the briefing file he used in his meetings with Gannon. He scrawled a note on a sticky pad that said simply, "Whitehorse," and stuck it to the front. Within minutes, the Whitehorse phone call was completely out of his mind.

Chapter 5

As word on the reservation spread that Danny Whitehorse had saved the Begay pickup truck, the 'many others' Robert Begay had spoken of started showing up. What began as a trickle of indigent *Diné* families became a river, then a tidal wave that threatened to overwhelm the scant resources of Danny's tiny practice.

"What are we going to do?" Kathy moaned after one of a seemingly endless series of client interviews. "I've got three more couples waiting in the hallway."

Danny shook his head. "I wish I knew. What's the client count up to?"

"I think we'll pass two hundred and eighty today."

When is this ever going to end? "Is Chaco having any success?" Danny used his cousin Chaco as a part-time investigator. Chaco was a man caught between two worlds. His father was Danny's uncle, the youngest of the previous generation of Whitehorse sons. But his mother was a blonde, blue-eyed white woman from Oklahoma. She, Chaco's father and Danny's father suffered from the same malady, too much affection for the bottle.

Chaco's mixed race heritage left him with a lighter complexion than most of the Diné and with striking blue eyes.

Two years after Danny's father died, Chaco's father suffered the same fate. On her way back to Oklahoma, Chaco's mother appeared at Uncle Samuel's home and thrust Chaco into Aunt Ona's arms, then disappeared, never to be seen by the family again. Chaco was the closest thing Danny had to a brother.

Lately, instead of investigations, Chaco was working full-time trying to find jobs for the hapless dry well families. It was an impossible task. There were too many unskilled clients and far too few jobs.

"He only placed three people last week," Kathy said.

*

Six months after the Begay visit, the case count was at five hundred and still climbing. The sheer volume of clients pushed everything else aside, including any consideration he had of a social life. The cases sucked up every penny of what little income Danny was bringing in, making it more and more questionable every day as to whether his overburdened practice would survive.

And then there was Amanda — Amanda Lujan — his girlfriend of over two years. They'd met at a Native American convention held at the Albuquerque Marriott. She was a member of the nearby Pueblo Sandia tribe.

He was smitten from the moment he laid eyes on her. She was the kind of girl he thought he could never have — too beautiful — too smart — too popular, but for some unfathomable reason, she was as much taken with him as he with her.

After the convention, there was scarcely a weekend that one or the other of them hadn't made the hundred-fifty-mile drive between Farmington and Albuquerque so they could be together. They had even begun to discuss marriage. Then came the dry well client onslaught. The more cases that came in, the less time there was for Amanda. Their time together dwindled from every weekend to a couple of weekends a month, then to once a month or less. Despite Danny's pleas for her patience, Amanda finally broke it off when more than six months had passed since they'd last seen each other. Danny was devastated, but there was nothing he could do and no time in which to do it.

Chapter 6

"*Ya' at' eehii* Brother," twenty-four-year-old Nathan Begay greeted as he slipped through the half-open barn door. The dim light cast by numerous candles and hanging oil lanterns revealed a cavernous interior filled with people. Most were seated on hay bales, overturned buckets — anything that could provide a seating surface, including the floor. The rest simply leaned against stall rails or roof supports, forming a rough circle around a tall man.

All were there to hear the words of the commander. The NALM was a rag tag assortment of mostly angry young men and women from dry well families whose commander was reluctantly recruited by elders who were worried that some of the young firebrands were about to bring trouble down on the reservation.

Calling on his own military experience, the Commander had organized the NALM into a quasi-military group with squads and companies and platoons that he wore out with relentless training, the purpose of which was to occupy their time and keep them out of mischief. He taught them military-style discipline and respect for a chain of command — and it seemed to be working. A loose lid of sorts had been placed precariously atop the furiously boiling cauldron.

"I know you are angry Richard Tso," the commander said to a man standing at the periphery of the crowd. "But what you wish to do would bring disaster down on the reservation. Have you not been told of the Fairchild Industries plant in Shiprock back in the seventies? Our brothers—some of them your fathers—attacked the plant openly and stupidly. Many ended up in a *Bilagaana* prison. The plant closed and Fairchild left the reservation forever. Those jobs have never come back."

"But how long do we sit back and do nothing?" Tso asked. "I have seen my parents grow old overnight."

A young woman spoke up. "When the well was drilled on our land, my parents thought their poverty was over. They tore down the *hooghan* and put up one of those prefab houses. What's going to happen this winter when it's ten below zero and they can't afford to fill the propane tank—like what happened to Eddie Nez's grandparents?"

An angry murmur rippled through the crowd. A young man across the room called out. "I'll bet Gannon Oil would turn those wells back on in a heartbeat if a few of them suddenly started to disappear."

"Who said that?" the commander asked as he shielded his eyes from the glare of the lanterns and peered into the crowd.

"I did!" Eddie Nez's cousin, Gilbert Yazie, stood so the commander could see him. It was the type of comment the commander feared most.

"A better question is, what happens when the FBI shows up at your door with a search warrant? Do you know they can detect explosives residue that is so tiny you can't even see it on your clothes or in your car? We must act wisely, not like our brothers did forty years ago."

Yazzie sat back down, but the commander could tell the man was not fully convinced. He tried another tack. "Our brother, Danny Whitehorse, is working in the white man's way, using the *Bilagaana's* own laws to try to get the wells turned back on. We must do nothing that interferes with his work. I ask all of you for a pledge as warriors of the *Diné* that you will follow the leaders of the NALM and not take things into your own hands. Let all who agree raise their fist so Changing Woman can see."

Invoking Changing Woman, the most sacred Navajo deity, made this a solemn commitment indeed. Quietly, dozens of fists rose all around the room.

Then the Commander said, "If any here cannot make such a pledge, let them raise their hands now. There is no shame in this. The only shame would be if you did not speak and let the rest of us believe you are one of us."

No one raised a hand, but in the room there were those who kept their hands down lest they reveal themselves.

*

It was after eleven p.m. when Eddie Nez, Albert Horseman, and David Nakai, lingered over coffee at the all-night café in Shiprock, discussing the NALM meeting. "It's all bullshit," Eddie spat. "They talk and talk as if talk is enough. As long as all they do is talk, Gannon Oil has no reason to do things differently."

Albert shook his head. "Some of the others just want to start shooting oilfield workers."

"That's crazy," David responded. "It would be just the excuse some of the *Bilagaanas* need to start coming over here and shooting us."

"You're right," Eddie said. "We need to put the squeeze on Gannon without hurting anyone else. We're the only ones who can do that. We just need to decide when and where."

"I say we do it right now, tonight," Albert said. "We've got all the stuff. We know it works. There's no reason to wait."

David nodded his enthusiastic agreement, then hesitated. "There's just one thing. What if we do this and they think one of their wells blew up all by itself? It would all be worthless."

"You're right." Eddie scratched his chin. "Any suggestions?"

David had obviously been giving the problem some thought. "I think we should go buy some magazines, cut out words and paste up a letter to Gannon Oil that says that what happened to their well was no accident—and makes it clear that the NALM is willing to do it again."

"We ought to tell that attorney, too," Albert said. "Give him an anonymous call or something."

"Good idea," Eddie replied. "It's going to take us a little time to get all of this right. Let's get some sleep. Our time has come, my brothers. We'll make tomorrow night a night this reservation will remember forever!"

Chapter 7

The morning's mail brought a forty-eight-hour shut-off notice from the electric company. As Danny read a copy of a client statement for what had to be the sixth or seventh time, he realized his mind was more on the bills than the case file. Without thinking, he cursed and flung the file across the room, leaving a trail of scattered pages all the way to his office door.

"What the hell?" Kathy shouted from the outside office. She sprang to Danny's door to see what was wrong.

"Sorry, Kathy. I'm just at the end of my rope. I hate to say it, but we've got to pull the plug on this whole Gannon case. If I don't start bringing in some money, fast, this law firm is sunk."

"But Danny, we've worked so hard."

Danny shook his head wearily. "I know, but we've ridden this horse to death—now we're trying to drag it along behind us. I'm going out to Robert Begay's place to tell him that. When Bri comes in, have her help you start putting all the Gannon case files into storage boxes."

Brianna Sanders was more than just a friend, she was Danny's *Bilagaana* sister, and had been since as a frightened twelve-year-old, he became a member of the Myron Sanders family.

Fresh out of his uncle's *hooghan*, Danny was cowed and over-whelmed by the comparative opulence of a white man's home. The Sanders took him in under the Mormon Church's Indian Placement Program and treated him as if he were one of their own. The program allowed him to attend school in Farmington rather than at one of the then lesser-regarded Indian boarding schools at the time. Bri was only eight years old. Her only sibling, Carrie Ann, was just one.

Redheaded and precocious, Brianna immediately adopted Danny as the big brother she'd never had. She followed him around wherever he went. He initially thought of her as his own personal pain in the butt, but had to admit she was actually kind of cute—so long as she didn't embarrass him in front of his friends. By the time he graduated from high school, their bond as brother and sister was inseparable.

While Danny was away at college and law school, the gangly, bucktoothed, carrot-topped little girl had grown into a tall, shapely, stunningly-beautiful strawberry blonde whose sparkling blue-green eyes engaged everyone and everything around her. Best of all, she still had her energetic, guileless personality that quickly drew people in and made them smile.

Now a high school accounting teacher, she came into the office every afternoon to maintain Danny's books and help Kathy with the prodigious task of keeping up with the dry well files. She also assumed the role of his personal caretaker. She cleaned his house, did his laundry, and made sure he got a good, home-cooked meal at least a couple of times a week.

"She'll be disappointed," Kathy said.

Danny shook his head. "I know. But it's either that or we start filling out our bankruptcy petition. She'll just have to understand."

*

As Danny and Robert walked to the well site a couple hundred yards from Robert's home, he spoke reluctantly. "It's going to be impossible to force Gannon to get your well back into production. I went down to Window Rock and checked the tribe's lease documents against the one you gave me. Their master lease confirms that Gannon Oil has the absolute right to control production on the wells. No matter how I cut it, the law is all on Gannon's side."

Robert was silent for a moment and then asked, "So is this the end of your fight?"

"That's what it looks like."

Robert's face fell. Danny could see the disappointment and concern in his eyes. "Look, Robert," he said, "I know you don't understand, and it kills me to have to tell you this. But I haven't been able to pay my staff, and the electricity at my office will be shut off day after tomorrow. I've got to start earning some money or I'm going to be completely out of business." Although Danny knew the effort was probably futile, he asked, "Tell me again everything that happened here just before production stopped?"

Robert repeated the now all-too-familiar story. "A man from company come to my *hooghan*. He say men have to come and work on the well. The next day many men come. They bring trucks and machines. A big truck with a tower tall as a tree was right here." Begay walked over next to the wellhead and pointed. "They dig down all around the well, then dig a trench over this way." He gestured toward the east. "We did not know it, but another machine from far away was digging toward this well. When the trenches meet, the men put a pipe in the ground and covered it up. They worked more than a week, then go away. Next month no check comes."

"Can you show me where the new pipe was laid?"

"Yes. Follow me."

The pipeline's path was marked only by a slight, nearly unnoticeable depression in the ground which extended just a few yards away from the well site. Then Danny lost track of it altogether. As much as he disliked the Gannon situation, he had to admire the care they had taken to obscure the scars they made on the land.

Robert, however, read it unerringly for nearly a mile, all the way to the top of a low ridge overlooking the area. "Is this how the pipeline looks from here on?" Danny asked.

"Yes. It goes to that well over there." Robert pointed southeast toward another well site a half-mile away that was barely visible over the sage brush.

Robert looked at Danny and asked, "Are you sure there is nothing else you can do?"

"I'm sure. I don't have enough evidence to even start a lawsuit, let alone win one. There's just no way to force Gannon to turn the wells back on."

Robert shook his head and said quietly, "If the law cannot help us, perhaps there is another way."

"What do you mean, my friend?"

"There are some on the reservation who believe the dry wells have cursed the *Dinétah* and should be made to go away. My oldest son, Nathan, joined some others in something they call the Native American

Liberation Movement. They use the initials, NALM. They are learning to fight like the Army fights. He told me that some in his group want to blow up the dry wells. I tell him 'No!' I say they must have patience. I say that you will find a way for us. But now you tell me there is no way."

Vague rumors had circulated of a shadowy paramilitary organization. But this was Danny's first actual confirmation.

"Robert, you keep your boy away from that group. If some of those hotheads start blowing up wells it could bring the FBI, the ATF, or even the U. S. Army onto the reservation. Who's running this NALM, anyway?"

Robert looked Danny directly in the eye and asked, "Do you ask as a warrior of the *Diné* or as a man whose heart lies in the world of the *Bilagaana*?"

Danny was dumbstruck by the insult. His surprise turned to anger. "You know damn well I always speak as a member of my people first. If you, of all people, question my loyalty to the *Diné*, then call your witnesses, Robert Begay, and we will determine upon this place who is worthy to be called a warrior."

"There is no need for witnesses my brother," the big man answered softly. "I have always known of your honor but felt it was time to remind you of it. Today you sound as if you are ready to stop fighting. We have fought the *Bilagaana* for more than one hundred and fifty years and lost many more battles than we have won. But we have never lost our spirit. We have suffered many defeats, but we have never been defeated. Gannon Oil will not defeat us either.

"I too have joined NALM. Six months ago they made me a leader of young men from our area. We are nearly two hundred strong now. Every day, more want to join."

Robert sat down on a juniper stump. "Let me tell you why I joined, Danny Whitehorse. You can just as well try to stop the San Juan River with your bare hands as to try to stop our young men and women from being angry. Young anger is very hot. So hot that unless it is tempered, it will destroy those who possess it, along with many other innocent people. I joined to cool the anger and divert it from a path that would harm our people."

Danny shook his head. *Two hundred soldier wannabe's getting organized and looking for a fight? Gannon Oil has no idea what they're provoking.* "Your

NALM could bring the whole reservation down around our heads," he said. You've got to stop them from doing anything stupid."

"Keeping these young people under control is very hard. That's why you mustn't stop working. You are the example we use to show there are other ways to win a battle. But time is running out."

"Robert, I need to know who the leader is. I need to talk to him directly."

"I'm sorry Danny. That information is secret. I will go and tell him what it is you want. Then I will tell you what he says."

"When?"

"Someone will bring you an answer by noon tomorrow. But for now, if you are through being angry, I'm sure Lena has supper almost ready. How about a plate of fry bread and some of my wife's excellent *atse'*?"

Danny was instantly hungry. To him there was no finer meal than Navajo Fry Bread, cooked crisp in rendered sheep fat, smothered in pinto beans and homemade goat cheese, with sliced *atse'* on the side. It was food to restore Danny's extremely frustrated soul.

Chapter 8

"Aieee—this is a great night for our people," Eddie Nez shouted over the roar of the engine as David Nakai's beat-up old pickup truck bounced its way along a rough, little-used track that snaked across the sagebrush flats just below Dead Horse Bluff. The jagged escarpment started about ten miles southeast of Shiprock and extended south and westward in a sweeping crescent shape for over twenty miles.

"Aieee, you are right, my brother." Albert Horseman hoped his bravado belied the tense nervousness gripping him.

They carried no firearms. This wasn't that kind of mission. Their weapon of choice tonight was three five-gallon Gerry Cans filled with the explosive concoction they'd worked on for months. It was not a mission sanctioned by the NALM. Indeed, the officers would have tried to stop them had they known. But the three were tired of waiting on the do-nothing NALM leadership.

Careful not to mention Eddie's grandfather's name lest the old man's *chindi* should find them, David said, "The heart of that man you found will sing tonight as he walks the Shining Way."

"Be careful." Eddie cautioned as the truck drew closer to his grandfather's property. "His *chindi* is sure to be nearby. But what you say is true, my brother. He would be proud to know that it is his grandson who strikes the first blow against the *Bilagaana* oil company."

Chapter 9

The soft door knock on the singlewide, sixties-era trailer at the end of Tachiinii Road on the west side of Shiprock, came just after ten p.m. Chaco knew who it was. He opened the door and said, "You're late tonight."

"I know," Kathy said as she stepped through the door into Chaco's immaculately clean, well-ordered living room. Chaco's disciplined Army-style compulsion for order and cleanliness had not deserted him as a civilian. As he closed the door behind her, Kathy turned, put her arms around his neck, and delivered a hot, probing kiss. It was an act utterly out of character with the way their relationship began.

Early on, Danny had enlightened Chaco on the subject of his hot-tempered secretary. He said that Kathy was born on the Rosebud Sioux reservation in South Dakota. Abandoned by her alcoholic parents at age fifteen, she somehow made her way to the West Coast where she'd grown up homeless on the mean streets of the Bay Area. Somehow she avoided the cesspool of drugs and prostitution that sucked so many of her friends to their destruction and fought her way to a paralegal Associates Degree from Contra Costa College.

Danny said he met her just days after he passed the California bar, when his law school scholarship obligated him to complete two years of practice at a non-profit legal clinic in Oakland.

She was a beautiful, profane, in-your-face paralegal who cut a wide swath at the clinic. Many there were terrified of her.

As the only two Native Americans, there was an instant attraction.

They started as lovers, but Danny told Chaco that Kathy's impulsive, volatile temperament clashed so much with his measured, orderly, peaceful nature that their tempestuous, six-month romance nearly killed their deep friendship. They both agreed that friendship was more important.

Danny said that when he announced his intention to return to New Mexico to start his fledgling law practice, Kathy insisted on coming along.

If anything, Danny's warning about Kathy's eccentric behavior was an understatement. Chaco was instantly put off by the woman's cold, often foul-mouthed temperament.

Kathy made it clear from the first day he arrived that she was the one running the office—no matter what Danny said. Under her arbitrary office rules, Chaco was never to touch her files. One day while Danny was out, Kathy returned from an errand and caught Chaco red-handed replacing a dry well file.

"What the hell do you think you're doing?" she screeched. Rushing over, she tried to grab the file from his hand but only succeeded in knocking it from his grasp and spilling its contents across the floor. Enraged, she drew back her hand to slap him.

He caught her arm mid-swing. It was not a gentle interception, but rather, painfully wrenched her shoulder, causing her to cry out. He held her arrested arm in an iron grip. "Let go of me," she hissed. She pulled violently, but to no effect.

"You picked the wrong man to try to slap, lady," Chaco growled. "You can be a cold-hearted bitch all you want, but around here, we don't hit people."

This was a side of the quiet-spoken, gentle man she'd never seen before, nor had she ever felt such raw strength. It frightened her and excited her at the same time. His grip was cutting off the circulation in her arm. "Let go of me," she spat,

"On one condition."

"No conditions. Let go of me or I'll call the cops."

"And tell them what? That I assaulted you while trying to protect myself from your assault? I've got self-defense and the fact that I'm an ex-cop on my side. Who do you think they'll believe? But if you insist, I'll help you dial the phone number."

She stopped struggling against his grip and glared. "So what's your condition?"

"Actually, there's two. First, you must agree that there's no more hitting in this office — ever. And second, we sit down right here and have a thirty-minute talk about you and me and this job. There is a third condition, but I'll save that until after our talk."

Kathy hesitated then finally said, "Alright. I agree to the first two. But I'm not agreeing to anything else until I hear it. Now let go of my arm. You're hurting me. I can't feel my hand anymore."

"Done," Chaco said as he released her hand.

"Ohhh," Kathy moaned as blood rushed back into her hand. She rubbed it furiously to rid herself of the pins and needles. Chaco opened the door to Danny's office and beckoned her inside. Once she was seated he said, "Kathy, I've never hit a woman in my life. I don't believe any man has the right to do that. But there's one exception and that's if the woman hits the man first. Believe me, you don't ever want to get hit by me."

"Then you'd better stay out of my files," she groused. "I work hard to keep them in perfect order. I warned you about that."

"And I said I would try to respect your wishes. But every rule has its exception. This was one of them. You were gone, and I had to look at that file. I can't put my work on hold just to satisfy one of your arbitrary rules."

Kathy raised an eyebrow. "Arbitrary? I don't think so."

"Okay then — unreasonable. An unreasonable rule is any one that prevents either of us from doing our work. Now, if you want to compromise and say that we need to put things back where they came from, that's fine. But it was your unreasonableness that spilled the contents of that file all across the office. If anything, Ms. Redhand, I'm just as compulsive about maintaining orderliness as you are."

"You're a man. I don't believe that."

"Come to my house someday. I'll prove it."

Kathy looked skeptical. "Not a chance. But okay, I'm willing to bend a little on that until you screw up."

"There's another thing. You're a very good looking woman — pretty face, very nice body — but how you act makes you seem ugly. You always growl at people. You hardly ever smile. And your potty-mouth makes it seem like you're mad at everyone all the time. Why are you like that?"

No one had ever dared to speak to her that way. The words stung the worse because she knew they were true. Her hands flew to her mouth in shock as she tried to think of something to say. Finally she stammered, "Wh—why I am how I am is none of your business. Danny's never complained."

Chaco shook his head. "That's because he's afraid of pissing you off, just like the rest of us. Professionals smile. Professionals try to make other people feel comfortable. You make people feel like they're walking through a minefield whenever you're around them. There's a difference between being a professional and being a bitch. I hate to say it, Kathy, but most of the time, you're just a bitch."

Kathy's cheeks flushed. "How dare you say that?" She started to stand.

"Sit down!" Chaco boomed. The force of his command put her back in her chair. "You want to know how I dare say it? It's because I don't deserve the way you treat me and neither do our clients. You think your potty-mouth makes you look tough, but what it really does is make you look petty and uneducated. It certainly doesn't gain you anyone's respect. I'm tired of hearing the F-bomb dropped around here all the time, especially when it's directed at me. I'm tired of the disrespect. I'm your fellow worker, and I won't stand for it even a second longer. Understand?"

*

Chaco's words bit deep. On the streets where she grew up, Kathy was a frightened little girl who could never let her vulnerability show for fear of being perceived as weak. It was a characteristic that carried over into her adult life. Though she had never let it show, she cared deeply for Chaco, but felt she had to hide those feelings from him in order to maintain her image of aloof professionalism. Now, for the first time, Kathy smashed head-on into the reality of how people thought of her.

My God. What to her was a necessary façade of strength and competence was actually coming across to others as making her seem harsh and unapproachable. She realized that she was maintaining her street toughness at the expense of those she loved.

In that moment of clarity, Kathy felt her carefully built, seeming impregnable wall of toughness crumble. She placed her face in her hands and sobbed.

It took her several minutes to regain a bit of control and look up at Chaco. "Chaco, I'm so sorry," she said. "I admit, I have been a bitch. I became one at fifteen because I had to and I've been one ever since. That's not who I really am. I didn't know it was hurting the people I care for. You and Danny and Brianna are the only family I have." She wiped her eyes. "I guess I need to learn how to become an un-bitch."

Chaco looked surprised. "Kathy, I didn't think you even liked me. I've spent the past year and a half trying to figure out what I do to piss you off so regularly."

Chaco's response cut her to the core. She launched herself out of her chair and threw her arms around his neck, her body wracked with sobs. Recovering her ability to speak, she said, "I love you, Chaco, I really do. You amaze me. You're always so nice and polite, but I've never been able to figure out how to do that myself. Please help me." She hugged his neck hard as her tears wet his collar.

*

Chaco circled his arms around her and let her cry herself out. The warmth and sensuality of having a woman in his arms for the first time since Caroline's death nearly overwhelmed him. Finally he pushed her back gently and said, "About that hitting thing . . ."

Again her lip quivered. "I promise I'll never try to hit you again."

"That's good," he said with a slight smile, "because if you do I'll have no choice but to spank you."

"You *what?*" Kathy raised her hand to her mouth in surprise. The shock of his statement staunched the flow of her tears.

"You heard me." He chuckled. "I'd just have to pick you up, turn you over my knee, and give you a good, hard spanking."

Kathy was speechless. How could he have known? It was one of her most closely held fantasies. "I . . .I . . . ." she said before words failed her.

Chaco stepped back a little. "Now about that third condition. You ready for it?"

Still unable to speak, Kathy simply nodded.

"Have dinner with me tonight."

The third condition was carried out at the Golden Slipper restaurant in Durango.

Since then, the office bitch only appeared in occasional unguarded moments. Kathy still turned a rich four-letter phrase more often than Chaco liked, but far less frequently, and almost never in the presence of clients. The "F"-bomb disappeared completely.

*

When their lips parted, Kathy purred, "I've needed that all day long."

"Me too," Chaco smiled.

"Have you eaten anything tonight?"

"I grabbed a quarter-pounder and some fries on my way out of Farmington around eight o'clock."

"Chaco Whitehorse, you're going to kill yourself eating that way. I told you I'd make supper."

"I know, but I had to make a stop or two. I picked up your new uniform pants with the butt let out to accommodate those very sexy hips, and then I had to talk to Nathan Begay and Matthew Tsosie. They're worried about a couple of Tsosie's men. Fix yourself something, then we've got to talk."

Kathy's first stop was the bathroom where she rid herself of her work clothes and underwear. She reached into her purse and pulled out a pair of light-weight athletic shorts and a nearly see-through cream-colored tank top and threw them on. *This is getting ridiculous. I should just bring some clothes over here and leave them.*

Rather than cook, she snatched a large apple from a bowl on the kitchen counter and returned to the living room, plunked herself beside him on the couch, took a big bite, and mumbled through a full mouth, "Okay, Commander, go ahead. I bet you're thinking the same thing I am."

"About what Danny said this morning about NALM?"

Kathy nodded.

"We're not going to be able to keep him in the dark much longer. With what Robert Begay told him about the existence of the NALM he's going to keep probing until he learns the truth. If he finds out before we tell him, he'll feel betrayed. He might not ever trust us again."

Kathy slurped apple juice to keep it from running down her chin. "He's going to be mad as hell. How do you think we should do it?"

"He asked Robert to arrange a meeting with the NALM Commander. I think it's time to let that happen."

"When?"

"In the next couple of days, before things spiral out of control."

Kathy looked concerned. "Has something happened?"

"Not yet, but you know how hard it's been to keep some of these young soldiers reined in. Tsosie has a couple of hotheads in his company talking a lot of trash and perhaps gaining a following. If those idiots do something stupid and it gets connected to the NALM we might all go to jail for RICCO violations. Those boys have no idea what kind of resources the government would bring to bear in a fight."

Kathy shook her head. "So what's Matthew doing?"

"Not a lot he can do at this point. He says those boys stopped talking to him about three weeks ago, and that's what's got him worried. He's doing his best to keep an eye on them, even has other members of his company watching their houses and following them when they can. But nothing's turned up so far."

"So if they do something stupid, what are you going to do?"

"Firing squad," Chaco laughed, then said more seriously, "There's not much we can do. We're certainly not going to hurt anyone. I'm really quite powerless. I just hope none of these young hotheads figure that out anytime soon."

"I hope so too, General."

"Commander," Chaco corrected. "The last thing I need right now is a promotion. I didn't want this job in the first place, remember? But speaking of promotions, I'm worried about you not getting your paychecks. How are you doing?"

"I'm okay. There's food in the refrigerator and the rent's only a couple of weeks behind. It's a good thing my car's paid off and gets thirty-five-miles to the gallon — otherwise I'd be doing a lot of hiking around town. How about you?"

"I'm fine. I've still got about half of the insurance money from Caroline's accident and all the money I got from selling the house and furniture in D.C. My Jeep was paid for before she died.

"Do you still miss her?" Kathy asked.

"Like the sky would miss the sun. I'm just sorry we never had kids. I'll tell you one thing, lady, you're never getting on a plane without me. If we go, we go together. Thank God Danny picked me up out of the gutter when he did. If it weren't for him, I'd be just another drunk Indian lying beside the road."

"And you'd never have met me," Kathy said, playfully poking him in the ribs.

Chaco gave her a warm squeeze and said, "True that. Look, I'm the only one of the three of us who has any money in the bank. Why don't you let me help out on your rent?"

Kathy recoiled and slid across the couch out of his reach. "I certainly will not take any money from you," she said. "If I need more money I'll get me a frickin part-time job."

"Okay, okay," Chaco said, holding up his hands up. "I just worry about you, that's all."

"Well, stop it! You should know me well enough to know I can take care of myself."

"Believe me, I'm well aware. You want me to bend over for a spanking or just sit here looking like a whipped pup?" He stuck his bottom lip out and made puppy-dog eyes at her.

"Oh, you," she said, breaking into a grin. She slid back across the couch, grabbed his arm, and draped it around her.

Chaco gave her an impish look. "The truth is that you're the one who deserves a good spanking, for real, not for play."

Her face flushed slightly at the thought. "There you go talking all romantic again. So just how long are we going to keep us a secret? I'm having a pretty hard time keeping my hands off you around the office."

"Yeah," he said. "I'm having the same problem. I just don't know how Danny will take it."

"He's a big boy, Chaco. I'll stick with him no matter what, but you know there hasn't been anything romantic between us for years. As far as he knows, I'm still the iron maiden — cold as ice."

"We both know that's not true," Chaco said. "If Amanda were still around, it would make telling him less worrisome."

Kathy nodded. "He's just so damn stubborn about calling her."

"Maybe we should tell him about us at the same time we tell him about the NALM. I'm tired of all this hiding and lying. I want to get it all off my chest once and for all."

"Sounds good to me," she said. But this is something I *don't* want off my chest," she squeezed his hand, placed it on her left breast, and turned to nibble his ear.

Chapter 10

"Do you think that stuff's all right back there?" David Nakai asked, the dull sheen of sweat covering his brow revealing his nervousness.

"Don't worry," Eddie reassured him. "Nothing can go off until I install the detonator. You could throw a match into one of those cans and it wouldn't explode."

Their destination was a well site that sat across a wide arroyo only a couple hundred yards from Eddie's grandfather's ruined house, its north wall now broken out and open to the elements in order to disperse the evil spirits and shoo away the *chindi* of Eddie's grandmother. The well sat back a hundred feet off the road in the middle of a clearing that was devoid of vegetation.

Nakai turned the truck so the headlights illuminated the well structure. "Let's do it." Eddie said as all three scrambled out. While his companions retrieved the three fuel cans, Eddie, carrying the canvas bag in which he'd stashed the detonator and all the tools and rope he needed to rig the bomb to the pipe structure, went straight to the well. Nakai and Horseman hoisted the cans up one by one and held them while Eddie tied them off with rope. Once they were securely in place, it was time to rig the detonator. Eddie nodded to his companions and said, "You two get out of here. There's no sense taking a chance on blowing all three of us up. Move the truck over to the other side of the arroyo."

With the truck safely away, Eddie connected the wires from each can to the negative side of the detonator. Then he set the timer for twenty minutes and connected the lead wires to the positive side. He had long ago learned that if he connected all the wires before he set the timer, the act of winding the timer could trigger the circuit.

Eddie felt every beat of his pounding heart as he completed the connection. If something wasn't right, he would simply cease to exist.

So far, so good. With the connection made, he grasped the little plastic tab he had inserted between the bell body and the clapper. This was the final, most dangerous step. He scarcely breathed as he delicately removed the device's one and only safety mechanism.

He was bathed in sweat as he viewed the plastic tab in the palm of his hand and heard the clockwork sound of the timer winding down. He scrambled off the well with canvas bag in hand and walked backward as fast as he could all the way to the road while obliterating his footprints with a sagebrush branch

"Yieeee," Horseman cried as Eddie leaped into the truck. "I'm happy to see you, my brother. I would not want your *chindi* following us home."

"Not as happy as I am." Eddie said. "Get us out of here, David."

As they drove, Eddie kept a close eye on his watch. With five minutes to spare, he said, "Stop. I want to see this!" The three gathered silently at the tailgate of the truck. In the distance, a coyote yipped softly then turned the yip into a high-pitched howl that was immediately answered by other coyotes around the area. "It is *Ma'ii*, the spirit of Brother Coyote," Eddie said. He rejoices that the warriors of the *Diné* have at last risen to fight and bring chaos to the *Bilagaana's* world."

The darkness was suddenly shattered by a huge column of first white, then yellow, then orange flame that turned into a fiery mushroom cloud that blossomed hundreds of feet into the air. As the glow of the explosion began to fade, the shock wave rolled over them. Even from nearly two miles away it pounded against their chests and assaulted their ears.

For a moment it looked as if the blast would fade away to nothing. Then Eddie detected a glow near the ground. The blast had raised an enormous cloud of dust and smoke that momentarily obscured the result of their handiwork. But as the cloud lifted up and away, it revealed a huge column of orange flame that illuminated the entire area

"Holy Hell" Horseman said almost reverently. "It's like the devil's own blowtorch.

"Looks to me like there's plenty of gas left in that well," Eddie said. He threw back his head and shouted a great "Aieeeee," then broke into a chant and started dancing the warrior's dance of victory. Nakai and Horseman joined him. It was an ecstatic celebration witnessed only by the three participants..

Chapter 11

Chaco's instincts woke him as he heard a vehicle come down the little-traveled road leading to his house. He gently extracted his arm from beneath Kathy's sleeping head, gathered his pants and shirt from the floor, threw them on and walked to the front door. He opened it just before a startled Matthew Tsosie could knock.

"Matthew, what brings you here?"

"I have bad news, Commander. It's happened."

"What's happened?"

"I told you members of my squad were sometimes following the three men I told you about. Tonight Richard Tso saw David Nakai and two others drive out of town in Nakai's old pickup truck. There were several fuel cans in the back."

"Who were the others?"

"One was Eddie Nez. Matthew couldn't tell for sure about the third guy, but thought it might be Albert Horseman. He turned off his lights and followed them out to Eddie Nez's grandfather's old place at Eagle Dome. They didn't go to the house — they went to the gas well just across the wash. They were there less than a half-hour. Matthew had to get out of there before they spotted him, but he said he only went a little way before there was a big explosion. Afterward, he saw a huge flame shooting into the air. He's sure it was the gas well."

A chill coursed through Chaco's body. "Who knows of this?"

"As far as I know, just Richard, me, and now you."

"Who do you think the ringleader is?"

"My money would be on Nez. He's the one who's been agitating to go after the wells."

"Any idea where they are now?"

"Last Richard saw, they were a couple of miles away from the explosion, apparently admiring their handiwork."

With a sigh of resignation, Chaco said, "Round up as many of your squad as you think you can trust and meet me at Nez's place — fast."

*

As the three exhausted, exultant men arrived at the outskirts of Shiprock, Eddie asked David, "Did you mail the letter?"

"I dropped it in the mail slot just before the post office closed."

"Good. Now Gannon Oil will learn the consequences of starving out the families of the *Diné*. Albert, when are you going to call Whitehorse?"

"First thing this morning. I'm going up to Cortez to call him from a phone booth."

Eddie stepped from Nakai's truck as a faint tincture of light showed on the eastern horizon. *Strange.* Three cars that usually weren't there were parked just down the road. *Neighbors must have company.*

Eddie stepped into his darkened living room and closed the door, so tired he didn't know if he would make it all the way to his bed. The couch was good enough and a dozen steps closer. He turned on the light — and leaped back in surprise.

"*Ya' at' eehii*," greeted the man seated on the couch. Another voice from down the hallway startled him. "Oh, my brother, what have you done?" Lieutenant Matthew Tsosie stepped into the light. "Have you brought trouble down upon the *Dinétah?*" Others filed into the living room from down the hall, members of the Black Lizard Squad.

"Two of you stay here with me and Lieutenant Tsosie," Chaco said as he rose to his feet. "Corporal Charley, you and the others go get Privates Nakai and Horseman and bring them here."

Turning back to Eddie, the commander said in a gentle tone, "It looks like you've had a rough night, my friend. I think we'd better put on some coffee and you can tell me about it."

Chapter 12

The phone rang just as Danny unlocked the office door. He hurried through the reception area to his office and answered. A muffled, unfamiliar voice speaking Navajo asked him to look out his office window toward the southwest.

"Who is this?" Danny asked, walking phone in hand, to the window.

"Call me the spirit of your ancestors," the voice said. "Look to the southwest and tell me, do you see the smoke?"

At first, Danny saw nothing unusual. Over the gray sandstone bluffs that formed the periphery of the San Juan River valley were the usual plumes of steam perpetually belched out by the huge Four Corners and San Juan coal-fired power plants. Further to the west he saw the distinctive outline of the Shiprock monolith thrusting its rocky mast high into the desert sky.

Then his mind registered another plume quite far south of the power plant stacks. This one was black rather than white. "I see some smoke down to the southwest. Is that what you're talking about?"

"The smoke you see is because the warriors of the *Diné* are fighting to give us victory over the *Bilagaana* evil. What you see is the new hope of our tribe rising from the earth to consume our enemies. It is the first blow struck by the NALM to reclaim our land and restore the dignity of our people."

At the mention of NALM, Danny's stomach dropped. "Who is this, and what the hell are you talking about?"

"I am the spirit of your grandfathers calling you to battle, Danny Whitehorse. What you see is the death of a Gannon Oil Company gas well. It burns quite nicely for not having anything in it, don't you think?"

"YOU IDIOTS! You reckless, stupid idiots!" Danny shouted. "You've no idea what you've done. You may have ruined what little chance I ever had of getting anything from Gannon Oil. You imbeciles think you're an army? Well, a real army with real guns and tanks will be on the reservation tomorrow and they'll be looking for you!" He slammed the phone down in disgust, cursed, then grabbed his stapler from his desk and threw it through the open door into the reception area. It hit the entrance doorpost with a bang just as Kathy came in carrying a cup of coffee and an armful of files. She screamed and dropped to the floor, her files flying everywhere, along with the coffee.

Danny rushed to help, "Kathy! I'm so sorry." Coffee now adorned the front of her cream-colored satin blouse, her gray skirt, and a good portion of the floor. Was she burned? He grabbed her arm and tried to pull her to her feet.

"What the hell are you doing?" Kathy jerked free and stood on her own.

"Sorry, but all our work on the Gannon case is literally going up in smoke right now." He led her to the window, pointed out the plume of smoke in the southwestern sky and told her of the phone call.

Kathy shook her head as she stared at the horizon. "What do we do now?"

"I don't know. Since I'm the only one who's been in contact with Gannon officials about the well problem, we'll probably get a visit from the local cops and possibly the FBI. They may try to seize our records as evidence." He looked around at the stacks of file boxes lining the walls. "We don't want to make it easy for them. I want you to get all the important Gannon file originals out of here right now. Rent a small storage unit and put them there. Call and see if you can get Bri to help. Tell her it's an emergency."

"Aren't we protected by attorney/client privilege?"

"I wouldn't count on that if some Gannon lawyer convinces one of their bought-and-paid-for local judges that all us Indians are a terrorist threat. I'm going out to Robert Begay's place. Try to track Chaco down and tell him I need to see him as soon as possible."

Chapter 13

The pressure-fed fountain of fire spewing from the earth reached at least three hundred feet into the air. The column spewed black smoke so thick that at times it covered the sun even where they were standing, more than a mile away. Looking through binoculars, Danny saw men and trucks surrounding the fire. Miraculously, the sagebrush around the cleared well site had not caught fire.

He spotted three fire trucks and three of the distinctive white with blue stripes Ford Expeditions driven by the Navajo Nation Police. He thought he saw a New Mexico Highway Patrol car as well—far less of a police presence than he'd expected.

"Why, Robert? How could your precious NALM let this happen?" Danny's face was rigid with anger.

"I told you my friend, young anger is hot. Sometimes it defies all reason and logic. This is the work of three young men, one who buried his grandfather recently. He blames Gannon Oil for his grandmother's and grandfather's deaths. You see his grandparents' house about a half-mile west of the well. The young man said this attack was a tribute to his grandfather's warrior spirit."

"It's a tribute to stupidity!" Danny spat. "Robert, listen to me very carefully. No one, not even a *Bilagaana* judge, can make me tell about our conversations. It's something called attorney/client privilege. Are any of your family members tied in with this?"

"No." Robert said.

"Thank God. By tomorrow, Shiprock could be crawling with FBI agents and maybe even the military. If they learn of the NALM, the government may impose martial law on the reservation. Spread the word that no one should talk to any of the authorities without me being present. If you learn someone is being questioned, send for me at once. What's the NALM doing to see this doesn't happen again?"

"Everything we can, but probably not enough."

"I hope the idiots who did this weren't stupid enough to contact Gannon Oil and brag."

Robert flinched and cast his eyes at the ground. "I'm sorry Danny. I'm afraid they did. Our commander learned that they pasted together a letter with words cut out of magazines. It said that the well had been blown up by the NALM. It was mailed to Gannon Oil last night."

Danny kicked a dirt clod in disgust. "Gannon could have it today or at the latest, tomorrow, and from there, it will go straight to the FBI. What does your precious NALM leader have to say about all this?"

"I haven't talked to him today, but I promise, he's just as upset about this as you are."

"You tell your tin-star general that we have to meet. And I don't mean tomorrow — tonight. I can't have my work interfered with by the very people I'm trying to help."

"I'll get word to him right away."

Danny placed a hand on Robert's shoulder. "For what it's worth, my friend, I know you've worked very hard to head off something like this. I'm angry at the stupid young men who did this, but you, my friend, have my respect."

"Thank you Danny," the big man said in a quiet voice. "Respect is a precious thing."

"You've never been without it. Just get me a meeting with this so-called commander of yours."

Chapter 14

The drive back to Farmington was torturous as Danny imagined the dire consequences sure to ensue. The Shiprock area would likely be crawling with FBI and ATF agents within a matter of hours. They would quickly unravel the mystery of the explosion and arrests were certain to follow. The arrests could trigger more resistance and perhaps even a full-fledged armed insurrection.

By default, all those arrested would become Danny's clients. Such a scenario would surely collapse the ability of his tiny law practice to cope as a new flood of indigent criminal cases would push aside the dry-well civil cases. Danny shook his head. *What the hell do I do now?*

On impulse, Danny detoured at Apache Street and then turned onto Airport Boulevard. Another left led him up the hill past the Air National Guard armory to where Gannon's headquarters dominated the landscape. Danny had come to think of the building more in terms of a black vulture about to pounce down on the city than as a symbol of Farmington prosperity.

As he cruised past, Danny spotted two large television broadcast vans and a couple of Farmington Police Department cruisers parked near Gannon's entrance. *That's weird. I thought there'd be a lot more police presence.*

Someone was making a statement in front of the TV cameras on the front steps of the building. He was tempted to swing in and join the crowd but changed his mind. "Best keep a low profile," he muttered to himself.

He rushed back to his house, expecting to hear live television bulletins and see extensive coverage, especially by the local stations. All he found were the afternoon soaps. He waited for the regular three o'clock news update.

"Problems in the oil fields," the pretty, blond talking head said. "A Gannon Oil gas well has blown its top not far from Farmington. Steve Mecham in the Channel 2 News helicopter has the story."

The picture switched to a reporter inside the chopper wearing a bulky headset and talking into a handheld microphone. "Darcy, if you ever used a Bunsen Burner in high school, multiply the size of that flame ten thousand times and you have an idea of what this three-hundred-foot tall inferno looks like."

The scene shifted to a close-up aerial view of the source of the conflagration and then panned back from the wellhead as the reporter continued. "As you can see, the flame is generating a huge plume of black smoke that can be seen for miles. Gannon Oil fire trucks assisted by the Shiprock Fire Department, are pouring water on the well, trying to cool down what's left of the structure, but out here, every drop of water has to be trucked in. The fire commander tells us it's likely that fire crews are going to be here for at least days, maybe even weeks, until gas well fire specialists will be able to snuff the blaze. Steve Mecham reporting for Channel 2 News."

"Thanks, Steve," the news anchor said. "A few minutes ago, a Gannon Oil spokesman commented about the fire. Our Shannon Henrie was there."

The scene switched to Gannon's headquarters to a close up of a sweating, older man the screen caption identified as Jim Parker, Gannon Oil's president. ". . . so it's too early to tell what the exact cause of this accident is, but we are happy to report that no one was hurt and property damage is confined to Gannon Oil equipment and property. There is no danger to the public."

"Can you tell us why this happened?" a reporter off camera asked.

"No. It's far too early to tell. Natural gas is a very explosive substance. Sometimes, despite all precautions, these things happen." Parker paused, pulled a handkerchief from his rear pocket and mopped his brow.

Shannon Henrie, pushed her head into the field of view, held a microphone practically against Parker's mouth and asked, "Is there any chance someone may have blown this well up intentionally?"

Parker looked as if he'd been slapped. "Absolutely not," he spat back. "That's a stupid question. This is just an unfortunate accident. I'm sure we will find that some kind of defective equipment is the cause."

"Are you saying that Gannon wells are defective?" yelled a reporter from the back.

"No! No! I did not say that and don't you dare try to put those words in my mouth. You'll know more just as soon as we do." With that the man spun on his heel and retreated to the safer environs of the Gannon Oil Building, leaving behind a stream of unanswered questions hurled at his retreating back.

"Gannon must not have received the letter," Danny mumbled.

*

Minutes after Danny returned to his office, Nathan Begay showed up. The young man politely declined Danny's offer to sit down. "Hosteen Whitehorse, my father asked me to tell you the meeting you requested has been set up. He asks that you please be at our place around eight thirty."

"Good," Danny responded with relief. "tell him I'll be there."

Chapter 15

Red Gannon's ranch, located on Highway 64, sixty-three-miles east of Farmington, was anything but modest. At thirty-two-thousand-acres, it was one of the three largest privately owned pieces of real estate in Northern New Mexico. Only a few hundred acres immediately surrounding the Gannon mansion were developed. The rest remained as pristine forest and range land that extended northward to just across the Colorado border.

Gannon's sprawling seventeen-thousand-square-foot Casa Grande-style mansion sat in a lush, green valley accessible only via a half-mile long driveway leading down from the highway. Entry was protected by heavy steel gates operated from inside a Castilian-style stone gatehouse that sat between the entry and exit lanes of the drive.

Further down the valley was the private airport where Gannon kept his jets. Sitting on a helipad beside the house was the sleek, black helicopter sitting on a helipad beside the house he piloted himself between the ranch and Gannon Oil headquarters.

Inside, five men were gathered around a thirty-thousand-dollar burled black walnut table in the conference room adjoining Gannon's huge home office. Gannon himself sat at the head. The others were Lucas Blackthorn, Jim Parker, Stanley Popeson—Gannon's personal account-ant—and Marlin Webster, mayor of Farmington City.

Normally these were pleasant meetings that included an accounting from Popeson, of how much their Cayman Project accounts were growing. But this afternoon, each held a copy of the pasted-together letter the rebellious NALM members had sent to Gannon Oil headquarters. Blackthorn was nervous. Would Gannon and the others blame him? He was, after all, the head of security,

Six-foot-four James Edmond Gannon looked more sixtyish than his true age of eighty-two. He possessed a full head of silvery hair touched just at the forelock with the last orange tinge of the flaming red hair that had given rise to his nickname. He was still vital, active, and possessed of a stature only marginally lessened by age.

Gannon's steely, blue-gray eyes projected a look of simmering rage directly at Lucas. "So just who the hell is this NALM, Blackthorn, and what are we facing here?"

Blackthorn cringed, knowing better than most that Gannon despised any appearance of weakness. "At this point, we have no idea, Red. Probably just a couple of hotheads trying to make us think there are more people involved than actually are. That's a classic wannabe-terrorist ploy."

"What about your cops, Webster? They ever heard of this NALM?"

The handsome, grandfatherly Webster was Gannon's — bought and paid for. With him came at least some control of virtually all the government institutions in San Juan County. To assure that Webster never entertained ideas of straying, the old man possessed a videotape of him frolicking butt-naked in bed with two women to whom he was most assuredly not married. A copy of the tape could be sent to the press or to the man's wife of more than thirty years anytime Gannon wanted.

Marlin's response sounded like a campaign speech. "Red, this is the first time I've ever heard of this NALM group. But the instant I leave this meeting I'll have a joint city/county task force organized and use every detective we have to find the answer. You can count on that, sir."

Blackthorn could barely stand the pompous, self-serving man in the best of times, but this time Webster's answer displayed his abject stupidity. "That's real good, Webster," Blackthorn snarled. "Your Keystone Cops don't have even an ounce of jurisdiction on the rez. What better way to spread word of this thing around the county than by having every cop for miles around investigating what we don't want anybody to know about?"

Lucas looked at Gannon. "This was most likely some pranksters who read up on how to make a bomb on the Internet and wanted to try it out. If it gets around that it was a bomb that blew up that well, we'll have the

ATF and the FBI in here instantly. They'll call in well experts we can't control and they'll find that secondary pipeline the first day they're on the site. We have to deal with this whole thing from the inside."

"Good call, Blackthorn," Gannon said. "Jim, how much heat you getting from the press?"

"A lot less than I expected. I dealt with the TV stations this afternoon. I've had requests for interviews from a couple of newspapers. As long as this thing looks like just another industrial accident, I don't think anyone's going to be all that interested."

Gannon looked back at Lucas. "So how do we prevent this from happening again?"

" The truth is that without making a lot of changes, there's not much we can do. You know how isolated those sites are. To start with, I'm going to put a lot more of our people on the ground, day and night. I don't care if all they do is polish the pipes. Just their presence will be a deterrent. We better put a security fence around every Cayman project well. We may even need to post security guards. I want to hire some private rent-a-cops to start patrolling the area. Who knows, we just might get lucky and catch these little peckerwoods red handed. If we do, we'll send that reservation the clearest possible message that it doesn't pay to screw around with Gannon gas wells."

"What's all this going to cost?" Gannon asked.

"Can't say for sure just yet, but it's going to be somewhere north of five million for the site clearing and fencing. The Cayman wells are bringing in around nine million a month, so we can afford it. "

"Anyone disagree?" Gannon asked.

No one else spoke up.

"Good," Gannon said. "Make it happen. I'm willing to have Gannon Oil foot the bill this time, but if it turns out that this NALM is for real and they blow up another well, the full cost's coming out of the Cayman account money, something that will cost all you gentlemen millions.

Chapter 16

Nausea threatened as Danny, blindfolded, was uncomfortably jostled between the driver, Nathan Begay, and Richard Tso, a man he barely knew. The pickup truck navigated what seemed to Danny to be an endless series of twisting, turning reservation roads.

Finally it slowed and made a hard left turn. Dogs barked as the vehicle stopped. Richard helped him step out, then he was led inside a building and seated at a table. When the blindfold was removed, he found Robert sitting beside him and Nathan standing nearby. Two other men were present who he didn't recognize. All were dressed in Army-style camouflage uniforms.

The building was a traditional *hooghan*, its interior so nondescript, so generic that Danny had no clue as to whose house it was. Articles that would have identified the occupants had been removed or covered.

Danny's back was to the hooghan's east-facing single door. Robert placed his hand on Danny's shoulder. "Don't worry, my friend, the man you wish to see will be here very soon. I am sorry for the blindfold. I would not have done that, but others don't know you as I do. Please do not take offense."

"He's right, Danny!" said a voice from the doorway behind him. "There was no disrespect intended."

The familiarity of the voice startled Danny. He stood and turned to see Chaco, who was dressed in the same desert camo uniform the others wore. Then, to his utter astonishment, Kathy stepped out from behind him wearing exactly the same.

"Chaco? Kathy? Where did you come from? I didn't tell you where this meeting was."

"You said you needed to talk with the commander of NALM," Chaco responded. "Here I am."

"Wait a minute," Danny grinned, expecting Chaco to grin back and reveal the joke. But Chaco held Danny's gaze with dead seriousness.

The world tilted under Danny's feet as the enormous reality of what Chaco said hit him. He reached out and touched the table to steady himself. How could this possibly be? He knew these people! They all worked together, played together, did almost everything together, yet apparently, they had a secret life. Was this a betrayal? Was this an abuse of their supposedly open, trusting relationships? Danny's mind simply couldn't fathom it.

A palpable silence hung in the air as Danny searched for an adequate reply. His first impulse was to be angry, but an angry reply would do nothing to help, and might forever damage his relationship with these people. Finally, he did the only thing he could think of. Though it was a white man's custom, it was one both of them understood. He strode forward, placed his left hand on Chaco's shoulder and extended his right in a gesture that confirmed both his friendship and his respect for the new position in which he now had to view his cousin. Then he turned to Kathy and said, "And as for you, I don't know whether to salute you or fire you."

"How about giving me a hug instead?" He was more than happy to comply.

Chapter 17

"There really was no choice," Chaco explained. "Everybody around Shiprock knew I was former Army. I discovered what was going on when one of the Tselakai boys from Tabletop Mesa invited me to an early NALM meeting. I thought there would only be two or three people there, but twenty-six showed up—some of them talking about doing some real stupid stuff, like learning bomb-making off the Internet. They already knew just enough to blow themselves to Kingdom Come. Others wanted to kidnap Gannon workers and hold them for ransom. A couple just wanted to start shooting oil field workers.

Some of the elders and I came up with the idea of the NALM more as a diversion than anything else. If we hadn't, I'm sure there would already be martial law on the reservation. Frankly, I'm surprised it's taken this long for somebody to blow up a well."

Danny struggled to keep his anger in check. "You should have told me about all this stuff. Don't you think I would have understood?"

Kathy responded. "You already had more on your plate than you could handle. If you had to worry about what your clients' kids were doing on top of everything else, it would have only made things worse."

"You may be right," Danny conceded. "But I should have at least had the choice. You do know that all of you have now officially broken the law. By not turning those young men in, you're engaged in a conspiracy for obstruction of justice. If I don't say anything, which I won't, I'm engaged in the same conspiracy. I could lose my license and we all could go to prison."

Chaco's response was curt. "Turning them in would destroy the

NALM's trust in me. I may be the only person standing between the NALM and utter chaos. I'm not that worried about the FBI. You know how it is out here. The *Bilagaana* come knocking, ain't nobody talking."

Danny leaned back and took a deep breath. "So now we not only have the dry-well families to worry about, but the NALM as well. How do you think this is going the play out with the rest of your wannabe soldier boys?"

"And girls," Kathy quipped.

"Probably not the way we'd like." Chaco said. "It's the first major break in discipline I've had. Those three young men are going to be seen as heroes, especially since they weren't caught. It won't be long until others want to become heroes, too. It could all spiral out of control very quickly. What's the reaction from the other side?"

"The television news says Gannon believes the explosion was caused by some kind of mechanical failure. There wasn't much of a police presence when I drove past their headquarters building this afternoon. I don't think that letter you said those boys pasted together has been delivered. My best guess is that everything will hit the fan tomorrow — Wednesday at the latest. The reaction could be anything from just a normal, routine police investigation to a full-fledged invasion of the reservation by federal agents. We better pray that one of your little renegade groups doesn't blow up another well.

Chaco nodded his agreement. "I just can't believe a dry well would burn so hard and so long," he said.

"Neither can I. But if that well was connected to other wells, that could explain it."

"It could until they isolated the gas flow to just the burning well. You'd think that's the first thing Gannon would do. Yet that fire's as strong tonight as it was when the boys blew it up."

"So what's your conclusion?" Danny had asked.

Chaco spoke the thoughts all had harbored for some time. "I think that well is far from being depleted. And I'd bet none of the others are either. Don't ask me how, but I'd bet next week's paycheck that all those wells are somehow still producing."

"That's not much of a bet," Danny chuckled. "I haven't been able to pay you for weeks. I've looked at dozens of those wells, Chaco. All the valve indicators say they're closed."

"They're wrong."

"How?"

"I don't know. I'm not a gas well expert."

"So how do we find out?"

"Blow up another well?" Kathy quipped.

"Don't even go there." Danny scowled.

"Did you ever see that movie about the Watergate break-in? Robert Redford and Dustin Hoffman?" Chaco asked.

"Yeah, a long time ago."

"That Deep Throat guy said something that, as an investigator, I've never forgotten; 'Follow the money.'"

"What are you trying to say?"

"Where's the money in this thing?"

"There's a lot of it going up in smoke out there right now," Kathy said.

"That's not what I'm talking about. Why would Gannon build a new pipeline to wells that already have one, especially if they were about to go dry?"

"We've asked ourselves that dozens of times,"Danny said, shaking his head.

"There's something those new pipelines are trying to tell us," Chaco said. "I think your idea of mapping them is very important."

"I agree, but it's going to take us a year or more to do that. After today, I don't think we have that kind of time."

Chaco smiled. "What if we put an army on the job?"

"An army? How can we . . ." Danny's eyes lit up. "That's right, we do have one."

"You got it! I need to have something for the my troops to do besides blow up gas wells."

They settled on a two-prong plan. The NALM would immediately start tracing the paths of the newly installed pipelines. The second prong was considerably more tenuous. "You've got to file a lawsuit against Gannon Oil," Chaco said.

"I'd love to, but it's far too soon. All we have are suspicions with no real evidence that could prove our case."

"Here's the problem, Danny. I keep using you as an excuse for my more difficult NALM members to hold off on actions against Gannon

Oil. They keep asking when you're actually going to do something. 'Soon,' I tell them, but they've heard that so much that some don't believe me any longer. If enough of them start to believe that working through legal channels isn't going to work, we're going to see a lot more wells blow up.

Danny shook his head. "I can file if you think we have to, but unless we can turn up some hard evidence during discovery, we don't stand a chance of winning. There's another problem. Even in the best of circumstances, civil law moves very slowly. If I file tomorrow, it's going to take years to bring the case to trial. Gannon will try to keep it from going forward at every step. The only hope for a quick resolution is if we turn something up in discovery that's so damning that Gannon will want to settle. And I don't hold out much hope of that."

Chaco sighed. "Our biggest issue is what's going to happen on this reservation tomorrow, or next week or next month, not what happens five or six years from now Filing that lawsuit just might make another group think twice about doing something similar to what happened last night."

"Yeah, I can see that. It goes against everything I've been taught, not to mention my better judgment, but if you think it's the only way, I'll file just as fast as I can."

The decision filled Danny with dread. It was too soon. The evidence was not yet on his side. Gannon's first move would almost certainly be a motion for summary judgment of dismissal. Unless he turned up some sort of smoking gun that showed the wells were still producing, the lawsuit might turn out to be a fool's errand, and an expensive one at that.

*

Danny's car sped back toward Farmington as morning dawned over the San Juan Valley. His tired mind reflected that in another era, Chaco would have been a war chief teaching young braves to become warriors. Then he realized that that's exactly what he was today.

And Kathy! He should have recognized the signs before now. It once appeared she could barely stand the man, but for the last while, the bickering had stopped. Kathy was acting strangely cheerful — humming around the office, smiling when there was no particular reason. The dry well cases so distracted him that he'd paid no attention.

When they disclosed that they'd practically been living together for more than six months, Danny was shocked. "Remarkable," he muttered to himself. "Just remarkable."

Chapter 18

Danny drove past the Gannon building several times the next day, watching for any changes. But other than one television van parked out front, there were no other signs of unusual activity.

News programs reported only straight-forward stories about an "accident" that took place at the well site. Could the letter have gotten lost in the mail?

The following day went by without reaction, then the next and the next. A week out from the explosion and the newspapers and broadcast media seemed to lose interest.

With no signs of unusual FBI or ATF presence, Danny's anxiety level slowly subsided. Gannon seemed to be content to let the whole incident fade from public view.

*

"Danny, I need you to come with me,"Chaco said as he came through the office door one morning, three weeks after the explosion.

What Chaco wanted Danny to see was evident long before they reached Eagle Dome. Roads leading to the gas field were choked with trucks carrying heavy construction equipment.

Danny and Chaco stood on the hill where Danny and Robert had viewed the burning well the day of the explosion. The fire continued to burn as strong as ever as the Red Adair crews made final preparations to snuff it out.

Streaming past the site were trucks hauling excavators, bulldozers and construction equipment of every sort. Some carried large rolls of chain-link fencing and spools of razor-sharp concertina wire. The vehicles raised huge clouds of dust as they made their way deeper into Eagle Dome.

"What's going on?" Danny asked.

"They're clearing everything within a hundred yards of the well sites down to bare dirt, and putting up chain-link fences topped with concertina wire. And it's not just here. The same thing's happening up at Tabletop Mesa too. Don't they need permission from the tribe to do all this?"

"They already have it," Danny said. "Their tribal lease gives them the right to modify and improve their facilities within the boundaries of any well site." He shook his head. "This must be costing millions. What do you make of it?"

"My guess is that Gannon got the letter."

"Then why no FBI or ATF?"

Chaco looked at Danny. "There's only one explanation. Gannon doesn't want them snooping around. I think he's hiding something, and by the scale of all this," Chaco gestured at the trucks, "it has to be really big. Otherwise, why would Gannon spend all this money on a bunch of dry wells, and why aren't the feds knocking on doors all over Shiprock?

"This isn't the full picture, Danny. A month ago most of these wells wouldn't see a Gannon Oil truck for weeks, sometimes months. Now Gannon crews show up at every well every day at some time or other. They're showing up at night, too. To cap it all off, they've got uniformed private security guards making regular patrols."

Danny shook his head. "This is going to make our mapping project far more difficult. We certainly don't want our mappers and the Gannon crews coming into contact with each other. Have there been any incidents?"

"Not so far. I've told our guys to keep their mouths shut, avoid contact, and act like they're clueless. Under no circumstances are they to try to mix it up with any Gannon people."

"It's working then?"

"So far, so good. But then, I told them not to blow up any gas wells either."

Chapter 19

Kathy and Danny mounted a large map on the wall in Danny's office that showed all the roads and pipelines in the county. But other than showing major roads, detail on the reservation side was sparse.

Despite the massive construction project, NALM mappers did their job. Every day or two, Danny and Chaco updated the map. Without exception, the new pipelines snaked from dry well to dry well in a generally eastward direction toward the reservation border where the major pipeline companies' trunk lines lay just on the other side.

Danny held twice-monthly staff meetings. Brianna was so intimately involved in helping that they had no choice but to tell her about the NALM. Danny worried what her reaction might be. All she said was, "How do I sign up?" Danny laughed, gave her a hug, and said, "You're far too pale to pass the physical exam, sis."

"This looks like a bunch of creeks and rivers," Bri said as she eyed the map.

"Looks like a tree lying on its side to me," Kathy said.

Danny chuckled. "You're both right. It's amazing how much progress we've made. It's going so fast, I'm worried about how to keep our NALM soldiers occupied a couple of months from now."

"How's the lawsuit coming?" Chaco asked.

"We should be ready to file in the next two weeks. Trouble is, it's all smoke and mirrors. We still don't have any hard evidence."

"That fire burned for nearly six weeks," Bri said. "Can't you use how long it burned as evidence?"

"Just proving there was gas from that supposedly dry well feeding the fire doesn't help our case. The lease relieves Gannon of responsibility for losses due to events of *Force Majore*, in other words, accidents that are not Gannon's fault. What we've got to prove is that Gannon is producing and selling gas from the supposedly dry wells."

Danny patted the map. "A big problem we have right now is that none of us know how gas fields work. We might already have the answer and not know it. We need a gas field expert to tell us what we've got or not got. But that costs money, and we don't have any."

Bri knew little about the law and nothing about oil and gas fields, so normally she was only a quiet presence during these sessions. But this time, she timidly raised her hand and said, "I think I know an expert."

"What?" Danny looked at her in surprise.

"Angie's husband, Vic. He's the general manager for Northwestern Natural Gas."

"Whoa," Danny said. "I know Angie's your best friend, but Northwestern has to have huge connections to Gannon Oil."

"I'm sure they do, but Angie was born and raised on the reservation. Remember?"

Danny was skeptical. "True," he said, "But what makes you think Vic would be willing to help us?"

Bri cast her eyes at the floor. "Please don't fire me, Danny, but I already asked him. You and I are having lunch at their place on Saturday."

Chapter 20

Bri was greatly relieved when she left the office. Maybe, just maybe, she could at last make her own contribution to everybody else's efforts.

But the lawsuit wasn't Bri's only worry. Danny hadn't been his normal self lately. He wasn't eating like he should — wasn't sleeping. She had never seen him so thin.

Most worrisome was that the sparkle had left his eyes. At times, he acted downright morose — a condition totally out of character for her normally affable, good-natured big brother. Was he sick? Was there something wrong that he wasn't telling her?

Then a passing comment Danny made about the rumor that Amanda was engaged pulled all the threads together. Bri realized that he wasn't sick, he was in mourning. Why hadn't she guessed it before? Danny was suffering like a teenage boy who just lost his first love — and in keeping with his character, suffered in silence, not telling anyone, not admitting weakness or need.

Asking him about it got her a surly reply. "I don't want to talk about it. She's gone and that's the end of it," he said.

Just voicing the question drove him into a deeper funk — so deep she was afraid to leave him home alone that night. She pretended to fall asleep on the couch, but was actually awake when he tenderly covered her with a blanket. Only after she knew he was deeply asleep himself did she quietly slip out of the house.

*

It was one thing to cook and clean for him, but this was something else entirely. Was she being a busy-body? Was she stepping into a place that was none of her business? Maybe, but she'd just have to chance it. If Danny knew she was calling Amanda, he'd most likely be furious. But he wouldn't stay mad forever, and who knew—it just might work. She scrolled to Amanda's name in her iPhone contact list and pressed "call."

"Hello?"

"Amanda?"

"Yes."

"This is Brianna Sanders."

"Bri!" Amanda responded, "It's so good to hear from you. How are you?"

"I'm just fine. I've been missing you. I just had to break down and call. If Danny finds out I've done this, he'll probably kill me. "

"Is he still that angry with me?"

"No, he's not angry with you at all, but he may shoot me if he finds out I've stepped into his business." Brianna's heart pounded. *Here goes nothing.* "I need to ask you a question. Rumor up here is that you're engaged. Is that true?"

There was a long pause before Amanda said, "Yes, it's true." She spoke so softly that Bri could barely hear her.

Bri's heart sank. The call now seemed pointless. Trying hard to keep the disappointment out of her voice she said, "I see—so, when's the happy date?"

"It's . . . uh . . . well, there was one, but now there's not. We're just letting things kind of settle down for a while."

"Oh, I'm sorry Amanda. I shouldn't have asked. It's really none of my business. But you're a friend. I think you should know that I have another friend who's really hurting too."

"Danny? How is he?"

"I wish I could say he's fine, but it would be a lie. He misses you terribly. He's not been the same since he heard you were engaged."

Another long pause. Finally Amanda asked, "Is he seeing anyone?"

"No. He's not had a date since you two separated. Remember how much time he was spending on all those families that began showing up at his office? Well, it's worse. He's working twelve to fourteen hours a day, seven days a week. There are over six hundred of those cases now, and none of his clients have any money. He's carrying the load all by himself. He's not only tired, Amanda, he's dead broke."

"He always did work too hard."

Bri detected a tremor in the woman's voice. "Amanda, I can't tell you how many times he's said little things that all add up to one great big thing. He wants to talk to you, but he says that all he's got to offer you is the same thing that caused you two to drift apart in the first place. Was it really that bad?"

For a moment, Bri thought the connection was dropped. Then she heard the unmistakable sound of Amanda crying softly. She allowed the woman a bit of space before asking, "Are you okay?"

"Yes," came an almost whispered reply. "I . . . I'm sorry. Just a moment."

Bri heard her blow her nose, away from the phone. She imagined her wiping tears and couldn't help the tear that slid down her own cheek.

"This is so hard," Amanda finally said. "I feel terrible. Danny must believe I abandoned him, and the truth is, I did. I guess I was being selfish. I thought the reason he wasn't seeing me was that he was tired of us being us. I felt like I was being thrown away. After what you've said, I guess he was doing all he could. Now I've gotten myself into a real mess."

"A mess?"

"Yes. Greg's a great guy but I just can't see myself spending the rest of my life with him. I think the only reason I said yes when he asked was that after Danny, I questioned whether another man would ever want me. Oh, Bri, what am I going to do?" The woman broke out in real sobs, and this time didn't try to conceal them.

When the crying subsided, Brianna asked cautiously, "What do you want to do, Amanda? What do you want *me* to do?"

"It's what I *don't* want to do that's the real question. God help me, Bri, I really don't want to marry Greg. I've known that for some time. I've been trying to decide when and how to tell him. It's so ironic that you called. You're the first person I've told."

Bri stepped out on a limb. "Why don't you call Danny and talk to him about it?"

"Talk to him about my troubles with another boyfriend? I don't know if I could do that. He'd hate me worse than he does now."

"Believe me, Amanda, he doesn't hate you."

"It just wouldn't be proper, Bri. At least as long as I'm still engaged."

"What if I could get him to do it? Would you take his call?"

Another long silence. "Yes," she finally said. "In fact, that might be helpful. At least we could talk some things out. I'd like that very much."

"Let me work on it from my end. You know how stubborn he is. Just don't you go doing something foolish, like letting this Greg guy put that other ring on your finger. I don't want my big brother chasing a married woman."

For the first time in the conversation, Amanda laughed. "I won't. I promise. Now let's quit talking about men, and tell me what you've been doing this past year."

When the conversation began, Bri felt the weight of every one of her thirty-one years. But as Amanda allowed the door to open just a little on possibilities with Danny, she felt the tension lift. Soon she and Amanda twittered like eighteen-year-olds, renewing a deep friendship that both thought was lost forever.

Chapter 21

"You are so wrong," Brianna chuckled as she reached across the car and slugged Danny playfully in the shoulder. "I may be thirty-one years old, big brother, but I certainly won't end up being an old maid! You, on the other hand, will probably be a lonely old hermit living all by yourself in a cave somewhere."

Danny's first instinct was to vehemently deny her prediction, but at the same moment, he was struck by the fear that she might actually be right.

They were traveling in Danny's fully-restored, candy-apple red 1968 Mustang Cobra convertible, the only extravagant indulgence Danny had ever allowed himself. Even at that, he'd been able to cobble it together over the years for a surprisingly small sum.

The body was a bit rusty, and nothing worked when he found the Mustang in the back of a junk yard near Santa Fe several years ago. He bought it for only two hundred bucks.

He replaced the original 289-cubic-inch engine with a huge 460-cubic-inch monster block he took out of a wrecked Lincoln. He installed full race cams and had the engine blueprinted and balanced. He tracked down a dual-quad manifold up in Durango and topped it with twin Holly four-barrel carburetors equipped with progressive linkage. The engine would run fairly economically during normal highway driving, but when he tromped down on the accelerator and kicked both carburetors in, it would explode to life and the Mustang would fly.

Danny's most exotic find was in the back room of an old tractor repair shop in Cuba, New Mexico. It was an eight-speed Mercedes GT racing transmission. The owner couldn't remember how he'd come by it and had no idea what it was worth. Sitting on the shelf of a foreign auto parts dealership on either coast, it would have fetched more than six thousand dollars. Danny got it for fifty-five bucks.

Back then the car still didn't look like much, but other than a lot of skinned knuckles, it had only cost him about two thousand bucks to put back on the road. He built a dual exhaust system. The street legal set of mufflers made the Mustang as quiet as a new Cadillac when running around town. But at the racetrack, he removed the diverter covers from a set of chromed straight pipes that allowed the powerful engine a huge, throaty roar.

Danny's need for speed was fully slaked the day his special racing speedometer nudged 160 miles per hour. It was the one and only time he'd actually had the car in seventh gear. With one more gear to go, he assumed the top end would be somewhere in the neighborhood of 200. But fear and his sense of responsibility convinced him that eighth gear would just have to wait.

Over the next three years, scrimping to save every dime he could spare, he paid for a beautiful candy-apple red metallic paint job, new upholstery, and re-chromed trim and bumpers.

Radar detectors were illegal in New Mexico. Danny's heavy foot and frequent trips between Farmington and Albuquerque made a powerful CB radio a necessity in order to avoid speed traps. The radio had long since paid for itself.

All in all, the now well-known Mustang had cost him just over five thousand dollars, but was worth over thirty thousand. It was all the equity he owned in the world.

*

Brianna shielded her long, blonde locks against the wind with a colorful scarf, but Danny was unconcerned that the warm summer wind mussed his hair.

Their destination was a mile past Bondad, a tiny town lying in the Animas River gorge barely across the Colorado border. The town straddled the river and consisted only of a collection of several scattered homes, a small gas station and a few far-flung mini-mansions belonging to the lucky few outsiders who had discovered the place.

Bri's next question stabbed straight to Danny's heart. "Heard anything from Amanda?"

It took him a second or two to reply. "Naw," he said quietly, hoping his emotions didn't show. "She's engaged, and it's probably just as well. I can't afford a girlfriend right now anyway."

"You should call her, Danny."

He winced. A thousand times he'd nearly picked up the phone to do just that. But each time he realized that his inability to nurture the relationship was what killed it in the first place. Dear God, how he ached to see her — to hear her voice. What he'd give to hold her again and smell the sweetness of her hair as she rested her head against his shoulder. He blinked and shook off the thought. If anything, the demands of the dry-well cases were worse now than when they'd drifted apart.

"What good would it do?" he asked. "I don't have a life anymore. All I could offer her is even less than what we had before. It just wouldn't work."

"Danny Whitehorse, you never know about a woman's heart." Maybe her engagement happened because she thinks you don't care anymore."

"Or maybe it's because the guy's great in the sack, and has money and time." Danny gave her a false grin. "Stuff that happens in the sack I can compensate for, but money and time? I don't stand a chance when it comes to those things."

"Oh, Danny, don't talk like that." Bri gave his shoulder another playful slug. "Maybe she's just waiting for a signal from you that you still care."

Danny resisted the impulse to give an angry retort. He didn't want Bri to know how much this conversation hurt. He tried to lighten things by saying with a chuckle, "Maybe she's packing a shotgun in case I dare poke my nose up again."

"I'm sure that's not true. How about if I call her and just casually check in? We were pretty good friends, you know."

Danny thought for several moments. Could such a casual, indirect contact somehow crack open a door? He didn't dare even hope. "I don't know, sis. If you want to call her, go ahead. But you better keep it between you two. Even if she was willing to give things another try, the timing for me right now is lousy." He smiled at her and winked. "I'll just keep on sprinkling saltpeter on my eggs in the morning, and avoid encounters with double-breasted fire hydrants."

*

Approaching the state border, Danny turned the conversation back on her. "Don't you worry about me, Brianna Sanders. You're the one who needs to settle down and give me some nieces and nephews to spoil. Time's running out, girl."

Bri winced. She had given her heart away once, shortly after Danny returned to Farmington, and it proved to be a disaster. For her, a man's character was everything. Her strong religious convictions dictated that she only marry a man of her own faith. She thought she had everything in the person of one Andrew Lloyd Jessop, an exceptionally handsome man who blew into Farmington from the tiny northwestern Arizona town of Fredonia and swept her off her feet. It looked like she had finally found her eternal companion, but eternity expired the very day they were to marry.

As she was reaching to open the door of the LDS Temple in Albuquerque, a very pregnant young woman stopped her and begged her not to marry Andrew, saying he was the father of her unborn child. The marriage was off. She later learned that the man had a wife in Fredonia he'd never bothered to divorce. How he'd come up with a temple recommend for the wedding, Bri never figured out.

The experience smashed her gentle, trusting heart to bits. Thereafter, she pushed away man after man as soon as she perceived them getting too close.

"Whoa, mister," Bri said. "I don't see any rings on your finger or children playing around your front door."

"Yeah, but I'm ugly, old and boring."

Bri laughed as Danny turned left off of the highway, just past the Animas River bridge. "Ugly and boring you're not, but old? You may be right!"

"At least I don't have to worry about my boobs sagging or hearing the alarm go off on my biological clock."

"Now listen here, buddy. You old men are on pretty shaky ground when you start talking about things that sag with age. I've got plenty of time to have a couple of kids if I want. When the Lord wants me to be married, he'll send an earthquake or something to announce it."

"Tell you what, Bri, you can call Amanda if you let me hook you up with Jason Stevens. He's single, a highly successful lawyer, and, according to what I understand, not a bad looking guy. Plus, he's a Mormon. You two should get along real well."

Bri knew that Stevens was Danny's best friend from law school days and now had a very lucrative practice in Utah. She had met him briefly a couple of years ago while he was down visiting Danny. He was indeed interesting, and quite handsome. But Danny's attempts to match them up had so far failed to overcome her reluctance to pay serious attention to any man, friend of Danny's or not.

"You keep bringing him up," Bri said, her mouth turning down in the beginnings of a frown." I'm sure he's a nice man, but the last thing I need right now is another 'nice man.' I'll call Amanda, but no promises about your Mr. Stevens other than to say that I'll consider it."

Chapter 22

The arched, wrought-iron gate read, *El Rancho de los Capaletti*. At Brianna's instruction, Danny turned onto a long gravel driveway leading to a Victorian-style mini-mansion situated a quarter-mile back from the road. The circular drive delivered them directly to a wide, round porch where Vic and Angie Capaletti stood waiting to greet them.

Danny knew Vic by sight, but that was about all. The short, stocky middle-aged Italian sported a thick shock of wavy salt-and-pepper hair. He greeted Danny with a hearty handshake and a quick smile as Bri gave Angie an affectionate hug.

Angie's tall, willowy figure, high cheek-bones and long, straight, raven hair reminded Danny of the singer Cher. The image was enhanced by the woman's stoic demeanor that was more a by-product of her natural shyness rather than any willful intent.

Danny vaguely remembered Angie being around the Sanders home as a little girl, but it took an adult introduction from Bri to fix the woman's identity in his mind. She and Bri were together so often that she and Danny had developed a passing friendship as well.

Danny first heard Vic's name when Angie started talking about him a couple of years before the dry well families began showing up. Vic's company had transferred him to Farmington from somewhere back east.

Angie said the West was "Love at first sight," to him. He loved the mountains, he loved the wide-open desert landscapes, he loved the heritage and culture of the Indian people, and he apparently fell instantly and completely in love with Angie Benally. They married just three months after they first met.

After Vic and Angie built *El Rancho de los Capaletti*, their dream home, Bri was an almost constant houseguest. The latest news was that the first Capaletti child was on its way.

*

As Danny stepped through the door, he caught his breath. He knew that Angie was an artist of some sort, but now for the first time, was able to witness the depth of the woman's talent. The walls were covered with stunning, hauntingly surreal depictions of her homeland and people, rendered in the soft tans, browns, pinks, corals, and charcoals of the southwest.

He remembered Bri showing him the near perfect pencil sketch Angie had made of her the first day they met in second grade. She said it had taken Angie less than ten minutes to draw it. Bri treasured the gift and to this day, kept it in a gilt frame above her bed.

To Danny's embarrassment it took only moments from the time they sat down to the sumptuous meal Angie had prepared for Bri to impertinently inform their hosts, "Vic, we're here because Danny needs your help."

"Jeez, Bri," Danny objected. "It'd be a shame to ruin this meal by having me flap my jaws all the way through it."

"Bullshit!" Brianna shot back. "What you have to say is far too important to wait. If you don't tell them, I will!"

Danny was shocked. It was one of only two or three times in his life he'd heard his Mormon little sister cuss.

"Go ahead, Counselor," Vic responded with a wry smile. "Bri won't let us take another bite in peace if you don't."

Other than asking an occasional question to clarify some point or another, Vic remained quiet and thoughtfully attentive through Danny's recitation. But by the end, Angie was sitting straight up in her chair, looking intensely angry.

". . . So the bottom line is that we have no money left to prosecute the case, no experts we can afford to pay to tell us if we're on to something or not, and a lot of families whose children are going to bed hungry tonight. I'm broke, desperate, and a little embarrassed. It was Bri's idea for me to come and talk to you."

Vic cleared his throat to respond, but Angie beat him to the punch. "Danny Whitehorse, why didn't you come to us sooner? The first thing we're going to do is get some food to those families. You and I both know what it's like to wake up hungry out on that reservation. I'll start a food bank operation and begin delivering groceries out there tomorrow. Bri, I know you'll help too."

"I certainly will," Bri responded. "But where are we going to get the money? I have a little in savings, but it's not going to feed very many people. There are a lot of people who would help if they knew the facts, but it'll take time to get donations and organize a food drive."

Angie appeared strangely thoughtful. She looked back and forth at Bri and Danny then said, "I'm going to tell you a secret Vic and I have that we've never revealed to anyone other than my accountant. But it absolutely must never leave this room. Do both of you promise?"

Danny and Bri nodded their assent.

"Bri, you've always known that I can get my hands on a little money if I have to. The reason is that I'm rich—really rich. I don't even know exactly how much money I have, but there's more than seven zeroes behind the number.

Brianna was dumbstruck. "You—rich? How?"

"People in New York like those little pictures I spend all my time painting, and they go absolutely nuts over them in Europe. They start selling at around forty to fifty-thousand dollars in New York and three times that in Europe. For the past five years or so, I've been selling two or three paintings a month. I recently sold one in London for more than three hundred thousand dollars. Don't worry about getting the food bank started. We'll start with ten thousand dollars and put more in as we need it. Besides, I can use the tax write-off.

"From this minute forward, Counselor, you take Brianna off of everything else and put her to work on getting those people fed!" Angie stood abruptly and walked out of the room. She returned moments later carrying her purse. She pulled out a checkbook and wrote a check while everyone watched, and handed it to Danny. He looked at it and nearly fell out of his chair. It was made out to him in the amount of seventy-five thousand dollars.

"This is your initial retainer for representing our people Mr. Whitehorse," Angie stated. "I'll place another seventy-five thousand in your account next week, as soon as I can arrange the transfer. If you eventually sue Gannon Oil and win, you can pay me back from the proceeds, but only once all the families have been reimbursed and you've been paid the customary legal fees for such actions. If you need more money and don't ask me for it I will be highly offended and shall strongly consider replacing you as our people's attorney. Is that understood?"

Danny stuttered in disbelief. "Uh, well, I'm, uh. . . I don't know what to say. You know, we might not ever recover a dime."

"That doesn't matter. If Gannon Oil has done what you suspect, we can't let them get away with it." She pointed at the check. "The first thing I want you to do with that money is pay Kathy, Chaco and Bri every dime of back pay they have coming. Give Kathy and Chaco a five-thousand-dollar bonus each and a five-hundred-dollar-per-week raise. Oh, and by the way, pay this little hussy here a couple of thousand and give her a raise, too. Pay off all your office bills. You can't work if you don't have telephones to talk on or lights to see with. If you need to hire additional office staff, hire them. If you need to associate other attorneys in the case, do it. I want you to take ten thousand dollars as back pay for yourself, and then I expect you to pay yourself a decent personal salary as well—no less than fifteen hundred dollars per week after taxes. Agreed?"

Danny was momentarily speechless. "Uh, sure. How in the world can I ever thank you?"

"By working your ass off and getting those wells turned back on. Now give me a hug and you and Vic go smoke a couple of those smelly old cigars he keeps in the den while Bri and I clean up this kitchen."

*

Danny declined Vic's offer of a cigar. "Do you mind if I indulge? "Vic asked.

"No, no. Go right ahead." Danny took a seat in a richly upholstered burgundy leather chair where he watched the man clip off the end of a fat cigar. He lit it with an ornate butane lighter, and puffed up a huge cloud of smoke.

"You say over six hundred wells have been shut off?" Vic asked.

Danny did his best not to cough. "Six hundred and forty-eight that we know of."

Vic shook his head. "That's damned dangerous."

"Yeah," Danny responded. "I wouldn't want to be facing over six hundred lawsuits at once."

"That's not what I mean. Keeping a well shut down for a long time makes it more dangerous. Gas wells are like a garden hose. As long as the water's flowing freely, there isn't much pressure against the sides of the hose. But close the nozzle off and the pressure builds up. Almost every blowout happens when wells are shut down and the pressure causes a pipe or wellhead part to fail. Having over six hundred of them shut down at once is like playing Russian roulette. That's probably why Gannon's had that blow-out last month."

Danny maintained his silence about the real cause of the blow-out as Vic leaned back in his office chair and blew a great halo of blue smoke. "There's another thing I don't understand," he said. "You say you're having a hard time following these new pipelines. Aren't they marked? If I'm not mistaken, it's against the law to not do that. The signs are supposed to say what kind of pipeline it is, who owns it, and have arrows that indicate the direction of the pipe. As I recall, they're supposed to be posted every quarter-mile."

The statement hit Danny like a bombshell. Slapping his forehead he exclaimed, "Of course! I'm such an idiot. I've seen those little yellow signs on top of pipelines all my life. You say the law requires them?"

"It's part of the county building code. I'm sure it's part of the tribal building code, too. If memory serves me right, there's even a federal requirement. I know we would never put in an unmarked pipeline. There's just too many people out there digging around with backhoes and bulldozers. Not posting signs is just plain foolish."

"So why would Gannon do that?"

"I can't answer that. But pipelines are put in to be used, not just left abandoned in the ground. I have a feeling that if you can solve the mystery of those unmarked pipelines, you just might solve your case. Danny, my friend, I want to take a good look at that map of yours."

Chapter 23

Kathy's eyes widened when Danny showed her Angie's check. "Holy cow!" she exclaimed.

"Go to the bank and deposit it, then come back and pay every bill we owe."Figure out back pay for you and Chaco and add five thousand dollars for each of you. Do the same with Brianna's pay and give her an additional two thousand."

Kathy began to weep. "Danny, you don't have to. . ." He reached out and touched a finger to her lips. "Shhh," he said. "I know you wouldn't take it from me, but it's Angie's orders. Look at it this way. Now we can get phones with a real intercom and stop having to yell back and forth."

Danny confirmed that the county building code required pipelines to be clearly marked, but ran into a blank wall at the reservation border. "I don't have any jurisdiction out there," the county's chief building inspector explained. "Show me an unmarked pipeline on the county side of the border and I'll issue somebody a citation. But I can't help you on the reservation."

Danny called Window Rock and caught the head of the Tribal Building and Housing Department just as the man was leaving his office. "Yes, oil and gas pipelines require a building permit and are all supposed to be marked," the man confirmed, "but we pretty much leave that up to the contractor."

"Isn't that a lot like leaving the fox guarding the henhouse?"

"Look, Mr. Whitehorse, there's only me and one other man to cover the entire reservation. We're running as much as six weeks behind right now just trying to keep up with the permits inside reservation cities. A lot of construction people get tired of waiting for us and just go ahead and build anyway. That's probably what happened with your pipelines."

"Can you tell me what information is asked in a pipeline permit application?"

"We want to know who they are, where they're going, what the pipeline will be used for and how they're going to build it. They have to give us a building plan that's signed by a certified pipeline engineer. Oil companies can either do the construction work themselves or hire an outside contractor. Look, Mr. Whitehorse, I'm in a hurry here. These permit applications are public records. You're welcome to come down and look at them yourself."

"Does the tribe have maps showing existing pipelines on the reservation?"

"We're supposed to. I don't know how current they are. The last updates I'm aware of are three or four years old, but you're welcome to a copy of whatever we have."

Danny was cautiously optimistic. Surely Gannon had taken out the proper permits, and maybe—just maybe—the permits would shed some light on what Gannon was up to on Eagle Dome and Tabletop Mesa.

*

He was wrong. An all-day search of tribal building permits going back over five years yielded nothing. The only usable record he came away with was a cell phone picture of a tattered reservation map he found hanging on the back wall of the Inspection Department. It showed roads and trails, chapter boundaries, and oil and gas pipelines—all dated five or more years ago.

He and Kathy spent three days transposing the well and pipeline detail from the tribe's map onto the map in the office, overlaying the mapping work that was taking place on the Eagle Dome field. "See any pattern yet?" Danny asked two days later as he and Chaco inspected their latest update.

Chaco shook his head. "Still too many gaps. My boys have been careful about crossing the rez border, but there aren't any fences or lines on the ground out there." Chaco pointed out three pipelines. "We inadvertently traced across the border to these wells, but that's as far as the new pipelines seem to go. Doesn't make much sense."

Danny shook his head. "Question is, does all of this really mean anything? The proof we need might be staring us in the face and we just don't know it. It's time for Vic Capaletti to see this."

*

The next afternoon, Vic stood before the map and traced the red lines indicating the unmarked pipelines with his finger. "I've never seen anything like this," he said. "You've found entirely separate pipeline systems that duplicate the function of the marked legal pipelines in significant detail. It just doesn't make sense."

Chaco pointed to a heavy, dark line that paralleled the reservation boundary on the county side. "I assume this is a trunk line. Wouldn't the unmarked pipelines need to connect up with one of these to do any good?"

"Yes. This one belongs to El Paso Natural Gas. Our trunks are further east and north. We carry some of Gannon's gas, but it's not from reservation wells."

Chaco pointed to one of the three pipelines they'd traced beyond the reservation border. "This pipeline runs east to this well, then it just seems to disappear. It's the same way with two others." Chaco pointed them out.

"Hmmm." Vic scratched his chin and looked closer. "All three pipelines appear to terminate at loners." He saw Danny and Chaco's puzzled expressions. "Sorry," he apologized. "That's an industry term for a well that connects directly into the trunk line with no other wells attached." Vic pointed at one of the loner wells. "In the case of this one, it actually would have been shorter for the pipeline to connect directly into the main trunk line than to go all the way to this well."

"So what do you think it means?" Chaco asked.

"I don't know for sure, but if these unmarked pipelines are actually carrying gas, as you suspect, the minute the new pipeline hooked up to the loner well, there would have been a huge jump in how much gas that well was delivering into the trunk line."

Danny immediately grasped the implications. "And you guys have records of all that, right?"

"Yes. Otherwise the producers couldn't get paid."

Danny could scarcely conceal his excitement. "What kind of records are we looking for?"

"It's called an SR-30 form. There's a meter at every trunk line connection point that measures the gas the producer delivers. Every month, a meter reader from our company and a representative from the producer read the meter and record the reading on the SR-30 form. Each man countersigns it and both get a copy. It's not a lot different than what happens with your gas meter at home."

"What do the meters look like?" Danny asked.

"You've probably seen them all your life and just didn't know what they were. They're housed in a hinged steel box attached to a two-foot-square concrete pad. The boxes are painted dark-green and are about eighteen inches square."

"So that's what those boxes are," Chaco exclaimed. "Remember when we were kids, Danny? We played on them, threw rocks at them, even shot them occasionally with Uncle Samuel's .22 rifle." He looked at Vic. "You mean we could have blown ourselves up?"

"Naw." Vic chuckled. "A .22 won't penetrate the box, but some of the more powerful deer rifles will. We replace a lot of them. The only part of the meter that's above ground is the face, and its set deep into the concrete and covered by a thick metal lid. Everything else is below ground inside the pipe."

"Those SR-30 forms could be our smoking gun," Danny said, "and we can get our hands on them. Once I file the lawsuit I'll get a discovery order that will allow us to examine them. Your information couldn't have come at a better time, Vic. That reservation is a giant ticking time bomb, and right now, I may be the only person alive who can keep it from blowing up."

*

Even as Danny was speaking, three figures lay hidden in the sagebrush on the brow of a small hill overlooking Mesa Verde Creek Canyon several miles west of the famous National Park. Two of the men gazed through binoculars pointed across the canyon toward one of the most remote gas well sites on Tabletop Mesa.

Beyond the well, they could see billowing columns of dust raised by the construction machinery used to clear the ground and erect the fencing around more distant Gannon wells.

"They're moving quickly," Raymond Takai said.

Andrew Zonnie nodded his head. "Three — maybe four days tops and they'll be at this site. We need to act now."

Billy Biakeddy was holding the horses nearby. "Everything's ready," he said. "Eddie Nez sent me one of his timers. I tested it yesterday and it works."

"Good," Zonnie said. "I rigged a pack-saddle to carry the cans. That old Jake's a good pack mule. He'll have no trouble keeping up."

"Sure would be easier to just drive in, like David Nakai did," Raymond said, "but it's just too risky with Gannon's patrols everywhere."

Billy kicked at a clod and said, "Hey, it's only a half-day ride, and our horses can go were Gannon's vehicles can't. It's worth being a little saddle-sore. So when do we do this?"

"Tomorrow night," Raymond said. "We can't chance them starting to fence this well."

"Tomorrow night it is," Billy said. He handed his companions their reins and said, "Let's get out of here. These horses will need a good rest between now and then."

*

The next night, just before one a.m., the stillness of Tabletop Mesa was rent by a resounding blast as the darkness was shattered by a roaring pillar of orange flame that seemed to touch the sky. Unlike the first well explosion, this blast ignited the nearby sagebrush. The blaze spread upward toward Mesa Verde Creek Canyon, but before it reached the rim, a short drenching thunder storm rumbled through, slowing the fire enough that arriving fire crews were able to prevent it from exploding up into the tinder-dry cedar forests of Mesa Verde National Park.

Chapter 24

The sickness in the pit of Lucas Blackthorn's stomach wasn't from the rolling and pitching ride of the helicopter, but rather, from his fear of Red Gannon's dangerous, unpredictable temper which Lucas feared would explode as they looked down on another huge, towering spout of flame. Gannon was at the controls, with Lucas in the front passenger seat, and Jim Parker seated behind.

Twenty or more vehicles surrounded the site. Two company-owned pumper trucks were pouring streams of water on the burning wellhead to little effect. The advance team of well fire experts would supposedly be here by noon.

"Well Blackthorn, you still think all this was caused by a couple of Boy Scouts playing with matches?" Gannon growled darkly.

The security chief put on the best front he could. "It was probably the same bunch who blew up the first one. I've still not heard a word about any group calling itself NALM, and we've been listening. We've got to find these little peckerwoods and deal with them, that's all."

"*How?*" Parker whined. "It's nearly impossible for us to get any kind of information off that reservation."

Blackthorn resisted the urge to turn around and smash the man in the face. Though his stomach churned, his reply sounded calm. "We have twenty or thirty Navajos from the Shiprock area working for us," Blackthorn replied. "I'll throw a little money on the table and see if any of them want to play James Bond."

"It better work, and fast," Parker said, gesturing toward the towering inferno. "We can't afford any more of these."

"See that pretty little bonfire down there?" Gannon barked." It's not costing me a thing. Every penny is coming out of y'all's Cayman accounts. You both better pray this is the last of these, because if your money runs out and I have to start spending mine, I'm going to mount a few new heads on my office wall, and I don't mean wild game."

It was no idle threat. Parker and Blackthorn knew too much to be simply "let go." They'd be considered loose ends, and Gannon dealt with loose ends quite permanently.

*

Chaco learned that the second group of bombers mimicked the actions of the first, including pasting up a letter to Gannon Oil, and immediately reported the fact to Danny.

Again all awaited the disastrous outcome that was certain to follow. Surely a second well explosion would force Gannon to reveal the real cause of the well fires and call in every possible police agency. But incongruously, Gannon's public explanation for the second explosion was exactly the same as the first — a mechanical equipment failure.

*

"This silence is unfathomable," Danny said as he stared out his office window. He turned to Chaco and Kathy and asked, "What are you guys thinking?"

Chaco's response was immediate. "It proves they have something really big to hide. Otherwise the feds would be swarming all over the reservation."

Kathy nodded her agreement. "Nothing else makes sense."

"It has to be huge," Danny said. "These well explosions have got to be costing the company millions. And if those wells were still producing, as we suspect, it's costing even more millions in lost revenues."

*

Gannon's lack of public acknowledgement didn't mean there was no reaction. There was an immediate rush to finish fencing all the remaining well sites. The desert darkness was increasingly punctuated with pinpoints of light as Gannon installed generators and security lights. Guard shacks were placed inside each well's entry gate, and two armed guards took up a twenty-four-hour watch. And through it all, Gannon Oil continued its deafening public silence.

End,
Part One

Chapter 25

Butterflies churned in Danny's stomach as he greeted a clamorous crowd of waiting television and newspaper reporters on the steps of the Federal Courthouse. Only four days had elapsed since the second well explosion, but Danny had to get the lawsuit filed in hopes of deterring the sabotage of more wells. He could have filed his pleadings electronically, but Danny wanted the filing to be as public as possible.

The lawsuit alleged seven separate causes of action and contained twenty-six affidavits of the named plaintiffs he needed to qualify the case as a federal class-action. Among the plaintiffs was Robert Begay.

Hoping to put Gannon off balance, Danny had Kathy contact every major newspaper and television station from Denver to Albuquerque to give them advance notice of the filing.

Danny nervously eyed the gaggle of reporters. Standing before the court was not nearly as intimidating as this. "I'd like to make a brief statement before taking any of your questions," he said. "Nearly three years ago Gannon Oil, headquartered right here in Farmington, arbitrarily began turning off natural gas wells on the Navajo reservation, to the great detriment of the families whose land allotments the wells were drilled on, and to the tribe.

"These capricious actions were unnecessary and unjustified. We have reason to believe that all the wells subject to this action are fully capable of producing commercial quantities of natural gas, and that in turning off the wells, Gannon has not only acted in bad faith, but with reckless and willful disregard of the rights of our clients—many of whom have been bankrupted. Gannon Oil's unwarranted, callous acts have literally taken food out of babies' mouths.

"We have just filed a federal class-action lawsuit against Gannon Oil on behalf of at least six hundred and forty-eight such families."

Danny's mouth suddenly went dry as he looked into the television cameras and realized he was likely speaking to an audience of thousands. He paused to work up a little moisture in his mouth, then continued. "We have it on good authority that shutting down perfectly good gas wells makes them far more dangerous than if the wells were turned on and producing. We've recently seen two Gannon wells blow up while they were shut down, endangering not just property, but lives. It's our position that the continued shut-down of wells subject to our lawsuit poses a clear and present danger to the reservation and to the families who live nearby."

He paused again, which prompted the reporters to hurl a barrage of questions at him. Danny raised his hands and said, "Please, please. I can only answer one question at a time." He pointed at the reporter from an Albuquerque television station. "Let's start right here."

"Mr. Whitehorse, you say you have six hundred and forty-eight individual clients. Why hasn't the tribe joined the lawsuit?"

Danny didn't want to say that getting the tribe to act as an original party plaintiff would have involved a ponderously slow tribal decision-making process. Rather he said, "We've had good consultations with tribal officers, and we expect the tribe's full support."

"How much are you suing Gannon for?" came a shouted question from the back.

"We haven't put a dollar figure to it yet. What I can tell you is that just the lost income of my clients over the past two years is in excess of fifteen million dollars. And that's only a quarter of what the tribe has lost. We expect total damages of fifty million dollars or more, not including exemplary and punitive damages."

Danny pointed at the reporter from the local newspaper.

"What does Gannon Oil have to say about all this?" the owlish-looking-man asked.

"You're going to have to ask them. We did that early in the process, but we now believe the excuse they gave us to be untrue. Gannon Oil could have stopped this action at any time by simply turning the wells back on and making a commitment to restore our clients to their previous condition. They've failed on both counts."

"You ever met Red Gannon?" came a shouted question from the back.

"No."

"I'll bet he wants to meet you," came the ominous reply.

The rest of the reporters laughed.

Danny answered question after question for nearly an hour before finally cutting the session off. "You're sweating," Kathy said as they settled into Danny's car for the short drive back to the office.

"That was pretty intense," he said as he wiped his brow. "How do you think it went?"

"Sounded fine to me. We'll see how it plays out on the news tonight."

Chapter 26

Red-faced and sweating, Jim Parker rushed into Blackthorn's office with a *Farmington Clarion* news reporter in tow. "We've got a big problem," Parker hissed. He turned to the reporter. "Tell him exactly what you told me."

The reporter, an owlish, nerdy looking kid who looked to be just out of high school, said, "I just covered a press conference over at the federal courthouse. This attorney, Danny Whitehorse, filed a class-action lawsuit against your company for turning off some gas wells out on the reservation. Says he has six hundred and forty-eight clients. I came to see what you have to say about that. Can you give me an exclusive?"

Blackthorn's eyes widened and he started from his chair. "We on the record or off?"

"I'd prefer on," the young man said.

"Well, I'd prefer *off* for the moment."

"Okay," the reporter said hesitantly. "But ..."

"Don't worry, kid, you'll get your statement," Blackthorn assured. "You two sit down." Lucas indicated two leather chairs against the wall behind them. He returned to his desk and said, "Young man, I want you to tell me exactly what happened."

Using his carefully taken notes to make sure he made no mistakes, the reporter told them about the press conference. "That's about it," he concluded. "Have you turned off those wells, Mr. Blackthorn?"

"Look kid, this is the first we've heard of this. We turn wells off and on all the time for any number of reasons. For the record you can report that we deny all Whitehorse's allegations. That's all I'm going to say for now." Blackthorn rose, walked over, and extended the reporter a handshake that in a single motion pulled the surprised young man out of his chair. "Thank you for coming in," Blackthorn said. "We'll have a full statement about this very soon. We appreciate all the fine work your newspaper does for our community." He literally pushed the reporter out of his office and said to his assistant, "Miss Serrano, please show this gentleman out of the building with our thanks."

"Son-of-a-bitch!" he shouted the instant the door closed. He began pacing the floor in front of Parker

"This is bad. What are we going to do, Lucas?" Parker whined.

Blackthorn regarded Parker as nothing more than a sniveling puppet who didn't deserve a penny of the Cayman project riches. He was timid, mousy, indecisive and supremely ill-fitted for crisis management. Blackthorn would have fired the man years ago, but for some unfathomable reason Gannon liked him, and that was the end of the story.

"First thing is to find out if that lawsuit has been served on us yet. If it has, I want a copy on my desk immediately. If not, get someone from legal down to that courthouse right now and get a copy. I think I remember this Whitehorse guy calling me a long time ago. He was bitching about one of the Cayman project wells. I gave him a quick song and dance and never heard from him again. I think Whittington did a run-down. Do you know anything about him?"

"Not a thing."

"Yeah, well, you wouldn't. That idiot from the newspaper is just the beginning. We're about to be avalanched by reporters. Work up a written statement that will put everything off for a while until we know more. Run it by me and get legal to sign off on it, then set up a press conference for this afternoon. We'll deny everything in the lawsuit. Now get out of here and get it done. I've got to call Red. He's going to blow his stack."

Chapter 27

Danny and Kathy met at his house for the 6:00 p.m. news, hoping coverage of the press conference would capture the sympathy of the public and start a ground swell of support for the plight of their clients. What they saw felt more like a kick in the stomach.

The story led with the handsome, wavy-haired, news anchor saying, "Danny Whitehorse, a little-known local attorney who purports to represent a large number of reservation Indians, filed a major lawsuit against one of Farmington's largest companies today." The background video showed Danny talking to reporters on the courthouse steps. "Whitehorse claims that Farmington's largest employer, Gannon Oil, has wrongfully turned off some gas wells on the reservation and is asking for more than fifty million dollars for his clients. News 4's Jaime Penrod has the details."

The scene switched to an equally handsome middle-aged reporter standing in front of the courtroom steps. "That's right, Gene. This brave, or foolish, attorney, depending on your point of view, is taking on a pillar of the Four Corners oil and gas industry. Here's what he had to say."

The scene changed to a close-up of Danny and picked up his statement in mid-sentence. ". . . total figure would be more than fifty million . . . it's likely to go much higher. And . . . does not include exemplary and punitive damages that are sure to be awarded in this case."

It was a clever piece of out-of-context editing sure to enflame every working-class person in the area.

"That's not everything I said," Danny shouted at the TV. He looked at Kathy. "What the hell's going on? They're chopping it up and taking it out of context."

"Here's what Gannon Oil had to say about the situation," the reporter continued.

The scene switched to a carefully coiffed woman in a business suit interviewing Gannon's president, Jim Parker, in the lobby of Gannon's headquarters. "So what's your reaction to this lawsuit, Mr. Parker?"

"It's patently frivolous, malicious, and ridiculously uninformed." Though his voice was calm, Parker's eyes flashed his anger. "These people obviously think they know more about how to manage a gas field than we do. Those wells were shut down for a good reason. We never once said there was no gas in them. But they're getting old. If we don't let them recharge for a few years, they'll become unusable. All we're trying to do is make it so that someday we can pay the children and grandchildren of Whitehorse's clients their fair share of what gas is left on the reservation."

"Gannon Oil is one of the area's largest employers," the reporter said. "Could this have an impact on Four Corners-area jobs?"

Parker pounced on the question. "Absolutely! A judgment the size Whitehorse is talking about would cause layoffs and curtailment of future drilling plans. What we do costs huge amounts of money. We're certainly not going to make future investments in San Juan County if we can't make good management decisions about developing and operating the oil and gas fields we already have."

"Well, there you have it," the reporter said as the camera panned in to focus on her mature, sculpted face. "Gannon Oil says the lawsuit is frivolous and could cost many people their jobs. Is your job one of them? Only time will tell. Now back to the stat . . ."

Parker interrupted. "Can I just say one more thing?"

"Certainly, Mr. Parker," she said.

"I don't believe this is really about Indian families getting royalty checks at all. They survived just fine before we ever drilled a single well out there. I believe Whitehorse's motivation is to line his own ambulance-chasing pockets at the expense of Gannon Oil and the hard-working men and women of our community. He should be ashamed."

"Thank you again, Mr. Parker." The corners of the woman's mouth crept up into just a hint of a wry smile that implied her agreement with Parker's closing shot. "This is Libby Sampson reporting. Now back to the studio."

It was all Danny could do to keep from throwing something at the TV. "Can you believe that?" he yelled.

"Those arrogant bastards," Kathy said, shaking her head. "That wasn't a news report, Danny. It was a hatchet job. I fear we've kicked a very large hornet's nest."

When Danny picked up the newspaper the next morning, the *Farmington Clarion* headline proclaimed, "INDIANS SUING AREA'S LARGEST EMPLOYER." The feature story was written in a way that would inevitably lead readers to believe the lawsuit threatened the jobs and economic security of every family in the Four Corners.

The editorial page was a masterpiece of fear-mongering, characterizing the lawsuit as an attempt by the Indians to "bite the hand that feeds them." It was cleverly crafted to make the public think the Indians were ready to sweep across the reservation border to take away the jobs and economic prosperity of every God fearing Anglo-Saxon family in the Farmington area.

Chapter 28

Even from a half-block away, Danny saw something was amiss. When he pulled up, he saw, "The Only Good Indian is a Dead Indian,"had been spray painted in bright red across the street-level glass door that led up to his office.. "That's going to piss the Landlord off," he mumbled.

As he stepped warily from his car, he spotted several shards of glass lying on the sidewalk. He looked up and found that his second floor office window was smashed. He climbed back into his car and moved it several blocks away, then walked back to the office.

As he and Kathy picked up the broken glass that three large rocks had deposited inside Danny's office, they heard loud voices coming from outside. Kathy stepped toward the window to investigate just as another rock came crashing through, barely missing her head. She screamed as Danny grabbed her and pulled her away. A trickle of blood ran down her cheek from a small glass cut just above the corner of her left eye.

"Stay in the other office," Danny commanded, "and lock the door." He cautiously approached the broken window from the side and looked down. Several dozen protesters shouting slogans, carrying signs and shaking fists up toward the second-story, paraded on the sidewalk below. The protesters spilled out onto the street, partially blocking traffic. At least two news cameras were present, filming the action.

Danny heard people tromping loudly up the stairs. Shouts filled the outside hall as someone tried the knob before pounding hard on the office door. "Don't answer that, Kathy," Danny warned. "Call the police."

Though the police station was only seven blocks away, it took nearly a half-hour for the first officers to arrive. With lights flashing, the police car parked in the middle of the street and chirped its siren. Danny watched cautiously from the window as two officers exited the vehicle and began chatting and laughing with the protesters. Clearly there would be few, if any, arrests made.

It took a long fifteen minutes before a rap came on the office door and a voice shouted, "Farmington Police Department. Open the door, please."

Danny cautiously admitted a rather portly redheaded officer in his late forties and a young, husky Hispanic officer. They introduced themselves as Officers Riley and Chacon.

Kathy, still holding a tissue to the corner of her eye, told them about the rock that nearly hit her.

"Did either of you see who threw it?" the older officer asked.

"No," they both said.

"Not much we can do about it then."

"But it was obviously thrown by someone in that crowd," Kathy said, pointing down toward the demonstrators.

"You want me to arrest all of them? That ain't gonna happen, lady."

"Don't be ridiculous," Kathy spat. "Just go down there and find out who threw it."

The officer shook his head. "The chances of someone in that crowd ratting out one of their own is zero, lady. They're not going to tell me squat."

"What do you suggest we do?" Danny asked.

"Stay away from the window, call your insurance company, and install some plywood." Riley said it with a sneer, that made it clear that he was not sympathetic to Danny and Kathy's plight.

"Look officer," Danny said, trying to hold his temper in check. "Maybe we can't identify the rock-thrower, but you can keep those people from blocking the entrance to this building. There's no way my clients are going to want to come through that mob."

"Come over here, Mr. Whitehorse," Officer Chacon invited. Pointing down at the sidewalk with his night stick, he said, "You're an attorney. Let me ask you. Who owns that sidewalk?"

"I assume the City," Danny replied.

"That's right. Those people down there are walking on a public sidewalk. As far as I can see, they're not blocking or inhibiting anyone else from using it. Now you tell me what law they're breaking?"

"So you're not going to do anything about this?" Kathy hissed.

"We *are* doing something about it," Riley answered. "We're here, aren't we? But understand this. Three members of my family work for Gannon Oil. As far as I'm concerned, you people created this mess and you're just going to have to find your way out of it." He turned to his companion. "Come on, Officer Chacon. There's no crime that we're going to be able to solve here."

The only concession to law and order the officers made was to use their patrol car's speaker to instruct the protesters that they couldn't block the entrance to the stairway or intrude on private property by taking their protest inside. They threatened to arrest anyone caught throwing rocks or damaging property.

Danny made an emergency call to a local glass company who showed up quickly to install a Plexiglas window pane that rocks couldn't break.

The first patrol car left after a time, but was replaced a few minutes later by another which hung around until shortly after two in the afternoon when the protest fizzled out and the people dispersed.

But the troubles were far from over. When protesters returned the next morning, Danny had to get the police to escort him and Kathy into the office. Their phone lines were jammed by hostile calls, some of which included death threats. It was clearly an orchestrated effort against them. After requiring another police escort into the building the following morning, Danny told Chaco and Bri to stay away from the office until things calmed down.

Danny's lawsuit dominated the local news broadcasts, which had a decidedly unfavorable editorial slant. Gannon was winning the PR battle.

The protests unexplainably stopped on the fourth day. But another development caused Danny deep concern for his and Kathy's personal safety. Looking down from the window of his office, he noticed that the two men who had been there all morning were still loitering on the corner across the street. Danny watched as Kathy emerged from the building entrance to take care of the office mailings.

The post office was just two blocks away. As she walked, Danny saw one of the men separate from the other and fall into step a few yards behind her. He watched until Kathy disappeared around the corner on Main Street. The man didn't appear threatening.

A couple of hours later when he again happened to be standing at the window as she went out. This time the other man broke away and followed her. That she was being intentionally followed was obvious and ominous. Was the same thing happening to him? When he told her about it, a deep sense of paranoia settled over them both.

*

That night, Danny watched his rear-view mirror closely as he drove home. He took a long, circuitous route with several stops—first the drive-up window at McDonald's—next, the Post Office for a booklet of stamps he didn't need—and then to a convenience store for a gallon of milk. By the second stop, he identified a dark-green Chevy mini-van discreetly tailing him.

The mini-van stayed with him all the way to his two-bedroom, wood-frame home in one of Farmington's oldest neighborhoods. He watched as it slowed at the intersection of the street he lived on just long enough to see him turn into his carport.

Once safely inside, Danny leaned against the door and realized he was sweating. "Damn, damn, damn," he cursed, furious that his privacy was being so rudely infringed. He locked and bolted all the doors and pulled his curtains closed. Too nervous to eat, he grabbed a cold can of Diet Coke and then sat in his recliner, staring at the walls until well after sundown, his mind working feverishly on what to do about the surveillance.

I'll bet someone's watching my house. Without turning on lights, he put on dark clothing and then slipped out the back door and down the alley. Two doors down, he moved quietly between houses to where he could see the street. *Be just my luck to be caught as a peeping tom.* He made his way to the end of the side-yard hedge that formed the fence between the two properties.

Nothing appeared amiss. Looking back toward his house, he saw only the familiar neighborhood vehicles parked exactly where they should be. He had to expand his search.

Moving carefully to avoid the wash of porch lights burning at some of his neighbors' houses, he dashed between the evenly spaced trees lining the curb. Five houses down, he spotted the minivan parked across the street just at the margin of light from a street-lamp. It was occupied by two men. As Danny watched, the driver occasionally raised a small pair of binoculars in the direction of the house.

The second man looked odd. When he leaned forward into the wash of the streetlight coming through the Van's windshield, Danny saw why. He was wearing a bulky set of headphones.

They've bugged my house! The implications sent shockwaves through his brain. The wave of paranoia that had dogged him all day turned into a tsunami. He fought down an attack of of panic, gathered himself, and made his way back home, determined to find any evidence of clandestine entry.

Once he realized what he was looking for, the search was not difficult. Books that had been in one place on the shelf for a long time had been moved, leaving tiny but recognizable voids in the dust patterns. The neat stacks of ordered priority in which he always placed his monthly bills on the little desk in the dining area were disturbed. Danny kept several houseplant pots in shallow terra-cotta pans that would catch the overflow when he watered. Three of the containers had been moved, as evidenced by the rings that showed on the surfaces where they sat.

He switched his television on and turned the volume up high, hoping the noise would mask any sounds he made as he searched. Within minutes he found three bugs—one under the coffee table in the living room, one under the lamp on his bedside table, and a third device in the mouthpiece of his telephone. If there were others, they were too cleverly hidden for him to find. He had little doubt that the same problem existed at the office.

What had they overheard? Danny reviewed all his conversations inside the house over the past few days. Bri and Kathy had both been here. Was there any mention of Chaco and the NALM?

Then a new thought sent a chill through him. Were these listening devices just corporate spying by Gannon Oil, or were they part of a court-ordered, secret wiretap investigation of the explosions?

Near as he could recall, he hadn't talked to Chaco on his home phone since the day he filed the lawsuit. He was confident the surveillance hadn't started before then. With Chaco immersed in the mapping project, since the filing, their one and only meeting had taken place at the café in Shiprock.

But then there was Kathy and Bri. He had to warn them—and do so without the attention of the two men down the street.

Chapter 29

Danny eased out of his driveway and turned as if heading to town. "Come on fella's," he coaxed. In his rearview mirror, he saw the minivan pull away from the curb a half-block behind.

At the second intersection, he turned left, hoping he had enough of a lead on his pursuers, who now hung back nearly a full block. The instant the van was out of sight he tromped on the accelerator and shot forward a short distance, then made a sharp right turn down an alley. He turned off his headlights as he traversed the narrow passage, relying on the street light at the end of the alley to guide him — praying mightily that no one was in the way.

He watched in the rearview mirror as the van passed the alley trying to catch up with the quarry they believed to be somewhere in front of them. When he reached the street, he turned right again, and with a squeal of tires, sped away in the opposite direction. A couple more twists and turns confirmed that he was free of his unwanted company. It was easy this time. His watchers weren't expecting him to run. But Danny knew it would not necessarily be so easy again.

He called Kathy's cell phone. "Kathy this is Danny. Don't say anything to me except 'yes' or 'no'. Are you at home?"

"Uh, yes."

Your house may be bugged and other people could be listening. Understand?"

There was a long pause before she practically whispered, "yes." Danny could sense her confusion.

"I don't want to frighten you," but people followed me home tonight.

I just discovered that my house is bugged and the people who followed me were outside, watching. Someone may be following you, too. We've got to get together in a safe place and talk. You know that neighbor of yours to the north?"

"Yes," she said again in a cowed voice. Danny could tell her confusion had become fear.

"Is she home?"

"I think so—I mean, yes."

"Good. She has an attached garage. Does she park her car inside?"

"Yes."

"I want you to turn some music up loud in the house and then go out your back door as quiet as you can. Try to stay hidden from the street. Go to your neighbor's back door and tell her you're worried about a stalker or you're playing a joke on someone—something like that. Ask her if she can take you somewhere. I'm parked three blocks away. When she pulls out of the garage, duck down so it looks like she's driving alone. As soon as you're away, call me. If for any reason you can't make that work, call me back right away, okay?"

"Yes," Kathy dutifully replied.

"Don't be scared. This is all going to work itself out." He hoped the encouragement would help. Trouble was, he couldn't define just what "working itself out" meant either for her or for himself.

*

"Are you serious?" Kathy asked as they drove east toward Bloomfield. Danny's call had caught her just as she was about to head to Shiprock and Chaco's house.

"As serious as I can be. They followed me home. Probably followed you too. But what's even more scary is that they've been inside my house. I already found three bugs."

"And you think my house is bugged too?"

"Wouldn't surprise me in the least. That's why I couldn't just come over to talk to you. We've got to warn Brianna as well."

"I'll call her right now. I assume you want her at the café, too."

"Yes. Try not to frighten her, but tell her she's got to make sure she's not being followed."

Kathy dialed Brianna's number and relayed Danny's instructions. "What now?" she asked.

"Call Chaco. I'm sure he knows a lot more about this kind of thing than we do."

Forty-five minutes later, Chaco slid into the restaurant booth next to Kathy. Bri had arrived five minutes earlier. "What's all this about bugs in the house and you being followed?" he asked.

Danny gave Chaco and Bri a detailed briefing. Chaco's face went rigid with anger, while Bri could scarcely contain her fear and disbelief.

"What did you do with the bugs you found?" Chaco asked.

"Left them where they were. I didn't know what else to do."

"Good. That will keep them occupied, at least for a while. Give me your cell phone."

Danny handed it over and watched his cousin disassemble the back, remove the battery and examine the instrument. "It looks clean," he pronounced. "Now girls, give me yours." He repeated the process.

"They all look clean," he said as he handed them back. "But that doesn't mean they're completely secure. These things are nothing but a radio. Anyone with the right monitoring device can pick up your conversations. They make cell phone scanners that work just like police scanners."

"This is bullshit," Kathy spat. "We can't live like this."

"Calm down, sweetie," Chaco said. "I'll get us some secure cell phones in Albuquerque tomorrow." He looked at Danny. "We need to establish some communications security protocols and change some of the ways we do things. I know a security firm in Albuquerque who can debug your houses, cars, and the office. I'll get them up here tomorrow. Until then, no one can even mention the NALM in any of those places.

"We can get scrambling devices for the office phones, but they only work between two phones with the same type of device attached. We might want to consider setting them up on your home phones as well. Calls to or from anywhere else won't be scrambled. Needless to say, Doing all this will tip off the bad guys that we're on to them, but it should stop them from trying to replace the bugs we turn up."

The waitress approached their table and asked if anyone needed refills. Chaco, the only one of them drinking coffee, nodded. Danny raised his near-empty coke glass and shook the ice.

"Now for the second thing, Chaco continued. All critical paperwork and records must be removed from the office, including your computers and all your storage disks." Chaco looked at Danny. "Are your computers password protected?"

Danny looked sheepish. "Yeah," he replied, "but I leave my computer on most of the time. All someone has to do is move my mouse and they're in."

Kathy shook her head. "I've been trying to get him to turn his computer off at the end of the day for years. There's not much important on his computer anyway. It's all on mine. I have a very secure password and I actually use it. All my files have passwords as does our storage media. Danny couldn't get into one of our thumb drives or DVD's if he wanted to. I also use a secure remote backup service in case the thing crashes."

Chaco looked at Danny. "This woman just may have saved your butt. Tomorrow we'll secretly move your computers and original documents and all our investigative notes on the Gannon case either to the rez or up to Vic and Angie's ranch. We'll run down to Radio Shack and buy a couple of cheap computers to use in the office."

"Better use the ranch, if we can talk Vic and Angie into it," Danny replied. "There's no reliable broadband on the rez, and I need Internet service for my legal research.

Danny looked at Brianna. "Do you think the Capalettis will let us make the ranch our new unofficial headquarters?"

"I'm sure they would. They've been after me to let them do more. They already have alarm systems installed on the house and the studio."

Chaco nodded his approval. "For the next few days, you need to make it look like the office is still our base of operations. Kathy, you'll need to erase the work product on both of your computers every day and carry it out of the office on thumb drives. We'll add the Capaletti location to our secure phone network.

"We can never go up there without making absolutely certain we're not being followed," Danny said.

"I'll buy us our own electronic sweeper and use it daily," Chaco said. Of course, that won't stop shotgun mics or laser mics."

"What the hell's a laser mic?" Kathy asked.

"They point a laser beam at a window and read the vibrations caused by conversations inside. Believe it or not, it actually works.

"Maybe we can rent a cement cubical somewhere," Danny groused.

"There's one other thing." Chaco looked at Brianna. "I want you to buy a gun. The office can pay for that, right?" He looked at Danny.

Danny nodded.

"Do you know how to use one?" Chaco asked.

"I used to shoot .22's when I was a kid, but I haven't shot anything in years."

Kathy put down her iced tea. "Do you really think it will get that serious?"

"I don't know, but I don't think we can take any chances." Chaco said.

Kathy looked at Bri. "You can do this, sister. I always carry a little .25 caliber automatic in my purse and have a concealed-carry permit to make it legal." Kathy reached into her purse and withdrew the weapon just far enough for Bri to see the handle.

Bri's eyes grew wide. "You carry that every day?"

"Every day. And I can shoot the eye out of a fly clear across this room. I can teach you to do the same."

"Well, well. A regular little Miss Annie Oakley," Danny chuckled. "I'm sure glad I've minded my P's and Q's and kept my hands to myself."

"I don't know, Counselor," she said with a wry smile. "Until Chaco wised up, on some of my lonelier nights I came close to wanting to shoot you because you did."

*

As Danny drove home, a wave of sorrow washed over him. It seemed as if he were living in the middle of a third-rate spy novel. Tonight made it abundantly clear that the people at Gannon Oil had no respect for the law or anyone's personal rights. In less than a week, the quiet, anonymous tranquility he once enjoyed was becoming only a remote memory. *Will I ever have my life back?*

Chapter 30

Odd, Danny thought on his drive to work the next morning. No one appeared to be following him. He was taken by the irony that only two days ago, he found it extremely strange that someone was. Could it be that one simple shake-off of whoever was tailing him last night was enough to discourage further surveillance? He doubted it. *They must be tracking me, but how? Time to take a good look at this car.*

He took a detour into the Quickie Lube. Tommy, the owner, was a friend of many years who lusted after Danny's immaculate red Mustang. "You ever decide to get rid of that thing, I get first dibs," Tommy frequently said. "Not a chance," was Danny's stock reply.

"Hey, you were just here last week," Tommy said, glancing around. "Don't know if I should be seen working on your car or not. You're none too popular these days." He winked to show he was kidding.

Danny gave the man a quick smile and said, "Don't need a lube job, Tommy. I need to take a good look under my car. Can you put it up on the rack?"

In no time, Danny spotted the black plastic box about the size of a pack of cigarettes that was magnetically attached to the inside of the rear bumper. The antenna wire dangling out left little doubt as to what it was.

"Is that what I think it is?" Tommy asked with a frown.

"I'm afraid so. Question is, what am I going to do with it?"

"Hey, you in some kind of trouble or something? I understand the feds use those things a lot."

"Believe me, it doesn't belong to the feds. Don't worry. I'm not in any trouble with the law."

Danny threw the signal beacon on the front seat and drove around, trying to figure out what to do with the device, then spotted the answer. Two Highway Patrol cars were parked at Dunkin' Donuts in a spot where the troopers inside could only partially see them. He couldn't suppress a smile as he parked next to the farthest one. He slipped behind it and placed the tracking devise on the chassis behind its rear bumper. "Let's see them get that one back," he chuckled.

An hour later, he and Brianna sat with Angie at the Capalettis' kitchen table. Vic came rushing into the house from work with a worried look. "What's wrong?" he asked.

"We've got troubles," Danny said. He briefed Vic and Angie on last night's events. The more he said the darker Vic's scowl became. Angie sat as still and quiet as stone. When Danny told about discovering the radio tracking device on his car, Vic shook his head in disgust. Angie's eyes narrowed and her jaw muscles clenched.

"So we developed a plan of sorts and it involves you if you're willing to help," Danny concluded.

"Of course we are," Angie said without looking at her husband for confirmation. "What do you want us to do?"

"Would you consider allowing us to secretly move our operations up here? My office downtown would actually become a decoy. I don't think it's safe to work on the Gannon case in Farmington any longer."

"My studio is way bigger than what I need," Angie volunteered. I'm only using part of it now. The rest is just overflow storage for a lot of stuff I haven't used in years. The floors are stained and it'll smell like oil paints and turpentine, but we can put a wall across the middle and make whatever other changes we need to make for you."

Vic led them on a tour. Indeed, it was a sizable building, five thousand square feet. It was located a couple of hundred feet from the house, half-hidden from view between the garage and the barn.

"I'll borrow a crew from the company and get that place cleaned out today," Vic boomed. "We can store Angie's stuff in the barn if we have to. What else?"

"I need to brief you on some security procedures and code words we'll be using from now on. No sense in taking any chances, even out here. I just hope we're not putting you folks in danger."

"Nonsense," Angie said. "This place has a lot more security than your office. This studio, the house, and garage are all on a state-of-the-art alarm system. We can start using the driveway's electric gate instead of just letting it stay open all the time. Neighbors might think we're getting a bit snooty, but that's their problem. If you think it's a good idea, we'll hire a security guard. Whatever it takes, we'll do it."

Chapter 31

Blackthorn stared unseeingly out the floor-to-ceiling windows of his office. Last night's meeting of the Cayman group had not gone well. Gannon was indeed charging all the expenses of the second well explosion against everyone else's accounts. His $11 million share of the Cayman account had been diminished by more than $2.8 million and counting. Two weeks out from the second explosion and the Red Adair team still had not put the fire out. Another week, they said, at more than $150,000 a day. Blackthorn's dream of the $5 million retirement estate he had his eye on at Cabo San Lucas was in jeopardy.

He was tempted to go out to that well site and kick some ass himself, but of course, nobody did that to the world-famous Red Adair team. If he stepped on their toes, the work would slow to a crawl and he'd have to watch more millions evaporate before his eyes.

There had to be a way to stop this damned lawsuit and deflect the anger of the Cayman group away from him. More importantly, he had to get back in Red Gannon's good graces. But how? Whatever he came up with had to be a real game-changer.

*

Danny stood in the reception area talking with Kathy when a large, balding man in his late fifties or early sixties, wearing a white shirt with no tie and a suit jacket that he couldn't button across his protruding belly, walked in. He carried a rolled-up document in his hand.

"May we help you sir?" Kathy asked.

Ignoring her, the man looked directly at Danny and asked, "Are you Whitehorse?"

"I am," Danny answered warily.

"I'm Lucas Blackthorn with Gannon Oil."

Danny tried to cover his surprise. He cast a quick glance at Kathy to confirm he'd actually heard the man right. She gave him a barely perceptible shrug.

"What can I do for you, Mr. Blackthorn?" Danny asked, keeping his tone cordial.

"I just came to see if we could chat a little about this." Blackthorn popped open the document he was carrying. It was a copy of Danny's lawsuit. "Is there somewhere we can talk privately?"

"I normally require appointments, but I could probably spare you a minute or two," Danny said, remaining coldly aloof. "Step into my office. Ms. Redhand, please hold my calls."

Kathy could scarcely keep from laughing at Danny's pompous role playing. "Yes, sir," she said in her best stiffly formal tone.

"Please sit down, Mr. Blackthorn." Danny gestured to one of the tattered wingback chairs as he closed his office door. "This is quite a surprise. I expected to hear from your legal department rather than someone such as yourself. Are you an attorney, sir?"

"No. I'm hoping that we can avoid the necessity of getting more lawyers involved in this problem. I'll get straight to the point. In order to stop this foolishness, my company has authorized me to make you what we believe is a very generous offer if we can settle this whole mess."

"Neither I nor my clients regard our lawsuit as foolishness, Mr. Blackthorn. Your company has seriously damaged the finances of both the tribe and the individual families I represent."

Blackthorn scowled slightly, recovered himself, waved his hand dismissively and said, "Of course, of course. The families will get something, but we're more interested in you at the moment. I've done a little research and found out you're a pretty impressive guy. We need people of your caliber working for our company.

We've looked into your law firm and know that it's — what's a good word here — struggling? We're in a position to help. If you'll just drop this lawsuit I'm prepared not only to give you a generous settlement for your clients, but to hire you to work for us at Gannon Oil. I can promise that you'll find our company very generous indeed."

Danny could scarcely believe his ears. The bribe attempt was so brazen and amateurish in both presentation and content that he was sure it had never so much as sniffed the inside of the Gannon Oil legal department. *How far are they prepared to go?* "Sounds interesting, Blackthorn," he replied. "What are you prepared to offer?"

The oil company executive took a deep breath and visibly relaxed. "Well, this is more like it," he said affably as he settled into his chair. Danny — do you mind if I call you Danny?"

"Call me anything you like."

"We're willing to pay each family a production severance allowance in the amount of one thousand dollars cash. That's over six hundred thousand dollars. Of course, there's the matter of your fees. We're sure you took this case on a contingency basis. The normal fee for settlement before trial is what, thirty percent? We're prepared to pay that in addition to what we pay to your clients. If I'm not mistaken, thirty percent would come to just north of two hundred thousand dollars for you. In addition, we're creating a new minority affairs department that needs a director. You'd be ideal to fill that position. Your starting salary would be one hundred eighty thousand per year with a three-year contract and considerable fringe benefits. We're even willing to allow you to continue taking private clients on the side. All in all, we believe this should solve the problems of all parties."

Danny was stunned. The sum Gannon was willing to pay to sweep everything under the rug was huge — over a million dollars total before their corporate attorneys even had a chance to answer the lawsuit. His lawyerly instincts practically jumped through his skin. How far could he push?

Turning a cold gaze on the man, Danny said, "That salary's too low. I'd need at least three hundred thousand annually. Three years isn't enough either. Make it ten. My secretary comes with me and she gets one hundred thousand a year. I'll want a new car annually, a Mercedes or BMW, a new home, nothing fancy, something in the two hundred to three hundred thousand dollar range, and last but not least, a stock portfolio that includes five percent of the outstanding Gannon Oil shares. In short, I want a seat on your Board of Directors, Mr. Blackthorn."

Blackthorn rose halfway out of his chair with a murderous scowl, caught himself, composed his features, and eased himself back down. When he spoke, his voice was flinty and strained. "My, you're a greedy little bastard, aren't you. The salary and the secretary are no problem, and the house and car I can guarantee. But the stock—hell, that's more than I own myself. I don't know if Red Gannon will go for it or not. But if I get those things for you, you'll settle this thing, right?"

"There's just a couple of other things, Mr. Blackthorn. My clients each get fifty-thousand, and the wells get turned back on—right now. And lastly, I want to know why you built secret, unmarked pipelines to every dry well just days before you shut them off."

Blackthorn leaped from his chair. "God damn it, Whitehorse, I've just made you a very rich man. What we do in those gas fields is none of your business. Now give me your answer! Do we have a deal or not?" For a moment, Danny thought the man might come right across the desk at him.

"Sit down," Danny commanded, realizing that he too now stood in reaction to Blackthorn's aggression. He leaned over his desk, eyeball to eyeball with his enemy, and said, "I have a few questions for you, Mr. Blackthorn."

"I didn't come here to answer no questions," Blackthorn said, backing off a little. "I came to settle this case. All I'm looking for is your answer, yes or no."

"The answer is no, Mr. Blackthorn. I certainly will not advise my clients to accept a settlement equal to less than a month's income on even the lowest-paying well out there, particularly since your company intends to leave those wells off for many years. But I will tell you this, we're going to find out what you and your company are up to, and when we do, we'll be able to get our hands on all the Gannon Oil money we want. Now if that's all, I have a lawsuit to prosecute against your employer."

Perhaps he'd said too much, but there was no recalling the words. The gauntlet was squarely thrown down.

"You're making a very big mistake," Blackthorn said in a cold and measured tone. "This is a fight you can't win. Red Gannon and I didn't get where we are today by letting two-bit, redskin legal eagles like you take advantage of us."

"Let me put you on notice, Mr. Blackthorn. This two-bit redskin legal eagle is going to kick your ass in court. Now good-day to you, sir." Danny sat down and contemptuously turned his attention to the papers lying on his desk.

Rather than leave, Blackthorn leaned over Danny's desk and said in a quiet voice, "Perhaps you'll change your mind about our offer if I tell you we know of your involvement with the NALM."

It took all the iron-willed control Danny could muster not to react. It was the single point of vulnerability that could bring his entire effort down. Did this man really know of the close relationship he had with Chaco and the NALM? Though his head was spinning, he had to answer. He calmly raised his eyes to the security chief and prayed neither his voice nor demeanor betrayed him. "I beg your pardon, Mr. Blackthorn? I'm not familiar with that acronym. Just who or what are you talking about?"

"You know God damned well what the NALM is," the man shouted. "If you think we're going to sit still for your renegades running around the reservation blowing up our gas wells while you try to pick our pockets in court, you're very, very wrong. You could also end up very, very dead! I'll put an army of my own in those fields and blow away every member of the NALM we find."

The man's tirade confirmed that Gannon had received the letters. Danny prayed the man's knowledge of the NALM was limited to what was contained in them. He struggled to maintain an appearance of calmness. "Mr. Blackthorn, what in the world is all this talk about armies and blowing up wells? As I understand it, you've had some trouble with faulty equipment. But if you're telling me that someone is deliberately blowing up your gas wells, I strongly suggest you go to the authorities. Have you tried the FBI or the ATF? As to your threat of personal violence against me or any member of my staff, I suggest you don't say anything more. I already have very damning evidence that could prove your illegal threats in court. Let me show you." He punched the button on the new intercom. "Kathy, I'm sure you've done your usual competent job of recording this interview. Would you mind playing back a little of Mr. Blackthorn's last statement?"

"Sure, boss," came the gleeful reply.

After a short pause, Blackthorn's deep basso voice came loud and clear over the speaker. "If you think we're going to sit still while your renegades run around the reservation blowing up our gas wells while you try to pick our pockets in court, you're very, very wrong. You also could quickly end up very, very dead! I'll put an army . . ."

"That's enough Kathy," Danny said. "Please take very good care of that recording. We may need to forward it to the authorities."

"Yes, sir, Mr. Whitehorse," Kathy's sickly sweet voice came back.

"I certainly hope I never have to use that recording, Mr. Blackthorn, but I promise you that if anything untoward happens to me or one of my people, it will instantly be in the hands of authorities who will shortly be on their way to arrest you. From this time forward, you'd better pray neither I nor anyone on my staff gets so much as a hangnail. And while you're at it, you'd better call off the people following us and quit spying on our homes and this office. Do I make myself clear, sir?"

"You bastard," Blackthorn croaked. "You didn't tell me we were being recorded. I want that tape! It's illegal to tape me without my knowledge. Besides, you're an attorney — you can't say nothin'."

"You're wrong on both counts, Blackthorn. First, in this state, so long as at least one of the parties to a conversation is aware it's being recorded, it's both legal and admissible. Second, you are not my client and not protected by attorney/client privilege. I would consider it an honor to testify against you. For your own good, I strongly suggest that the next contact between us be through your attorneys, who are much more likely to know what they're doing than you. Good day, Mr. Blackthorn."

The security chief slammed out of Danny's office and out of the building. Kathy rushed in the instant he disappeared. "Do you think he really knows about the NALM?"

"Of course he does. We now know for certain that they got those two letters. But if he's made the connection between us and the NALM, we could be in serious trouble."

"What are we going to do?"

"Nothing, for the moment. I think he was here on a fishing expedition. The existence of that recording should keep things from getting physical. But I'll tell you this, if we weren't getting close to the truth, Blackthorn wouldn't have been here offering us over a million dollars."

Chapter 32

Danny could tell Kathy was excited the instant she walked through the door. She held up a manila envelope and said, "It's from Gannon Oil. Do you want to open it or should I?"

"Be my guest." Danny gestured for her to do the honors.

The envelope contained Gannon Oil's formal answer to Danny's lawsuit. It was a short, non-committal, general response that denied all causes of action. It could have come directly from the pages of any first-year tort law text book. It contained no affirmative defenses or other arguments that gave the slightest hint as to how the company intended to proceed.

But the issue was now joined and the door open to begin discovery.

"So what's next, Counselor?" Kathy asked.

"Let's open Gannon's records up like a can of sardines. Grab your notebook." Danny headed for his office.

Two hours later, Kathy placed the final document on Danny's desk. It was only three pages long but was one of the most powerful instruments available to the legal profession. It's formal title was, "Request for Examination of Books and Records Under Title V, Rule 34 of the Federal Code of Civil Procedure." It would require Gannon to give Danny access to all books and records that were pertinent to the case.

"Good," Danny said, approving the final draft. Get a copy of this in the mail to Gannon. I'll go to the courthouse and file a copy." He turned toward the window and shouted out, "You've got thirty days, Red Gannon. Thirty days until I'm going to know you better than you know yourself!"

Chapter 33

Red Gannon sat behind his huge home office desk facing his four fellow conspirators. Each held their own copy of the examination request. "Parker, how vulnerable are we to this thing?" he growled.

"Depends on how deep they dig. As you know, everything associated with the Cayman project is buried several layers down in the bookkeeping. We can hide any of the records we need to on our side, but there's nothing we can do about the delivery and payment records from the pipeline company if he subpoenas them. And he's almost certain to do that."

"He'll not turn up anything there," Popeson said. "The wells we're actually delivering the gas from aren't on the reservation and no longer show up as belonging to Gannon Oil. We should be safe as long as they don't figure out the relationship between us and the ownership of the delivery wells. As a precaution, the company should carefully vet its records to make sure no path leads to my doorstep."

"Get that done today," Gannon barked at Parker. "I want you to personally review every document related to the project and make sure Stan's name doesn't appear anywhere. Now let's get to the source of the problem. We've got to deal with this damned redskin attorney. That means you, Blackthorn. Why haven't we done something about this guy?"

Blackthorn knew the question was coming, but didn't know exactly how to answer. Under normal circumstances he would just make Whitehorse disappear. But there was that nightmarish meeting between him and Whitehorse that no one knew about, and that cursed recording that Whitehorse dangled over his head. Lucas had to steer very carefully.

"The truth is, we've never faced a situation like this before, Red. The way Whitehorse went public makes everyone identify him with us. If we take him out, it's got to look like an accident. That means no screw-ups and a lot of planning. I'm working on that now."

"Wait a minute," Webster shouted. His face turned pasty white. "It sounds like we're planning a murder here. It's one thing to steal a little gas, but it's something else to kill someone. I won't be a party to anything like that. There has to be another way."

"Listen to me, you slimy little political prick," Gannon sneered. "I'm not going to prison for you or anybody else. If the hundreds of thousands of dollars I've paid you under the table over the years and the millions at risk on this Cayman project aren't enough for you to understand how important it is to cover all our asses, maybe we better think about terminating you from this group — permanently!"

Webster withered and backpedaled. He knew what 'permanently' meant. "Red, uh, look, I'm sorry. I didn't mean to convey the wrong impression here. Of course I'll go along with anything y'all decide. I just want to make sure the course is well thought out and considerate of all possible outcomes, that's all, just like Lucas says." Webster nodded his head agreeably, hoping to disarm the tension and shift attention from him back to Blackthorn.

"That's more like it," Gannon barked. "Anyone else want to tell me they're afraid to hurt Whitehorse's feelings? No? I didn't think so. Where were we, Blackthorn?"

"If we take out Whitehorse, we have to take out the secretary, too. An attorney's legal secretary knows everything about every case. If we get rid of him, we can't have her taking this case to another law firm.

"That's going to make it a lot harder. The two of them don't seem to hang out together much. In fact, we're not seeing much of either of them in town anymore. We suspect they're both staying out on the reservation where we can't get to them."

Gannon steepled his fingers in thought. "Maybe Webster's right. Perhaps we're being a bit hasty. Let's give Whitehorse one more chance. Get your hands on him, Blackthorn, and show him it's not in his best interest to screw around with Red Gannon. We'll give him a chance to back away. If he doesn't, we drop the hammer."

Gannon raised the request copy in his hand and said, "I want it done before this thing ever comes up for a hearing. I can deal with state and local government, but that federal courthouse is the one place I don't have any control."

Chapter 34

It was a great day for a top-down ride in the Mustang. Chaco's mapping project was going smoothly, and with the request to produce filed, there was little to do but wait. Gannon's lawyers were sure to file an objection, but such objections were rarely sustained. Today he would see for himself what was going on in the gas fields — and maybe snap a few pictures for his evidence file.

As Danny drove through Shiprock and turned south on Highway 555, he couldn't help but chuckle to himself. The road used to be called Hwy 666 and was known as the Devil's Highway. The U.S. Department of Transportation thought many people refused to use the road for that reason, so they changed the number designation. As far as Danny could tell, the change hadn't affected traffic at all.

Driving south toward the turnoff to Eagle Dome, Danny's mind slipped back to the subject he'd been fighting himself over more and more lately — the idea of calling Amanda.

Brianna was vigorously stirring that long-dormant pot, pestering him over and over to make the call. Could she be right? Was there enough of a spark left in her that it might somehow burn again if he just had the guts to call? *Should I? Shouldn't I? What would she say if I did? What about the fiancé? How do you start a conversation with a woman who's about to be married to someone else?*

He missed so many things about her — the sound of her voice, the late-night phone conversations, and her several-times-a-day emails. He missed the way she chewed the end of a pencil when she was worried or thinking about something too hard. He especially missed the feel of her lips on the back of his neck when she thought he'd been ignoring her for too long.

Most of all, he missed those wonderful, delicious, passionate weekends at her place or his. He missed her twinkly laugh, the soft warmth of her skin when they lay together. He even missed the clouds of baby powder that made a mess all over his clean bathroom counters and floor as she dusted herself, fresh out of the shower. But call her? The thought terrified him more than all the goons Gannon could send.

Wrapped up in his thoughts, he nearly missed the turn off to Eagle Dome, twenty miles south of town. He was surprised by what he saw. The road had been widened and freshly graveled. It was a virtual freeway compared to the bumpy, dusty narrow track it used to be.

He passed by several well compounds where the fencing and construction were finished. Each enclosure had a single electronic gate that was opened by guards stationed in a shack just inside.

Even though he had every right to be there so long as he stayed outside the fences, he could easily be spotted by Gannon's guards while getting his pictures, an act they might consider provocative. *Maybe this isn't such a good idea."*

He was about to turn around when he passed a well site that looked promising. It was situated on level ground next to a gently banked, ten-foot-deep ravine that ran between the road and the fence. Just past the site, the road dropped into a shallow canyon just deep enough to conceal his car from the guards. He could leave his car down there, hike up the bottom of the ravine to a spot where he could pop up from the sagebrush just long enough to snap a quick photo or two, then duck back into the ravine and make his way back to his car. He would be visible from the roadway, but only visible to the guards inside the compound for the brief few seconds it took him to take the pictures.

He was intently at his task when he registered the sound of a vehicle coming up the gravel road. He turned and saw a dust plume some distance away that told him the vehicle was traveling fast. *Time to get out of here.* He started back to his car, moving as quickly and quietly as he could.

He made it nearly to the back corner of the compound when a white crew-cab dual-wheel Chevy pickup truck typical of Gannon work crews, roared through the little canyon where he'd left his car and topped the rise so fast its wheels left the road's surface.

The driver spotted Danny and brought the vehicle to a sliding stop amidst a billowing, choking cloud of dust that momentarily obscured the truck Danny's view. He scrambled out of the ravine to higher ground. When the dust cleared, he saw that three men had exited the vehicle and were approaching. They appeared to be ordinary oilfield workers except that one carried a baseball bat, the second a three-foot-long piece of pipe, and the third a lengthy piece of chain. They fanned out, flanking him as they crossed the ravine. With the fence at his back, Danny was boxed in.

The men moved menacingly, countering any move Danny made to escape. The inevitability of a confrontation settled into his mind. Danny calmed himself and looked around for a weapon. Ten feet away, a three-foot length of 2x4 lay at the base of the fence, apparently left over from construction. He picked it up and turned to face his attackers.

The trio advanced slowly, cautiously. The man in the center, the one carrying the baseball bat, wore an ugly grin that revealed a huge gap where his front teeth should have been. He was huge, several inches above six feet tall, and weighing at least two hundred eighty pounds. He had a scruffy beard and approached with a casual swagger that told Danny he felt no concern whatsoever about losing this fight.

The second man, an African-American, was only slightly smaller and carried his pipe cocked like a baseball player ready to swing. The third man, the one on his right, was short and thin, with a narrow, ferret-like face. When Danny moved in his direction, he flinched back and looked to his companions for support.

Danny still retained his college football player stature, thanks to regular running and workouts. With Chaco's martial arts training over the past year, he was confident he could handle one man, was fairly sure he had a chance against two, but three? It was likely he would suffer some considerable damage even if he managed to win. If he lost — well — he didn't want to think about that.

Maybe he could talk his way out. He smiled and addressed the man in the center. "Howdy, mister. Strange place for a baseball game, but I'll pop for the hot dogs if you guys brought some beer."

The men stopped their advance as their leader considered the words. "I ain't heard nothin' 'bout no baseball game, Mr. Smartass, but we're damn sure gonna get in some battin' practice."

The other two men chuckled. The little one said in a high, squeaky voice, "Yeh Monte, his head does look a lot like a freaking baseball."

"Damn it, Pug, no names! Remember?" Monte shot the little man an angry glare.

Danny jumped on Monte's error. "No, no, Pug's right. I'm the ugliest one here, so with that settled, let's call this little game off, all shake hands, and go have a drink. Like I said, I'm buying. What are you guys so upset about, anyway?"

"We ain't upset 'bout nothing," Monte said. "We're jest keepin' trespassers off our wells. You're trespassin', boy."

"Oh I don't think I'm trespassing," Danny said, looking around. "I might be if I was inside that fence. But out here it's definitely reservation land. I'm an attorney. I know about these kinds of things. I'd hate to see you make such a mistake, so if you don't mind, I'll just leave now and you boys can be on your way. No harm, no foul, right?"

"You ain't going nowhere, Whitehorse. We got orders to bring you in. We ain't making no mistake 'bout you trespassin', either. Once we drag you inside that fence, you'll be trespassin' fer sure."

Danny's mind constantly assessed his options as he tried to stall the impending assault. He held two weapons, the sturdy 2x4 in his right hand, and his camera, with its powerful, fast-recovery strobe flash, in the left. As a battle plan began to form in his head, he knew there was a third weapon, perhaps his best — the element of surprise.

"Well, hell, boys," he said, trying to show no signs of aggression, "if that's the way it's got to be, I might as well get a shot of all this while I can." He raised the camera and set it off in Monte's face.

"Hey!" the big man hollered, raising his arm too late to avoid the myriads of bright spots that suddenly danced before his eyes. Danny rapid-fired the device at the other two men. The man on the left raised his arm in time to ward off the blinding flash, but gave Danny the opening he needed. He skipped left and brought his 2x4 down hard on the arm carrying the pipe. The arm broke with a resounding crack and the pipe tumbled from the man's hand. He let out a bellow of pain and went to his knees, clutching his useless appendage.

Danny whirled, released the camera body from his grasp, caught it by its strap, and whipped the heavy instrument mace-like into Monte's ribs. Again, Danny heard bones break as the big man gave out a great whoosh of air and crumpled to his knees, unable to inhale or even give voice to a scream. He shoved the man with his foot and sent him over backwards, writhing and clutched at his ribs. Then Danny turned to the attacker he was least worried about.

*

As Pug's vision cleared, he was struck by terror at the sight of Monte rolling on the ground, obviously in great pain, and Mike, his other companion, on his knees, groaning and clutching what looked to be a broken right arm. But most terrifying of all was the sight of the big man advancing toward him with a 2x4 in one hand and the camera, swinging weapon-like in the other.

Without his companions to bolster his courage, Pug backed along the fence, holding the chain he once intended as a weapon before him as a wholly inadequate shield. "N — now look Mr. Whitehorse, this wasn't my idea. The c — company — they're the ones. They ordered us to grab you. Monte, he . . . he's the who wanted to hurt you, not me! In fact, I told him not to . . ." The jabbering words trailed off as the little man cowered before Danny's advance.

Pug failed to see the protruding rock behind his left foot as he backed. His heel caught and he tumbled backwards. Now completely vulnerable, he curled unto a fetal ball and screamed pathetically, "No! No! Don't hit me mister! Please don't!"

Danny glanced over his shoulder at the other two attackers. Both still appeared to be incapacitated. He turned back to Pug. "All right you little freak, I'm only going to ask you once. I want every one of your names — now."

Pug let out a whimpering moan. "I — I can't tell you. Monte'll kill me. We'll all get fired."

"Danny gave the man a solid jab in the ribs with the end of the board, prompting a fearful scream. He hissed again, "You'd better worry a lot more about me right now, because I'm about to put this 2x4 right through your little pea brain." He gave him another sharp poke.

"Okay, okay. I'm Gene Pugmire. They call me Pug. And the others are Monty Jasper and Mike Olson."

"Why did you attack me?"

The man slowly uncurled. "We were only doing our job. They said to watch for you in the fields and to try to bring you in. They passed a picture of you around and told us we'd earn a reward."

In the far distance Danny heard another vehicle approaching from the same direction the first had come. He could ill afford another Gannon crew showing up.

Pug's gaze flickered to the side for just an instant. His lips twitched slightly toward a smile. Danny didn't know if he heard something or simply sensed a presence behind him, but he instinctively ducked just in time to avoid the full force of a crushing blow aimed at his skull from a heavily swung baseball bat. The blow caught him hard across the left shoulder, knocking him to the ground and sending agonizing bolts of searing hot pain down his arm. He rolled to his right and attempted to come back up, but the arm refused to support him. He rolled again, just in time to avoid a second descent of the bat, and this time regained his feet. He turned to face Monte Jasper, advancing slowly, drawing wheezing, labored breaths, and favoring his left side.

When the bat struck, Danny lost his grip on both his weapons. His left arm now hung uselessly at his side. But Monte was injured, too. Danny broke a rib during a football game once, and if Monte was hurting like he had then, the big man was nearly disabled. One more punch should put him down for good.

The other vehicle was almost here. Monte closed to within striking range and with one hand, heaved back on the bat. It was a classic mistake many big men made—relying on their strength and size while under-estimating the speed and strength of a smaller opponent. As the bat began its forward motion, Danny stepped inside its arc and delivered a crushing right fist to the exact spot his camera had smashed just a few minutes before. Monte again let out a scream and crumpled to the ground, clutching convulsively at his torso.

Danny continued his motion to where Pug was curled against the fence. He seized the smaller man with his good arm and dragged him to where Monte lay writhing. Pug recoiled and screamed himself as Danny raised his one good fist to smash into the man's face. As he did, he heard the terrifying sound of the charging bolt of an AR-15, the civilian version of the military M-16 assault rifle, slam a cartridge into the breach.

He froze. A Gannon Oil security guard stood on the other side of the fence pointing the deadly weapon squarely at his head. Another uniformed guard ran up behind the first and aimed his rifle at Danny's chest.

"Put both hands on top of your head." The first guard shouted. "Take five steps backward and kneel. Now!"

There was no option. "I can't move my left arm," Danny explained as he slowly backed away and knelt in the sand

"Then put your right hand on your head. If I see that left arm move the wrong way, I'll blow it off at the shoulder, understand?"

Danny nodded.

Neither Monte nor Mike were in any condition to realize their change of fortune, but Pug was ecstatic.

"Well, now. Would ya looky here!" he screeched as he stood and strutted closer to Danny. "Looks like I got me a prisoner after all. Now Mr. High and Mighty Attorney, let's see how you like getting busted up." He smashed his fist into Danny's face, crumpling him to the ground.

"Stand away, Pug," the first guard barked as Danny shook his head and woozily righted himself. "I'll not allow torture by you or by him."

"Ah, Jesus, Adams, look what he done to Monte un Mike. He deserves to be knocked around a little."

"You're mighty brave with my gun backing you up," the guard said with obvious disgust. "But you're a real chicken shit on your own." He looked at the younger guard and said, "Calvin, go out and check those injured men. I'll stand here and protect Whitehorse from our brave little field hand."

"Yes sir." The young guard spun and took off for the distant gate at a trot.

The guard glanced toward the road as the approaching vehicle, an older, brown pickup truck, topped the rise and slowed to maneuver around the Gannon truck stopped in the middle of the road. Danny chanced a sideward glance.

It was one of Chaco's mapping crews returning from a more remote site. "Lie down flat," the guard hissed at Danny. Swallowing hard, Danny did the opposite. He stood up.

The driver was paying attention to the vehicle blocking his path, but Danny's movement attracted the attention of the others riding in the open bed. One of them pointed at Danny and shouted, "Whitehorse, what's happening, brother?" The man's grin turned into a grimace as he noticed the guard with a rifle trained on the Navajo attorney. The man pounded on the pickup cab and shouted something. The truck slid to a halt directly across the ravine from where Danny stood and was enveloped in a blinding cloud of dust. When it cleared, a line of five men had formed a few paces apart who were advancing toward the fence.

"Now you men just get on out of here, the older guard shouted. He waved the gun menacingly toward the group.

No one in the line faltered. All kept their hands visible and smiled broadly at the guard. The man at the right end of the line spoke. "Hey, no sweat Mr. Rent-a-Cop. We ain't here for no fight. The man bent over and scooped up Monte's fallen bat. All we see is a couple a guys lying around looking like they want to play a little baseball. We figured you needed a few more players, that's all. I must say, you make one hell of an umpire. Ain't nobody going to argue with your calls, not with you holding that big, ol' gun."

As the line reached Danny, the men closed ranks protectively in front of him and stopped. Danny recognized three of them, including the speaker, Richard Manyhorses, and marveled at their bravery. "There's another guard coming around the fence from the main gate," Danny said through clinched teeth,

Manyhorses shouted the message in Navajo to the truck and pointed toward the other side of the compound. Danny watched someone small but very fast slip away into the sagebrush.

*

Harold Adams was indeed a rent-a-cop, an ex-policeman from Albuquerque, and a partner in his small security firm. He knew the three Gannon field hands and cared little for their type. He now regretted making the radio call that summoned them to the site to check out the man snooping round the outside of the fence. The man obviously had no idea he was being watched by a high resolution security camera atop one of the tall light poles, almost from the moment he parked his car. "You're Whitehorse, right?"

"Yes. But you knew that, didn't you."

"I was pretty sure. Your picture is posted in the guard shack. Three days ago, the company offered a five-thousand-dollar reward to any crew who brought you in. I've been worried about that reward. There are crews out here who would kill for that kind of money."

Adams shifted his gun barrel, pointing it toward the ground, then he addressed Danny's rescuers. "Okay boys! I'm only going to say this once. I don't want to shoot anybody, and I don't want anyone else hurt. Why don't you take your friend here, nice and quiet like, and get on out of here."

"That's mighty white of you Mr. Rent-A-Cop," Manyhorses said, "considering that if you change your mind, you'll be the first one to go down. Take a close look at our truck."

Adams looked at the pickup and blanched. Over the hood of the pickup he saw a scoped rifle trained directly at his chest, while over the bed he was staring down the bore of what looked to be a long-barreled .44 magnum handgun.

"I get your point fella," Adams said in a quiet voice. "How bout I put this here rifle on the ground and you have your boys point their firearms in some other direction. No sense anyone getting killed here."

"Sounds good to me," Manyhorses replied cheerfully. "How about you Danny?

"It's the best idea I've heard in the past hour or so," Danny's voice was just above a whisper. The pain in his arm and shoulder was so intense that it sickened his stomach.

Manyhorses shouted something in Navajo to the men behind the pickup. "Okay, mister, put that rifle down."

Adams slowly set his rifle on the ground and backed one step away, making sure to keep his hands well clear of his utility belt containing a holstered pistol. Then he asked, "Mr. Whitehorse, are you okay? Do you need an ambulance or anything?"

"I don't feel much like dancing, but I don't need an ambulance. But you better get one out here for those other two men. That black guy has a broken arm, and your friend Monte has broken ribs. The way he's breathing, he may have a punctured lung. You better get that other guard on the radio and stop him before he walks into a gun fight here."

The security guard's face went ashen. "Oh crap, you're right!" He looked at Manyhorses and croaked, "Tell them not to shoot. I'm only getting my radio!"

Richard again hollered to the truck in Navajo, then said, "Use your left hand. You make one move toward that pistol and it will be your last."

Adams retrieved the radio and spoke loudly into it. "Calvin! Come in — over!" No reply. "KXJ-356 Calvin, come in, damn it!" Still no reply.

From just beyond sight around the far corner of the fence line, a voice shouted from the ravine, "Calvin's a little tied up right now. He'll talk to you in a minute." Moments later young Calvin came walking through the sagebrush, hatless, and wearing his own handcuffs. Behind him marched a small but wiry figure, Johnny Birdsong, a tough little guy who was the group jokester. Johnny wore Calvin's service cap despite the fact that it was many sizes too large for his head. The guard's utility belt adorned Johnny's hips, drooping nearly to his knees. Birdsong carried the guard's rifle military parade style over his shoulder. Upon reaching the group, he called out loudly, "Prisoner, halt!"

"Where'd you learn that, little brother?" one of the men chuckled.

"John Wayne. I saw it on TV."

"Looks more like the Three Stooges," said another.

The pain in Danny's shoulder was worsening. "Richard, we need to get out of here. There's no telling when another Gannon crew might show up." He turned to the older guard. "Your name tag says your last name is Adams. What's your first name?

"Harold. Adams and Slade Security Services.

"Are there any other Gannon crews coming?"

"I sent the call out on an open company channel, so I have no way of knowing."

"As you know, I'm an attorney. If you want to save yourself and your company from one hell of a lawsuit, you'll tell me who gave the orders to have me picked up."

"All the security teams received a memo from Mr. Blackthorn. It had your picture and orders for us to detain you if we spotted you messing around the well sites."

"You have a copy of that memo?"

"It's hanging on the wall of the guard shack."

"I'll relieve you of that document. How interested are you in saving your company?"

"What do you mean?"

"I mean, are you interested in keeping me from suing you from here to Sunday?"

"Ah, hell, Whitehorse, you don't want to do that. I didn't hurt you — I saved you. Why would you want to sue me?"

"I don't, but I want you to tell the truth about what happened out here when the time comes."

"I've never lied in a courtroom in my life, but you'd best remember this. Outside this fence, you can do anything you want, as far as I'm concerned. But if I or any member of my company catches you inside, we'll deal with you like a common criminal. Now please get away from here and let me get these men some medical help."

"All right brothers. It's time to leave," Danny said politely in Navajo, "Someone will have to come with me. I don't think I can drive my car. Thomas, would you do that? I need to find Chaco as fast as I can."

Thomas' eyes lit up at the prospect of driving the fabled red car.

*

"Ouch," Danny cried as the Mustang jostled over a pothole.

"Sorry, man," Thomas apologized. "I'm missing as many of them as I can."

"You're fine," Danny replied through gritted teeth. "Makes me regret putting in that stiff racing suspension."

Five miles of gravel road remained before they reached the paved highway. Danny could move his arm just enough to confirm there were probably no broken bones, but his range of mobility was limited by excruciating pain the higher he tried to raise his arm.

The physical assault shattered all the rules. There appeared no lengths to which Gannon wouldn't go to keep him from discovering the truth. Danny had to be very, very careful from now on.

Chapter 35

Blackthorn trembled with rage. Not only had his security guards let Whitehorse slip through their fingers, but two good field hands were out of commission to boot. Apparently Whitehorse was tougher than anyone thought.

Lucas' telephone rang. He'd instructed his secretary not to put any calls through. Then he noticed that the line being lit up was the red button at the end — Red Gannon's direct line from the ranch.

Gannon was the person Lucas Blackthorn wanted least to talk to at the moment, but he had no choice. He reached into his desk drawer and took out an always-present bottle of antacids, popped one in his mouth, chewed it quickly, then picked up the receiver.

"Blackthorn," Gannon barked, "I heard a radio call a few minutes ago. Something about one of our crews being attacked by a bunch of Indians, and two of our men now in the hospital. What the hell's going on?"

There was no sense trying to put polish on it. Gannon would eventually hear it all anyway. That big communications console in his ranch office was wired into every phone line and radio frequency the company had, allowing Gannon to know everything that happened at the company almost the instant it took place.

". . . So the bottom line is that our Boy Scout security guard let Whitehorse go. We have no idea where he is right now, but he doesn't appear to have left the Shiprock area, otherwise we'd have spotted that red Mustang."

There was ominous silence before Gannon said, "This guy's far too dangerous. We can't let him get us into court. I want him dead, Blackthorn, and I want it now."

"I agree, Red. We've completely underestimated this guy."

"No, you've underestimated him, just like you underestimated the significance of that first well explosion. There's an old saying, Lucas. 'What you do thunders so loudly in my ears that I can't hear what you say.' Don't tell me what you're going to do, show me. If you can't get rid of this guy, I'll find somebody who can." Gannon clicked off without saying good-bye.

Blackthorn's stomach churned. Maybe the ulcers would kill him before Gannon had the chance. He popped a couple more antacids into his mouth and turned his chair to the window before pulling out his cell phone. He didn't want this call going out over the company telephone system even though the man worked in the security office just two floors below.

"Sonny?'

"Yeah."

"This is Lucas. Remember that wildcatter from Midland we had to deal with a few years ago? I've got another job for you just like it."

"Who and when?"

"Not over the phone. Come up to my office and we'll talk."

*

"Not to look a gift horse in the mouth," Sonny Wilcox said, "but why don't you just off the guy with a sniper or something? Sure would be cheaper." Sonny Wilcox was one of the most cold-blooded men Blackthorn had ever known. He also was good at keeping his mouth shut.

"That's true, Sonny, but the way he's been so public about filing his lawsuit, people would automatically assume we did it. That's why this has to unquestionably look like an accident."

"So when are you thinking this should go down?"

"Tonight. As soon as possible. After the scare we gave him today, I doubt Whitehorse will use the expressway to get back to town. My gut tells me he'll probably try to sneak back on old Highway 57. Go out there and scout out the best place to pull this off. Twig was on his way to Albuquerque with a load of drip gas but I've turned him around. He and I will set it up wherever you say."

"Sounds good. I'll use Halverson again on my end. He's a good driver and keeps his mouth shut. We'll need a couple of fast, unmarked vehicles. Better make them four-wheel drive, in case Whitehorse tries to go off-road."

"No problem. I'll deliver the vehicles to the Razorback warehouse. There's no time to get secure radios put in, so we'll use CBs. We'll call the operation Jackrabbit Stew. Your handle will be 'Hound Dog One.' Halverson's 'Hound Dog Two.' Twig will be 'Matchstick,' and I'll be 'Elmer Fudd.' The target will be 'Jackrabbit.' If he uses that highway tonight, I want this thing set up so tight that there's no way we can miss."

"So what we talking here? How many zeros?"

"Six all around. One hundred thousand each for Halverson and Twig and three hundred thousand for you. That good enough?"

"Whew, five hundred big ones. I knew this guy was a pain in the ass, but I had no idea he was that big a deal?"

"Yeah," Blackthorn said as he reached for another antacid, "Jackrabbit is definitely that big a deal."

Chapter 36

Danny's first thought was to go to Robert Begay's *hooghan*, but there was a well with guards not far away. "Take me to Chaco's house," he instructed. On the way Danny called Chaco and briefed him on the attack. "Damn it, Danny, I told you not to go into those fields alone. How bad are you hurt?"

"A few bumps and bruises, but the big problem's my left shoulder. I can't tell if it's broken or not. When I try to move my arm, it just about puts me on the floor."

"I'm on my way. I'll try to get you some help by the time you arrive."

*

"*Ya' at' eehii* brother," Chaco greeted as Danny ascended the porch steps, his left arm dangling uselessly. "That's one beautiful shiner you got there, Cuz. Gonna give you something to talk about with whoever sees you the next couple of weeks." He held the door open.

Inside was an attractive woman Danny didn't recognize. "This is Beverly Benally, Angie's cousin," Chaco introduced. "She's an emergency room nurse over at the BIA hospital in Farmington, and the NALM's Chief Medical Officer."

"*Ya' at' eehii*," Danny said, his face pale from the pain.

"Let's take a look," the woman said. Chaco, help me get rid of that shirt.

Beverly determined that Danny's shoulder was severely dislocated. She enlisted Chaco and Thomas to hold him steady. "This is going to hurt," she said. "Keep your arm relaxed and don't tighten up." She took a firm two-handed grip on his hand. "You ready?"

"As ready as I ever will be," Danny replied, gritting his teeth.

Beverly gave his arm a sudden sharp pull and twist.

Danny screamed as joint and sinew popped back into place, but almost in an instant, he felt relief. Within minutes the pain was down to a dull throb rather than the sharp, searing waves he'd endured before.

"Now let's take a look at your back," Beverly poked and prodded, eliciting occasional yelps from Danny. "This bruise makes your shiner look puny. I think I can read the printing from the baseball bat. At least the guy used a Louisville Slugger," she chuckled.

Danny smiled. Despite the pain, he couldn't help but be conscious of a woman's hands on his skin for the first time in over a year. He shuddered. *It's been way too long.*

"Okay, let's check out those shoulder bones." Beverly placed her hands around Danny's shoulder and had him move his arm back and forth and up and down. It hurt, but at least his full range of motion was restored. "I think you're okay," she said. "Keep your arm in a sling for a couple of days at least. Everything inside that shoulder has been stretched and pulled, maybe even torn. It could easily pop itself out again. Don't lift anything heavier than a milk bottle until the pain's completely gone.

"I'll leave you some of my illegal pain pills," she said with a wink. "Take one now and another in four hours. After that, take one when you need it, but no more than six in a day. I'll connect with you tomorrow and see how you're doing."

"Can I drive?"

"Does that Mustang have power steering?"

"Yes."

"Then you'll probably be okay. Steer one-handed as much as you can."

*

Chaco had Thomas take Beverly home. On one hand, he was sorry for Danny's pain, but on the other, he was pleased that something had happened that would change the perception the members of the NALM that his cousin was just a white-collar desk jockey. His fight with Gannon's goons would "blood" him in the NALM's eyes and give him a reputation of being a field fighter — just like them.

Chaco and Robert urged Danny to stay on the reservation, but argue as they might, Danny said he wanted to sleep in his own bed. He assured them that his car could easily outrun any bad guys. He said he would stay off the expressway and return instead via old Highway 57, a road hardly anyone used anymore.

Chapter 37

Lucas Blackthorn dropped the key to a shiny, new Dodge Durango into Sonny Wilcox's hand, then did the same to Rex Halverson. He would have preferred black vehicles, but the best the dealership could do was two medium grays. Both vehicles' huge, big-block Hemi engines would provide more than enough speed for tonight's job. "You boys get this job done right, and those Durangos are yours," he said. They're waiting for you out at the Razorback warehouse." The two looked at each other and grinned.

Blackthorn had driven the route earlier with Wilcox. It lay in the valley but close to the hills on the north where cell phones would be useless most of the way. Before delivering the vehicles to the Razorback warehouse, he had them run through the motor pool shop where they installed a couple of good CBs and attached long whip antennas to their bumpers. Blackthorn had the warehouseman stand by while he drove out to his waiting spot to do a radio check. The CB's worked fine.

"Let's go over radio protocol again." Blackthorn said. "We'll use channel twenty-four. Most likely we'll have it all to ourselves, especially way out there. Matchstick and I will have everything set up on the other end. The only thing you have to worry about is delivering Jackrabbit to us. I'll be about a mile down the road from where it's going to happen. Any questions?"

"What if he doesn't come out this way?" Halverson asked.

"He might not, but after the scare we put in him this morning, I'd say it's a fifty/fifty chance. We're pretty sure he's holed up in Shiprock. The expressway is the most obvious route back into Farmington. If he suspects we're after him, that's where he'll expect us to be. If we don't see him by dawn, we'll pack up and call it a day. If nothing else, breakfast is on me."

*

A bright full moon hovered at mid-sky, making things so bright that one could easily walk around without a flashlight. As Danny pulled out of Shiprock just after one a.m., he could see the detail of the silvery hills bounding the south side of the river valley over a mile away.

Old Highway 57 tracked considerably north of the newer, more modern expressway that ran east out of Shiprock straight toward Farmington. Danny stayed on the expressway only about two miles, then turned off where Highway 57 wound around the southern tip of Razorback Ridge, a sharp, rock-spined hill that marked the reservation border. The road ran north past the old Razorback Inn, a dilapidated bar and grill that used to serve hundreds of travelers every day before the expressway was put in. Now it survived by serving drinks to oil field workers and a small cadre of local customers.

Then the road turned eastward again onto the stretch Danny liked best. For nearly fifteen miles, it ran wide and straight through alkali flats until the track was interrupted by a meandering, lazy "S" curve that threaded between a couple of low-lying hills not far from the western outskirts of Farmington.

Danny always kept his speed down on the reservation. A sheep becoming road kill might create a food crisis for a family who counted their annual income in the hundreds rather than thousands of dollars

But once past the Razorback and onto the alkali flats, he could safely blow some carbon out of the Mustang's engine and let it exercise some of the speed for which he'd created it.

Turning off the expressway, Danny saw only a couple of cars and an old pickup truck as he passed the Razorback Inn. But just past the dim light of the parking lot's single pole lamp, his headlights illuminated the back of a gray Dodge Durango. Other than the fact that the temporary license in the rear window showed the vehicle had been recently purchased, Danny couldn't put a finger on why he noticed it at all. Perhaps it was the glow of dash lights or some other telltale hint that told him the vehicle was occupied and running.

After weeks of being followed, Danny's instincts were honed to an edge. He checked his rearview mirror after he passed. Strange — the Durango was no longer visible. What *was* visible against the dim light was a cloud of dust where the vehicle had been.

Had it pulled down a side road or into a driveway? Danny tried to spot it moving away from the highway, then remembered that the only side road out here was a mile farther down the road. He checked for taillights to see if the vehicle had made a U-turn. Nothing!

Why hadn't the driver turned on his lights? He accelerated and watched his rear-view mirrors closely. Twice, he thought he caught the glint of metal reflected in the bright light of the full moon, but he wasn't sure.

Unease turned to alarm when Danny spotted another Durango, identical to the first, sitting at the stop sign of the only side road before the alkali flats. Could it be the same one? Impossible. There was no way it could have gotten around him that fast. This one, too, had interior light glow but displayed no running lights.

They had to be Gannon vehicles. Danny shifted into fifth gear and watched his rear view mirror, trying to see what the second vehicle did.

Darkness swallowed the Durango the instant he passed, but this time, he caught a distinct flash of taillights as the vehicle shifted into gear. Moonlight reflected off chrome as it moved onto the highway, but it too failed to switch on its headlights. Danny was certain both vehicles were following close behind.

Danny's mind ranged up the road, trying to think of where he could take evasive action. Already, the alkali flats, muddy from summer thunderstorms earlier in the afternoon, had closed in on each side. The barrow pits still had puddles, and were a sure barrier against his type of vehicle. Going off-road was not a consideration.

Maybe they were just tailing him, like all the times before. Danny dismissed such optimism. A few hours ago, peaceful surveillance had painfully evolved into hostile pursuit. This lonely, isolated stretch of highway was the perfect location for not just pursuit, but perhaps much worse.

He processed all he could remember about the two vehicles, but something didn't make sense. The Durangos wouldn't stand a chance against him. His car was simply too fast. The best they could hope for was to somehow box him in, which meant there had to be someone or something up ahead that would enable them to do that.

Danny recalled that the first Durango had a long CB whip antenna attached to the rear bumper. If they were using cell phones or company radios, he was sunk. But CBs? It was a long shot, but worth a try. If he could overhear their communications, he might be able to figure a way out.

He put his CB on scan. At channel nine, two kids were talking trash. *Why did they have to use such language?* On channel nineteen, the most frequently used channel, he heard distant trucker's chattering to each other. At channel twenty-two some guy was shouting a fire and brimstone Christian sermon. At channel twenty-four, the signal meter pegged at full strength. ". . . udd, Elmer Fudd, this is Hound Dog One, over."

"Go ahead Hound Dog One." Danny recognized the voice. It was Lucas Blackthorn.

"Elmer Fudd, Jackrabbit is in sight running about a half-click east of Two's watch point. He's unaware the dogs are loose. Over."

"Roger Hound Dog One." Danny could hear the excitement in Blackthorn's voice. "Give me speed and ETA to my location. Over."

"Speed is sixty-five and steady. ETA at your location in approximately nine minutes. Over."

"Matchstick, Matchstick, you copy that? Over."

A third voice answered. "Ten-four Elmer Fudd. The barbeque is hot! Repeat, the barbeque is hot. Jackrabbit stew on your signal. Over."

"Hound Dog One, maintain cover for . . ." There was silence on the channel for a couple of seconds as Blackthorn apparently checked his watch. "Seven minutes. Repeat, seven minutes. Then move up and let him know you're there. As soon as he jumps, keep me posted on his speed. What's his status now? Over."

"Still sixty-five and steady."

"All right boys, this is it.!" Blackthorn sounded ecstatic. "I want Jackrabbit's hide hanging over my fireplace in about seven and a half minutes. Elmer Fudd out."

The implications were all too clear. Trouble was, Danny was already trapped. He couldn't stop or turn off the road, and the two Durangos made it impossible for him to turn back. Apparently, their plan would take at least some degree of coordination in order to pull off. His arrival in a certain place at a certain time was apparently the event trigger.

Timing appeared to be the weak point in Blackthorn's plan. If Danny could somehow destroy it, he might be able to shoot through their trap before they could close the door. To do that, he had to disrupt their communications. He placed his CB mic under his leg in such a way that the talk key was depressed. The 250-watt linear amplifier in his trunk would blow anyone else off that channel for miles around. Did they have a backup channel? He couldn't afford to think about that.

He tromped his accelerator all the way to the floorboard. Even at sixty-five MPH, the burst of power momentarily broke his tires loose and caused a slight fishtail. Then the tires grabbed and shot the vehicle forward, pressing him into his seat.

Then came the action he feared the most. He turned his own headlights off.

*

Sonny Wilcox could scarcely believe his eyes. Jackrabbit's car had disappeared. One moment it was there, and the next it was gone. It took him a couple of seconds to realize that Jackrabbit had turned off his lights and was on the run.

He ripped the CB mike out of its dashboard socket and tried to hail Blackthorn. "Elmer Fudd, Elmer Fudd, Jackrabbit's spotted the dogs. He's on the run—I repeat, he's on the run!" When he released the mic key, his ears were assaulted by a piercing burst of feedback static. He keyed the mic and released it again with the same result. His signal strength meter was pegged off the scale. Someone was broadcasting a signal far more powerful than the radios he and the others were using.

He threw the useless mic on the seat and took out his cell phone. *Damn, no bars!* In desperation, he turned his headlights on, rolled down his window, and gestured frantically for Hound Dog Two to follow him. He floored his accelerator and took out as fast as the big Dodge Hemi engine could propel him toward where he last saw the Mustang's taillights.

Chapter 38

Despite the bright moonlight, darkness crashed around Danny like a pall. He knew his eyes would adjust, but for the moment, he was completely blind.

He concentrated hard on trying to keep the car straight until he once again could see the road. He heard the left tire begin to pick up shoulder gravel and corrected slightly — at least, he thought it was only slightly. Perhaps he was careening toward the barrow pit on the other side, but didn't know it.

The engine's whine told him it was time to shift gears. As he shifted into sixth, he felt gravel on the right. He corrected again. He had to be doing somewhere near one hundred — and still he couldn't see the road.

Then slowly, the white stripe at the left side of the road came into view. He was nearly over it. He corrected. Then other lines began to materialize. The contours of the land took shape and he could finally discern details. Telephone poles whizzed by. He could finally see the yellow lines that marked the center of the road.

He glanced in the rearview mirror. Two sets of headlights flared some distance behind him, probing the darkness, but he rapidly out-paced them. Danny settled in and began thinking about the road ahead as he shifted into seventh gear — his speed now upwards of 130 MPH — and climbing.

It was a gentle hump where the road rose a few inches to allow a culvert to pass under, barely noticeable at normal speed. But at close to 140 MPH, it launched the Mustang like a catapult. The impact felt like an artillery shell exploding under his seat. The engine screamed as the undercarriage clunked away and all four tires free-wheeled in the air.

Danny took his foot off the accelerator just as the car came back to the pavement with a jarring thump. The rear tires tried to reestablish their grip on the road, but broke loose and threw the car into a severe fishtail. The car became a monster under his hand, careening back and forth, threatening to roll. Despite his tender shoulder, his hands moved faster than he ever thought they could as he countered each swing and fought to regain control.

The combination of lowering power slightly and his skillful maneuvering finally overcame the violent seesaw motions, and he found himself again going straight down the road, albeit at breakneck speed. *This is fast enough.* He eased back on the accelerator.

Once the terror subsided, Danny's mind returned to his puzzle. If it were him, where would he set up some kind of trap? *Blackthorn? Matchstick? Where are you?*

Then he thought he knew. The bright moonlight was just beginning to illuminate the outline of the two low hills that signaled the road's transition from a long straightaway to a lazy "S" curve that snaked between them. Coming into the curve at night was no problem at normal speeds or during the daytime, but at night at his high speed it would be impossible to see around the curves, and impossible to stop if something were in the way.

The hill closest to Farmington was the taller of the two and had a dirt road leading to a flat area at the top. It was a favorite Lover's Lane. When Danny was in high school, he and his friends called it Pregnant Point. It was also a favorite place for Highway Patrol troopers to set up radar traps.

Truckers who knew about the place occasionally pulled up there to update their log books or catch a few winks in their sleepers. If Blackthorn had set a trap, more than likely, that's where it was.

As he got closer, Danny thought he saw something at the top of Pregnant Point. It took a few seconds to recognize what it was. He was looking at the ghostly outline of the twin tanks of a fuel hauler.

So that's how they're going to try to pull this off. There was no backing out or backing up. His only choice was to keep going and praying that he'd successfully disrupted their timing.

He knew the "S' curve was not far away, and that he was traveling far too fast to attempt to negotiate it by moonlight alone. Despite that it would reveal him, he reached down and turned his headlights back on.

*

Blackthorn hung his CB mic back on its hook, leaned back, and stretched luxuriously. Everything was going perfectly. Whitehorse had come out of Shiprock just as he predicted. He wasn't losing his touch after all. He looked toward the top of the hill where, even from here, the bright moonlight allowed him to see the silver tank trailers. The rear one was the instrument of Whitehorse's death. It held 4,000 gallons of highly-flammable drip gas — an unrefined form of natural gasoline that collected in small amounts as a condensate at natural gas wellheads, where it was collected and stored until there was enough to fill a tanker truck.

Twig Lusk — Matchstick — was reliable. His nickname came from his stringy, rail-thin, six-foot-six body. Blackthorn once told him in jest that he was the only man he knew who could lay in the shade of a barbed-wire fence.

It took the two of them nearly an hour to precisely position the rear tank so it balanced precariously on its center of gravity at the apex of the hill. The pin on the trailer hitch would slide out easily, then be replaced after the fact with one that was broken.

It would require only a single hard push to send 4,000 gallons of instant death careening down the dirt road and out onto the highway. Even if the tank arrived before the car, the tank would crash into the other hill, blocking the roadway and spilling its contents. If Whitehorse entered that first curve at more than sixty MPH, there would be no way he could avoid the wreckage. If the tank didn't ignite on impact with the hill, Hot engine parts and the sparks from tearing metal from a car hitting the wreckage certainly would do the job. But if by some miracle even that didn't work, Matchstick had a flare gun that would do the job. The plan was more complicated than a simple bullet to the head, but it would make Whitehorse's death look like just a tragic accident.

Yes sir! In about five minutes, my life is going to get a whole lot easier. Blackthorn rubbed his hands together in anticipation.

Then he noticed that his CB radio was acting up. A dull rustling and rumbling sound came from the speaker. He checked the signal-strength meter. It was jumping around crazily. He took the mic off its hook and tried to hail Hound Dog One.

145

"Hound Dog One, Hound Dog One, Elmer Fudd. Over." His call was answered only by a loud burst of static. He keyed the mike and tried again. Same result.. "Cheap damn radio," he muttered as he threw the useless instrument to the seat in disgust. He pulled out his cell phone. One and a half signal bars. It wasn't much, but if the two hound dogs were close enough to Farmington, it might do the job. He punched the speed dial with Wilcox's number and waited. The call failed to connect.

It was an irritating problem, but not critical. Once the chase actually started, the radio was no longer needed. He and Matchstick were using a visual signal to start the process anyway. He would simply flash his headlights three times and the tank of drip gas would be on its way.

Lucas got out of his car and peered down the road. Sure enough, several miles back, two sets of headlights were coming his way. He glanced at his watch. They were a little earlier than expected. He was about to climb back in when he heard something. It sounded like a car approaching, but there were no headlights. He strained his vision in the direction of the sound.

Suddenly, a blinding set of headlights flared right in front him. A vehicle traveling at tremendous speed swept past, its wind whipping up a hailstorm of sand and pebbles that assaulted his exposed face and arms. His mind held the impression of the vehicle as being red. The car was red!

It's him. But how? Blackthorn dived for the open car door. He flashed his headlights with one hand and honked the horn with the other. "Hurry, Matchstick, hurry," he repeated over and over.

*

"What the hell?" Matchstick bolted upright and stared into the valley. A pair of headlights had suddenly flared from out of nowhere near where he'd been watching for Blackthorn's signal. At first he thought it was Blackthorn's car, but these headlights didn't flash. *That car's really moving.*

In the next instant, another set of headlights flashed three times, paused, and flashed three more times. A car horn blared up from the valley floor. It was the signal — but it was too soon. It wasn't supposed to come for another two minutes. The fast-moving headlights must be the target. It was perilously late to try to close the trap.

Matchstick sprang to the hitch pin to uncouple the rear trailer. As he reached for it, the stillness of the night exploded with a thunderous noise that came rumbling up from the valley floor. It startled him so much so that he missed his grab and smashed his thumb into the rough metal of the hitch, tearing his nail nearly off. Pain shot all the way to his elbow. He cried out, jerked his hand back and shook it to alleviate the pain. Then his mind came back to his task. He made another grab, this time successful, and yanked the pin free. Then he threw his shoulder into the huge tank and pushed. It shuddered and slowly began to roll. One-inch, two-inches, four-inches, a foot. As the tremendous weight of the load shifted past the center of gravity, the tank gained speed. He pushed with all his might until he was running to keep up. Then his foot caught a rock that sent him sprawling headlong to the gravel. Cut, scraped, and bruised, he raised his head and watched as the tank traveled faster and faster down the hill toward its rendezvous with the speedy Mustang, just now rounding the first curve. "Hurry," the man urged. "Hurry!"

*

As Danny's headlights flared to life, the person of Lucas Blackthorn appeared out of nowhere. Even as fast as he was going, Danny could see the startled expression on the man's face.

But there was no time to wonder, the first curve was closer than he'd thought. He glanced at the speedometer which registered one hundred and thirty-four miles per hour. There was simply no way to slow enough for the curve in the short distance left. He was going to die — it was just a matter of where he would leave the road.

Position and timing were everything if he were to have any chance at all. He had to find that one tiny spot in the road from which to dive to the left, and then hold a perfect line through the first curve. At precisely the right moment, he had to find another such tiny spot that would allow him to change the direction of his momentum and hold another perfect line through the second half of the "S." Danny recognized that even with an uninjured left shoulder, he was not a perfect driver.

He slammed the car from seventh to fifth gear and applied all the brakes he dared. If the tires broke lose now, it was all over. If the road didn't get him, Blackthorn and his goons would.

Gearing down the huge engine so violently created tremendous backpressure on the exhaust system. The engine spun up more RPMs than it was ever designed to handle. The burst of backpressure blew the diverter covers off the straight pipes and unleashed a barrage of noise that exceeded any his vehicle had ever produced, even at the racetrack. The sound thundered through the area all the way to the top of Pregnant Point.

For a split second Danny's mind was overloaded by all the critically timed choices he had to make. Then his mind shut down and instinct took over. The world seemed to go into slow motion and he knew exactly where the setup spot was, and it felt as if he had hours to get there. His mind's eye saw the car drift slightly to the edge of the pavement on the right, then, at the precise moment, dive sharply left at the beginning of the curve where it began a screaming, four-wheel drift through the first curve. Tremendous cen-trifugal forces clawed at him, but the car held its line and stopped the drift just as the tires began picking up gravel at the right shoulder.

There was just enough of an interval for him to make a quick maneuver to the left to position himself for a dive to the right into the second curve.

But just as he started his low dive, a huge object, big and silvery and moving fast, careened onto the highway from the dirt road leading to the top of Pregnant Point. It was going to hit him. He nudged the car as far left as he dared and held his breath for the impact. The bulky end of a tank trailer seemed to fill his passenger-side window. He cringed in anticipation of the impact, but only felt the car shudder a bit as the tanker lightly brushed his rear bumper and disappeared into the darkness.

Though the impact was ever so light, it threw his car slightly off-track. Belatedly, he tried to nudge the car farther to the right, but felt the rear tires get squirrelly as they strained to maintain their tenuous grip on the pavement. More pressure on the steering wheel would send him into a deadly skid. He drifted farther and farther left — toward destruction — and there was absolutely nothing he could do about it. Danny heard shoulder gravel thrown up into the wheel wells just as he felt the rear tires slip.

He pictured in his mind his beloved car careening out into the desert, rolling over and over and over, disintegrating into a thousand pieces as it encountered the rocks and sagebrush of the field beside the highway.

Chapter 39

He didn't know just how long it took for his awareness to fully return. One moment Danny believed himself to be hurtling off the road, then in what seemed to be the next instant, he found himself stopped over a half mile from the hills; his car facing in the wrong direction. He was gripping the steering wheel savagely and staring wild-eyed straight ahead.

Then the contents of his stomach began to rise. He slammed hard against the door, sending a fountain of pain through his already injured shoulder. He dimly realized that not only was his seat belt still latched, but he'd forgotten to pull the door handle. He ripped the belt off, found the handle, and tried again. The door flew open, tumbling him out of the car and rolling him down the ten-foot embankment. He landed face-first in several inches of dirty, smelly, barrow pit mud, and there puked his guts out.

When the waves of nausea subsided, he climbed to the top of the barrow pit and sank to his knees, hugging himself, trying to quell the violent shaking that wracked his body as the terror of the past few minutes caught up with him. He looked up and saw columns of flames leaping more than a hundred feet into the air between the hills. By all rights, he should have been in the middle of that conflagration.

He heard sirens coming from Farmington. As a convoy of emergency vehicles streamed past, his terror turned to anger — dark, boiling, white-hot anger. In a single day, he had won two separate confrontations with Lucas Blackthorn and Gannon Oil. Without being fully in control of himself, Danny Whitehorse, a grown man, a highly-educated attorney, but most of all, a warrior of the Diné, instinctively released his terror and showed his defiance to his terrible enemy the best way he knew how.

*

More than one fireman would later remark about the crazy man covered with mud doing some kind of dance beside a vintage Mustang parked on the side of the road that night. Had to be some kind of nut case, they said.

They didn't understand because they were not Diné. Only a fellow warrior would recognize the mud-covered man's gyrations as the warrior's dance of victory.

"Too bad about that guy up on the hill," they said. The tank that broke loose and exploded sent a geyser of hot metal and flaming liquid right back to the top of Pregnant Point, where a piece of burning shrapnel punctured the second tank and sent torrents of flaming drip gas cascading over him and down the hill in all directions, igniting a large brush fire as it went.

Chapter 40

Danny's first instinct was to go straight to Kathy's house and tell her what happened. But he immediately rejected the thought as far too dangerous — not just for him, but her as well. Same problem with Bri's place. With his car so recognizable, and now so loud, he didn't even dare take a chance on driving through town to get to Vic and Angie's ranch.

He thought of Uncle Samuel's place, but rejected it against the possibility that Gannon knew more about his family connections than he thought.

He could find refuge on the reservation, but had little doubt that every road in and out of Shiprock was being carefully watched. The one choice that made sense was to get out of the area and stay as far away from the people he loved as he could until things settled down.

Driving gingerly, trying to keep his noise level as low as possible, he drove into Farmington only far enough to duck across the river and onto the reservation on the Bisti Highway. He drove south past the road that led to Chaco Canyon National Monument and on to a connection with Highway 555 near Gallup. He doubted Gannon's goons would be looking for him this far south — at least not yet.

Sunrise found him parked in the trees just off a secluded dirt road on the outskirts of Gallup trying without success to catch a few winks. Sleep was impossible with his mind churning over the question of what in the world to do next.

As the morning's golden light touched the cedar-covered hills, a plan percolated into his mind. Unfortunately, the first step involved one of the most painful things he could possibly do.

He found an auto parts store and bought a set of diverter plates, installed them, then circled Gallup on surface streets and picked up Interstate 40 five miles west of town. He used the last cash he had on him to buy three-quarters of a tank of gas, then drove on to Holbrook, Arizona a hundred miles to the west.

He needed money. But going to his bank, using his debit card, or swiping his one and only credit card might expose him to someone with Gannon's resources. His only available liquid asset was his car. The car was as much a part of him as anything had ever been. It was worth at least thirty thousand dollars. Unfortunately, it also marked him. He had to get rid of it.

He sold the famous Mustang to a very pleased Holbrook car dealer for the ridiculous price of seven thousand cash. Danny wrote an option clause into the sale contract that said the car could not be sold to anyone else for two weeks. The clause gave him an option to repurchase it for ten thousand—a neat $3,000 profit for the dealer. If he missed the repurchase date, the car belonged to the dealer, no strings attached.

Danny told the dealer he needed the money to get to Los Angeles. If anyone checked the Holbrook Greyhound Station, they would find he had indeed bought a one-way ticket all the way to LA.

He took the bus only as far as Flagstaff, where he spent thirty-two-hundred of the money to purchase a beat-up ten-year-old Ford Pickup that ran well and would look perfectly at home on the reservation or in any of the towns around it. He paid cash for a room at the Ramada Inn and collapsed into bed for his first sleep in almost forty hours.

The maid tapped on his door shortly before ten the next morning. After a quick McDonald's breakfast and a trip to Walmart to buy a couple of changes of clothing and other personal necessities, Danny returned to his room armed with several legal pads and began to write out his plan.

Sometime after eleven that night, with the floor littered with wadded-up yellow sheets of paper and a cold, half-eaten pizza sitting atop the dresser, Danny finally nodded off to sleep, fully clothed, and with his pen still clutched in his hand.

Chapter 41

Blackthorn came to work Monday morning so tired, worn, and worried that he could barely function. Red Gannon was not one to countenance failure, and his failed attempt to get rid of Whitehorse was the biggest failure of his life. All day Saturday and Sunday he expected the phone call or a knock on his door that would signal the worst from Gannon. But he heard not a word from the man.

Twenty minutes after his arrival, that much feared red line button on his phone lit. He let it ring long enough to pop two antacids into his mouth, then took a deep breath and tried to compose himself.

"Good morning, Red. You're up and at it early today."

"This ain't early. I've been up for hours. What's on your schedule?"

Lucas was relieved. The man sounded hearty and chipper — not at all in a foul mood. He made a charade of checking his schedule. "Let's see. I'm fairly clean today. I have a security briefing with department heads and well-site security contractors at nine thirty, then nothing else until around three o'clock." *Could it be that Red was unaware of the Jackrabbit Stew operation?*

"Good," the old man said. "It's time for us to count the Cayman money. Cancel your security briefing and be out here at ten thirty. Webster, Popeson and Parker will be here at noon. I'll have Juan barbeque up some short ribs. After you screwed up your chance at jackrabbit stew Saturday night, I thought some ribs would just about hit the spot!"

Blackthorn's blood turned cold.

*

Lucas paced outside Gannon's office door for nearly half an hour. He was convinced that the old man was inside mocking his distress. To his surprise, Gannon burst through the front door wearing riding pants and carrying a crop. He shouted instructions over his shoulder—something about putting his horse away. Then he spotted Blackthorn.

"Lucas," the man bellowed. "Sorry to keep you waiting. We were running a couple of coyotes up on Diamond Back Ridge. I completely lost track of time. Come into the office and let's have a drink."

Blackthorn nearly collapsed into one of the high-back leather chairs in front of Gannon's desk. He knew better than to relax.

"There you go," the man said as he handed Lucas his drink. "Bottoms up." Gannon hoisted his own glass in salute, then retreated behind the huge antique Spanish Colonial desk, asking almost as an afterthought, "Let's see, where were we? Oh, yes. Jackrabbit stew! Start at the beginning and tell me everything." Gone was even a hint of warmth, replaced in an instant by the man's infamous cold, unblinking stare.

". . . That's about the size of it, Red. There was simply no way any of us imagined that Indian going so fast with his lights off. Both the Hound Dog units thought he ran up the road a mile or two and somehow turned off into the flats. They looked for him all the way, but by the time they reached me, it was already too late."

Gannon digested the information for a few moments then asked, "So where's Whitehorse now? Anyone seen or heard from him?"

"Nothing. It doesn't look like he ever went home after the accident. I've got several people checking every town from here to Albuquerque, especially the reservation border towns like Gallup, Grants—even Flagstaff.

"Trouble is, we have a huge blind spot out on that reservation. We've made some inquiries around Shiprock, but it's like talking to a wall. The minute you mention the guy's name, people clam up and won't say a word. We're just going to have to wait until he surfaces again."

Gannon turned his chair to the window and stared out while Blackthorn endured the man's silence with apprehension. Finally, Gannon turned back and spoke with cold calmness. "Let me tell you something about coyotes, Lucas. I got a couple of shots off at one this morning, but missed. Now that it's been shot at, I'll never get close enough to that animal to shoot at him again. It will most likely be the same with Whitehorse." Gannon shook his head. "Lucas, you've let me down again. Quite frankly, I don't know if I can trust your judgment any longer. I think it's time to bring in outside help to deal with Whitehorse. Help I can rely on."

"Ah, come on, Red," Blackthorn pleaded, "you know you can trust me. Look at all the years we've had together. Hell, anybody can . . ."

"Don't argue with me!" Gannon flung his drink glass past Black-thorn's ear, spilling liquid across Lucas' face and shirt and shattering the glass against the wall. "You're not listening. I'm not asking—I'm telling you how it's going to be. The full cost of that little jackrabbit stew operation of yours is coming out of your share of the Cayman account. You're paying Wilcox and Halverson every dime you promised them, plus, you're giving Twig's widow a million bucks to make sure she keeps her mouth shut. Now argue with me some more and I'll consider retiring you right now. Today. You'll never leave this ranch and you'll never spend a dime of that Cayman account money."

Blackthorn reeled. Over a million and a half dollars gone from his Cayman account. It was a severe blow, but the money mattered far less than getting out of this terribly dangerous situation. He wiped the stinging liquid from his eyes and tried to sound calm, but his voice betrayed him. His words came out squeaky, fearful. "Jeez Red. No need to talk like that. You—you're right. This *is* my fault and I should pay for it. Nobody could have predicted what Whitehorse did out there, but I'm not going to argue with you. I just don't want you to give up on me, that's all. Give me another chance. I promise I'll hand you that Indian's head on a platter the instant he pokes his nose out."

Gannon underwent one of his legendary changes of demeanor. His color returned to normal, his eyes softened and he broke into a grin. "That's great Lucas." He beamed. "You'll be a great help to the two men I've hired. For the time being, I'm placing them in charge of the search for Whitehorse. They're waiting at your office. Get them set up at Looking Glass as soon as you get back. Now, what say we join the others? I'll bet Juan has those short ribs ready to come off the grill."

Blackthorn's stomach turned on a wave of nausea. All he wanted was an antacid and a bathroom where he could relieve his tortured bladder. Nonetheless, he put on his best face and followed the old man outside, trying to act as normal as possible. Sometimes with Red Gannon, putting on a good performance was everything.

Chapter 42

Something banged against the motel room wall. Danny leaped from his bed, sure that Gannon's men were about to come crashing in. Then he heard the sound of a squeaky-wheeled cart. His pounding heart slowed as he realized it was only a maid who had clumsily interrupted his sleep.

It was seven fifteen on Monday morning, and he needed coffee. The motel offered a free hot breakfast so he dressed and hurried to the lobby where he devoured two blueberry bagels, some hash browns and bacon, and washed it down with a steaming cup of wake up. Second cup in hand, he returned to the room to review his notes.

A half-hour before checkout time, he took the first step in his plan. It was perhaps the longest shot of all, but it was the one thing that everything else hinged on. All he had to do was to talk his best friend since law school, Jason Stevens, into giving up all the money and seniority he enjoyed as an equity partner in Salt Lake City's most prestigious law firm, and convince him to come to Farmington to work for a pittance, and perhaps risk his life in the process.

Were Jason married, Danny wouldn't have considered making such a request. He was a decorated former Navy Seal, and more importantly, possessed the same passion Danny had for using the practice of law to help people who couldn't afford legal representation.

Maybe he would come, maybe he wouldn't. But Jason Stevens was the only attorney Danny knew who might even remotely consider such an unappetizing proposition.

Here goes nothing. Danny dialed the phone.

*

It was all Jason could do to maintain his focus on the business partnership agreement before him. He'd seen so many of them that his mind just sort of glazed over. It was becoming the same way with real estate contracts, patent royalty agreements, even pre-nuptial contracts – all the fancy documents that made businesses run or defined the lives of his well-to-do clientele.

When his secretary announced the caller, Jason smiled and put aside his yellow legal pad with only four unused pages remaining on it. Danny Whitehorse. It had been nearly two months since they'd last talked – a long time considering that they'd never gone more than two weeks without one or the other calling ever since law school. "Danny, you old horse thief, how are you?"

"Hello Jason. Glad I caught you."

Jason sensed a subtle, seriousness in Danny's greeting that told him this call was going to be different than their usual light-hearted, laughter-filled conversations. Danny's tone seemed tentative, guarded. Danny started talking about how well they used to work together at the legal clinic where they'd met, about how much fun it had been, and how satisfying it felt to both of them to be helping people who otherwise could never have afforded legal representation.

Jason agreed and said it was indeed the most satisfying practice of law he'd ever experienced. Then Danny blindsided him. "Jason, how would you like to get that feeling all over again?"

Jason didn't know how to answer. He'd been asking himself just such a question for at least the past two years. Nonplussed, he asked quietly, "What do you mean?"

The door was open, and for the next twenty minutes Jason listened and furiously scribbled notes on the remaining four pages of his legal pad as his friend unveiled the story of a company called Gannon Oil. "So the bottom line is," Danny finally concluded, "I've been flooded with a huge number of clients who can't afford to pay me. Thankfully, I have a donor whose deep pockets are keeping the office operations alive. I've filed a class-action lawsuit that I may not have enough evidence to sustain through a routine motion for summary judgment, let alone a full-blown trial. The lawsuit has stirred up public sentiment against me so strongly that there have been public protests outside my office and death threats against me and my staff."

"Holy cow, Danny."

"There's another thing, Jason. Some of the young hotheads on the reservation have already blown up two gas wells. If I don't get ahead of this thing fast, the whole reservation could literally go up in flames."

"What about you? Are you all right?"

Danny paused long enough that Jason could tell his friend was struggling for an answer. Finally he said, "Hey, what's a couple of bumps and bruises? Other than the fact that the whole world hates us down here, things are good!"

Jason could tell there was much left unsaid. But knowing his friend as he did, he knew that if Danny wasn't ready to reveal everything yet, there was good reason.

"The only upside to all this," Danny continued, "is that my clients' damages are potentially in the hundreds of millions if we win, and Gannon Oil has the money to pay the judgment. I know all this can't sound terribly attractive to a guy in your position, but the reason I'm calling is to ask if you would consider leaving your life of prestige and luxury to come down here and join me as an equal partner in Farmington's least profitable law firm."

There it was—the choice—lying naked on the table, just waiting to see what he would do. The choice was between the mind-numbingly boring, safe and predictable practice of law he'd become accustomed to or or stepping dangerously out on a very thin limb in order to help Danny. Choosing the latter was crazy, insane, completely irrational— and Jason was not by nature an irrational man. There was only one answer. He said, "Of course I'll come, Danny. How soon do you need me?"

"A. . .a . . . how soon as you can get here?" Jason could tell that Danny was not expecting such a quick, affirmative response.

"I'll turn in my resignation today." It'll take me a day to settle my partnership interest and turn my cases over to someone else, and a couple more to pack up and hit the road. I can probably be down there by Thursday night or for sure by Friday. I assume you can put me up at your place until I can find something of my own?"

Jason heard Danny hesitate. "Um, how about I meet you in Durango on Friday night? There's a restaurant on the south end of town called the

Golden Slipper. Does seven o'clock sound okay?"

The response perplexed Jason a bit, but didn't seem unreasonable. It was obvious that Danny didn't want him to come to Farmington. He would find out why when he got there. "That works for me," he said. "And Danny, thanks man! You've no idea how much I've needed this change."

Jason's mind swirled as he hung up the phone. The firm wouldn't like him leaving, but there were at least four senior associates who were dying to become partners.

As Jason reviewed his conversation with Danny, he realized that what was not spoken contributed as much to the swiftness of his acceptance as what actually was. It was very unlike Danny not to tell him everything. There was an uncharacteristic urgency in his friend's voice that whispered to Jason's mind that his friend was in trouble — serious trouble.

Chapter 43

Lucas silently cursed when he found that indeed, two men were waiting for him at his office. Although he'd agreed to work with them, he didn't have to like it. But one didn't disagree with Red Gannon and expect to live a long and happy life.

The man who appeared to be the leader was a tall, swarthy-looking Italian who called himself Tony. His companion, his polar opposite in almost every way, was Max, a short, pear-shaped man of German extraction with a fringe of thick, medium-brown hair around an otherwise bald head. Max's round face was dominated by a pair of equally round, thick-lensed eyeglasses that magnified his eyeballs into bulbous-looking orbs.

He verified their identities with Gannon, then escorted the pair to Looking Glass. "This is quite a setup," Tony said in a thick Bronx accent as they looked down two twenty-foot-long, six-foot-tall racks of electronic equipment with dozens of LED lights winking and blinking to signal activity.

The comment gave Lucas a chance to brag. "There's not a phone line, radio frequency or company-provided cell phone we can't monitor from here," he said. "Thanks to a man we have inside the phone company, we have a direct fiber optic link into their main switch. We have access to not only our employees' home phones, but anyone else who lives in this end of the state.

"But what you're interested in is over here." Lucas directed the men to a dual workstation console with an array of flat-screen video monitors and a bewildering collection of buttons and knobs. "These consoles allow us to monitor up to a dozen active wiretaps at a time. There are remote taps on all the lines going into Whitehorse's office, his house, and his secretary's house. The taps are voice activated and can be used either as a full-time sound surveillance system or just for call monitoring. Everything's digitally recorded."

"What about on-premises devices?" Tony asked

"We had them, but they caught on right away. Whitehorse found our bugs the same day they were installed. We've tried to reinstall, but it looks like they're using an electronic sweeper. Somebody over there knows what they're doing. They've installed scramblers on all their landlines."

"What about cell phones?" Tony asked.

"They're using encrypted cell phones. We're only able to hear what they want us to hear."

"Then you're a bit behind the technology curve," Tony said.

Blackthorn wanted to smash his face, but held his tongue. This pair had Red Gannon's ear.

"We have a source for a mobile decrypter that might unscramble those cell phone conversations," Max said, "but it will take seventy-two hours to get it here. Now, Mr. Blackthorn, if you'll step outside, we'd like to show you what we have."

Blackthorn couldn't imagine what they could possibly show him that would be of interest, but once outside, he had to admit the pair's one-ton Dodge van was a marvel. The powerful vehicle was armored against small-arms fire, including a bullet-proof windshield and side glass. It was equipped with the most sophisticated mobile surveillance equipment Blackthorn had ever seen. He asked them about the strangely configured winch on the front bumper. "Actually, it's an original invention of ours," Max said. "It's a locking claw that will attach to another vehicle's bumper. All we have to do is give a car or truck a little nudge from behind that attaches the claw, and the chase is over."

They had an arsenal of sophisticated weaponry and ammunition, some of which Blackthorn had never laid eyes on before. He was grudgingly impressed. If Whitehorse poked his nose out anywhere in the Four Corners area, these men would surely be able to gather him in.

Chapter 44

Danny was elated. Jason was coming. But his elation was tempered by the thought that when the man found out just how dangerous this case was, he might turn around and head right back to Utah.

Time to let everyone know I'm alive and well. There was only one reasonably secure way to do that. He found the Flagstaff public library and used a public access computer to let Kathy know what was going on. He detailed what had happened to him Saturday morning and gave precise instructions for her and Chaco to follow until he could meet with them again. The one thing he didn't reveal was where he was.

Two days in the same motel was stretching his luck to the limit if Gannon was putting his considerable resources behind the task of looking for him.

Time to move. But there were two more things he needed before leaving Flagstaff. The first was a good handgun. He would never again be caught in situations like he'd faced Friday without some heavy-duty personal protection.

He found the second item at Betty's Magic Scissors Boutique & Salon on the northeast side of town. The salon's Yellow Pages ad prominently listed what he was looking for.

Twenty minutes later, Danny emerged carrying a tall, round box, the contents of which would enable him to accomplish the second phase of his plan, which was to make Danny Whitehorse, the attorney, disappear.

*

At six thirty that evening, Danny checked into the Blue Mountain Inn at Monticello, Utah, under an assumed name. The town was an hour west of Cortez, Colorado, and two hours from Shiprock. It wasn't likely that Gannon would be searching for him so far from the reservation. He spent the next four hours putting the final touches on his plan and then relaxed for the first time in many days.

It took him two hours working on the wig he's acquired at the beauty salon to create the long side braids that would transform him from a clean-cut, short-haired attorney into a properly braided reservation Indian.

Around midnight, confident that he had done everything he could do, he dozed off into a deep, peaceful sleep.

He awoke at eight fifteen Tuesday morning, loaded his few belongings in his truck and drove to Cortez. At the Goodwill Store he bought a pair of cowboy boots, a pair of blue jeans, a plaid flannel shirt, and a black felt cowboy hat. He changed into his new old clothes at the Shell station and took a look in the mirror. The transformation was complete. He looked exactly like what he really was, a reservation born and raised Navajo Indian. No one would recognize him. His newly acquired derelict pickup truck only complimented the image.

Shortly after eleven, he called Kathy to have her arrange a meeting with Chaco.

Chapter 45

Seventy-two hours without a hint of Whitehorse's whereabouts. Blackthorn's nerves were strung to the breaking point. He'd tried all morning to break away from his office duties and get down to Looking Glass, but it was eleven fifteen when he finally swiped his electronic passkey to open the door. As he stepped in, Tony put a finger to his lips, shushed him, and pointed at Max who was listening intently to a set of headphones.

After a few long moments Max took a deep breath, reached over and flipped a switch, then peeled the headphones off and said, "I think we've got him!" He clicked his mouse on his computer screen several times, then pushed a button on the console. The sound of Danny's baritone voice filled the room.

"*Kathy, this is Mr. Plumber.*"

"*Yes Mr. Plumber, I've been expecting your call.*"

"*Did you get the information I sent concerning our problem?*"

"*Yes, sir. I followed your instructions precisely.*"

It was obvious by their cautious conversation that Whitehorse and his secretary suspected others might be listening in.

"*Did you get in touch with Mr. Canyon?*"

"*Yes, sir. He's standing by.*"

"*Think carefully on this. Do you recall the 'Top Job' project, the one I update on a daily basis?*"

"*The one you and Mr. Canyon have been working on?*"

"*Yes, that's it. Have him meet me at Red-22 at seven o'clock tonight. That's*

Red-22 at seven o'clock. Do you understand where that is?"

The woman's voice paused. Finally, she replied. *"I think I understand that location. It's near that major gas facility, is it not?"*

"That's exactly right."

"I don't think it would be wise to contact Mr. Canyon from here Sir."

"I agree. You have to reach Safe Harbor. You'd better leave immediately. Don't take anything with you and make sure you shake your tail. Understand?"

"Perfectly, sir. May I contact you to confirm your meeting?"

"No. He'll either be there or not. Have you heard from Paleface today?"

"No, Sir."

"Good. That means he's on his way. Tell Prudie I want her to meet him on Friday night at seven where I took everyone for last year's Christmas party. Have her bring him directly to Roundtree. Understand?"

"Yes, sir"

"Get out of there, Kathy. Do it now!"

The recording went silent as both phones hung up.

Blackthorn trembled with excitement. "Yes!" he shouted. "That's him! Who we got tailing that secretary of his?"

"Unit Three, Jamison and Carter," Tony said. He seemed surprised at Blackthorn's sudden commanding tone.

Blackthorn grabbed a radio mic hanging from the front of the console, keyed it, and shouted brusquely into the instrument, "Unit Three, Unit Three. This is Papa Bear, what's your ten-twenty? Over."

"We're westbound on Broadway. We just pulled out following Redbird. Looks like she's in a hurry. Over."

"Stay close and let me know if she leaves town. I want a face-to-face with her and I want it now. You copy? Over."

"Roger, Papa Bear, but if she's headed for the reservation again, that's not likely. Over."

Blackthorn cursed. The man was right. The reservation was like a giant "do-not-pass-go" zone for his surveillance crews.

"Do your best, Unit Three. Papa Bear out."

Blackthorn turned to Max and asked, "Can you type out a transcript of that conversation? We've got to figure out where that meeting is going to happen. Tony, get the phone book. Start looking for any place that has the name Red-22 or anything like it. Max, you and I will start going through the stuff we copied from their office."

Blackthorn glanced at his watch. Five minutes after twelve — less than seven hours to move heaven and earth in order to become the uninvited guest at Whitehorse's meeting.

*

Kathy was barely out of town on the Shiprock Expressway when she noticed the surveillance behind her. *That's strange.* This time, the team was making no attempt to conceal themselves. She picked up her cell phone. "Richard, there's a white Ford Fusion riding my bumper. I'm pretty sure it's a Gannon surveillance team."

"No problem," came the reply. "We spotted them almost as soon as you left the house. Don't worry, little sister. We'll take care of it."

A few seconds later, an old GMC pickup inserted itself between her car and the Fusion. At the same time, an older gray Chevy Lumina van pulled up in the inside lane and boxed the car in. Kathy tromped on her accelerator and shot off toward the reservation border. She had to chuckle. Her followers apparently had no idea that they themselves were being followed.

Chapter 46

Four ten in the afternoon and Blackthorn was beside himself. Unit Three had lost the secretary. Worse yet, he still had no idea where or what Red-22 was. They'd tried phone book listings for bars, restaurants, motels, anything, without results.

Max believed the secret was buried in the paperwork that was surreptitiously copied from Danny's office. "Obviously the terminology 'Top-Job' is a crude code word for Whitehorse's lawsuit," he stated. "I believe the files will tell us exactly where Red-22 is."

The three divided the copies between them and began the arduous task of reading as fast as they could, realizing it could take days. They only had a couple of hours.

"Damn it," Blackthorn shouted. "Somebody find something!" He grabbed a handful of discarded papers and flung them across the room. For several moments he sat in his chair, staring dejectedly at the mess until a single piece of paper caught his eye. He picked it up. It was a sheet of the cream-colored parchment paper on which Gannon Oil printed their letterhead. Just a few minutes before, he had read part way through it before realizing that it was just a memorandum he'd sent to the regular Looking Glass crew that somehow became mixed in with the copies from Whitehorse's office.

He crumpled the useless sheet and flung it in the general direction of a wastebasket, but before it completed its arc, Blackthorn leaped from his chair and shouted, "That's it. I think I know what we've been missing. Where are the blow-ups of that map from Whitehorse's office?" Tony pointed to four cardboard tubes leaning against the far wall.

Blackthorn grabbed them and extracted the contents. Max let out a yelp as Blackthorn swept the man's neatly stacked papers off the console and into the mess on the floor as he spread out the oversized sheets and arranged them in order. He immediately discarded two of the sheets, and repositioned the other two. Finally, he stabbed a finger at a spot on the map section on the right and exalted, "There! That's it! That's Red-22."

Max and Tony eyed each other then looked to see where Blackthorn was pointing. The map showed an area on the reservation just east of Eagle Dome nearly thirty miles straight south of Farmington on Reservation Highway 301. He pointed at a well designated as Eagle Dome #22. It was not a Gannon Oil lease.

"I don't understand," Tony said as he scratched his head. "I see the twenty-two, but where do you get 'red' out of that?"

"Right here." Blackthorn pointed to a wide red line drawn around the area by a felt-tipped marker. Other large areas of the map were demarcated with blue, green yellow and black lines.

"What tipped you off?" Max asked.

"This." Blackthorn showed them the crumpled memo. "It's an original, not a copy. My signature was in blue ink so it stood out in contrast with the rest of the page. I realized 'red' was probably a place, not a name. The only thing we've got of Whitehorse's with color on it is the map copies."

"I'll be damned," the big Italian swore. "Blackthorn, you're smarter than they said."

Blackthorn winced at the backhanded compliment but let it slide. "You two get out to that well site before Whitehorse gets there. I'll cover the road from where the pavement ends at the turn-off to the gas plant. Stay out of sight until you positively identify him. I've no idea who this Mr. Canyon is, but we need to avoid involving him if possible. An unexplained body would make things too complicated.

"You guys move it! Let's see if you and that wonder van of yours are worth what Gannon's paying you."

Chapter 47

The well site belonged to Tenneco Corporation and sat at the bottom of a mile-wide bowl-shaped depression. There were no security fences or guards. In fact, it appeared to have been weeks since anyone had visited the site.

Danny arrived fifteen minutes before he spotted Chaco walking in through the sagebrush from the south. Chaco looked at Danny, did a double-take and smiled. "I'm supposed to meet a guy named Whitehorse out here. You seen him?"

Danny chuckled. "*Ya' at' eehii,* brother."

"*Ya' at' eehii* yourself. Where'd you come up with the hair?"

"Found it over in Flagstaff."

"What's going on, Danny? Kathy told me Gannon people tried to kill you. Is that true?"

Danny recounted all that happened after he left Shiprock early Saturday morning. As Chaco listened, his look became more grim.

"So as I see it," Danny said, "Gannon's escalation from legal confrontation to a willingness to kill tells us two things. First, it confirms that we're headed in the right direction and touching some very tender nerves. Second, if I want to live to see the end of this thing, I've got to change tactics. That's why we're here."

*

Tony wanted to scream, to jump up and beat at his pants. Some kind of bug, probably one of the large red-and-black ants he'd seen around the area, had crawled up his pant leg and was munching happily on the back of his thigh. He chanced holding his binoculars with one hand while smashing the offending insect between his fingers with the other.

The van was stashed in a deep arroyo behind where they lay. On the outside, the vehicle looked like any other tan-colored Dodge that a building contractor or service company might use, but it had four-wheel drive and was powered by a huge, turbo-charged Hemi engine capable of over 600 horsepower.

Upon arrival, he and Max donned camouflage sniper-style ghillie suits and took up a position at the rim of the depression. Anyone looking their way from the well site would be looking directly into the low-lying sun.

While Tony trained powerful binoculars on the site, Max pointed an ultra-sensitive parabolic shotgun microphone toward two men conversing near the well. The microphone could pick up conversations over a mile away so long as no intervening noise overpowered it.

"Quick, which one's talking?" Max hissed?

"You got something?"

"One of them just called the other 'Danny.'"

"Which one?"

"How the hell should I know? You're the one with the field glasses. Here—you hold the antenna and give me the glasses."

Max adjusted the expensive electronic binoculars to compensate for his thick glasses and upped the magnification so he could clearly see who was talking. After a time, he said, "Well I'll be damned. It's ponytails himself. Must be wearing a wig. We got him, Tony. Call Blackthorn and tell him we're about to bring home the bacon."

*

"I'm going to Roundtree tonight." Danny said. "I want to brief everyone on my plan." He checked his cell phone for service and was surprised to see that he had three bars. *Must be because of the gas plant.*

Kathy answered her cell phone on the third ring.

"It's me," he said. "Would you call Brianna and the Capalettis and arrange a meeting at Roundtree tonight? It's important."

Kathy answered with a simple, "Yes."

"Good. I'll be up there around ten. Tell Angie not to cook for me. I'll grab a bite on the way through Aztec."

"Are you okay?" Kathy asked.

"I'm fine — still sore, but fine. I'm with Chaco right now."

"Tell him I love him."

"I'll tell him. Thanks, Kathy. Goodbye."

"Poor misguided woman says she loves you," Danny said as he holstered his phone.

"You know it's true, brother." Chaco said with a grin. "Do I know this Stevens guy?"

"He's been down here several times, but only twice since we started these dry-well cases. You don't have to worry about Jason. I trust him with my life."

"You might be doing just that. What's to stop Gannon from going after him like they have you?"

"That could happen, but right now, Gannon thinks I'm just a lone wolf. We'll put the word out that we've expanded the company, created a hydra with many heads. To make the story believable, we'll make Jason the face of what will appear to be a larger firm. It's a lot easier to kill a single lawyer than it is to eliminate an entire law firm."

"Sounds reasonable to me. Meantime, my problem is protecting you and Kathy."

"Don't worry. Even my own mother wouldn't recognize me right now. But we've got to protect Roundtree. I figure you and the NALM can handle that."

Danny glanced at his watch. Eight thirty-five. The sun was just touching the western horizon. It would be dark in a half hour. "I'm going to slip up to Aztec and grab a bite to eat on the way. I'll see you at Roundtree."

"Danny?" Chaco said as he turned to go.

"Yes?"

"Don't let anybody steal that hair. You look far too becoming in it."

*

As Chaco walked toward his vehicle, parked just out of sight on a little-used track about a half-mile away, his mind was a jumble of conflicting thoughts — none of them good — especially in view of what had happened to Danny on Saturday night. He had to step up the protection levels dramatically for both Danny and Kathy. Neither would like it, but they were going to have to live with it. Danny was naïve. The man thought a good handgun would be enough to protect himself. With his specialized military training, Chaco knew better. The kind of resources available to Gannon could bring forces and weapons to bear that would make Danny's pea shooter seem like a toy.

Chapter 48

"Grab the other two and I'll put the sign up," Max directed as Tony wrestled two more road barricades out of the van and lugged them into place. He glanced up at the dust trail left by the old pickup truck. Tony put the final road barricades in place and then helped Max finish hanging the "Road Closed" sign that would prevent any north-bound traffic from interrupting their deadly mission.

They scrambled into the van. Tony floored the accelerator, spraying gravel and raising a large cloud of dust while Max punched the speed dial of his cell phone.

"Blackthorn?"

"Yeah."

"Any south-bound traffic?"

Lucas Blackthorn was parked at the intersection where the turnoff to the gas plant marked the end of the pavement, fourteen miles to the north. The road the van was a broad, smooth gravel surface that allowed vehicles to safely travel at speeds of fifty miles per hour or more.

"Couple of cars have turned east toward the gas plant," Lucas said, "but nothing's gone south."

"Go ahead and close the road then start driving south toward us. Looks like we've got him boxed.

Blackthorn's heart raced. "On my way." He threw the cell phone on the front seat and sprang to the trunk of his car where he extracted the two barricades Tony and Max had given him. He quickly set one up in each lane and hung a detour sign between them with an arrow pointing toward the gas plant road. Then he dove back into his car and headed south. As he drove, he laid his .45 Caliber Colt automatic on the seat, vowing that last Saturday's failure would not be repeated. One way or the other, Whitehorse would not get off this road alive.

Chapter 49

Confident that his disguise would thwart detection, Danny drove casually, almost leisurely toward Farmington, his mind reviewing the details of his plan. Attorneys often stepped very near the edge of the law during the course of their practice, but this plan might require him to go well beyond it.

Cut it out, he chided himself. *If you worry more about getting caught than making this work, you may as well quit now.*

Earlier, he'd spotted the dust plume from another vehicle far behind him. He checked his rear-view mirror and was surprised to see that a gray van had nearly caught up. *Those boys must be late for dinner.*

When he checked his rear view mirror a couple of minutes later, all he could see was the billowing dust cloud behind his truck. *Must have turned off somewhere,* he assumed. *Good, Now I won't have to eat their dust all the way to the pavement.*

Suddenly, he felt a slight bump from behind. It wasn't hard—just solid enough that it jerked his head back a little and made the rear tires a bit squirrelly. He looked in the rear view mirror. *What the . . .?* To his astonishment, the mirror was filled by the hood of the van. They hadn't turned off after all, but were so close that their dust cloud had mingled with his.

"You SOB!" Danny shouted as he turned his head to try to see the vehicle better. Were they trying to pass and didn't see him through the thick dust? *Good thing they weren't traveling any faster.* He watched the van back off and disappear into his dust cloud.

Then he felt something else—a tug that threw him slightly forward against his seat belt. His truck began to slow as if a giant hand were holding it back. He pressed harder on the accelerator, but his truck continued to slow.

What the hell? It was almost as if his truck had run out of gas, but the tank was nearly full and the engine was straining hard, as if pulling a heavy load.

Danny feared that his rapidly falling speed might cause the vehicle behind to crash into him again. He looked in the mirror, expecting the worst. Then something caught his eye. He could just make out a black line extending from the rear of his truck and disappearing into the dust cloud.

With sickening clarity, Danny realized that his truck was somehow tethered to the heavier vehicle like a fish on the end of a line that was slowly being reeled in. He tromped on the accelerator, hoping to break the grip of whatever was holding him captive, but only succeeded in spinning his wheels on the gravel surface, causing him to lose traction and slow more rapidly.

There was nothing he could do to prevent the van from bringing him to a full stop. With resignation, he reached into the glove box and grabbed his newly acquired Smith & Wesson .44 Magnum revolver and prepared to do battle.

*

Blackthorn's cell phone, rang. "Go ahead," he shouted.

"We have him stopped!" It was Max's voice. Blackthorn heard a strange popping noise in the background.

"Where are you?"

"About four miles south of you. You better haul ass. He's got a boomer, a big one, and he's good with it. We're pinned inside the van. We could kill him, but then it wouldn't look like and accident. We'll need you to help flush him out."

"I'm on my way. Don't damage the merchandise."

Even though he was already traveling over fifty MPH on the gravel surface, Blackthorn pressed the accelerator harder. "All right you son-of-a-bitch," he muttered, "let's see you get your ass out of this little sling."

*

Danny bailed out of his truck the instant it came to a halt and leveled his gun at the van. The driver's side door began to open, but quickly

177

closed as Danny fired three rounds that ricocheted off it. He fired the next three into the windshield, directly at the driver. Though the bullets cratered the glass, they did not seem to pass through.

Whoever was inside stayed put. Danny crouched behind his driver's door and reloaded as fast as he could. He had to see what held him captive. He snapped off three quick covering shots into the windshield and leaped to the back of his truck. His bumper was captured by a heavy claw-type clamp attached to an inch-thick, tautly drawn steel cable. Danny fired twice at the cable, hitting it once, but the soft lead bullet simply pronged off and ricocheted away, doing little damage.

He fired the last bullet at the van's windshield and then ran to reload behind the cover of his truck. Half his ammunition was gone.

He looked around for any avenue of escape. The truck was stopped half-way down a small hill that formed one side of a wide depression. A small arroyo bisected the depression a little over a hundred yards further down the road. If he could reach it, the low walls might afford him some cover. The arroyo appeared to deepen as it meandered west. If he could use the protection of its walls to make it across to the other side, he could hide in the tall sagebrush that lay beyond.

It was well past sundown. Another ten minutes or so and darkness could help cover his escape. For protection, he would keep the truck between him and the van while he ran down the road to the arroyo. He didn't worry about the van trying to follow. So long as it was attached to his truck, it too was immobilized.

He finished reloading and stuffed the remaining cartridges from the box in his pocket. Time to run—but first he'd give whoever was in the van something to think about. Until now his shots were aimed at whoever was inside. Perhaps it was better to go after the vehicle itself.

Then he heard a van door open. He peeked around the side of his truck and saw that it was the rear cargo door. *Uh oh.* He had hoped to keep everyone inside the vehicle while darkness fell, but someone getting out of the van changed the equation.

He fired four rounds into the van's engine compartment and two toward the open cargo door. *Okay feet, do your stuff!* He spun and ran straight down the road, running faster than he ever had.

*

Lucas Blackthorn roared down the gravel road at nearly seventy miles per hour. The slightest steering error could send him careening off the road and out into the desert. His car topped the far side of the depression where Whitehorse's pickup and the van were stopped. He slammed on his brakes in panic. While he fully expected to see the van with Whitehorse's vehicle stopped, what he didn't expect was to see someone running toward him with a gun in hand. Although the man looked different, it had to be Whitehorse.

The car skidded to a stop in a huge cloud of dust. Blackthorn grabbed his automatic, leaped from the vehicle, and ran forward blindly, trying to peer through the choking dust cloud.

*

Danny was halfway to the arroyo when a car exploded over the top of the hill to the north. It came to a sliding stop just yards from where the arroyo crossed the road. He recognized the driver. Blackthorn.

Running straight to the arroyo was now out of the question. He had but a single option — a bad one. He broke left and dashed down the open slope in a zigzag pattern, hoping to throw off the aim of anyone who might try shooting at him. Perhaps he could sprint across the open ground to the safety of the arroyo farther out.

"Hold it, Whitehorse," Blackthorn's voice boomed from the direction of the car. Then he heard the roar of the man's handgun. A bullet ripped the ground just ahead and to his right. He kept running. Blackthorn was not inviting him to stop for tea.

He was over halfway to the safety of the arroyo when he heard a strange "whump" come from the direction of the van. Then he heard a soft thump as something struck the ground ten yards ahead and to his left. A thick, white cloud of smoke erupted from the spot. He jagged right to avoid it.

Then came another "whump," and another, and another. The first thump hit to his right, then in quick succession, two more exploding, misty clouds appeared directly in front of him. He was bracketed by the vapor.

He gulped a great lungful of clean air, hoping it would last him until he emerged on the other side of the cloud. If this stuff was nerve gas, it wouldn't make any difference. He'd be dead in seconds.

As he entered the cloud, Danny heard more whumps from the van. He was somewhat surprised that the mist didn't burn his eyes or skin. It wasn't tear gas. If he could just get through it, he might come through this okay.

But as more thumps hit the ground, the cloud seemed to go on and on. His now oxygen-starved-body screamed for air. He couldn't see where he was running. Suddenly, his foot caught a protruding rock that spilled him headlong to the desert floor. The force of the fall expelled everything left in his lungs, and his body instinctively gasped for more.

He realized in an instant what he had done and tried to expel the breath. He scrambled up to run again, but as he rose, his feet suddenly felt like lead. He stumbled forward a few steps, his body not obeying as it should. Try as he might, he couldn't resist taking another breath.

Then, it seemed foolish to be running. He stopped and looked around at the white brightness surrounding him.

Why am I holding my breath? He opened his mouth and inhaled once again. *Why am I falling?* The ground came toward him in surrealistic, slow motion. It didn't hurt when he hit. As he rolled to his back and looked up he could see stars in a strange, wavy, swirling sky. Then the world turned into a long, dark tunnel that passed him into oblivion.

*

"Is he dead?" a jubilant Blackthorn asked as he stood over the inert body.

"Naw, just sleeping like a baby," Max explained. "If we were to let him, he'd wake up in about a half-hour with one hell of a headache."

Blackthorn looked around nervously as the last grenade gave up its final wisp of smoke. "Shouldn't we be wearing gas masks or something?"

"No need," Tony replied. "MZ Gas changes chemical composition and becomes harmless within a few seconds of being exposed to air."

The answer mollified Lucas' concern. "All right, men, let's get rid of this pain in the ass." Blackthorn gave Danny's body a hard, satisfying kick. "So what are you going to do now?"

"Car accident," Tony replied. "We'll make it look like another drunk Indian crashed his vehicle. That rock outcropping up there should be just about perfect. If we roll the truck off the road and down into those rocks, it should cause enough damage to look real."

"There has to be a fire," Max said. "The impact damage might not look bad enough to have killed him. But if his truck catches fire, nobody's going to question the cause of death. Besides, the coroner can't read the blood alcohol content if a body is mostly consumed by fire."

"How long will it take?"

"Not more than fifteen or twenty minutes," Tony replied. "We have a drug in the van that almost instantly paralyzes the heart and dissipates in the blood in less than a half hour. He'll be dead long before the truck ever hits those rocks."

"Get it done!" Blackthorn commanded, barely able to contain himself. "Then you two disappear. We'll wire your money wherever you say. I'll get back and let Red know the good news. You men have certainly earned your keep."

*

Blackthorn's ride back to Farmington was slow and pleasurable. The security measures meant there would be no more well explosions. The death of Whitehorse meant there would be no more lawsuit. Despite his recent losses, the money would just keep pouring into Grand Cayman Island.

He glanced into his rear view mirror and spied the red glow of the fire in the distance. "So long Mr. Danny Whitehorse, Esquire." He chuckled as he tipped his finger to his brow and snapped off a mocking, half-hearted salute. "That'll teach you to screw around with me and Red Gannon."

Chapter 50

"Where's Danny?" Bri demanded. Worry etched her face as Chaco came through the door alone just before eleven p.m. Bri's concern over her big brother's safety ratcheted itself through the roof after Kathy recounted the story of Danny's harrowing Saturday-morning attack.

"He's not here?" Chaco asked.

"We haven't heard from him. Kathy said he wanted all of us here at ten."

"He said he was stopping in Aztec to grab a bite to eat. I'm sure he'll be here shortly."

They waited for over an hour, the tension growing. Finally Chaco said, "I'm going to look for him. He's driving an older pickup truck. Maybe he broke down or something."

"I'll go with you," Brianna volunteered.

"No, you stay here. If Danny's in some kind of trouble, it could be trouble for us too. I don't want you in the middle of it."

At five a. m. Chaco stumbled back into the house, bearing devastating news. He told of driving out toward where he and Danny met earlier and found himself in the midst a collection of fire trucks and cop cars that surrounded the burned-out hulk of Danny's pickup. Dozens of people milled about the scene, including the press. The police took him to a white-sheeted-body, and pulled back the covering. The corpse was burned beyond recognition. They showed him a badly scorched wallet they said they'd taken from the corpse. It was Danny's.

Friday morning, four days after the crash, the body was buried in the desert a half-mile away from Uncle Samuel's home. The site was well marked so that thereafter, people could avoid it. The NALM took care of the burial, sparing Danny's mother and Uncle Samuel the ominous task.

Bri, Angie, and Vic were the only non-family members allowed nearby. They viewed the burial from a safe, respectful distance that would keep them out of contact with the *chindi*. Kathy wasn't there. No one had seen her since the morning Chaco delivered the terrible news.

Bri wanted to go down and throw her arms around Uncle Samuel and Danny's mother to comfort them, but Angie explained that such an outward show of emotion would only cause the family more distress by inviting Danny's *chindi* to come closer and remain longer.

Still distraught at not being able to see and touch Danny one last time, Bri faced another awful responsibility. She was supposed to meet Jason Stevens in Durango. Only instead of delivering him to his friend, she would have to deliver the awful news instead.

"I can't do it," she wailed when the group got back to Vic and Angie's house "We just buried him."

"I know," Vic said gently, "but we can't let the man just sit at the restaurant and wonder why Danny doesn't show up. Kathy's not here, and you're the only one who would recognize him. You've got do this, Bri."

Bri dabbed at the tears streaming down her face. Angie walked around the table and gathered the heart broken woman into her arms. "I know it's hard, honey, but you can do it. Just bring Mr. Stevens here where we can all cry together and figure out what to do next."

END

PART TWO

Chapter 51

It was Thursday, just before seven a.m. when, Jason Stevens, driving his fully loaded Escalade, towing a medium-sized U-Haul trailer behind, cast a last look in his rearview mirror at Mount Timpanogos. It would be strange not seeing that familiar mountain every day.

He'd had no trouble negotiating a $1.8 million buyout of his partnership interest, but truth be known, if the partners had refused, he would have simply walked away.

Mom took the news surprisingly well. Since her recent remarriage, she took *everything* surprisingly well. His sisters cried and fought over who would cook him dinner the next two nights. They both won.

As Jason drove up U.S. Hwy 6 through Spanish Fork Canyon and on toward the city of Price, he remembered meeting Danny for the first time. He was fresh out of the UC Berkeley Boult Hall law school, had just passed the California Bar Exam, and was wondering what to do with the rest of his life. Out of curiosity, he wandered into the Oakland free legal clinic managed by Danny. "Why don't you come work with me?" he asked. "The pay's lousy, but it's a great way to get little guys some legal representation they couldn't otherwise afford."

Jason liked Danny, and the idea appealed to him so much that he not only struck a deal to work at the clinic, but that he and Danny would share the two-bedroom flat Danny had been struggling to pay the rent on. He, Danny, and Kathy, Danny's paralegal, became known by their fellow workers as the Three Musketeers. Together they ran the clinic like a rodeo and generally raised harmless hell all around the Bay Area.

Then Danny announced that he was going to return to Farmington to open a law office to benefit the Indian tribes around the Four Corners area. Jason and Kathy convinced him that he couldn't get along without them, but just as the move was to take place, Jason's father passed away suddenly. He had to return to Utah to take care of his grieving mother and deal with his father's considerable estate.

That was ten years ago. Between taking care of his aged mother and managing the estate, Utah just kind of sucked him in. He ended up an equity partner in one of Salt Lake's most prestigious law firms, with a salary just north of three hundred thousand dollars, plus his partnership bonus. Last year's bonus came in at just over $1.2 million. That, combined with his eight-figure inheritance, made Jason a respectably wealthy man. But no matter how lucrative his practice, he longed to get back to the kind of law he and Danny had practiced at the clinic years ago.

When Danny called, the family estate was essentially running itself. With his aged mother unexpectedly remarried, the shackles of his life were falling away.

The most painful shackle to fall happened just over a year ago when his one and only stab at marriage ended disastrously. He came home one day to find his house empty and a note from his beautiful, young wife of two years, saying that she had left to "find herself." Apparently, her aerobics instructor lost himself in the same place. Jason considered the half-million-dollar lump-sum divorce settlement to be a bargain.

*

Jason stopped to fill his Escalade at the southwest Colorado town of Cortez, just twenty-five miles north of the Four Corners National Monument, marking the only point in the U. S. where the borders of four different states—Utah, Colorado, Arizona, and New Mexico—came together at a common point. Farther south was Shiprock and the vast Navajo reservation. It would have been faster to head to Shiprock and take the short drive east into Farmington, but for some reason, Danny preferred they meet in Durango, an hour to the east. Jason didn't understand, but Durango it was. He eagerly looked forward to the reunion.

Chapter 52

In summer, Jason slept in his underwear with only a sheet covering him. Last night, with the scent of the nearby pine forests wafting on the evening breeze, he opened the bathroom window to allow the pleasing scent to defuse the slightly musty smell of his motel room. But in the pre-dawn hours, the crisp mountain air coming off the surrounding eleven-thousand-foot peaks turned freezing cold. Jason awoke Friday morning feeling like he was inside a refrigerator.

Shivering, he wrapped himself in a blanket and went to close the offending window. Then an even more shocking encounter with an impossibly cold toilet seat brought him irretrievably awake.

As Jason emerged from his motel after wolfing down the continental breakfast the establishment offered, he swore he heard the whistle of a steam engine locomotive. He had to investigate. His search led him to the fully restored, narrow-gage, Durango/Silverton Railroad. He bought a ticket.

The all-day train ride to the restored mining town of Silverton, altitude more than ten thousand feet, was spectacular. It was the first time in years Jason felt simply like a tourist rather than a buttoned-down, prim and proper, suit-wearing lawyer.

At 5:00 pm, He debarked the train in downtown Durango feeling refreshed and reinvigorated. With two hours until his meeting with Danny, he decided to wander the historic Main Street district for a while.

It was the middle of Durango's summer tourist season, and the sidewalks were crowded. He browsed the large number of art galleries and curio shops on Main Street. He passed the famous and stately Strater Hotel, restored to its 1890's grandeur. There was an old-fashioned restaurant on the ground floor with waiters wearing stiffly starched white shirts, and sporting old fashioned haircuts. All had long handlebar mustaches that were obviously part of the dress code. He wondered what they would do if they hired a woman for the job.

At the south end of the historic district, he ended up in front of a quaint-looking, turn-of-the-century drug store complete with an old-fashioned soda fountain. It brought back memories of the old Salmon Drug Store where he used to stop for a chocolate root beer every night after his paper route.

He couldn't resist the urge to wander inside. Maybe this modern replica could actually make a chocolate root beer.

As he stepped past the counter, a newspaper stand caught his eye. The headline of one of the papers proclaimed, "**FARMINGTON ATTORNEY KILLED IN ONE-CAR ACCIDENT.**" The picture showed a blackened, burned-out hulk of an old pickup truck with a white-sheeted body lying next to it. The caption said the dead man's name was Danny Whitehorse.

The room spun. Jason had to grab the counter's edge to steady himself. *No! This can't be! It just can't be!*

Chapter 53

Jason rushed back to his motel, hoping against hope that the story was wrong. Surely this could not be *his* Danny. He tried Danny's cell number. No answer. Next he tried his home. The phone rang until a message came on saying Danny's voice mailbox was full.

He tried Danny's office number. The answering machine confirmed his worst fears. He recognized Kathy's recorded voice informing callers that due to the death of Mr. Whitehorse, all office activities were suspended until further notice.

How could this possibly be? He had to talk to someone — anyone. He called information for Kathy's home number, but there was no listing. A second call to information, requesting a number for anyone whose last name was "Whitehorse," returned only Danny's home number.

Torn between crying out in anguish or screaming in anger, Jason finally settled on the only thing he could think of. He would be at the Golden Slipper at seven p.m. on the off-chance that someone would show up and tell him more. One way or another, he was leaving Durango tonight and would be in Farmington tomorrow morning, trying to figure out what to do with the rest of his life.

*

"I'm expecting someone," Jason told the hostess, trying to conceal his agitation. "Could you place me where I can see the door? Let me give you my card in case anyone asks for me."

While he waited, Jason read the newspaper article again, wanting it to be wrong. He picked absently at his salad, but had no inclination to eat a thing.

In the middle of reading the article for the third time, he looked up to see the hostess leading a strikingly attractive, blond-haired woman toward his table. She looked vaguely familiar.

"Mr. Stevens, this lady asked for you," the hostess said.

"Thank you," Jason said as he stood and extended his hand to the woman. "I'm Jason Stevens."

The woman's hand trembled as she returned his handshake. "I'm Brianna Sanders. We've actually met before, but I'm sure you don't remember. Do you mind if I sit down? I'm afraid I have some very bad news."

"Please do. " Jason indicating the booth seat opposite him. The woman was struggling to hold her composure. He broke the awkward silence by saying, "I do recall meeting you, Miss Sanders. I assume its 'miss.'" Bri nodded, but refused to hold his gaze. "Danny mentioned you to me a number of times. I think he was hoping to play a bit of a matchmaker. I assume you're going to tell me that this newspaper story is true." He laid the newspaper face-up on the table.

Bri's lip quivered and a tear escaped her eye. "I'm afraid it is. Danny was killed Tuesday night. We had his service today." Her tears flowed more profusely and her body was wracked by a sob. "Pardon me," she whispered as she dabbed at her eyes with a handkerchief. "I thought I'd done about all of this I could today." Then she held the handkerchief to her mouth and turned her eyes to the window as a flood of silent tears streamed down her cheeks.

Jason swallowed a huge lump in his own throat and said, "Danny spoke of you often, Miss Sanders. I could tell the two of you were very close. He was my best friend. I just can't believe he's gone. Is there anything I can do to help?"

Bri turned away from the window and looked at him. "I don't know what anyone can do at this point. Danny always spoke of you in the best terms. I'm sorry you have to learn of his death this way, Mr. Stevens. It's been a terrible shock for all of us."

"Please, call me Jason. Does anyone know what happened?"

"All we know is that he crashed on a dirt road several miles south of Farmington. There was a fire. The body was badly burned."

Jason shook his head. "How did you know to meet me?"

"Danny got word to his secretary that you were coming. We've tried to reach you, but didn't have your cell phone number. I'm so sorry."

"Under the circumstances, I'm surprised and grateful you even remembered. I came down to help Danny with a case that was giving him problems. Now it looks like I'd better hang around to help settle things in his law office and with his estate. I remember that he called you his little sister. If it's not too much to ask, could you tell me a bit more about your relationship with him?"

Brianna recited their history. "Danny called me his little *white* sister," she concluded. "He was my big brother and my dear, dear friend. Now it's your turn, Counselor. You and Danny apparently had quite a history. Care to tell me about it?"

By the time he finished telling his story, they had laughed and cried and laughed again. The tension of their first awkward moments passed and a comfortable commonality settled in. "Did you have anything to do with Danny's practice?" Jason asked.

"Only at the most peripheral edge. I'm actually a high school accounting teacher. I introduced Danny to some friends of mine who were trying to help him with his Gannon Oil case. I wanted to get more involved, but Danny wouldn't let me. I don't know if he told you or not, but there were two serious attacks on him in the last week. All of us believe Gannon Oil is behind his death."

"That's the case Danny called me down here to work on. I could tell there was a lot more going on than he was saying, but I had no idea there'd been physical violence. I want to help, but I don't quite know where to begin. Any suggestions?"

"That's why I'm here. I was sent to fetch you. I'm staying with those friends I told you about and they'd like to put you up at least long enough for all of us to get our feet back under us and figure things out. Their place is a few miles south of here."

"That's very generous, especially from people who've never met me."

"It's true that none of us know you, Jason, but we all knew Danny. He valued your friendship greatly. We'll respect his judgment, unless and until you prove that we should do otherwise."

Chapter 54

Jason followed Brianna's VW Toureg nearly twenty miles south toward the state line. A highway sign indicated they were entering the town of Bondad. The deepening twilight showed that there were no commercial businesses—only a few widely scattered homes.

Brianna signaled and turned right onto a road leading west. She drove less than half a mile to the end, and turned left into a gated private driveway leading to a large, two-story, Nuevo-Victorian-style home set far back from the road. It was too dark to see the rest of the grounds.

As Jason pulled his Escalade to a stop in front of the house, a tall, dark-haired woman stepped through the front door and eyed his vehicle. She was joined by a shorter, swarthy-looking man with a stocky build and thick salt-and-pepper hair. Brianna performed the introductions. "Angie, Vic, this is Jason Stevens. Jason, this is Angie and Vic Capaletti."

"Mrs. Capaletti," Jason greeted as he stepped forward and offered the woman his hand. She locked Jason's eyes in a hard stare that conveyed no warmth nor even a hint of a smile. She nodded aloofly, barely returning his handshake.

Taken aback at the chilly greeting, Jason turned and offered his hand to her husband. "Mr. Capaletti, I'm glad to meet you, sir. I wish it were under different conditions. I appreciate your invitation."

Vic's response was considerably warmer. "Glad to have you, Mr. Stevens. Lousy set of circumstances. Come on in. Let's get acquainted and try to figure out what we're going to do."

*

The instant they entered the house, Brianna grabbed Angie by the

192

arm and propelled her up the stairway leading off the entry foyer, leaving Vic to host Jason. Vic showed the way to the back of the house and into his combination office/study. It was a woody, masculine man cave with French windows and doors looking out on a large redwood deck.

"Take a chair, Stevens," Vic invited, indicating one of the maroon-leather, wingback chairs against the wall. "Can I get you a drink? I've got about anything you want."

"No, no, Mr. Capaletti. I'm fine. But you go ahead if you wish."

Vic poured himself two-fingers of brandy then leaned against his desk.

Judging by the look of his richly appointed office, the man was doing quite well. "Brianna tells me you're in the oil business." Jason said.

"Not oil, natural gas. I run the Northwestern Natural Gas operations around here. We're a pipeline company that transports gas from the fields to metropolitan distributors all around the western U. S."

"You must have been a great help to Danny."

"Not near as much as I wished. I helped him a little with a lawsuit he had against one of our more prominent local oil companies."

"Would that be Gannon Oil?"

Vic looked mildly surprised. "Yes it would. Are you familiar with them?"

"Only that that was the case Danny wanted me to come down and help him with."

"I think he was on the right track, and that may have been what got him killed." Vic cast a glance out the office door. "Sorry the women are acting a little weird, Jason. It's been a really tough day."

"I can only imagine."

"It's been hardest on Bri. She's used to nice Christian funerals held in a church, with flowers and tributes and sermons about how the dearly departed have gone to a 'happier place.' She feels like she's been cheated out of saying good-bye to Danny in the way that means the most to her. It's that closure thing — and she's never going to have it. "

"Hate to say it, but I'm sort of in the same boat."

"I don't know how much you know about the Diné, Stevens — Diné is the real name of the Navajos. Let me tell you about their funerals.

"Their funerary tradition is basically a four-day affair. Today is the fourth day after Danny's death, the day the dead are buried, and the last day they will ever be spoken of directly again—even by their family.

"Unlike our cemeteries, where we can visit the grave over and over again, Danny was buried in an out-of-the-way place the family will avoid forever. My wife is full-blooded Diné. You may be wondering why she's not here while we discuss this subject. She's not being rude—it's just that the Diné consider it very bad luck to directly discuss the dead after the fourth day. They believe the *chindi*, the ghost of the dead person, remains close after death, and that saying the name of the dead person can cause their *chindi* to haunt whoever spoke it.

"Angie doesn't really believe all their hocus pocus like she used to, but the culture is still strong in her. Aside from the fact that all of us were very close to him, she'll have a hard time talking directly about Danny as if he were still a person."

"That's right Mr. Stevens," came Angie's voice from behind them. Jason turned and found her standing in the doorway, her red, puffy eyes showing that she'd been crying. Bri stood behind her, dabbing a tissue at her own eyes.

"I apologize for how coldly I greeted you," Angie said, still not looking directly at him. "It's not Danny's *chindi* I fear, I'm having a hard time even thinking about someone replacing him. Vic's correct about my people. Though many of them still believe in witches and skin-walkers and ghosts, you don't have to worry about me, I'll be happy to share any information I can."

"I appreciate that, Mrs. Capaletti. Perhaps the first thing everyone can do is start calling me Jason. The only time people call me 'Mister' is when I meet new clients or I'm in a courtroom."

"Jason it is," Vic replied, and we're 'Vic' and 'Angie.' If you were as good a friend to Danny as we've been led to believe, then the first thing we should say is, welcome to the family."

"Thank you. Needless to say, I'm completely at loose ends. I closed all my interests in Utah in anticipation of working with Danny. Obviously that's no longer an option. Bri tells me that all of you worked with him on this Gannon case. Under the law, the case didn't die with him. If I can be of any help, I'd like to try. I just can't leave here without being sure Danny's interests are taken care of, and that includes his clients. Do you mind if I ask a few questions?"

"Not at all," Vic replied, "but why don't we adjourn to the den? There's a very nice Merlot uncorked and on ice. Or, if you prefer, there's cold beer in the refrigerator."

"Thanks, Vic. You folks go right ahead. Some of us Utah folk are a little weird when it comes to alcohol. Perhaps a Diet Coke?"

"Oh, ho!" Vic crowed, raising an arched eyebrow in Bri's direction. "I suspect we have another one of those Mormons amongst us. Brianna will finally have a soul brother to commiserate with while the rest of us pass around our uncorked vessels of sin."

Jason glanced curiously at Bri, who nodded her confirmation. Then he looked back at Vic and confessed, "You found me out. Bri and I can both now serve as your permanent designated drivers."

It took the better part of an hour to bring Jason completely up-to-date. Finally, Vic summarized. "Danny was under almost constant attack of one sort or another from the day he filed the Gannon Oil lawsuit. There have been riots outside his office, his home was broken into, and he and Kathy have been followed almost constantly. A week ago today he was attacked and beaten out in the oil fields, then nearly killed in another attack that same night. They finally got him on Tuesday."

Something bothered Jason ever since he arrived. He finally figured out what it was. "I kind of expected to talk to Kathy before anyone else," he said.

"She's disappeared," Bri said quietly. "We haven't seen or heard from her since the morning Chaco told us Danny had been killed. She wasn't even at Danny's service."

"Is that normal for her?" Jason asked. "Do you think something's happened to her as well?"

"I doubt it," Vic responded. "At least, Chaco hasn't said anything about that. They're quite an item—Chaco and Kathy—if you know what I mean. If something was wrong, Chaco would be out looking for her, not hanging around to bury Danny. She's kind of peculiar, that one. I'm sure she'll turn up when she's good and ready."

"I see," Jason said, remembering Kathy's strangeness from years before. "This may sound like a stupid question, but I have to ask. Do you think there's any chance Danny's death was just a tragic accident rather than something more sinister?"

Vic's answer was sharp and immediate. "There's no way, Jason.

Danny had driven that road hundreds of times. We have a lot of unanswered questions too, like, where's that car of his? It was his pride and joy. None of us have ever seen that pickup truck he was killed in. Another thing—the police said there was alcohol involved. They even produced a scorched bottle of Jack Daniels to prove it. But Danny hated alcohol. He watched his own father kill himself with it. He wouldn't allow it in his house or his office. He even gave us a bad time about having a glass of wine with dinner. There's simply no way Danny was drunk."

"Brianna tells me no one's seen the police report."

"It won't make any difference," Vic groused. "Gannon owns the local police. They'll write up the report to say anything they want, regardless of the facts."

"Sounds like we'd better do our own investigation. Where's this Chaco guy?"

"You won't be able to talk to him for at least three more days," Angie said. "He was one of those who buried Danny. When my people's burials are over, those who had direct contact with the body call a singer to perform a Blessing Way. It's a four-to-seven-day-long purification ceremony intended to cleanse their souls, ward off the *chindi,* and restore their *Hozho,* their harmony. They started the sing this afternoon."

"I see," Jason said. "Then I'll want to do some investigation on my own. Has it rained around here since the accident?"

The others looked at each other quizzically. "I don't think so," Bri said.

"Good. Maybe we can take a hard look at that accident scene before all the evidence gets washed away. I want to go out there first thing in the morning, and could use some help. Anyone interested?"

Bri caught her breath and covered her mouth. "Ohh," she gasped.

Vic didn't hesitate. "Damn right we'll go along. That okay with you, Ang?"

Angie looked darkly distressed, but said, "Yes. I'll go."

"I will too," Bri said. Her voice quavered and the hand covering her mouth trembled. "You may have to hold me up when we get there, but I'll go."

Chapter 55

It was not difficult to identify the accident scene. Lengths of yellow police tape remained in several places. All around the area were red plastic flags on lengths of wire pushed into the ground — markers for accident scene artifacts.

Brianna began to weep quietly as soon as the Escalade stopped. Angie put an arm around her shoulder and told the men they'd join them in a few minutes.

"Apparently this is where the truck ended up," Vic concluded. The place was marked by a white outline on the ground. He and Jason stood before an outcropping of chest-high rocks thrusting through the surface of the desert floor some two hundred feet down the long, gentle slope from the road. When they compared the newspaper picture to their surroundings, Jason realized he was standing in nearly the exact spot where the white-sheeted body had been.

Evidence of the fire was clear. Had there been any significant amount of grass, the crash surely would have resulted in a wildfire. Patches of whitish powder still remained, residue from fire extinguishers the fire fighters had used.

A profusion of tire marks and footprints told much of the story. Virtually all the emergency vehicles had turned off the road some distance north of the crash site and traveled across the face of the gentle slope.

"That's strange," Jason said as he walked around the spot where Danny's truck had stopped, observing it from all angles.

"What?" Vic queried.

"We're a long way from the road. If you were traveling up there and suddenly found yourself off the road for some reason, what's the first thing you'd instinctively do?"

"Hit the brakes?"

"That's what I'd do. How fast do people normally travel that road?"

"It's a pretty good road. Probably forty, fifty miles an hour or so."

"Take a good look at Danny's truck in this picture, Vic. Tell me what you think of the collision damage."

Vic examined the newspaper. "I'll be darned," he said softly. "The fact that it's all burnt out distracts you. There's not much damage at all. It doesn't look like the windshield's even broken."

Jason scratched his head and looked up the path the vehicle had traveled. "There's nothing between here and the road that would have torn a gas line loose or punctured the gas tank, so why the fire?"

"You got me, Counselor. What's your conclusion?"

"That truck wasn't traveling at any significant speed. Let's go up and take a closer look at where the truck came off the road."

They paralleled Danny's tire tracks back up the hill, keeping them at a safe distance to assure they disturbed nothing. For the first twenty feet, Danny's tire tracks were completely obliterated by the tracks left behind by emergency vehicles and personnel, but were easy to pick up a little farther on.

When Vic and Jason reached the road, it was easy to see where the pickup's tires had plowed through the small berm of soft soil that road graders had made at the edge of the road.

The girls exited the Escalade. "Be careful," Vic cautioned. He pointed at the tire tracks. "don't disturb anything."

Jason examined the tracks a bit longer, then looked at the others and said, "Danny's vehicle was traveling very slowly, maybe barely moving, when it left the road."

"How do you know that?" Bri asked.

"By the angle at which the tracks leave the road. The wheels would have had to be cramped all the way to the left and the truck barely moving in order to go off at such a severe angle. If he'd been moving at any speed at all, the wheels would have plowed out much more of the berm, and the tracks would have stretched out in a longer arc."

Vic walked down the road and looked for himself. "You're right," he confirmed.

Angie appeared to be conducting her own study. She stepped off the side of the road and went a little way down the hill. "I think I know why Danny was going so slowly," she called to the others. "The truck couldn't go fast because it was being pushed. Come look."

Angie pointed to a set of footprints that were parallel with the driver's side. Then she pointed at another set in the middle between the two tire tracks. Both sets followed the path of the truck down the hill in the same positions.

"How can you tell they were pushing the truck?" Jason asked.

"I've been reading tracks in the sand since I started herding sheep when I was five years old. These footprints were made by people pushing something very heavy. Look how they're only using the balls of their feet and leaving mounds of sand pushed up behind, especially the footprints between the tire tracks. It looks to me like one person was pushing from outside of the truck on the left side, and the other was pushing from behind. The person on the left was most likely pushing and steering at the same time while the person at the back had nothing to do but push,"

"Good job!" Jason praised.

Angie smiled. "I'll bet it gets clearer the farther down we go."

She led them forty-feet or so down the hill and stopped. "See how the tracks are changing? We're starting to see heel prints, and the tracks are farther apart."

"They're starting to run, right?" Jason asked.

"That's right."

Another fifty feet on and the prints on the left curled out and away, into the low sagebrush. The prints between the wheel tracks continued a bit further before ending abruptly in a kind of a smear in the dirt.

"Ooh," Vic commented. "Looks like this guy took a pretty good spill."

"I believe this confirms that what we have here is a murder, not an accident," Jason pronounced. "Most likely, the collision and fire were the cover-up, not the cause of death. Let's go up and give the road a good going-over to see if we can spot anything else. We'll work both ways for a half mile or so. Vic, Angie, you two head south. Bri and I will work our way north." He gathered several of the nearby marker flags and divided them. Handing one set to Vic, he said, "Mark anything you think may be suspicious."

Jason took the left side of the road, Brianna the right. Vic and Angie did the same in the opposite direction. Two hundred yards north of where Danny's truck left the road, Jason spotted where the footprints of a number of people led west, down into the valley — but away from the crash site. *"One of the emergency vehicles must have parked up here."*

A few steps farther on, Brianna asked Jason to come over to her side. "I'm not sure, but doesn't this look like Danny's rear passenger-side tire?" The tread mark had a distinctive cut that matched one on the tracks leading down to the crash site.

"I think you're right. If he made it this far up the road, why would his tire marks leave the road way back there? Let's flag this spot and keep looking."

Just a couple more steps and Brianna called Jason over again. She pointed at several shiny expended pistol cartridges lying in the road just past where the front of where Danny's truck would have been.

"Don't touch anything," Jason instructed. "I'm going back to the Escalade for the video camera and something to put evidence in."

When he returned, he said, "We just may be able to determine who these belonged to. The brass of a firearm cartridge holds fingerprints quite well. If the person loading the cartridge wasn't wearing gloves, the oil from his fingers is left on the cartridge and gets burned into the surface when the cartridge is fired. You usually only get a partial print, but it can be enough to confirm someone's identity. Do you know if Danny owned a handgun?"

"I never saw one at his house."

"We'll gather these anyway. Even if the cartridges were fired by someone else, they could be important." Jason carefully marked and videoed the location of the tire track and the cartridges, then he picked the cartridges up with a pen and placed them in a numbered plastic baggie, which in turn, he placed inside a large paper bag. Then they resumed their search.

Half way between where the cartridges were found and the spot where a little arroyo crossed the road at the bottom of the depression, Jason spotted another set of footprints, these also led west off the road.

Whoever made them was running. He decided to trace them out.

The runner's route was a peculiar one. Every few steps, the tracks abruptly changed direction, then changed back again after a couple more steps — but always leading generally downward to the floor of the shallow valley.

It took Jason little time to recognize the pattern. He'd used it himself as the whine of bullets sprayed all around him. It had worked, right up until that one golden bullet in a hail of hundreds of others ended his Navy SEAL career.

Further into the valley, the footprints were overlaid by the tire marks of several heavy vehicles. The runner had crossed the area before the emergency vehicles arrived.

Jason found the footprints on the other side of the vehicle tracks and followed them a dozen steps farther. They abruptly ended in a smear in the dirt, indicating that the runner had fallen. A number of other sets of footprints converged at the same spot. Several came down from the road south of where the runner had left it, and one set came from farther north, past where the little arroyo crossed the road.

Jason shouted at Brianna to come down. He had little doubt that he was standing at the place from which Danny had not been able to run away.

*

"What do you think, Angie?" Jason asked. "You're our resident footprint expert."

Angie concurred with Jason's conclusion. "But something happened to the runner between here and where his tracks get lost in the jumble of tire tracks. "The zigzags get progressively smaller and the stride length gets shorter. By the time he reaches this point, the runner is barely running and is going in a straight line, maybe even stumbling. Look how his right foot comes down all the way across the left a couple of times right up to where he fell.

"Could he have been shot?" Brianna asked, her lip quivering.

"Maybe, but there's no blood.".

"I can tell you from first-hand experience that chest wounds don't bleed much externally," Jason said, "particularly if there's no exit wound. Someone shot in the chest with a low caliber bullet could be killed with practically no external bleeding. Was Danny's body autopsied?"

"The family wouldn't have asked for one," Vic said. The Diné are very reluctant to have a dead body handled more than absolutely necessary."

"Not to mention that the medical examiner wouldn't waste county money on an autopsy of a drunk Indian," Angie added.

"How would the family feel about an exhumation so we could have an autopsy done ourselves?"

Angie shuddered. "It would be the end of any cooperation you could ever expect from the reservation. There's nothing more frightening to the Diné than the prospect of someone disturbing the *chindi* of their dead."

"How about if the police or the D. A.'s office were to do it on their own?" Jason asked hopefully.

"No jurisdiction," Angie said. "This is reservation land and the tribe is its own sovereign."

"Whew," Jason sighed with exasperation. "Nothing about this is going to be easy."

"Not when it comes to the dead," Angie agreed.

Jason shook his head. "That's a shame. I'd be willing to bet Danny's lungs show no evidence of him dying in a fire, but I guess it is what it is. We need to conduct a systematic search of this whole area."

Jason retrieved a yellow legal pad from his vehicle and had Angie sketch a map of the shallow valley. Then he had her draw a grid pattern into the sketch that they could use to identify the relative position of anything they might find. Once done, they resumed their search.

Brianna was the first to shout that she'd found something. Jason had everyone carefully mark where they stood, then gather to view her discovery.

A chill coursed through Jason the instant he saw what it was. It wasn't exactly the configuration he remembered, but it was very similar—and painted exactly the right color. Half-buried in the sand was a dome-shaped object a little over two inches in diameter with a hollow brass stem protruding from the top. The dome appeared to be made from some kind of hard cellulose material. The bottom half had been torn or blown off.

Jason inserted his pen into the top of the tube, and picked it up. "If this is what it looks like, it's what's left of a rifle grenade. Be very careful of anything like this you see lying around."

They flagged the location, marked it on their search grid, tagged and bagged it, then resumed their search.

Vic, positioned farthest out from the rest, suddenly shouted, "Everybody stop! Jason, you'd better take a look at this."

There in the sandy soil, buried nearly to the trigger stem, was the olive-drab dome of what appeared to be another grenade. "Everybody stand back," Jason warned. "Be careful where you step — there could be more.

When the others were safely away, Jason gently excavated just enough dirt from the side of the device to determine that it was unexploded.

"You say this is reservation land?" Jason asked as he withdrew and joined the others.

Angie nodded.

"Good! That means we can get the FBI involved instead of the locals. The military and the ATF are going to have a whole lot of questions about where that thing came from and who brought it out here." Jason unclipped his cell phone and was surprised to find cell coverage in such a remote location. "I have a friend who might be able to help," he said as he dialed 411.

"City and state, please," the operator asked.

"Albuquerque, New Mexico."

"What name, please?"

"United States Attorney's Office."

"Doyle Stewart, please," Jason said when a receptionist answered, Stewart, an old high school friend, was now senior deputy U. S. attorney for the northern district of New Mexico.

"I'm sorry sir. Mr. Stewart is in a meeting. May I connect you with his assistant?"

"Yes." Jason tapped his foot impatiently.

"Julie Thorson," a woman's voice finally answered.

"Ms. Thorson, this is very urgent. My name is Jason Stevens. I'm an attorney. Mr. Stewart knows who I am. I'm standing in the middle of a major crime scene on what we believe is either BLM or Navajo Reservation land outside Farmington, New Mexico. There is unexploded military ordinance on the scene. It's urgent that I speak with Mr. Stewart immediately. Would it be possible to interrupt his meeting?"

"I'll be glad to get a message to him, Mr. Stevens. What number are you calling from?"

*

Less than ten minutes later, Jason's phone rang. "Jason Stevens, as I live and breathe," boomed Stewart's hearty voice. "Where in hell's half acre are you? Julie tells me you're here in New Mexico at some sort of crime scene."

"I'm standing near an unexploded rifle grenade on the Navajo reservation just south of Farmington. A friend of mine, a Native American, died here a few days ago and the evidence I've uncovered leads me to believe it was murder. Doyle, I have reason to not trust this information to the local police It looks like several of these grenades exploded in the area. What I know is that this grenade will be of great interest to the ATF and certainly to the military.. You're the only one I could think of to call. Let me give you the details."

Jason could hear Stewart scribbling notes throughout the conversation."It sounds like you've uncovered a whole kettle of worms,"Stewart said when Jason finished. "Stay put. I'll call you right back—and stay away from that grenade!"

Fifteen minutes later, Jason's phone rang again. "Tell me exactly where you are," Stewart commanded.

Jason read the navigation coordinates off of his iPhone.

"The Army is dispatching military police and a bomb disposal unit right now," Stewart said. The ATF has their collective tails all in a knot. There's no FBI field office in Farmington, but I've got three agents out of Albuquerque on their way. They'll be in Farmington in three hours or less. I'll leave as soon as I can clear my desk. Jason, you did exactly the right thing by calling me."

Chapter 56

The FBI arrived first, followed within minutes by AFT agents. Doyle Stewart and the Army ordinance specialists were nearly an hour behind. Jason briefed Doyle and walked everyone through what they had uncovered, then turned over all the evidence they had gathered.

It was dark before Jason and the others were released from the scene. The Army unit stayed behind to guard the site until the FBI could process all the evidence. Only then would they attempt to recover the grenade.

After a gritty day in the desert, Vic suggested they all take a plunge in the large spa behind the house before going to bed. Jason and Brianna hurried to their rooms to change.

Vic and Angie were buried to their necks in the spa's hot, frothy, water when Jason came down. He climbed in, found a massage jet to place his back against, lay his head back and said "Ahhhh, let's move the office out here."

"I have a rule against talking about work stuff in the spa," Vic said sternly. "Anybody who tries it gets summarily dunked – repeatedly if necessary."

"That's a great rule," Jason chuckled. "If I break it I'll go down voluntarily. Pull me up just before I drown."

"Maybe we will, maybe we won't," came Bri's voice from behind. "Depends on whether you're a repeat offender."

Jason turned to respond but his words caught in his throat at the sight of Bri in a simple, black, French-cut swimsuit. From his perspective, the woman's long, exquisite legs seemed to go on forever. Shapely hips curved to a slender waist, and the suit top simply could not contain the woman's ample *décolletage*. He couldn't help but stare.

"Jason!" she remonstrated softly as she stepped into the spa, her face blushing at his obvious attention. "If you keep staring at me like that, I'll go back up and put on coveralls!"

"Oh . . . I . . . I'm sorry." His own face turned bright red at being caught. "I didn't mean anything by it." He tore his eyes away.

"Oh, leave the poor man alone," Victor chided. "As you recall, I used to stare myself till I got used to you two good-looking heifers prancing around my backyard with practically nothing on."

"Heifers!" Angie snapped. "Get him Bri!"

Bri slapped a splash of water into Vic's face while Angie did the same from her side. "Okay, okay," Vic sputtered. "I give up! I give up!" He held his hands up in surrender.

"You'd better behave, Victor Capaletti," Bri scolded. "You ever call us heifers again and there'll be another bull sleeping in your barn. Right Ang?"

"You'd better believe it, and I have it on good authority that none of our cattle would even consider you as a bed partner."

"Whoa there!" Vic protested. "You been talking to the livestock again?"

"That's right, and you're going to be learning their language yourself if you're not careful!"

"I already know how to tell them to get out of my way. You just say 'Mooooove' over!"

"Oh, Vic," Bri snickered. "That's awful."

"Well, pardon me." The stocky Italian feigned insult. "I'll just go to my corner and pout!" He slid far to the left, folded his arms resolutely, and stuck out his lower lip.

"I know what will cure him," Angie said. "A little wine and cheese does it every time. Come with me, Bri."

Jason was shocked as Angie rose from the frothy water without a stitch on. She made no attempt to conceal her nudity. For the second time in minutes, Jason was rendered utterly speechless. He averted his eyes.

As she ascended the spa steps, Angie hesitated and said, "You're perfectly safe, Jason. My people are pretty self-conscious about their bodies, but after spending a good deal of time in Europe, I prefer their bathing traditions. Europeans aren't nearly as hung up about social nudity as we Americans. If I ever jump into a spa at your house, I assure you that I'll be as fully clad as our blonde friend is right now, if that's your preference. But at our house you're going to have to get used to how the natives dress — or undress. It's nothing sexual, believe me. It's simply our lifestyle. In about ten minutes, you'll get over the compulsion to stare, and in twenty, you'll basically not even notice anymore. Bri," she called to her friend, "let's go."

As the women swept away, Vic chuckled at Jason's confused discomfort. "Hey, buddy, it's okay. Believe me, what she said is right. In ten or fifteen minutes you won't even notice."

"That's hard to believe," Jason said. "Don't get me wrong, this is your house and you have the right to do anything you want. It just caught me a little unawares, that's all. How about you? Are you . . ."

"Yup, naked as a jaybird, but don't worry, old man; they don't call me Shorty because of my height."

Jason laughed. "Are you trying to say that if you're arrested for indecent exposure I'll be able to successfully mount your defense on the basis of insufficient evidence?"

"Oh, ho, ho," Vic guffawed. "Only from the mouth of an attorney."

After the girls returned, the conversation turned serious. Vic looked at Jason and said, "When we were out there today, you seemed to know a lot about military stuff. Care to enlighten us?"

Jason lowered his eyes. His military service was something he didn't talk about much, especially his Purple Heart, Silver Star, and Metal of Honor nomination. But it was important that he gain these people's full trust.

"When I was in high school, I was a lousy student. I was much more interested in football, girls, and cars than anything academic. My dad was a famous attorney and was absolutely determined that I follow in his footsteps. However, the last thing in the world I wanted was to be a boring, old attorney like my dad, so when I turned eighteen, I joined the Navy. Dad was furious and demanded that I withdraw. But you can't unenlist once you've sign up, so it was off to basic training for me."

"Did your dad ever get over it?" Bri asked.

"He started speaking to me again in a year or so, but I don't think he ever really got over it. It just didn't fit his plan for my life.

"On my ship I was able to go back to school. I worked hard and got my Bachelor's degree, which earned me an officer's commission before I re-upped..."

"What's that?" Angie asked.

"It means that I reenlisted after my first hitch was over. The next year, I became a Navy SEAL."

Vic whistled. "Tough outfit."

"They don't get any tougher. I loved it. I was on my way to being a SEAL for life when my platoon was ambushed on a beach in Iran on a mission I can't talk about. I caught a bullet right here," Jason pointed at a small, round scar on his upper chest. There's a worse scar on my back where the bullet came out. It nearly killed me. It came so close to my spine that it shocked my spinal cord. I couldn't walk for nearly three months."

Jason didn't tell them that he caught the bullet as he single-handedly rescued three of his platoon members before going down himself just as he was boarding the rescue helicopter.

"I was in the hospital and rehab for nearly five months. The Navy wanted to give me a desk at the pentagon, but back then, I wasn't a desk kind of guy. I mustered out, and for reasons that to this day I don't fully understand, I went to law school the same place my dad did—UC Berkeley. That's where I met Danny."

There was silence in the spa as the occupants digested Jason's story. Bri was the first to speak. "Jason," she said softly, "Thank you for your service to our country." She caught his hand and gave it a squeeze.

"Yes, thank you," Vic and Angie chorused.

"Hey, it was no big deal," Jason said, embarrassed by the attention. "But Vic, I'm going to break your rule. I think it's clear to all of us that what we saw out there today was a murder scene. Like I said last night, Danny's lawsuit didn't die with him. It's a federal class-action lawsuit that's now under the control of the court. With Danny gone, they could actually solicit or appoint another attorney to take over.

"I don't know about you folks, but I don't want someone who doesn't give a damn taking over here. This case is Danny's legacy. I want to make sure it's a monument to him and a benefit to all his clients."

"What are you trying to say, Jason?" Vic asked.

"I'm trying to say that I want to stay on. I want to take over the case and finish it for Danny. Not to sound arrogant or anything, but I'm a damn good trial lawyer, one with no job and no clients at the moment. I'll do it on a pro bono basis."

Again there was silence. Brianna finally spoke. "You'd do that, knowing that the case likely killed Danny?"

"That's why I *have* to do it."

"You sure you're up to it?" Vic asked.

"Yeah. My wounds healed a long time ago. Believe me, I'm a lot tougher than I look."

"I'm the one who actually paid Danny's retainer," Angie said. "So I guess you could say I hired him. I think that gives me the right to have a little say in this. I accept your offer, Mr. Stevens, with the provision that you're on probation until further notice. Chaco and Kathy each deserve a vote, too, but if you turn out to not be who or what you purport to be, I'll fire you immediately and promptly cut your balls off." She wasn't kidding.

Chapter 57

Long after Vic and Angie retired, Bri and Jason lingered in the spa, talking and getting better acquainted. "Not to be impertinent, Bri, but I'm surprised you're not married. You're a very attractive woman with a good job and a lot going for you. Are the men here in Farmington blind or just plain stupid?"

"Neither." She chuckled, "and thank you for the compliment. For your information, I'm thirty-one and unmarried not because of a lack of potential suitors. It's my choice." She held up her left hand. "I came within minutes of putting a wedding band right here a few years ago. I was saved on the steps of the Albuquerque Temple by a very pregnant seventeen-year-old. My intended was the baby's father. They'd been carrying on all the time he and I were engaged. I've been very, very careful about men ever since. What about you? Do you have a wife or two and some kids stashed away that I should know about?"

"No, no, much to my mother's chagrin. I took a stab at the eternal institution of marriage a couple of years ago. Her name was Karen. I guess she thought being married to me for time and all eternity was too much. She ran off with her aerobics trainer. The divorce was final six months ago."

"I'm sorry, Jason."

"Yeah, me too. But like you, I'm not very anxious to go through that meat grinder again."

They sat silently in the swirling hot water, lost in their own thoughts until finally, Jason reached over the lip of the spa and retrieved the watch he'd set on the deck. "Holy cow," he said. "It's twenty minutes past one."

"Oh, my!" Brianna stood up. "I'm teaching Sunday School today. I'll be dead on my feet." She grabbed a towel from the deck and began drying off. Jason tried his best not to stare, but only partially succeeded.

"I'm going to get out of this wet suit," she said. "In case you haven't noticed, our bedrooms adjoin off the back balcony. When all the lights are off, it's absolutely dark, and the stars are amazing. I like spending a few minutes looking at them before I go to sleep. If you promise to be a very good boy, you can meet me there in ten minutes and I'll show you. But not for long. I've got to get some sleep."

The five-foot-wide balcony extended the entire length of the rear of the house. They leaned against the railing, enjoying the cool mountain breeze. He had donned a pair of slacks and a pull-over knit shirt, but no shoes. She was clad in a silky, aqua-green, robe with an apparently matching nightgown underneath. The robe was securely tied at the waist with what appeared to be an impenetrable knot.

Indeed, the stars were breathtaking. Bri pointed out her favorite constellations. Jason, in turn, impressed her with his extensive star knowledge gleaned from his Navy experience. Jason took care to not encroach on her personal space. At a lull in their conversation, he delicately inquired about a subject that still had him befuddled – the Capalettis' nudity.

Bri laughed and said, "It's not just the spa, Jason. Both of them go prancing around the house in the 'altogether' quite frequently. Like Angie said, they just look at nudity a little differently than you and me. It's okay for them, but I'm more than a little shy when it comes to stuff like that. Can you imagine how embarrassing it would be to have to confess such a lifestyle to your bishop?"

"You can say that again," Jason responded.

"I'm glad you're here, Brother Stevens," Bri said, looking into his eyes. "I need the reinforcement."

He gently reached out to brush back a lock of hair that had fallen in front of her left eye and was startled when she recoiled as if he were about to strike her. "Oh, I'm sorry," he said. "I didn't mean to frighten you."

"It's not you," Bri said, visibly trembling. "I've built some pretty high walls around myself when it comes to men. The only ones I've ever allowed inside are my dad, Danny, and Vic. Welcome to my world, Mr. Stevens."

Jason stepped back and said, "Bri, I want you to know that I don't ever go where I'm not invited. I never want to do anything that makes you uncomfortable."

" I didn't mean to be so gun shy, Jason. Let's just leave it at this. I could use a hug—and nothing else." She stepped forward, put her arms around his neck and drew him into a quick but warm embrace. He made sure his hands didn't go anywhere questionable. Then she quickly withdrew, leaving behind just the lingering, subtle scent of herself.

Jason lay awake long after turning out his light. When sleep came, it was only fitful, knowing that just a thin wall and their well-defined senses of morality were the only things that separated them. He could not know that Bri did the same.

Chapter 58

"Jason. - Jason." The sound came to him dimly through a deep haze of sleep he didn't want to interrupt after finally being able to capture it the early pre-dawn hours. He turned over and tried to ignore the sound he wasn't sure was even real.

A hand shook his shoulder. "Jason, Jason, wake up!"

Jason groaned, rolled over and opened his eyes to find Angie standing over him. "Uh. Oh, g'mornin Angie. Wha . . . what's wrong? What time is it?".

"It's seven fifteen. You have a phone call. I think it's that U. S. attorney guy. He said he tried your cell phone, but you didn't answer."

"Oh!" Jason said, sitting up and remembering that he'd failed to plug it in before going to bed.

Angie carried a phone in one hand and a steaming cup of brown liquid in the other. "He's on hold," she said, handing him the phone. "I brought you a cup of Postum. I assume you have the same unfathomable Mormon attitude toward coffee as Bri."

"Yes," Jason chuckled. "But the Postum is most welcome."

"I don't know how the sun can rise without a cup of coffee in hand," she said as she turned to leave. "You Mormons must have far stronger morning constitutions than Vic and I." She closed the door quietly behind her.

Jason took a long sip of the steaming drink to wash away the foul taste in his mouth. It was only as he was about to push the talk button that it dawned on him that Angie wore the sheerest of nightgowns, and all too obviously, nothing else. "This is going to take some getting used to," he muttered as he brought the phone to his ear. "This is Jason."

"Jason, Doyle Stewart. I'm out here at the crime scene with the FBI and a bunch of others. How soon can you get here?"

Jason rubbed a hand through his rumpled hair and said, "I'm about twenty miles north of Farmington. Give me a chance to shower and shave and I can probably be there in just over an hour."

"I need you to walk us through this crime scene again."

"No problem."

"You said you were staying with the people you had with you yesterday. Can you bring them along?"

"I'm sure I can."

Jason stumbled down the stairs with cup in hand and found Vic and Angie in the kitchen. Thankfully, Angie had put on a bright, flowery silk robe considerably more opaque than the nightgown. Vic, wearing a dark brown terrycloth robe, sipped a large mug of coffee. Bri was nowhere in sight.

"Good morning, folks," Jason greeted. "Doyle Stewart wants us to meet him again and walk him and the FBI through everything. Any problem with that?"

"Not a bit," Vic boomed.

Angie nodded. "I'll wake Brianna right now. She usually goes to church on Sunday mornings, but I'm sure she'll make an exception for this."

*

A number of military vehicles and government cars were parked along the road when Jason and the others arrived. Several uniformed military people were scouring the sagebrush in the area where the grenade fragments were scattered. A number of people were dressed in civilian clothing. *FBI or ATF,* Jason supposed, *maybe Homeland Security.*

Jason parked the Escalade on the road. He spotted Doyle talking to a tall, African-American man near where he and the others thought Danny may have fallen.

Sure glad I videoed this place yesterday. With all this activity it would be much more difficult to sort out which tracks were evidence and which were not.

Doyle looked up and motioned for Jason and the others to join him. He introduced the man he was talking with as Agent James Wooley, special agent in charge of the Albuquerque FBI office. "Glad to meet you folks," Wooley said. He pointed out two men in civilian clothes who were marking evidence. Those men are Agents Carter and Hernandez. They're permanently assigned to the Navajo reservation."

"Your grenade has shaken up a lot of people," Stewart explained as Jason and the others walked him and Agent Wooley through the area where the unexploded device was found. "The army people say it looks like somewhere between ten and fifteen of them were used."

"What kind of grenade is it?" Jason asked.

"Until a month ago, I couldn't have told you. It was just declassified. "It's a prototype gas grenade not yet deployed in the field. A pallet from the first production run was stolen from the Redstone Arsenal in Alabama six months ago. That grenade and the other fragments are the only evidence of them that has ever turned up."

"Gas grenade?" Jason asked with concern.

"It's called MZ gas. It's a non-lethal experimental weapon that's like an advanced tear gas. Only instead of just burning someone's eyes, it knocks them out cold. It goes inert a few seconds after exposure to air, but anyone who breathes the active vapor gets a nice half-hour nap."

"That explains a lot." Jason indicated the set of running footprints leading down from the road. "The only interpretation we could put to these is that for some reason, Danny abandoned his truck up there and ran down to here. Angie believes he was injured, perhaps shot, but being knocked unconscious would look the same."

While the FBI agents labored over the grenade fragment area, Stewart had Jason and the others retrace their steps through the rest of the scene. Jason led them to where Danny's truck and the body were found. He explained his interpretation of how the truck arrived where it did and why he and the others were skeptical about Danny dying as a result of a collision with the rock outcropping. When he showed Agent Wooley the newspaper picture, he too, was doubtful the collision could have been the cause of death.

It was mid-afternoon before Stewart and Wooley were ready to release Jason and the others from the scene. "For a bunch of amateurs, your crime scene investigation skills are pretty good," Doyle complimented. "Agent Wooley, do you have any more questions for these folks?"

"About a million," Wooley replied, "but we have to finish processing this crime scene first. We'll be able to tell a lot more when we get our hands on Whitehorse's body and on that truck he was driving."

"I'm sure the truck was impounded," Jason said. "I should be able to find out where it is by tomorrow. But the body's going to be a problem. Angie, tell them how the Diné feel about handling dead bodies."

Angie explained the Navajo death taboos. ". . . So if you want any cooperation from the reservation or Danny's family, you can't touch that body," she concluded.

"Agent, can you live with that?" Doyle asked.

"We can for the time being, sir. But if you want more than circumstantial evidence for murder charges, we're going to need a forensic examination of the body at some point."

"We need to hear the full detailed story about what led up to all this. Jason, can we go back to where you're staying?" Doyle asked.

Jason looked at Vic, who nodded his approval.

*

Kathy was waiting at the ranch when everyone arrived. She was accompanied by a tall, dark-haired, blue-eyed man Jason didn't recognize. Jason greeted Kathy warmly. She, in turn, introduced him to Chaco.

The group spent more than three hours briefing the government agents on the events leading up to Danny's fiery crash. Kathy and Chaco gave inside information that the others had no way of knowing.

It was well after dark when Stewart stretched and said, "This certainly gives me a lot to chew on. It's going to take a few days for us to sort it all out."

"What can we do to help?" Jason asked.

"Find Whitehorse's truck," Agent Wooly responded.. "It would be better if you do that than us. If what you said about local law enforcement is true, I don't want anyone knowing a federal investigation is taking place just yet."

"I'll be staying in Farmington for a day or two to coordinate what we've got with the military and ATF investigators." Stewart said. "Let me know the minute you find that truck."

The federal people's exit left Jason with one more task – talking with Chaco and Kathy. He worried about their reaction to his taking over the case. "Kathy, you know me, and you know how close Danny and I were. But Chaco, we don't know each other at all. Danny asked me to come down and help because he trusted me and was confident I could do the job. With what I've learned, I absolutely believe Danny was murdered. I've already told Brianna and the Capalettis that I intend to stay and finish the job Danny started, but I can't do it on my own. You both know much more about the Gannon case than I do. I hope you'll trust me enough to help me finish this lawsuit."

Jason saw Kathy's jaws tighten. "Jason, you know I don't take orders very well."

"I don't give orders. When I say 'work together,' I mean just that. We're just people trying to do what's right on behalf of a friend."

To Jason's surprise, Angie spoke up. "Kathy, don't be a little bitch! I already hired him. He's exactly who and what we need right now. Okay?"

Vic chimed in. "Jason's offered to work for free and use his own money to continue the Gannon lawsuit. He's already called in personal markers with people he knows to get the feds involved. If we don't give him our full trust and cooperation, we'll be letting the case clients down badly."

Kathy looked at Jason. "It didn't take you long to make converts. Don't worry about me. We worked well together before and I'm sure we can do it again. I'm just reminding you that I can be a bit hard to handle sometimes. Can you deal that?"

Jason chuckled. "And, as I recall, you used to use some pretty interesting four-letter words now and again. Don't change a thing for me, Kathy.

"No, no, no," Chaco said with a thin smile. "We do want her to change. She's been doing much better lately. I haven't had to wash her mouth out with soap in more than a month."

Kathy elbowed him in the ribs.

The exchange confirmed to Jason that Kathy and Chaco were indeed more than just co-workers. He looked at Chaco and said, "I understand you're an ex-cop."

"Military MP and ACIS . . . twelve years. I was the staff judge advocate general's chief investigator the last four. Decided I liked the rez better than D.C. Haven't worn a uniform in four years."

"I didn't much like uniforms myself."

"What branch?"

"Navy."

"What outfit?"

"SEALS."

"Tough outfit." Chaco responded. "I won't need to worry about you taking care of yourself. Welcome aboard, Navy. Glad you're the commander of this outfit and not me."

"Ahh, but you're my first officer. All investigative duties I hereby gladly delegate to you."

"Aye, sir."

"Kathy, where does the case stand right now?"

"Danny filed a Request to Produce two weeks ago. They've got two-weeks left to respond."

"Under the circumstances, the court will grant a continuance on the court's own motion until there's a new attorney of record on our side," Jason said. "That will buy us a couple of months while I get my feet under me and familiarize myself with the case. For now, I want to remain anonymous as long as possible. Since you're using this place for the office, I think I'll rent a room in Durango."

"You'll do nothing of the sort," Vic bellowed. "You have a room. You slept in it last night. Hell, this house is big enough that I could put all of you up and have a couple of bedrooms left over. You're staying here, and that's final."

Jason was embarrassed. "I can't impose like that."

"Of course you can," Angie replied. "We already have Brianna living here more than she does at her own apartment. It'll be nice to have you around." She looked at Kathy and Chaco. "Why don't you both just move in here for a while, at least long enough to get this case handled?"

They cast each other quick glances. "Thanks, Ang," Kathy said, "but I'm out on the reservation near Shiprock. That's where I feel safest right now."

"That's a very generous offer, Angie," Chaco said. "But I'm working on the mapping project every day, and my place is much closer."

Angie looked disappointed, but nodded.

"My first order of business will be to go into Farmington tomorrow and check a few things out," Jason said. "I need to get a copy of the accident report from the sheriff's office. I'll let the local authorities believe I'm just here to close out Danny's estate. Then I want to go by the federal courthouse to see if there are any new filings in the case. Let's meet back here tomorrow night and I'll give everyone an update. Folks, it looks like we have us a law firm."

Chapter 59

The trail of clothes bothered Chaco less and less each time it appeared. His strict military sensibilities were offended by the disorder, but walking behind and watching her all the way to the bedroom was ample reward for the compromise to his sense of order.

"So tell me about Stevens," Chaco asked as Kathy cast her top aside and reached behind for her bra clasp.

"You'll like him." He heard the zipper of her jeans open as he struggled with the buttons of his fly. "He's a very good lawyer and easy to get along with. He's tenacious as hell and sees a lot of things that other people miss. You two are a lot alike that way."

As Kathy entered the bedroom door, she stepped grace-fully out of her jeans without missing a beat. Chaco tried the same, missed, and became entangled with his pant leg. He banged his shoulder painfully on the door frame and hopped one-legged into the bedroom while struggling to free himself. He succeeded only in toppling unceremoniously onto the foot of the bed, his jeans only half way off. "I don't know how you do that," he said.

"What?" Kathy asked, trying to suppress a snicker.

"Walk right out of your jeans the way you do."

Kathy laughed as she slid out of her tiny lace thong. "You've got to be able to walk and chew gum at the same time."

She screamed as Chaco caught her by the waist, and tackled her onto the bed. "I may be slower out of my pants," he said, " but I'm quicker on the draw. Otherwise, you'd still be standing up instead of lying down."

"You'd better not be too quick," she purred. "I have big plans for you for the next hour or so."

*

Bathed in sweat and enjoying the warm afterglow of their lovemaking, their conversation returned to Jason. "You and Stevens were friends a long time ago, but how much do you know about him today?" Chaco asked.

"Not a lot since he went to Utah, but he's a good guy. Your ears really perked up when he told you where he served in the service. Why?"

"SEALS are about the toughest warriors in the world. It's a very elite outfit. They're highly trained and have instincts honed to a fine edge. Being a Navy SEAL is a huge accomplishment."

"With what Danny had to go through, that may come in handy."

"The real question for us is whether or not we tell him anything about the NALM. I don't think I'm comfortable with that just yet."

"I agree," Kathy said as she yawned and snuggled deep into his neck. "When the time's right we'll know it."

Chapter 60

Jason pulled out of Bondad just before nine a.m. He was struck by how Colorado's beauty seemed to exhaust itself almost the instant he crossed the state line, giving way to flinty hills, dry, dusty canyons, and sand. Even the Animas River was different. It seemed lost, anemic, almost exhausted as it clawed out a hard-scrabble path toward its confluence with the San Juan River in the heart of downtown Farmington..

At the town of Aztec, the county seat,. Jason found the sheriff's office and emerged with the accident report in hand. Then it was back on the highway to Farmington, just twelve miles to the west.

Soon the industrial buildings beside the highway grew in size and number, many belonging to oil companies or oilfield service companies. Jason dubbed the stretch "Oil Row."

Close to town, he spied a huge complex on the north side of the road that was surrounded by a ten-foot-tall chain-link fence with privacy strips. The large metal building bore the name "Gannon Oil." Vic had said that Gannon's headquarters was on the west side, near the airport, so this had to be the company's workshops and equipment yard.

Just past the Gannon property, the road climbed a small hill. A sign at the top announced the presence of a historical scenic overlook. Jason couldn't see anything scenic the place overlooked, so he drove past.

Farmington's downtown area was bounded by steep sandstone bluffs that confined the river valley. The south bank of the San Juan was reservation, while the north side was a bustling *Bilagaana* city. The river wasn't just a city boundary—it was a boundary between sovereign nations, and two distinctly different socio-economic cultures.

Jason's objective was the federal courthouse, a large four-story granite and glass building set squarely in the middle of town. When he opened the case file, the first item was something Kathy must not have known about. Gannon had filed an objection to Danny's Request to Produce. It requested a hearing date for Thursday, four days from now. A letter from Kathy, notifying the court of Danny's death would take care of that. The court would grant a continuance on its own motion. But Jason would call the court's scheduling clerk to make sure the hearing was taken off the court's agenda.

He dialed Kathy with the news. "Include reference to the hearing date on their objection in your letter," he said. "How does Danny's office get its mail?"

"We have a Post Office box."

"Better pick up the mail and check the office email just in case there's anything else we should know about."

As he walked to his car, Jason debated his next move. By the time he unlocked the door, his mind was made up. "What the heck?" he muttered to himself. While he was still anonymous, he decided to poke around a bit in the most unlikely of places—Gannon Oil's headquarters.

Chapter 61

As Jason drove along Airport Boulevard, a sleek Southwest Airlines 737 touched down just three hundred yards to his right. Between him and the runway, the general aviation area held the usual array of Cessnas, Pipers, and Beechcrafts, but was also home to several executive jets, some bearing names of oil companies.

That has to be Gannon Oil headquarters. On the left side of the road, directly opposite the airport terminal, he spied a six-story, oval-shaped, office building perched on the brow of the bluff.

Feeling a bit like Daniel walking into the lion's den, Jason walked through the glass front doors and found himself beneath a domed thirty-foot-high ceiling that protected dark gray marble floors. Small trees were planted in large marble urns scattered about the lobby, interspersed with couches and chairs for the convenience of waiting visitors.

At the center of the lobby was a multi-tiered fountain. The sound of cascading water masked the background noise of clerical workers busily toiling in a maze of cubicles behind the foyer. The building presented a panoramic impression of money and efficiency.

Jason took a seat on one of the lobby couches in an out-of-the-way spot, and sat back to observe. People scurried in and out the front doors—men in suits carrying briefcases, UPS drivers and others of indeterminate occupation. A number of women who were dressed to the nines and clutching what appeared to be résumés gave Jason an idea. Perhaps there was a way to get a glimpse into the inner-workings of the company so that he'd at least have some idea where to start once he began discovery. He stood and approached the receptionist, a pleasant looking young woman. "Miss, I have a friend who's moving to town soon and needs a job. How do I find out what might be open?"

"You need to visit our personnel department, sir," she replied with a syrupy sweet voice and good company smile. "Take the elevator to the third floor and follow the signs."

He soon stood on the third floor before another receptionist who gave him the company's standard employment application form. "Do you have any information I can send to my friend that would help her customize her résumé?"

"Certainly, sir," the bleach-blonde thirty-something with big hair replied. "Let me get you a corporate information packet."

The woman stepped through an office door behind her desk and reappeared bearing a colorful portfolio with the company logo on it. "This should be what you need."

"Thank you, miss. By the way, how are your openings for book-keepers and executive secretaries?"

"We always have openings in bookkeeping." She leaned forward and whispered conspiratorially. "But the high skirts — that's what we call the boss' secretaries around here — that's another story. Pretty tough to land one of those jobs, but not impossible. Mr. Blackthorn's staff is out of the question. He only promotes from within. But Mr. Parker — that's where she'd have her best chance. His staff turns over quite a bit." The woman lowered her eyes and looked around, then practically whispered, "Frankly, Sir, he likes to chase skirts around his desk, if you know what I mean. I'd tell your friend to steer clear of his office. "

"Well, thank you very much, miss," Jason said as he pulled a twenty-dollar bill from his wallet unobtrusively as possible and slipped it into her hand. "I'll certainly let her know. You seem to know a great deal about what goes on around here. Mind if I ask your name?"

"Oh," the woman blushed a little at the unexpected compliment. She glanced quickly at her palm to determine the size of the gratuity. "Pamela — Pamela O'Brian. And I do know a lot. Truth is, this company couldn't run without me. I'll bet I know more about this place than Old Man Gannon himself. It's nothing but a big ol' Peyton Place, if ya know what I mean." She gave Jason a none-too-subtle wink. "What's your friend's name? I can make sure she gets a good job around here. You're not married are you? I mean, you're not wearing a ring or anything."

Her eyes gave Jason's body a quick once over before finding his eyes again.

Jason chuckled. "Her name isn't important right now, and no, I'm not married. Are you?"

"Not on your life. Was once, and that's why I'm not now. Are you new to town? I don't think I've never seen you around here."

"You've never seen me, and yes, I'm new to town. Perhaps you could show me around some time, maybe go to dinner."

"Sure," the woman replied a little breathlessly as she scribbled a number on a Post-it Note. She started to hand it to him, but pulled back. "You gotta promise not to give this number to anyone else. It's unlisted. I get too many calls from heavy breathers, if ya know what I mean. By the way, what's your name? I don't just give my number out to folks I don't know!"

"Jason." He smiled. "Jason Stevens."

"Well, Mr. Jason Stevens," she said, winking as she handed him the note. "you'd better call soon. You never know when that number might change."

"Thanks Pamela. I'll do that." He offered a handshake and held it just a little longer than necessary, being sure to give the hand a tender squeeze before turning and walking away.

*

Jason sat in the parking lot of McDonalds, reading the accident report while sipping a Coke and munching the last of his fries.

The medical examiner's statement totally contradicted what Jason already knew. It cited the recovery of a partially full whiskey bottle from inside the truck. It said that the body was too thoroughly consumed to be a good candidate for forensic examination, so on the basis of circumstantial evidence, the MEs conclusion was that the victim died accidentally after losing control of his speeding vehicle as the result of alcohol intoxication. The time of death was fixed as nine seventeen p.m.

The report dovetailed neatly with what had been reported in the press. The last page was a copy of the towing release for Danny's truck.

Jason couldn't believe his eyes. The towing entity listed was Gannon Oil Services, Vehicle Maintenance Div. It listed an address on the Farmington/Aztec Highway. *That has to be the complex I passed on the way in.*

Jason rushed up the highway and past the Gannon complex. Indeed, the address was the same one listed on the towing release. He turned around and drove past the other way, trying to see what was in the acres and acres of equipment behind the building. But his view was blocked by the high chain-link fence. He needed a better vantage point. The scenic overlook he'd driven past at the top of the little hill was perfect.

The roadside monument directed visitors' attention across the highway to a spot near the river where a couple of settlers had been killed by Indians in the 1870s. Jason's interest was in another direction. Using the high-powered digital binoculars he always carried in the Escalade, he began a methodical, section-by-section examination of the Gannon equipment yard. "Where are you?" he mumbled.

It took several minutes, and even then he almost missed it. The truck was parked in the back, its burned out body blending almost perfectly with two old, badly rusted hulks of machinery.

The headlight holder on the driver's side was broken and the bumper was bent upward into the grill, but that was all the collision damage he could see. He turned his binoculars to their highest setting to zoom in on the license plate.

"Damn," he cursed. Rather than a numbered front plate, truck had only the Arizona Starburst plate that resembled the state flag. The color on the right side of the plate was burnt off, but the left side was intact.

Jason sprang to his vehicle and snatched the newspaper he'd bought in Durango. *Good.* The picture clearly showed the half-burnt front plate. The newspaper photo confirmed that what he was seeing through his binoculars was indeed Danny's truck.

He needed a picture. He popped the cargo door of his SUV and rumbled around for his camera case. He pulled out his SLR digital camera and his most powerful telephoto lens and snapped several close-ups of the front of the truck. Then he shot a few more photos of the yard, the buildings and the entry gate.

As elated as Jason was, his excitement was tempered by the reality that the vehicle was still in enemy hands. There was no guarantee the truck would be around next week, tomorrow, or even an hour from now. He had to get back to Bondad fast.

As he raced up the highway, Jason dialed Vic's home. Angie answered.

"Angie! You're just who I wanted to talk to. You've got to reach Chaco and tell him we need a tow truck operator we can trust. I just found Danny's truck. I want to pick it up in the morning."

"I'll certainly try, Jason. Anything else?"

"Yes. Get hold of Kathy, too. I have some papers she needs to prepare—tonight. I'm on my way back to your place. I'll be there in a half-hour."

Next he dialed up Doyle. "I've found the truck," he reported. "Believe it or not, it's at the Gannon Oil storage yard right here in Farmington. I'll get a writ of possession in the morning."

"Mind if I tag along?" Doyle asked.

"Not at all. I'd love to have the backup."

When he arrived at the ranch, Angie met him at the door. "I reached Chaco," she said. "He has access to a tow-truck out of Shiprock. He'll have it in the Walmart parking lot at ten in the morning. He said that Kathy's on her way."

"Thanks Ang. I need someone to fetch Danny's mother. We're going to court tomorrow morning for a writ of possession, and I want her to be there in case we need Danny's next-of-kin to testify."

Without hesitation, Angie said, "I'll leave for Nageezi right now."

Chapter 62

The nightly plunge in the spa was already a ritual. Once they'd all settled into the relaxing waters, Jason told of his day, including venturing into Gannon Oil's headquarters.

"That was brazen," Vic said.

"Not to mention dangerous," Bri said, submerged to her neck in the bubbling water and sitting closer to Jason than the night before.

"I was perfectly safe. They have no idea who I am. It gave me a good feel for just exactly what size and type of company we're dealing with. While I was there, I came up with a plan that could help us learn a lot. Want to hear it?"

All nodded.

"Danny's Request to Produce is a procedure that opens up the books and records of an opponent so they can't hide evidence from the court. But as powerful a legal tool as it is, you can't just go in and rummage around blindly, hoping to find something. You have to know what you're looking for, and it must be relevant to your case. The information we need to know won't be lying around on someone's desk for all the world to see, it's going to be buried. In order to find it, we need to know how Gannon's bookkeeping systems work."

"That's a pretty tall order," Vic said.

"I know, but I think I have a way. We need a spy inside Gannon Oil. One who knows bookkeeping and who would never be suspected."

Brianna looked around the tub. "The only one's who know what we're looking for are us four. Vic and Angie are out, and Chaco's no bookkeeper. Kathy would be recognized instantly."

"I wasn't thinking of them," Jason replied.

"Then who? I'm the only one who knows anything about book-keeping or account . . ."Brianna's eyes widened as Jason's intention became clear.

"I know it's probably unfair to ask," Jason said. "I'd jerk you out of there the instant we perceived any danger. But your background would virtually assure you getting a job right where we need information from the most. Would you be willing to consider it?"

Bri shook her head. "I want to, Jason, but school starts in a couple of months, and I'm a teacher, remember?"

"Of course," he said. "All we need is a snapshot of how their bookkeeping is organized, and particularly, how and where they process their SR-30 records. Once we can learn that, I can use discovery procedures to trace the records of all our dry wells. That shouldn't take long. You can quit anytime you want and go back to your teaching job.

"Then of course I'll do it. I've been racking my brain, trying to figure out how I can do something of value amongst all you geniuses. It'll make me feel like I'm not just a fifth wheel anymore. I'll just pretend I'm Mata Hari."

Angie scooted around the tub and gave her friend a hug. "You've never been a fifth wheel around here, my dear, and you're much prettier than Mata Hari. Better yet, you won't have to sleep with any smelly old German generals.

Chapter 63

Danny's mother was seated with Jason, Kathy, and Doyle in the judge's chambers promptly at nine a.m. Mrs. Whitehorse verified that Jason was the family attorney. The matter was settled quickly when Jason offered a $1000 cash bond to assure that any outstanding towing fees or other costs would be paid. Angie took Danny's mother back to the reservation while Jason and Doyle hurried off to meet Chaco and the tow truck driver.

Jason stood between Chaco and Johnny Two Shoes, the tow truck driver who looked more like a grizzly bear than a normal person. They were at the scenic overlook.

"Danny's truck is parked between those two large pieces of machinery," Jason said, pointing down at the yard.

"You sure this is legal?" Two Shoes asked. "I paid a lot of money for this truck, and I can't afford to lose it."

"There's nothing to worry about. New Mexico law provides for access to private property for the purpose of vehicle recovery."

Doyle nodded his agreement.

"Getting in will be easy," Doyle said as he looked down at the complex. "They leave the gate wide open. But getting out might be another story. They may try to stop us with that electric gate. Chaco, Johnny, if someone does try to stop us, you two just keep hooking up the pickup. Jason and I will deal with them. When you're done, get that truck out of there—fast."

*

Jimmy Olivera smiled as he walked back to the office from visiting the burnt out old truck, relishing his coup. Although the cab was pretty messed up because of the fire and the bumper was pushed in a little, the rest of the truck was in pretty good shape. He'd make a couple hundred bucks just off the engine accessories. But the transmission was the answer to his prayers.

His pickup was the same age and model as the burned-out hulk, and his truck transmission was slipping a little more every day. Without another one, he'd soon be bicycling to work.

Then the solution dropped right into his lap. He was getting ready for another night at the Las Conchos Bar when Mr. Blackthorn himself called. Blackthorn ordered him to take the tow truck clear to hell and gone down Highway 302 on the reservation to tow in a wrecked pickup truck. It was kinda weird. The tow truck was supposed to be only for company vehicles. But orders were orders and overtime was overtime. The Las Conchos Bar would have to wait.

Jimmy called Blackthorn the next morning to ask what to do with the thing. Blackthorn's answer surprised him. "Sit on it for two or three days just in case someone comes looking for it, but no longer. After that, turn it into scrap. Keep your mouth shut and there'll be a little something extra in your paycheck at the end of the month."

Olivera knew how to keep his mouth shut.

Then things got busy. The truck had been here for a week, but that was no big deal. It was just a burned out old piece of junk and all he wanted was the transmission. Tonight he'd go out with the forklift, lift the thing up, and rip that transmission out. Tomorrow he'd see what else he could salvage. What was left would go through the metal shredder. The scrap dealer always gave him a nice little kickback. Life was beautiful if you played your cards right.

*

Hey! What the hell? A big red tow truck swept into the yard, followed closely by a white Cadillac Escalade. Vehicles were supposed to check in at the office before going out back. *What do these guys think they're doing? Nobody comes into this place without dealing with me first!*

Jimmy trotted after the offending vehicles. Then his anger turned to panic. They drove straight to the burned-up pickup. Two men got out of the tow truck and started hooking the thing up. He broke into the fastest run his two-hundred-seventy-pound body could muster.

Two suits got out of the Escalade. "Hey!" Jimmy shouted as he wheezed to a halt. "What the hell do you think you're doing? Get away from that truck or I'm going to call the cops."

Chaco quietly stepped away from what he was doing and took a backup position three yards behind the man while Jason said, "We are the cops. I'm an attorney for the Whitehorse family, and this man is the deputy U.S. attorney." Doyle flashed his badge. "Who are you?"

Whoa. This sounds like heavy stuff. "I'm Jimmy Olivera, the yard manager. You're not supposed to be back here without checking in with my office." The tow operator continued his work, completely ignoring Jimmy's command.

"Mr. Olivera, this is for you, the first attorney said, slapping a folded bunch of papers into Jimmy's chest. It's a copy of a writ of possession signed by a judge an hour ago, giving us the right to secure immediate possession of this truck. You're probably going to want to show that order to your bosses. "

Jimmy looked at the document. Legal gobbledygook, but it certainly looked official. This was a lot more serious than what he had authority to deal with. Worst of all, he'd screwed up. Blackthorn ordered him to get rid of the truck and he hadn't done it. As fearful as it seemed, he had to get hold of Blackthorn rightnow. *If I still have a job after this, it'll be a miracle.*

"You men just stop what you're doing. I'm going to call my boss and see about this." Jimmy turned on his heel and lumbered toward the office, noticing that the tow truck guy was nearly finished.

Jimmy slammed through the rear door of the yard office and ran for the phone. He stabbed out Blackthorn's number. Gasping for breath, he shouted at the man's secretary, "Let me talk to Blackthorn, fast!"

"Who may I say is calling, sir?" a sickly sweet voice cooed.

"It's Jimmy Olivera down at the equipment yard. We got a real emergency here. Get Blackthorn on the phone now, damn it! Tell him it's about that truck he had me bring in from the desert."

Jimmy heard the woman catch her breath at his curse, but she calmly replied, "Yes, sir. I'll transfer your call."

Blackthorn listened as Jimmy babbled out the story. "You stupid son-of-a-bitch," Blackthorn yelled. "I told you to lose that truck a week ago! Where are they now?"

"Still in the yard."

"Get your ass out there and stop them. You hear me? I'm leaving right now. If they get out of that yard, you better be gone with them, and hope I never lay eyes on you again!" Blackthorn slammed the phone in the yardman's ear.

"Oh, God!" Jimmy muttered as he tried to catch his breath before sprinting toward the back door. He threw it open and was reaching for the switch that closed the gate as the tow truck swept past in a swirl of gravel and dust. Right behind came the Escalade. The ponderously slow ten-foot-high chain-link gate closed impotently behind the fleeing vehicles as Jimmy watched helplessly while they rolled west up the highway toward Farmington.

Chapter 64

When will they return? When will they bring the sweet tea? Not the bitter tea. Please, No more bitter tea. Bitter tea brings the monsters. I've told them everything over and over even though at first I thought it was wrong. I don't remember why I thought that way.

They said the monsters were people – people who said they were my friends – but they were really monsters. I see that now. I told them how evil the monsters were.

My real friends give me the sweet tea. It's not wrong to help real friends. They keep the monsters away."

I feel my arms, my legs. Why can't I move them? My body feels warm. There's softness all around me, like a cocoon of velvet cement.

What was that. . . ? Is it time? Are you bringing the tea? Oh please, not the bitter, make it sweet. I'll tell you everything you ask.

"What's your name?" a voice whispered.

He said his name. His lips reached out as he felt the small trickle of glorious sweet tea.

"How old are you?"

Again he answered eagerly, correctly. The reward was sweet.

And so it went, like so many times before. *They're right. They are my friends. I'll do anything they ask – tell them anything they want to know. How stupid to think the monsters were my friends. They are, after all, monsters! And monsters bring bitter tea, not sweet.*

*

"Any problems with our prisoner?" Chaco asked Alan Chee, the attending NALM officer. "No. He's been completely docile and talking his head off. He's told us some amazing stuff. It's all on the recordings."

"Enough to use against him if we need to?"

"Oh, yeah. Enough for the death penalty several times over."

"You've learned well, Alan. Tomorrow we'll start progressively relaxing his restraints. The hardest part will be weaning him off the tea. The withdrawal is worse than heroin."

"Too bad he doesn't know more about the gas wells."

"True, but what we've got is what we've got. Just don't let him see your face. You'd better get back in there. I'd hate to have him get sick and drown in his own vomit or something. We need this guy alive and willing to testify."

Chapter 65

Trying to balance her trepidation against the exhilaration she felt over her new assignment, Bri walked through the doors of Gannon Oil as the newest addition to the accounting staff. It took her two hours last night to decide what to wear. She settled on a sky-blue blazer set off by a light yellow blouse tucked into sharply creased navy pants.

It was only nine days since Jason submitted her application through some woman named Pamela. Bri was surprised at being more than a little discomforted when Jason took Pamela to dinner, though she knew she had no right to be. After all, she and Jason weren't dating—officially—even though it sort of felt that way. For the first time in years, she found herself wishing her relationship with a man could be more 'official.'

The call from Gannon Oil, asking her to come in for a pre-employment interview came seven days ago. Jason must have done something right with Pamela—but she didn't want to think about that, let alone ask him about it. Now here she was, walking through the tall front doors of the Gannon Oil Building.

She was taken to the accounting department for the obligatory introduction tour where she met her twenty-three co-workers. Then she was escorted to a cubical and given a stack of employee policy manuals to read and sign by the end of the day. As she watched her HR escort walk away, the weight of her undertaking sank in. For other people, these first few hours would have been a cause for celebration. But for her, they were sobering, daunting, and a bit frightening.

Then she thought of Danny. Somewhere in this building were the people who took him away from her. Somewhere in this building was the evidence that would bring Danny's murderers to justice. Her heart lifted at the thought that she was no longer just along for the ride, but was an integral part of obtaining justice for her big brother.

Chapter 66

It took Jason two weeks to review all the case files. He'd set Kathy and Chaco to obtaining signatures on the Substitution of Attorney agreements he needed from each of the named plaintiffs.

Jason watched curiously as Chaco added information to the big map on the wall of the office. He knew the map's purpose, but had no idea where the new information was coming from. One day he asked.

"Oh, I've hired some kids out on the reservation to help," Chaco said.

Jason envisioned two or three high school students. "Are you sure the information they're giving you is good?"

"Don't worry, Jason. I ride herd on them pretty good."

*

From her first day, Brianna made it her business to discover where the SR-30 forms were processed. It wasn't difficult. The entire accounts receivable department revolved around them. During her orientation, she stated a preference to work in accounts receivable. "I was raised on a property that had a Gannon gas well on it," she told her placement interviewer. "I want to work where I have a chance to really feel the pulse of the gas flowing out of the ground and through our company."

Her interviewer was mildly surprised at her enthusiasm. "Most of our newbies don't really care where they work," she said.

"It's just that when I was a kid, a guy from Gannon and a guy from some other company would come out and read a meter on our property. I used to watch them. They'd fill out some kind of paper and both of them would sign it. They acted like it was real important. I always wondered what happened to it. Is this where those papers come?"

"Oh, you mean the SR-30 forms. We get a copy of them," the interviewer replied. "It's our job to reconcile our internal well production figures with what the SR-30s say."

"Would it be possible for me to work with them? I think it would satisfy my childhood curiosity."

Bri got her wish. Her first job was to log the production of a block of just over five hundred wells and their associated SR-30 meter reports. When she typed the meter number of the SR-30 into her computer, it would automatically bring up a report form that listed all the wells that meter served. Unfortunately, she had no way of knowing where the wells were located. She asked her supervisor, Suzanne O'Neal, a perky woman with a perpetual smile, but she didn't know either. "We don't care where they're at, honey," Suzanne said, "we just plug in the numbers like the good little worker bees we are."

Gannon's computer procedures were strict. Bri received a login code that only allowed access to the records for her block of wells. "It used to be better," Suzanne explained. "About three years ago they got this brilliant idea to compartmentalize and assign everyone blocks of meters. Then a few months ago, they gave us these damn passwords. It sure creates a mess if someone gets sick or takes a vacation. If I can't cover their station myself, I have to shuffle people around. But every time I do, I have to change the password at both stations. It seems like I spend half my life just creating and deleting passwords, but if some bright little worker bee like you could come up with a way to solve this password problem, I'd be forever grateful." The term "worker bee" was one of Suzanne's favorites.

"Let me think about it," Bri said.

Chapter 67

Early on, Chaco gave Bri a list of all the wells and meters he suspected were carrying gas from the supposedly dry wells. None corresponded with the wells or meter numbers to which she was assigned. Nearly six weeks into her job as a spy and she had nothing to show for her efforts.

Taking a cue from her first conversation with Suzanne, Her second week on the job, Bri wrote a formal suggestion showing how departmental efficiency would be improved by not having to change security codes every time someone took vacation or became ill.

This morning Suzanne unexpectedly called her into her cubicle. "Bri," she said, beaming, "you've solved one of my worst problems. I just received word that the suggestion you turned in has been approved. I've asked them make you my new assistant department manager and they said 'yes.' Congratulations!"

"Wow!" was the only thing Bri could think of to say. She truly was flattered.

"From now on, you'll take over all department work scheduling and help me supervise the other data entry technicians. You'll handle vacation and paid time off scheduling and, as much as possible, cover the work load of anyone out sick or on vacation."

"But what about the security passwords?" Brianna asked.

"That's what got you this new job. The company had no idea how much time it was taking just dealing with those silly passwords. "Here." Suzanne handed her what appeared to be a credit card attached to a lanyard she could wear around her neck. "This is your new master passkey card. It's just like mine and will allow you to remotely work on any computer in the section. You're probably not aware of it, but before giving you this position, the company did a security check on you to make sure you could be trusted with this new responsibility."

"I had no idea." Bri smiled, but was immediately concerned. She'd noticed nothing. It must have been only a credit and prior employment check. If they'd been following her around, she might have led them straight to the ranch. She resolved to be far more careful.

"You'll receive a new computer this morning that has a card reader. Your card authorizes access to all accounts receivable files related to the SR-30s. Here, let me show you." Suzanne turned to her computer, called up a screen, and typed in a password. The screen that came up was a list of all the employees in the accounts receivable section. Suzanne selected a name and hit "enter." Instantly, an SR-30 report form materialized. Brianna watched with fascination as letters and numbers appeared on the form.

"That's Kathryn Clark's station. You'll have the ability to monitor anyone else's workstation in real time. That's how I supervised you. If they're sick or on vacation, you can actually work off of their workstation from your desk."

Bri was astonished. She had no idea she was being so closely monitored. "That's amazing. Do they watch you this closely?"

"I'm sure they do, but I don't care. I just do my job and let the higher-ups do the worrying. Now, let's get you up to HR and get your pay records updated. This new job comes with a very nice raise. Oh, and by-the-way, the dress code requires that management level women wear skirts just like management-level men have to wear ties. It's a bummer, but that's why you've never seen me in pants."

Bri could scarcely contain her excitement. At last she'd have access to all Gannon's well production records. But her elation was short-lived. Using her newly granted powers, she systematically monitored every data entry clerk, hoping to see one of them processing a form that contained one of the target wells or meter numbers on Chaco's list. None ever showed up. It was like they didn't exist. After two frustrating weeks, she had to conclude that none of the clerks were processing SR-30's from the meters Chaco suspected were serving the dry wells.

*

"I thought for sure that within a day or two, I'd be able to find the SR-30's for at least some of our meters," Brianna complained to the group as they assembled at the ranch in front of the wall map. "I've searched and searched and haven't found a single SR-30 that covers any of them. Anyone have any ideas?"

"Does anyone outside your department process SR-30s?" Angie asked.

"Not as far as I know. I think our section gets them all."

"That doesn't make any sense," Vic groused. "Those meters are being read every month and the report has to go somewhere."

"But would that be true if there was no production coming from the wells?" Chaco asked.

"That's not terribly unusual," Bri replied. "We get several reports each month that show zero production for one reason or another."

"Hmm," Jason said. "I assume you call up your records by simply typing in the meter number."

"That's right."

"What if you just typed in one of Chaco's meter numbers?"

"I don't know. If I make a mistake, the computer gives me an error message, but I can give that a try and see what happens."

"Maybe there's a back door," Jason said.

"A back door?"

"Yes. It's a way of calling up information if the normal way of accessing it doesn't work for some reason. Most database programs have that feature built in. Try this—tell your supervisor you're having trouble accessing one of the meters and ask if there's another way to access those records."

"It's worth a try," Bri said. "At this point I'm willing to try anything."

Jason gave her shoulder an encouraging squeeze. "I do have some important news for everyone," he said. "I finally heard from Doyle this afternoon. The FBI is finished processing Danny's truck. They concluded that the impact speed with the rocks was between twelve and fifteen miles per hour, far below the threshold necessary to cause any sort of major injury to the driver. As for the fire, they think an accelerant was poured over the outside and in the cab. The fire burned up and away and never reached the engine compartment or the undercarriage. That's why the gas tank survived. It was intact and almost three-quarters full. They don't believe the engine was even running when the truck hit the rocks."

"Whoever started the fire has to be who killed Danny," Angie whispered.

"That's the way the feds see it too. The FBI and Doyle's office are ramping up a full-scale murder investigation."

"What does that mean for us?" Kathy asked.

"It means we can quit worrying about pursuing the criminal side of Danny's death. If involvement goes as high up the Gannon food chain as we think it does, Red Gannon and his gang will be much more worried about the criminal investigation than our civil lawsuit. Maybe they'll drop their guard."

Jason, school starts in two weeks. They're expecting me . . ."

Jason knew this day was coming and feared it. He took her hand, squeezed it and said. "None of us can tell you what to do. Your career's an important part of your life. If you need to quit Gannon and get back to a normal life, I'll support you all the way."

Angie walked over and put her arm around Bri's shoulder. "We will too, my dear. We'll just have to find another way to get that information.

For your peace of mind, Bri, if you stay, I promise you'll never have to worry about having a job," Jason said. "Every law firm needs a book-keeper and I can't think of one I'd rather work with. But you decide what you think best."

"Oh, you guys," Bri said, wiping a tear about to escape her eye. "What I was about to say before Jason so rudely interrupted was that I mailed my resignation letter to the District yesterday. Of course I'm staying on. I just thought you should know, that's all.

Chapter 68

"Mr. Blackthorn, there's a Mr. Stewart here from the U. S. attorney's office."

Blackthorn's heart raced. What could the U. S. attorney's office possibly want with him? The situation with the two well explosions seemed contained. The seizure of Whitehorse's truck had taken place weeks ago with no apparent repercussions. Should he call the legal department and have them send up one of the company attorneys? Better find out what the man wanted first.

"Tell him I'll be right with him." He took a moment to compose himself, popped in a couple of antacid tablets, then had Jennifer escort the middle-aged, powerfully-built man into his office. "My name is Doyle Stewart," the man said as he extended his business card. "I'm the deputy U. S. attorney for the northern federal district of New Mexico."

Blackthorn offered the man a chair. "What can I do for you, Mr. Stewart?"

"I'm here on a small investigative matter. Before we get started, just for my own recollection, I normally record these conversations. You don't mind, do you? It's no big deal. It helps me keep my mind straight." Stewart held up a small recording device and placed it on Blackthorn's desk.

Blackthorn's mind screamed, *Danger, Danger.* Of course he objected, but until he found out why this man was here, he didn't want to appear to have anything to hide. "That's quite all right," he said, not meaning it.

"First things first." Stewart spoke into the recorder. "This recording is of Doyle Stewart, Deputy U.S. attorney, interviewing Mr. Marion Lucas Blackthorn." Stewart watched Blackthorn wince at the mention of his first name. "To answer your question, Mr. Blackthorn, my office is investigating a homicide that took place here in the Farmington area a little over two months ago. We're hoping you can answer some questions related to it. I'm sure you recall the incident. The victim was a local attorney by the name of Danny Whitehorse. I believe he was in the process of suing your company at the time of his death."

The air went out of Blackthorn. His instinct was to flee, but flight was impossible and would only make him look guilty. Struggling to show no reaction, he said, "I do recall hearing about Mr. Whitehorse's death, but I understood it to be a tragic accident, not a homicide. Why would the U.S. attorney's office be involved? Isn't a murder investigation the job of local authorities?"

"Normally it would be, but Mr. Whitehorse was a Native American and the killing took place on reservation land, which places it under FBI jurisdiction."

"Wha . . . what could that possibly have to do with me or Gannon Oil?"

"A few weeks ago, the pickup truck in which Mr. Whitehorse died was recovered from your company's equipment yard. We've been processing it for evidence. I'd like to know how your company acquired possession of that vehicle."

"Our possession?" Blackthorn said with mock surprise. "We had it? Now that's a real mystery! I have no idea how that truck could have ended up there."

"You're saying you didn't instruct anyone to place that truck in your yard. Is that correct?"

"Yeah, that's correct."

"Is your yard an authorized and licensed impound yard, Mr. Blackthorn?"

"I don't think so. We're an oil and gas company, not an auto salvage outfit. Our tow trucks are only supposed to be used for our own vehicles. As you may know, we have quite a fleet.

Doyle reached into his briefcase and pulled out a document. "This is a copy of the sheriff's department report on the incident." He flipped to the last page and turned the paper around where Blackthorn could see it.

"See this box right here?"

Blackthorn nodded.

"That's where the name of the towing company is written. This report lists Gannon Oil as the company. Can you explain that, sir?"

"No, I can't explain it. One of our employees may have been moonlighting with our equipment. I'll have to look into it. I know they listen to a police scanner down there. Since the truck was found on our property, that's probably what happened."

Doyle brought out another document. "This is a copy of the receipt the sheriff's department had the tow truck driver sign when he picked up the truck. The signature says the man's name was James E. Olivera. Is that the same Olivera who's the foreman of your storage yard?"

"He's on suspension for insubordination. Now it looks like I'm going to have to fire him over this Whitehorse truck thing."

"That's a pity, Mr. Blackthorn, particularly if he was simply carrying out the orders of someone higher up. A couple of my agents are interviewing him right now. Whether you continue to employ him or not, I'd strongly suggest that he remain healthy and available to us. If anything were to happen to Olivera, guess who we'd come looking for first?"

"I don't think I care for your implication, Mr. Stewart. Are you threatening me, sir?"

"Not at all, Blackthorn. I'm merely suggesting that you treat Mr. Olivera in a very friendly way. That's all. How well did you know Mr. Whitehorse?"

"Can't say I knew him at all. I saw him on the news and read about him in the newspaper, but I never met the man."

"That's a lie!" Doyle thundered. "I'm advising you that lying to a federal officer in the process of an investigation is considered obstruction of justice. If you lie to me again, I'll have you taken out of here in cuffs and we'll finish this little chat down at the federal building."

Blackthorn recoiled. Being led out of the building in handcuffs would be a disaster. "No! No! You can't do that. I'm sorry, I misspoke. I did know Whitehorse."

"The fact is you knew Whitehorse well. You hated the man—didn't you."

"I had nothing personal against him, but he was an enemy of our company."

"We have it on record that you personally met with him at his office on," Stewart paused and consulted a notebook from his briefcase, "May ninth of this year at approximately ten a.m. You were in his office for the better part of an hour, and when you left, you were very angry. In fact, you threatened Whitehorse's life. Isn't that so, Mr. Blackthorn?"

Blackthorn was dumbstruck. Stewart had to have his hands on that recording. He began to tremble. Even in death, that damned Indian was coming back to haunt him.

He had to say something, but what? He couldn't tell the truth. When he finally opened his mouth, words would not come. He swallowed hard and tried again. "I . . . I do recall that meeting. But I didn't knowingly do anything wrong. I said some things I shouldn't have said and certainly didn't mean. Look, I'm no attorney. I've never done anything like that before. I got a bad temper, see. Sometimes I say things I don't really mean. Gimme a break here, will ya?"

"Mr. Blackthorn, where were you on the evening of Tuesday, June seventeenth between the hours of seven and ten p.m.?"

"I'd have to look at my planner to figure that out." Then his mind registered on the date. "Hey, wait a minute! That's the night Whitehorse was killed, isn't it? You guys aren't trying to try to pin that on me, are you? The papers said it was an accident."

"I can tell you with certainty, Mr. Blackthorn, that it was no accident. Were you anywhere in the vicinity of Highway 302, south of the gas plant that night?"

Blackthorn felt beads of perspiration popping out on his brow, but for appearance's sake, hesitated to wipe them away. "Like I said, I'd have to check my planner."

"What's your cell phone number, Mr. Blackthorn?"

"My cell phone number? Why do you want that?

"Never mind. Excuse me while I make a quick call." Stewart took out his cell phone and punched in a phone number. The cell phone on Blackthorn's belt rang. "No need to answer that," Stewart said as he ended the call. He shook his head in wonder. "You know, these things are amazing. People use them now without even thinking about it. What they don't realize is that even the ones without GPS capacity can tell us where they've been. For example, if you made or received any phone calls on the night of June seventeenth, we can pretty much tell where you and any of your callers were by the cell towers the calls were switched from."

Blackthorn fought to appear calm. He indeed had made and taken several calls in the area of the gas plant that night. Thank God the two men Gannon had hired were smart enough to get rid of their disposable cell phones. Strange that he never heard back from them. Maybe they were talking to Gannon. "That's very interesting, Mr. Stewart. But I can assure you that if I was in the gas plant area that night, it would have been on company business. We have a lot of wells down that way. I certainly didn't see Mr. Whitehorse out there on that night or any other."

Doyle took a deep breath and said, "That brings me to my main purpose in coming here, Mr. Blackthorn. I think you can see the direction our investigation is going. There are a lot of people in my office who are already convinced that you and Gannon Oil are directly involved in Danny Whitehorse's death. We know that if you were, you weren't alone. Here's something you may not know. In almost every murder conspiracy, there's one person who fares better than anyone else, and that's the person who turns state's evidence first. While everyone else goes down hard, that person gets off light. You need to consider what I'm about to say very carefully. You're a smart man, but not a young man. If you get sent up for murder and don't get the needle, the best you can hope for is to die in your prison cell. But if you cooperate, all that might not be necessary. You give us what we want, and you might someday get the chance to play with your grandchildren. The bottom line here is that if there was ever a time to cut a deal over this Whitehorse thing, it would be right now." Doyle leaned back, folded his arms, and welded his eyes to Blackthorn's.

The silence between them seemed to stretch forever. Blackthorn was the first to look away. He leaned back in his chair and gazed at the ceiling in thought, then seemed to reach a decision. "One last time, Mr. Stewart," he said, "I wasn't there. I didn't order that tow truck to go out there, and I didn't have anything to do with Whitehorse's death." Each phrase seemed to stiffen the man's resolve. "If you believe I had something to do with that, then either charge me and read me my Miranda rights or get the hell out of my office. I've nothing more to say to you, not without my attorney present. I'm calling my legal department right now." Blackthorn placed his hand on his telephone.

Doyle closed his little notebook with a sigh. "I'm sorry you feel that way, Blackthorn. In my experience, that's not how innocent men act. As they say in the movies, 'Don't leave town.' If I suddenly can't find you, I'll have an arrest warrant issued." Stewart retrieved his recorder from the desktop, turned it off with a 'click,' and said, "Good day to you, sir."

The instant the door closed, Blackthorn wilted. Bathed in sweat., he sat and stared transfixed out the window for several minutes. Then he angrily swept everything off his desk, sending it flying across the room. "All because of that damned Indian," he shouted. A cold fear crept into his gut. With the feds involved, things were spinning out of control.

Is this the one? Is this that step across the line that brings me down? For the first time in Lucas Blackthorn's life, he truly didn't know.

Chapter 69

A lull in her work schedule finally gave Bri a chance to try Jason's suggestions. When she typed in one of Chaco's meter numbers, the computer's response was different than she expected. Where other times she received an input error message for an incorrect number, this time the machine seemed to recognize the number and flashed up a blank SR-30 response form. However, the blank form wouldn't accept data input.

"Hmm. What if I type in one of the well numbers?" Consulting Chaco's list, she typed in a well number. Again, the computer seemed to recognize it, but this time it flashed back a blank, nonresponsive well production report form. She tried several others with the same result.

Not working. Time to try Jason's second suggestion. She walked to Suzanne's cubical and said, "Sorry to bother you, but I'm having trouble with one of my SR-30s. It's happened a few times lately. I don't know if it's a program bug or if my computer is acting up. Every now and then when I input a meter number, the record just won't come up. It's making it so I can't reconcile my total production numbers. Is there a way to access the records more directly?"

In her sing-song voice, Suzanne said. "Let's see what the Bible says." She opened a desk drawer and pulled out a thick manual Bri had never seen before. She consulted the table of contents and flipped pages to the section she wanted. After a few moment's study, she looked up and said, "Yes, you can do that, but it's a procedure authorized for supervisors only. Since you're my assistant supervisor, I'd say you qualify. I'll make you a copy of this page, but it's strictly confidential, okay?"

"Sure Suze," Bri replied without hesitation.

"There's just one thing. It takes a password to access this portion of the program. You know how this company is about passwords. I wouldn't be surprised to see them start requiring one to open the bathroom door. I'll write my password on the bottom of the copy, but it's for your eyes only. Understand?"

*

Bri waited until Suzanne took her lunch break before trying to access the program. In a matter of seconds, she was viewing a spreadsheet showing every meter the company dealt with. "Holy cow," she whispered.

The first column listed the months, starting with the current one and going back row by row for what appeared to be forever. The second column listed the meter numbers in descending order. Next came monthly production figures, then a running total of production for that meter.

The fifth column caught her eye. It said simply, "wells," and had a drop-down arrow. She clicked on the arrow and a new spreadsheet appeared, containing the production information for all the individual wells associated with that meter.

She clicked on one of the well numbers and the standard production sheet form appeared. She watched with fascination as the figures changed. Someone in the section was updating that particular record in real time, as she watched.

She could scarcely contain herself. This was the Holy Grail—the final home of all the data entered by her and the other accounts payable workers.

She returned to the original spreadsheet and scrolled down until she found the first meter on Chaco's list. To her great disappointment, although the meter showed a total production figure, the current month's production read "0"—as did the previous month and the one before that, and the one before that.

How long has this has been going on? Scrolling down rapidly, she discovered that three years prior, the information changed. A marker flag was attached to the spreadsheet cell. From there back, the production cells contained numbers. She clicked on the marker. A text box appeared that said, "Production Transferred."

Transferred where? Maybe one of the well records would tell her. She clicked on the 'wells' drop down arrow list. When the spreadsheet appeared, in the same month that the meter record said "Production Transferred," every well was flagged with a comment box that said, 'Transferred to the Sunshine Group.' She checked three more wells and found the same.

What's going on here? Every well she looked at had normal-looking production numbers right up to the date of the transfer notice. This was a puzzle.

Suzanne's lunch break would soon be over. Bri printed out a half-dozen screen shots showing what she'd found, folded the papers, and stuffed them into her purse. She exited the program less than a minute before Suzanne reappeared. For the rest of the afternoon, she could barely concentrate on her job. She couldn't wait to show Jason her discovery.

Chapter 70

"Mr. Olivera, my name is Special Agent Martinez," the man said as he held his FBI credentials up to the screen door. "This is Special Agent Hawthorn. May we come in, sir?"

Jimmy blearily looked through the doorway, his vision fogged not just by the screen, but also a terrible hangover. There wasn't much to do except drink since Blackthorn suspended him — other than screw Wanda. She might be kinda big and sloppy, but she wasn't that bad-looking. And man, did that woman ever like to put out. She even brought her own booze. Right now, that was the only kind of dating Jimmy could afford.

"Whaddya want?" Olivera slurred. He was just sober enough to be alarmed when the men said they were FBI.

"We need to talk to you for a few minutes."

"Whadabout?"

"We understand you work for Gannon Oil. Is that right?"

"Them mother f . . ." Jimmy thought it better not to finish the curse. "Yeah, I work for 'em, but I'm laid off right now. Am I in trouble or somethin'?"

"No, not you, but we're investigating them. We'd like to ask you some questions. May we come in, sir."

"They in trouble?" Jimmy asked hopefully. The thought raised him to a higher level of soberness. Suddenly he needed a cup of coffee.

"We're not at liberty to say, Mr. Olivera, but it would be helpful if we could chat with you about your experiences there."

Olivera knew cop doublespeak when he heard it. *Yes, by God, Gannon is in trouble. Otherwise these monkeys wouldn't be banging on my door.* He swept the door open and said, "Come on in fellas. I'm always willin' to help the FBI."

He didn't know if Wanda heard anything or not. She was pretty smashed last night. He hoped she didn't come wandering out of the bedroom lookin' like usual—boobs showin' through her holey T-shirt and ass hanging out of those barely there thong panties.

He indicated the couch. "Have a seat. I just gotta tell my girlfriend not to come out here with nothing on. I'll put on a pot of coffee." Then he realized he was dressed only in a thin T-shirt and boxer shorts. *Hope neither of those guys are queer,* he thought as he retreated to the bedroom. *After all, I do look pretty good.*

*

"So you're saying that your company has never acted as a towing company before?" Martinez asked.

Jimmy had pulled on a pair of sweat pants and was sipping at a large coffee mug. "Not since I been there. We used those wreckers to retrieve company vehicles that were stalled or broke down."

"Have you ever been asked to retrieve a private vehicle before?"

"Nope. Not once. "

"Tell us how you got the call."

"I was at home here just getting ready to go out that night. Mr. Blackthorn calls and tells me he needs me to go out past the gas plant and pick up a truck that just wrecked."

"What time was that?"

"Oh, about nine, maybe nine thirty. I remember I had my good clothes on. I was going dancing."

"Did he tell you who the truck belonged to?"

"Naw. Just said it was a wrecked pickup. That's all."

"Did he say how he knew it was out there?"

"Didn't say that either. With Blackthorn you don't ask questions. You just do it."

"Did he give you any instructions?"

"Yeah. He said to bring it back to the yard and keep it out of sight. I asked him about it a couple of days later and he told me to get rid of it. He seemed real nervous about anybody knowing where that truck was. He offered me a good bonus if I kept my mouth shut about the whole thing. Then before I could get rid of it, those guys come and snatched the truck out of the yard. Instead of getting my bonus, I got suspended for ninety days. I'm pretty pissed about it."

"And you're certain it was Blackthorn who ordered you to pick that truck up?"

"Dead certain. Because in all the years I worked there, Blackthorn had never called me at my house. You remember stuff like that."

*

The lead agent dialed Doyle the minute they got back in their car. "Mr. Stewart, this is Agent Martinez. We're on the right track. Blackthorn knew about the wreck long before he should have. The 911 call came into dispatch about ten fifteen. Olivera claims Blackthorn called and told him to take the wrecker out there between nine and nine thirty—says he's certain about that time. The only way Blackthorn could have known about the wreck that early was if he was there.

Chapter 71

Bri arrived at the ranch just as Kathy was leaving. "You may want to hang around for a bit," she said.

Jason was elated. "We have to find out who this 'Sunshine Group' is."

They searched local phone books and every available Internet phone directory, but turned up nothing. Finally, Jason slapped his forehead and said, "What am I doing? Let's see if this outfit is registered to do business in New Mexico. Kathy, call up the state's website.

The New Mexico Department of Commerce's corporate registrations web page quickly returned a hit—"The Sunshine Group, S.A." Jason didn't like the S.A. designation. That meant it was an offshore corporation. Indeed, the address showed the company to be head-quartered in the Bahamas.

"Well at least there's something," Jason said. Kathy, clicked on the "officers" link. Another page appeared, but rather than giving names, a message box popped up, stating that disclosure of officers of Bahamian corporations was protected under Bahamian law. The only information listed was the name and telephone number of the corporate solicitor's office.

"Solicitor?" Bri looked puzzled.

"It's a type of attorney under British law," Jason explained. "In the Bahamas, corporate officers can hide their identities so long as a solicitor certifies that they are 'known to the Crown,' Which means they can only be identified to an official of the Government or by court order."

"There might be another way," Jason said. "Every corporation doing business in this state has to declare a local registered agent."

"What's that?" Brianna asked.

"Someone who resides in the state who can accept service of subpoenas and other legal documents if the corporation can't be served in any other way. Registered agent's names and addresses are public information. Kathy, go back to the Department of Corporations website."

At the page listing the Sunshine Group, Bri spotted it first and pointed. "Right there at the bottom." Kathy clicked on the link.

"Stanley J. Popeson," Jason muttered. "Either of you ever heard of him?"

Both women shook their heads.

"It lists a Farmington address," Kathy said, "but it's only a P. O. Box. Let's try the phone book."

There was no splashy Yellow Pages ad, just a simple line listing that said Stanley J. Popeson, Certified Public Accountant. The address was a non-descript, rather seedy downtown location on Animas Street just a short distance from Danny's office.

"Hmm – I'm curious," Jason said. Let's see who is Gannon Oil's registered agent."

When the webpage came up it read:

Stanley J. Popeson
135 N. Animas, Suite 202
Farmington, NM 87474
(505) 329-2300

"Interesting," Jason said. "Let's see if Popeson shows up as a corporate officer."

The officer information page listed James E. Gannon as the chief executive officer and James R. Parker as president. No one recognized the name of the Secretary/Treasurer, but Popeson's name didn't appear.

"Looks like registered agent is as good as we're going to get," Jason said. "Let's Google this guy."

The Google search returned several hits on the name "Stanley J. Popeson" and its variations. Most were articles about a college tennis player from New Jersey who set several NCAA school records. Finally, tucked away among all the references there was one obscure item that hit home. It said, ". . . audit conducted by Stanley J. Popeson." The reference was a link to a publication called *The Oil & Gas Professional*.

Kathy called up their website.

It was an oil industry trade magazine. Paging through back issues, they found a puff-piece article on Gannon's operations in the Four Corners area. "Here it is," Kathy said, pointing at a table on the second page. Just below the table graph, in very small red letters almost lost in the tan background of the page it said, "*Gannon Oil audit figures provided by Stanley J. Popeson, accountant and certified petroleum association auditor.*"

"Well, look at that," Jason said. "This guy's Gannon's auditor. That means he sees all the financial records. This gives us a point of commonality between Gannon and the Sunshine Group that we can exploit since it's highly likely the production records we're looking for are now going to Sunshine."

Jason straightened and said, "Kathy, I want you to withdraw our request for continuance of the hearing on Gannon's objection to our request to produce and get it set on the court's Law and Motion Calendar for as early as possible. It's time for me to come out of the woodwork and get this case moving again."

*

Jason was amazed at how the walls that Bri had built around herself appeared to be crumbling. He recalled the night she'd flinched away from him as he tried to brush back an errant lock of hair. Today their touching had become almost as natural as breathing. Though he was still reluctant to enter her personal space, it was becoming far less so for her with him. She took his hand as they walked and frequently put her arm around him. But out of an abundance of caution he only did so after she did.

There were occasional kisses, but only soft, chaste ones that lightly brushed cheeks or lips.

In the spa they allowed arms and legs to occasionally tangle. When Jason's arm went around her, he was careful to touch only her shoulder and nothing else. She would lean her head against his shoulder and they would talk — or not, as the mood would take them.

Both were inclined to playfulness in the spa, but even in their play, Jason was careful to not let an errant touch go anywhere she might consider intimate. It was driving him crazy.

As they snuggled close in the spa later that night, Jason asked, "Do you know how to use a USB drive?"

"Yes. I use them all the time in my school work."

"Is there a USB port on your work computer?"

"Two of them, right on the front."

"How closely are your computers monitored?"

"I don't know for sure, but the company's very tight on computer security. There's a rule against employee's using removable memory devices unless the company provides it."

Jason paused in deep thought, then said, "When I go to court on this request to produce, I may have to show documentary evidence that Gannon records have been transferred to the Sunshine Group. How dangerous do you think it would be to copy that spreadsheet file?"

As he talked, her hand found his thigh and rested there without hesitation or embarrassment for the first time. "I've no idea, she replied. Wouldn't that be illegal?"

"No. Cops work undercover all the time." He was having a hard time keeping his mind on the subject. "So do whistleblowers. But just to be on the safe side, I'll get Doyle's blessing on it first thing tomorrow."

Bri took a deep breath and removed her hand. "If he says it's okay, I'll do it. All they can do is fire me, right?"

"Normally, yes," Jason said with a worried look, "but this *is* Gannon Oil."

"Tell you what. The day I copy it, I'll carry a decoy USB drive. I'll put the real copy in a place they wouldn't dare look and you'd better not dare to ask me about. If they catch me, I'll give them the decoy, cry like a baby, and tell them I'm sorry."

Her plan seemed sensible and minimally risky. "We'll do it a couple of days before the hearing."He pulled her closer and brushed her hair with a soft kiss.

Chapter 72

Several huge flat-screen monitors lit the security room and rotated images from half a hundred surveillance cameras located inside and out of the building. Operators could watch every square foot of the building and grounds, and at the same time monitor the hundreds of computers used by Gannon employees. The instant Bri plugged the foreign USB drive into her computer, an alert warning flashed up on the security monitor screen of John Snell, the assistant shift supervisor. Six minutes after the alarm appeared, Snell returned from the restroom and spotted it. "Hey, Larry, we've got a USB sync up on station 436," he shouted.

"That's accounts receivable," Larry Larson, the shift supervisor, responded. "Whose computer is it?"

Snell checked the computer registry book. "Brianna Sanders, the assistant department manager."

"I'll throw a camera on her," Larry said. It took several seconds for him to identify the surveillance camera group in Brianna's work area, and more time to select a camera and pan it over to her station.

"Oops! It's gone now," Snell called out as the alarm disappeared from the security monitor.

Larry's camera finished panning and focused in on Bri's workstation just as she got out of her chair and walked away. "She's leaving her station," Larson said. "Let's see where she goes."

"The way she looks, I wouldn't mind following her around a while," Snell said

"Damn. Women's restroom."

"In your dreams," Snell chuckled. "Only way we turn those cameras on is with the blessing of God Himself."

"You mean Blackthorn?"

"Isn't that how you spell 'God' around here? Better write her up. I'll go down and get the drive—you call Parsons."

*

Snell intercepted Bri on her way back to her desk and demanded she turn over the USB drive. Then he escorted her directly to the office of Bradley Parsons, Gannon Oil's computer security director. Parsons was a perpetually suspicious man who bore a striking resemblance to Woody Allen. When it came to his computers, he regarded nothing as being innocent or inconsequential.

At least this woman is nice looking, not like a lot of those other stupid cows HR hires for data entry. Parsons instructed Bri to sit down in front of his desk. "Ms. Sanders, approximately twenty minutes ago, you committed one of the most serious breaches of computer security possible." Parsons picked up a sheet of paper from his desk, turned it toward her, and said, "According to your computer activity log, at eleven twenty-six a.m., a portable memory disk was inserted into computer workstation #436, and was disconnected approximately seven minutes later." Parsons picked up Bri's confiscated USB drive and wagged it at her.

Bri tried to look sheepish. "I'm sorry, Mr. Parsons. I didn't think it would hurt to listen to a little music. I know I shouldn't have done it. I felt so guilty that I didn't even listen to the whole song. It's a long one. Have you heard 'Stairway to Heaven?'"

"I'm going to let you in on something, Ms. Sanders. No one in this company has secrets from me. I can see every keystroke you make, every Internet page you visit. I can read all your email and, as you have just found out, I know every time someone plugs any sort of unauthorized memory device into one of our computers. You've committed a firing offense. That's very clearly stated in our employee handbook."

Brianna tried to look shocked. "Really? No, I didn't know that. If I'd had any idea, I never would have done that, Mr. Parsons. I love Gannon Oil, and I really need my job. You can have my USB drive. All that's on it is music." Bri allowed a tear to slide down her cheek.

Parsons picked up another sheet of paper and handed it to her, determined to not be swayed by the woman's tears. He scribbled something on it and handed it to her. "You are to take this to your supervisor. It's a two-day suspension without pay, beginning right now."

Bri caught her breath. "Oh, I don't mind the suspension, Mr. Parsons, I deserve it, but today's a really bad time. My supervisor's going on vacation and I'm the only one who can cover for her."

Parsons grabbed the paper back. "When will she be back?"

"She'll be gone for a week."

Parsons crossed out the date and scribbled a new one. "Your suspension starts the day she returns." He shoved the paper back at her.

"Thank you, Mr. Parsons," Brianna said demurely, giving him her most wounded look.

"Get back to your work station, Miss Sanders," Parsons commanded, "and never let this happen again!"

*

"What a twit," Parsons muttered to himself. "Only reason you've still got your job is because you're one stone-cold fox." He plugged the woman's confiscated USB drive into his laptop computer. No way was he going to take a chance on giving the potentially virus-infected device access to his mainframe. *"Now let's see what this baby's hiding."*

All he found was an assortment of nine songs. He checked his laptop's registry tracking program. No new registry entries had been recorded. His virus scanner detected no executable programs, and there appeared to be no spyware aboard. The disk seemed harmless.

Either she's just another dumb broad, or she, or someone else, is very, very smart. Parsons didn't assume for a second that this thumb drive was the same one she'd plugged into her computer.

This one bears watching. Parsons made a note to have security direct a recording camera at her workstation. Watching her for a few days would not be an unpleasant task.

Then he turned to his computer and typed out a series of commands. "Let's see what she's really been up to." The program he activated ran on all Gannon computers. It logged every keystroke and mouse command made by the computer over the past seven days. He ordered a printout of her last week's activity. He would take the report to his three o'clock meeting with his boss, Lucas Blackthorn. Brianna Sanders' name was now on the agenda.

*

When Bri returned, she found Suzanne Dean standing with purse in hand, her sweater draped loosely over her shoulders. "I'm so sorry," Bri said. "I know you're ready to leave." She knew that Suzanne's one and only reason for coming in this morning was to give her a short briefing on what needed to be done in the woman's absence. Now Bri had the embarrassment of having to tell her boss about her two-day suspension.

"Oh, don't you worry about that," Suzanne said. "Bradley Parsons is just an old poop. He nailed me for that, too, one time. But he's right. Don't do it again. They'll just come without warning and boot you out of the building. I've watched it happen."

"There's just one other thing I forgot to tell you about," Suzanne glanced at her watch. "We have a special batch of SR-30s that don't get processed in our office." She handed Brianna a sheaf of papers bound by a thick rubber band. "Put them in an envelope and mail them here." The woman handed her a sticky note with an address written on it.

"That doesn't sound too hard." Bri smiled.

"It's not. But for some reason, it's very important to the high muckety-mucks. If those SR-30s don't get where they're going on time, I get yelled at."

After appropriate hugs and wishes of bon voyage, Brianna waived her good bye then took a good look at the note. Her breath caught and her heart began to pound. It said:

Stanley J. Popeson
135 N. Animas, Suite 202
Farmington, NM 87474

She knew immediately what had to be done. She grabbed two large manila envelopes, walked out of the office and down to the department copy center, where she made a photocopy of each SR-30. She stuffed the originals in one envelope and the copies in another.

Back at her desk, she addressed the envelope with the originals as ordered and dropped it into her 'out' box, but waited until the end of her shift before slipping the other envelope into her briefcase while trying unobtrusively to block the view of the camera pod near her cubical. At five o'clock, briefcase in hand, she joined the crowd streaming out of the building, fearing with every step that she might be stopped and searched.

It was only when she was out of the parking lot and driving away that her fear began to subside. Even at that, she kept a fearful eye on the rearview mirror while taking many twists and turns all the way to the highway. As best she could tell, no one was following. Only after she passed Aztec and was well up the road toward Bondad did she allow a triumphant smile to touch her lips. Her time as a spy had finally paid off.

Chapter 73

"There is one other thing, Mr. Blackthorn," Bradley Parsons said as his security briefing concluded. "As you know, we have a very strict policy about employees plugging outside portable electronic media into our computers. We had an incident today, a USB drive plugged in by one of the accounts receivable employees, a Ms. Brianna Sanders. She claimed she was just listening to music, but I suspect the USB drive we took from her was a decoy. Since we don't do strip searches, I had no way to verify if she had another.

"So did you straighten her out?"

"Oh, yes. I spoke with her very firmly and gave her a two-day suspension. But there's more. After the interview, I called up her keystroke log. At the time she plugged in the USB, she had the Master Well Production Spreadsheet open. Not the data entry program, but the raw production database spreadsheet. How she got into it, I've no idea. The bottom line is that she may have made a copy of the file."

"What?" Blackthorn's immediate thought was of Stewart and the FBI. Could they have already infiltrated the company? Was this woman working undercover for them? Or perhaps it was some sort of industrial espionage. That sort of thing happened all the time. "Who do you think she's working for?" Blackthorn asked.

"I've no idea, sir. I checked her personnel file. She looks clean as a whistle. Before working here, the only job she ever had was as a local school teacher. Should we fire her?"

Blackthorn wanted to say yes, but if she were working for the feds, it might not be the best choice. Better to just isolate her instead. What was that old saying? "Keep your friends close and your enemies closer?"

"Let's keep this under the surface for now. Monitor her computer in real time and listen to her phone calls. Keep a camera on her every second she's in the building. I'll arrange to keep an eye on her when she's off-premises. She's bound to tip her hand."

After the man left, Blackthorn dialed the internal security office and asked to speak to Ed Rollo. "Ed, this is Lucas Blackthorn. I've got a job for you. I want a very discreet tail put on one of our employees. I want to know where she goes and who she sees. I'll have her file sent down from HR, and as always, keep this under your hat. "

"Of course, sir," Rollo replied.

Chapter 74

Bri could scarcely contain herself as she arrived at the ranch carrying the USB drive and copies of the Sunshine Group's SR-30s. Jason was flabbergasted. "This is huge," he said as he flipped through the copies. "If any of our dry wells show up in these production figures, it will be prima facie evidence of fraud."

"They do," Bri said. She handed the USB drive to Kathy and had her scroll to the dropdown lists that showed which wells contributed to the SR-30 readings. "It's all right there. Every one of those wells are on our dry well list.

"I don't want Gannon's attorneys even suspecting that we know about the Sunshine Group or the connection to Popeson's accounting office until after we have our order on the request to produce," Jason said. "Unless I don't have a choice, those names will never come up in my arguments."

"What if it doesn't work?" Bri asked.

"Then I'll need you to testify about how we learned the origin of these records. We may get bogged down in a fight over admissibility, but we'll most likely win. On the day of the hearing, I want you in a car outside the building, ready to testify."

"There's something else," Bri said. "They caught me when I plugged in that USB drive. I almost got fired."

Jason's concern soared. "Tell me about it, and don't skip a thing, no matter how insignificant you think it might be."

After listening, Jason said, "I've got more than enough ammunition to get our discovery order. You, my dear, have worked your last day at

Gannon Oil."

"Oh, Jason, I can't just up and leave. Suzanne's on vacation, and I'm the only one in the department who can cover for her. Since they didn't fire me, I don't think there's any danger. Suzanne will be back in a week, and then I'll quit. That will give me a chance to get my personal things out of there."

The resolute look on her face told Jason there was no sense arguing. "All right. We'll leave you in until Suzanne gets back, but not a minute longer. If you get any sense at all that something's wrong, you stand up, walk out of that building and get the hell away from Gannon Oil as fast as you can."

*

The spa didn't seem its normal place of refuge that night. Jason was preoccupied by the fact that Bri had been caught. He could tell she sensed his unease. Finally she said, "Jason, quit worrying. This is why we placed me there in the first place. I'll be very careful, I promise.

"I know you will. It's just that there's so much in there that you don't have any control over, no matter how careful you are. I wish I could be in there with you."

Bri leaned her head against his shoulder, put her arm across his chest and drew him into a tender hug. "I know you do," she said, "and I love that about you."

*

There was still a subtle tension as they met for their usual good-night on the balcony. Whether fueled by Jason's worry or Bri's unease at his discomfiture he didn't know, but tonight something was different.

Jason leaned back against the balcony rail, his arms wrapped safely and discretely, around Bri's middle. Her back was against him, her hair slightly damp and fragrant from her post-spa shower.

Bri wore the same silky aquamarine robe and nightgown as she had their first night on the balcony, he, a fleecy, maroon, terrycloth robe.

He softly kissed the back of her head. "I've got to tell you that I feel like we're making a huge mistake. Every minute you're at work this week, I'll worry that Gannon will somehow find you out. I don't know what I'd do if something hap . . ."

Brianna turned, leaned back a little in his arms, put a finger to his lips and said "Hush, Jason. I know how you feel. I'd feel the same if anything

269

happened to you." A tear formed at the corner of her eye. "If I've learned anything these past couple of months, it's that you can easily and suddenly lose the people you care the most about. You have to treasure every moment you have with them and not waste a minute of it."

She pushed herselfback and held him at arm's length. Looking into his eyes, she said, "Jason Stevens, I don't know what you've done to me, but you've got me feeling things I never thought I would again. You make me feel needed, like I'm somehow important in figuring out what really happened to Danny. But right now, you've got me feeling something else entirely. Want to know what?"

"Of course I do."

"I want you to kiss me. Not one of those little pecks we give each other every night, but a real kiss — like it matters more than anything else in the world, and I want it right now."

Their lips came together with a trembling tentativeness. Then came a second kiss, and a third that opened the floodgates of their repressed emotions. Each kiss was more intense than the last, as if someone were turning up the thermostats of their very souls. They held each other fiercely, like they'd never held anyone before.

It was electrifying, dizzying, overwhelming. She pressed hard against him despite his obvious ardor. They were engulfed in a delicious velvet oblivion where consciousness was defined only by the depths of hot, probing, kisses and the searing points of intimate contact between them they had tried so long, so hard to avoid.

Time became meaningless. Their repressed passions turned into a tsunami wave of unrestrained hunger and need that threatened to devour them. But somewhere in the middle of it all, Jason perceived there was no time left. If he didn't stop now, it would be everlastingly too late. Summoning his last ounce of restraint, he pushed her gently back. Her robe was off her shoulders and a nightgown sleeve had fallen, threatening to expose her. Jason pulled it back up, restoring the threat to her modesty. In a choked voice he said, "Bri, we have to stop."

"What?" she whispered, still lost in the fog of her emotions. "Noooo," she moaned, pulled him back to her.

The act nearly crumpled his will, but there was no choice. He would not risk losing her respect. He again pushed her back and said, "Bri, if we don't stop right now, we're not going to be able to, and you'll end up hating me for it."

She sagged a little in his arms. "Ohh," she groaned, "You're right." Pulling away, but not letting go, she said, "Thank you for being strong enough for both of us. Please forgive me."

"Forgive you for what? The fact that you have the same feelings for me that I have for you? We're both adults, Bri, and there's nothing I want more than to go into that bedroom right now and spend the rest of the night making love to you. But that can only happen for us when it's right. Remember the space you've reserved on that special finger on your left hand? As hard as it is, the best way for me to show you how much I want to claim that space for my own is for me to kiss you and walk away, right now."

In that moment, Brianna Lynne Sanders fell completely and utterly in love with Jason W. Stevens.

*

The delicious residue of their mutual passion kept Bri's touch, feel, and smell fresh and exquisite on his mind as Jason futilely fought for sleep that never fully came. He tossed and turned, acutely aware that the only thing separating him from the delicious consummation he'd had the smallest taste of on the balcony was the strength of his sense of morality, the love he now had to admit for Brianna, and that damned bedroom wall that seemed to get thinner and thinner every night.

Chapter 75

As Jason and Kathy took their chairs at the plaintiff's table in courtroom number two, he was uncharacteristically nervous. A request for production of documents and records was a straightforward legal procedure that many times required no court hearing. The only reason they were there was because of Gannon Oil's objection to the request.

At the defendant's table was a distinguished-looking, fiftyish man wearing a dark suit, white shirt, and red tie, G. Benjamin Whittington, senior staff counsel for Gannon Oil. With him was a younger man wearing a similar dark suit with a distinctive purple striped tie, and an attractive young woman, also in a dark suit, but with a stylish yellow and navy polka-dotted scarf over a cream-colored silk blouse. It was a larger showing of legal power than was necessary for what Jason knew would be a fairly scripted and predictable fifteen-minute hearing.

The Sunshine SR-30 copies were in his briefcase. Bri was parked outside, dutifully awaiting her summons should that become necessary.

There was no need for theatrics. The law was all on Jason's side. His legal points had already been made in the statement of points and authorities he'd filed in support of the request to produce. Restating them in open court would only irritate the judge, who would assume that Jason believed he had not read the document. Jason's oral argument-in-chief was short and to the point, and in less than five minutes, it was the other side's turn.

Whittington rose and addressed the court. "Your Honor, the principal grounds of our objection is that the plaintiffs' request to produce is overly-broad and does not define with sufficient clarity the specific records the plaintiffs expect the defendant to produce. Additionally, it does not limit discovery to only the documents and records relevant to the subject matter of this case. If approved in its current form, the order would constitute judicial license to conduct a fishing expedition through virtually all of Gannon Oil's files. The Court has a copy of our written objection and our citations of the numerous and persuasive points and authorities that support our objection. Therefore, defendant moves that the plaintiff's service of the request to produce on the defendants be quashed and that his request for an order to examine documents and records thereunder be denied."

"Thank you, Counselor," Judge Evon Oliver said. "Mr. Whittington, I have examined your written objection and your points and authorities. They are the normal pro forma objections I usually hear and turn down, I find nothing compelling in either your written objection or your oral arguments sufficient to persuade me to deny these plaintiffs their order. Can you cite any particular documents you object to and your grounds for wanting them excluded?"

It was a question every judge asked and every objecting attorney hated. Jason knew that Whittington would avoid identifying specific documents at all costs, because doing so would guarantee that the other side would move heaven and earth to try to gain access to them.

Whittington back-pedaled. "We wish not to designate specific records at this time, your honor, but we do want to make the Court aware that many of the Defendant's records contain trade secrets and information of a confidential nature that would detrimentally affect their ability to negotiate future contracts and protect their special relationships with corporate vendors and contractors. At the very least, we would ask that Mr. Stevens' order be amended to preclude public disclosure of any such documents."

It was a magnificent and dignified capitulation that prompted Jason to ever so slightly smile.

"I'm going to deny your motion to quash, Counselor," Judge Oliver said with a tap of her gavel. "My ruling on your motion is that Mr. Stevens' order is reasonable, relevant, and not overly broad. However, your request regarding public disclosure of trade secrets does seem reasonable. Mr. Stevens, what say you?"

"As the Court is aware," Jason answered, "the defendant and their counsel have the right to be present during any on-site discovery visit and has the opportunity to object to any record or document they believe should not be disclosed. We would stipulate to an amendment of the order to the extent that if in good faith, the defendant believes any particular document comprises a trade secret, we bring the document back to the court for an *in camera* judicial review and ruling as to its relevancy."

"Mr. Whittington, that solves our problem, does it not?" the judge asked.

Reluctantly, Whittington said, "Yes, Your Honor."

"Does that about sum it up, Mr. Stevens?" the judge asked.

"There's just one other matter, Your Honor." Jason was taking a chance, but not an unreasonable one. "We are informed that some of the production records relating to the wells in question have been removed from the Gannon building and are now in the hands of third parties. We fear that unless we can gain immediate access to them to at least tag and identify those records for future reference, those documents may be rendered inaccessible to us. We would request that in accordance with Rule 34(C) of the Federal Code of Civil Procedure, the order extend to all relevant records in the hands of third parties, and that the order be made effective immediately."

Jason held his breath. If the other side forced him to show evidence of specific instances of such record transfers, he would have no choice but to produce his copies of the Sunshine SR-30s and bring Brianna in to testify.

"What about it, Mr. Whittington?" the judge asked.

"One moment, Your Honor." Whittington looked worried. One of the first rules of the practice of law is that you never ask a question you don't already know the answer to. He turned to his co-counsels, who appeared as confused as he. Jason knew that Whittington now suspected Jason knew something which he did not.

After a hurried, whispered discussion, Whittington, seeming less then comfortable, addressed the Court. "We are unaware of records being held in the hands of any third-party, your Honor. Nonetheless, we object on the grounds that no such provision in the order is necessary. We intend to comply fully and completely, and shall encourage—no—make that 'insist,'" the man wagged the first two fingers of each hand as if putting quotation marks around the word, "that any vendors or third-party contractors cooperate and comply as well. We see no reason for any hurried, reckless, or precipitant execution of the order."

Whittington's answer was tantamount to walking into Jason's verbal right cross. "Your Honor, if, as they say, my opponents believe there are no records in the hands of third parties, they should have no objection to including that provision in the order. If it doesn't apply, the provision will simply be moot. If it does apply, then it is all the more wise and prudent for the Court to allow our timely access to such records and to identify the custodians of the same. In either case, the causes of justice and equity would be served by inclusion of such a provision in the order."

The judge nodded and said, "I agree, Mr. Stevens. I'm going to overrule the objection and allow the order, as amended, to take effect immediately in regard to third-party custodians as well. But I caution you, you do not have free license to unreasonably disrupt the business operations of any person or firm in possession of relevant records, or to extend your discovery efforts beyond the scope of this order. Is that understood?"

"Yes, Your Honor, we understand completely."

"Anything else, Mr. Whittington?" the judge asked.

"No, Your Honor," Whittington responded with resignation.

"How about you, Mr. Stevens?"

"That's all, Your Honor."

"The order will stand as amended," the Judge pronounced. "Mr. Stevens, if you want your order today, you will prepare it and have it in my hands by eleven fifty-nine for my signature. That gives you just over an hour. You will also provide opposing counsel and the clerk with conformed copies." The judge banged her gavel and said, "So ordered! Next case."

*

Jason walked to Bri's car, parked at the far end of the courthouse parking lot, to give her the good news. On his way he called Chaco. "We've got it," he said. "Meet us outside Popeson's office and we'll all go in together. The Sunshine Group is about to have a visit they won't

275

soon forget."

*

Ed Rollo picked a parking spot across the street, a few yards behind the Seven-Eleven because it commanded a good view of the courthouse parking lot. The Sanders woman left work around nine thirty and had driven to the federal courthouse where she parked far away from the building and other cars. Then she just sat there. It didn't make any sense.

A full bladder prompted him to interrupt his surveillance long enough to go into the store to take care of that problem, and get himself another cup of coffee, but then he saw a rather tall, sandy-haired man wearing a dark suit approach the woman's car. The guy got in like he belonged there. Rollo picked up the camera with its long telephoto lens and began snapping pictures. A couple of them showed the pair kissing. *Maybe the dude's married and they're having an affair.* In his profession, he saw a lot of that sort of thing.

Rollo had no idea who the man was, but he would find out. It wouldn't take long to uncover the secrets of Ms. Sanders' life and roll them out in the open for everyone to see. If this hot-looking babe was bent, he would soon know.

Chapter 76

Jason, Kathy, and Chaco swept unannounced into the reception area of Popeson's second-floor office. Barring their way was a customer counter guarded by a stout, silver-haired receptionist.

The work area behind was a fluorescent-lit open office area where three female clerks were working. A slight, bespectacled man whose thin, sallow face, narrow, hawkish, nose, and under-slung chin gave him a distinctive bird-like appearance, was in discussion with a matronly woman at one of the desks.

"May I help you, sir?" the aged receptionist asked.

"I'm looking for Stanley J. Popeson," Jason responded.

The man looked up and said, "I'm Popeson."

"Mr. Popeson, my name is Jason Stevens. I'm an attorney representing a large number of clients in a lawsuit against Gannon Oil. I'm here to execute a court order granted this morning that gives us a right to examine, identify, and copy certain records that are in your possession and under your control."

Popeson's eyes widened. "Please step into my office," he said. He indicated a door to the right of the main office. "Ladies, please carry on your work."

Jason turned to Chaco. "Bring the scanner in from the car and set it up on the counter." He looked at Kathy. "I want you to keep an eye on these women. If they start doing anything that doesn't appear to be normal office work, like packing boxes or shredding documents, come and get me immediately."

Stepping into the man's private office, Jason could tell that Popeson was a person caught between worlds. The outside office was up-to-date with modern computers and office machines, but his private office was like stepping back forty years. No computer adorned his desk – only a bulky seventies-era mechanical desktop calculator. The walls were lined with old, wooden filing cabinets topped with neat rows of cloth and leather bound ledgers. As Jason handed him a copy of the signed order, Popeson hastily closed one such ledger lying open on his desk.

"I don't know anything about this, Mr. Stevens," Popeson said after nervously perusing the order. "Gannon Oil is not a client of mine. I've never had anything to do with their records." Beads of sweat popped up on Popeson's bald head. The man's hand shook noticeably as he rid himself of the document by handing it back to Jason.

"Cut the crap, Popeson," Jason barked. "We know you're Gannon's corporate auditor and agent for service of process. If you fail to comply with this order or interfere with its execution, it will be considered contempt of court. We didn't come here randomly, sir. We know of your intimate working relationship with Gannon Oil."

Jason watched the man's eyes grow wider as he spoke. "I have in my possession copies of a large number of SR-30 documents transferred to you as recently as this past week. My order is enforceable not just on Gannon Oil proper, but upon all third parties in possession of those records, including Gannon's successors or assigns. That means you, Mr. Popeson, and the records you hold in behalf of the Sunshine Group."

The mention of the Sunshine Group seemed to send a shockwave through Popeson. "Y – Yes, Mr. Stevens," Popeson stammered. "I am the Agent for Service of Process for both companies, and we do receive certain records from Gannon Oil on behalf of the Sunshine Group, but I'm not sure if any of those records are still here. I'll have to check my file index and have my girls pull them for you. I could perhaps have them ready for your review first thing in the morning."

"Not a chance, Popeson," Jason said. "This order gives us the right to immediate access. Either show them to me right now so my people can start tagging and cataloging them, or we can go straight down to the court and have the judge cite you for contempt and obstruction of justice."

Popeson appeared to be on the verge of panic. "It—it's not that easy," he said as his eyes flitted to the file cabinets around the room. "It's such a volume of information. and it's all in order. You mustn't get it out of order."

Jason's gaze followed to where the man was looking. It was instantly clear why he was so nervous. The top drawer of the cabinet to Jason's left had a hand-lettered label that said "SR-30 #248 – #293." The drawer below that one said "SR-30 #294 - #345." Jason pulled a list of meter numbers from his pocket compiled from the SR-30 copies Bri had given him. Meter numbers on the list matched numbers on the file cabinets.

"Mr. Popeson, it appears that what we're looking for is right here. Your SR-30 labeling conventions are an exact match to those we already know are in your possession. I presume you have no objection to me calling in my colleagues so we can get started with our work?"

"I . . . I . . . I don't . . . uh . . ."

"You'd better cough up the keys to these cabinets, Popeson. You know as well as I do that I'm going to get a look at what's in them anyway. Either give me the keys or we call in an FBI agent to baby-sit this room while we all take a quick trip down to the federal courthouse to talk to the judge. It's your call. What's it going to be?"

The accountant, sweating profusely, appeared to have little experience in dealing with production requests, otherwise, he would have been on the phone to his attorney seconds after Jason presented himself. Jason banked on an intimidation factor to help him. He reached for his phone, and as he dialed, he spoke to Popeson. "This call is to the U.S. attorney's office, Mr. Popeson. This order is a federal court matter. I happen to know that there are a couple of FBI agents in Farmington right now who can help me enforce this." Jason did everything except press the "call" button. He raised his finger to shush Popeson as if the call had connected. "This is Attorney Jason Stevens. May I speak to Mr. Stewart, please?"

Popeson shook visibly. Rivulets of sweat poured off his brow. "Mr. Stevens . . . don't . . ." he pleaded

"Mr. Stewart, this is Jason Stevens. I'm in the office of Stanley J. Popeson..."

"Stop!" Popeson shouted. "You win, Mr. Stevens. You win."

"Hold on, Mr. Stewart." Jason looked Popeson in the eye and said,

"You have something you want to say?"

Popeson reached into the center drawer of his desk, pulled out a black velvet drawstring bag, and flung it at Jason. "There. Those are the keys. Satisfied?" He collapsed back into his chair so suddenly and completely that Jason feared the man had suffered a stroke. Popeson's chin fell to his chest and he seemed to physically cave inward. He didn't seem to notice as Jason holstered his phone without ending the call.

*

Popeson raised his eyes to his own phone. He had to call someone – but who? He feared to call Gannon with this man present. He thought about going out of the room, but wasn't about to leave the attorney unattended to rummage around. He thought of calling Blackthorn, but Popeson regarded him as a buffoon. Perhaps the best thing was simply to watch and see where this would all go. These people would undoubtedly take a break from their work, and when they did, as much as he feared doing so, he would call Gannon for help.

•

Chapter 77

G. Benjamin Whittington thrust a copy of Jason's order into Blackthorn's hand and asked, "Mr. Blackthorn, is this company forwarding any of the records of the wells we're being sued over to an outside firm?"

"I have no idea," Blackthorn lied, "and even if we are, I don't see that as being any of your business."

"Well, it may be everyones business now because this new attorney, Jason Stevens, blindsided us with an implication of just that at this morning's hearing. We weren't prepared for it. He got a clause included in his order specifically giving him immediate access to records held in the hands of third parties. I had the distinct impression that he knows something we don't."

Blackthorn's heart raced. Could they possibly know about Popeson? "Did he say anything specific?"

"You mean, did he name names?"

"Yeah, that's what I mean."

"No, but sometimes you can tell as much from what an attorney doesn't say as from what he does. I ask you again. Is Gannon Oil placing records related to this lawsuit into the hands of third parties?"

"How should I know?" Blackthorn growled. "I'm the security chief, not the head of accounting."

"I'd strongly advise you to find out fast," Whittington said. "I don't think it's in anyone's interest to have Stevens rummaging around in the records of one of our vendors without us being aware of it."

Blackthorn's anxiety rose, but he could say nothing to this man. He had to contact Popeson right away. "You're right, Whittington. I totally agree. I'll check into it. Is there anything else?" Blackthorn's response was a clear dismissal.

"No sir, nothing that can't wait."

"Well, thank you," Blackthorn said as he clapped the man on the back and guided him to the door. "Good job today, Whittington. We appreciate the work you do for us." He politely but firmly shoved the attorney out of his office and then dove for the phone.

Popeson's phone was answered by the accountant's ancient, cantankerous receptionist. "This is Lucas Blackthorn," he barked. "I need to talk to Stan."

"I'm sorry, Mr. Blackthorn, but Mr. Popeson is in a meeting at the moment."

"For how long?"

"I'm sorry, sir, he didn't say. Can I have him call you?"

"Yeah, you do that." Blackthorn knew better than to argue with this woman who took her job as Popeson's gatekeeper very seriously. "You have him call me the minute he's through."

Blackthorn hung up. If Popeson didn't call right away he'd drive over there himself.

Chapter 78

Jason saw that Popeson was a very meticulous man. Each file jacket carefully annotated each meter number, and below that, all the Gannon well numbers whose production the meter secretly carried. Jason was elated to be holding proof that the supposedly dry wells were still in production, but at the same time, somewhat sad that Danny wasn't here to see it.

Chaco and Kathy quickly developed a routine. She removed a file, noted its contents in her laptop, and handed it off to Chaco, who then scanned the contents into another laptop computer. While Chaco copied the file contents, Kathy photographed each file jacket, preserving a copy of Popeson's meticulous annotations.

Once Jason saw that the operation was going smoothly, he decided to see what else he could find. He strode directly to the last cabinet on the right-hand wall, which was labeled differently than the rest. The first drawer was labeled "Capital Security Improvements." The second, "Accounts Payable." It was the third and fourth drawers that caught his attention. The third said, "Well Transfer Documents." The fourth said, "Sunshine Banking/Corporate Filings."

As Jason unlocked the cabinet, Popeson started from his morose lethargy and wailed, "No! No! No! You cannot open that!" He jumped up and tried to push Jason aside. Jason chuckled at the man's feeble attempt. "Mr. Popeson, there's obviously something you wish to hide in here. I can see from the labels that these drawers contain Sunshine Group financial documents. They're discoverable under our order." He turned the key and went immediately to the fourth drawer.

"Mr. Stevens, I demand that you close that drawer."

Jason reached in and removed the first file, which was labeled "Gannon/Sunshine Transfer Account." He held it up for Popeson to see. "This file has the name of both Gannon Oil and the Sunshine Group on it. If you are certain the contents of this drawer are not related to my lawsuit, we have a very simple solution. We'll bag this stuff up, take it down to the courthouse right now, show it to Judge Oliver and let her decide whether I get to see it or not."

"I . . . I . . ." Popeson searched for words in rebuttal, but none came. He had to call Gannon right now. But it was a conversation that couldn't take place in front of Stevens. Perhaps he could get just a short delay.

"Mr. Stevens, it would be best if I contacted my client about this matter. I demand that you stop what you're doing until I have a chance to consult with him."

"You're certainly free to talk to your client, Mr. Popeson. I assume you're talking about Red Gannon. There's nothing he can say or do that will stop this process."

"Bastard!" Popeson screamed. He leaped from behind his desk and sprinted out of the office.

*

Popeson scurried down the stairs to the sidewalk as fast as his aged but spry legs could carry him, stabbing out Red Gannon's private number on his cell phone as he went. All he got was the man's voice mail. "Red, Red, this is Stan. Call me! For God's sake, call me back as soon as you get this message."

He tried Gannon's cell number and got voice mail there as well. He tried three other numbers that were possibilities to no avail. Though he found it distasteful, Popeson turned to his only other choice, Lucas Blackthorn.

"Mr. Blackthorn's office. This is Jennifer."

"Blackthorn. Give me Blackthorn," Popeson shouted.

"Who's calling, sir?" Blackthorn's assistant was maddeningly calm and deliberate.

"Stan Popeson. I must speak to Mr. Blackthorn immediately."

"I'm sorry, Mr. Popeson. Mr. Blackthorn stepped out for a moment."

"Well, page him or something. Look, young lady, I know you don't

284

know who I am, but trust me, I'm very important to Gannon Oil. I've got to talk to him this minute. It's a matter of life and death."

"I'm sorry, Mr. Popeson. The best I can do is give him your message and have him call you as soon as he's back."

*

Jason's eyes widened as he thumbed through the first file from the fourth drawer. It contained statements from a bank in Albuquerque, all of them neatly arranged from the newest to the oldest. In front of the statements was a small bank register book. He opened it and discovered two entries per month, a credit and a withdrawal in identical amounts. Dutifully recorded with each withdrawal was the notation of a wire transfer number and destination name. He opened a second file and four a bank book and bank statements from the Royal Bank of the Bahamas, complete with similarly annotated wire transfer information. The trail continued through the Bank of Scotland, then to a bank on the Isle of Wight, then through three additional European banks, finally ending up at the Old Dominion Bank of Grand Cayman Island.

"Holy Cow," Jason said when he saw the Grand Cayman bank balance. $677,934,082.00. "Kathy, you're not going to believe what I've just found."

While the file had the numbers, to be truly damning, the numbers had to be connected to names. While Chaco and Kathy hurriedly copied the new-found banking information, Jason went searching. He remembered how quickly Popeson had closed the ledger sitting on top of his desk. He opened it, and flipped through the pages.

The first few pages were filled with what appeared to be journal entries for some sort of construction project, one that used a lot of fencing. Seven pages from the end, he came to a journal section entitled "Cayman Account." The first column said "Month." It began with a date almost four years ago. The next column said "Gross Receipts." As Jason glanced down the column, the monthly numbers grew at an impressive rate. The next five columns had names: Red Gannon, Stan Popeson, Lucas Blackthorn, Jim Parker, and some guy named Marlin Webster. Under each was a dollar figure that likewise grew month by month.

The journal entries continued for two more pages, right up to the previous month. The figures under the names had grown to tens of millions of dollars for each. His hands shook. "Kathy, Chaco. This is it!"

He tipped the ledger in their direction. "This has all the names and dollar amounts from Gannon on down. It nails them all to the wall. These ledger sheets are too big for our scanner, so we need to get them out of here long enough to get to a copy machine that can handle them. We need to do that before Popeson gets back."

"That won't fit in our banker's boxes either," Kathy said. "We don't have any sacks or anything. What should we do?"

Jason looked around and thought for a moment before a solution hit him, but Kathy wouldn't like it. She wore the same suit she'd worn to court that morning. It had a tailored-looking skirt that wasn't form fitting, but neither was it full. It just might work as long as she was careful and no one looked at her too closely.

Jason tore at the post binding clasps and removed the ledger's hard cover, then carefully extracted the one-inch-thick stack of sheets. "Kathy, close the door a little, but not all the way, then step behind it and turn your back to me. Chaco, stand in front of that door so no one can come in.

Kathy did as instructed while Chaco watched curiously. Jason held the sheets of paper up behind her. "Yup," he said. "I think it'll fit. Where's your jacket?"

"On the chair in the foyer. Why?"

"Chaco, could you grab it?"

When Chaco returned, Jason said to Kathy, "You're our means of transporting these papers out of here. We need to put them under your skirt and make them secure enough for you to walk them out of here.

"We've got our court order," she protested. "Can't we just take them somewhere else to be copied?"

"I don't want Popeson to even know we've seen them. I'm sure he's calling his lawyer, who will do everything he can to stop us. Rather than having to take a chance on his lawyer somehow blocking us, I want the issue to be a matter of *fete accompli*.

"Okay, okay," Kathy relented, "but just remember whose rear end you're messing with here. Get cute and you'll be eating those papers."

Jason chuckled. "What, with Chaco standing right here? Truth is, I'm a lot more worried about what Bri might do if she were watching this. Turn around, girl, and let's get this done before Popeson comes back."

With Jason's help, it took only a few seconds for Kathy to install the long ledger papers under her waistband and cover them with her skirt. Once all was settled in, Kathy looked nearly normal, except for a slightly rectangular hump in the place of her normally round derriere. She put her belt back on and cinched it tight so that none of the papers would work loose as she walked.

"You're a little lumpy in the backfield," Jason chuckled, "but I think you're good to go." He handed her the keys to his Escalade and said, "Take them there. Chaco, you take the box of stuff we've copied so far and use it to block the view from behind. We need to get everything we've copied away from this building."

Chapter 79

This gentleman wants you to call him, Jennifer said as soon as Blackthorn strode back into his office, "He said it's urgent." Blackthorn looked at the name on the note and called immediately.

"Lucas!" the man screamed in his ear as soon as the call connected. "You've got to do something. They're going through my records right now!"

"What?" Popeson talked so fast that Blackthorn could scarcely understand. "Slow down, Stan. Say it again."

Popeson took a deep breath and started over. "A little over an hour ago, an attorney and two other people showed up at my office with a court order that gives them access to all my Gannon Oil records. They know about the Sunshine Group." The panic in his voice rose. "They're in there right now going through everything."

"What do you mean 'everything?' Tell me what they've got so far."

"I mean *everything*. They started with the SR-30 reports on all those collector wells we transferred. It's like they knew exactly what to look for. A few minutes ago, that attorney found the bank statements that lead from Albuquerque all the way to Grand Cayman Island. They're making copies right now! Red promised me nothing like this would ever happen. I'm too old for this, Lucas, you've got to . . ."

Blackthorn cut him off. "Shut up, Stan! I don't care what you were promised. I'll get one of our attorneys over there as fast as I can. You get your ass back in there and slow them down. Understand?" He clicked off and dialed another number.

"This is Blackthorn. Give me Whittington — now!"

"I'm sorry Mr. Blackthorn," Whittington's assistant apologized, "Mr. Whittington has taken our other staff counsels to lunch."

"Lunch?" Blackthorn thundered. "I told him to stay available. Where'd he go?"

"I believe they went to the El Papagallo over in Aztec."

"Give me his cell number. You page him at the restaurant and tell him to call me immediately. Got that?"

"Yes, sir." She gave him the number.

After five rings he got a recording saying, "We're sorry. This phone is out of our service area or is currently unavailable. Leave a message at the beep."

"This is Blackthorn! Call me!" Lucas shouted, then slammed the receiver down. There was nothing to do but wait.

Six agonizing minutes later, his phone finally rang. "Whittington?"

"Yes, it is. I understand you're looking for me."

"You're damned right I'm looking for you. I told you to stay available. That Stevens guy is taking apart a friend's office right now. You need to get over there and stop him."

Whittington paused, then asked, "Is this the third party I was concerned about earlier?"

"Yeah, yeah, so I'm busted."

Whittington paused again, then said, "I'll do what I can. Give me the address."

"135 South Animas. Hurry!"

"I'm on my way.

*

Kathy and Chaco were nearly at the bottom of the stairs when Stanley Popeson burst through the door and rushed up, seemingly oblivious to their presence. He flung his office door open just as Jason placed a ledger that looked like the one whose contents had been pilfered back on Popeson's desk.

"No you don't!" the man shouted. He rushed over and jerked the ledger from Jason's hand. "My attorney is on his way. You are not to touch another scrap of paper in this office until he sees it first." Popeson pushed Jason aside, opened a drawer in his desk, shoved the ledger in, and slammed it shut just as Chaco returned.

Popeson wagged a finger in his direction and said, "You just stay right where you are, Mr. What-ever-your-name-is. Don't you touch one more thing."

"I have a suggestion," Jason volunteered. "Why don't we all leave until your attorney gets here? You can lock up this office. We'll wait out in the foyer."

"I'll do it on one condition," Popeson replied, "and that's that you give me back the keys to those cabinets."

Jason tried to look reluctant before tossing the now unnecessary key bag to the accountant. "I guess it's okay for now," he said, "but I'll expect them back once your attorney's here."

*

"Nice job, Kathy," Jason said as he slid into the driver's seat of the Escalade. "I know it was embarrassing, We'll have to give the original copy of the ledger back. I want you to go straight to the court clerk's office and have them make two certified copies. File one with the court and we'll keep the other in Vic's safe. Bring the original back here."

Watching her drive away, Jason couldn't help his nervousness. The smoking gun they'd been hoping for was riding with her in that SUV.

Chapter 80

Lucas Blackthorn bounded up the stairs three steps at a time. Out of breath, he flung open the door to Popeson's office and found the accountant pacing behind the counter. A man in a suit—Stevens, he presumed—and another guy who looked vaguely familiar, stood chatting in the visitor's area. "Downstairs—now," Blackthorn barked at Popeson.

"Give it to me straight, Stan." Blackthorn said once they were outside. "Tell me everything."

Popeson's normally strong voice shook. "They got here just after noon." He described his office and how he kept his files. The more he said, the worse Blackthorn realized things were. "What about the Cayman accounting? Are they going to discover names?"

"He's got the banking information, but not the names to go with it. Trouble is, my master ledger has names, dates, amounts, everything. It's locked in my desk drawer right now, but Stevens knows it's there. If he gets his hands on that, it's over. We're all going to prison."

Ben Whittington pulled up in front of the building. "We've got to talk." Blackthorn hissed as Whittington exited. "That Stevens guy has been going through records for a couple of hours. There's a whole lot you don't know, and it can't be said in front of anybody but us. Let's walk." The trio set out at a brisk pace up Animas Street toward Main. "This is Stan Popeson." Blackthorn said to Whittington. "He's your new client."

Whittington hesitated. "I'm a staff attorney for Gannon Oil, not a private practitioner. I can't just take on an outside client without the company's written permission."

"Popeson does a lot of business for the company—stuff that's directly tied to the lawsuit the Indians filed. You'll get that written permission, but this guy needs an attorney right now. I'm officially authorizing you to represent him. Is that good enough?"

"If his work appears to be interrelated with that lawsuit, then yes, I can ethically represent him." He looked at Stan and asked, "Mr. Popeson, do you wish to retain me as your attorney?"

"Oh, yes," the man replied. "You've got to stop what's going on up there."

"Then anything you tell me from this point forward is protected by attorney/client privilege."

"That has to go for me too," Blackthorn said. "We've got to tell you some stuff you're not going to like. But I won't say a word unless I'm covered with that attorney/client thing too."

"As an officer of the corporation, you're covered as well unless you've willfully engaged in unlawful acts. For that you would need your own attorney. The same goes for you, Mr. Popeson. If what you tell me falls outside the legitimate business interests of Gannon Oil, I cannot represent you."

"Excuse us for a moment." Blackthorn said. He grabbed Popeson's arm and pulled him a short distance away. "What do you think?"

"I don't see that we have much choice."

"But how much do we tell him?"

Popeson mopped perspiration from his brow. "Just enough that he stops Stevens."

"But if he sees those records, he's going to know everything."

"I don't see how we can prevent that. Stevens saw me lock up that ledger and that's the first thing he's going to go after the instant he gets back in my office."

Blackthorn scratched his head. Then his features relaxed, "I think I've got a way out of this."

"How?"

"You let me worry about that. Let's talk to Whittington."

". . . so here's the bottom line," Blackthorn said. "That office contains the records of a very secret operation we've been running for over three years. I'm not going to give you the details, all I'm going to tell you is that it's critical that you stop this Stevens guy from going any further today. Can you do that?"

"No, Mr. Blackthorn, I can't. He has that court order, and you and Mr. Popeson both admit the records he's discovering are relevant to his lawsuit."

"Just what the hell can you do?" Blackthorn thundered.

"The best I can do is slow him down. I can object to everything he wants to look at and demand he not copy any more documents. He won't sit still for it, and we'll end up back in front of the judge in very short order. The judge will side with him."

"That's good enough. You and Popeson get up there and delay him as long as you can. If you can get him back to the courthouse, do it. Understand?"

*

Jason's patience was growing thin when he heard footsteps tromping up the stairs. G. Benjamin Whittington stepped through the door with Popeson.

"Well, well, Mr. Whittington. Are you the attorney of record for our friendly little accountant here?"

"Gannon Oil and Mr. Popeson's firm have interests in common that relate to your lawsuit, Mr. Stevens. Mr. Popeson is covered under an indemnification arrangement between his office and Gannon Oil."

Jason shook his head and said, "Fair warning, Counselor—the water here is much deeper than you probably know. How would you like to proceed?"

"The first thing is to review what you've already seen. I want to see every file you've opened and every page you've copied. Where are your copies, Mr. Stevens?"

"Not in this office, Mr. Whittington. They're in a very safe place."

Chapter 81

Blackthorn normally farmed this type of work out, but there was no time for such precautions. Thank God Marlin Webster was the mayor and had good control over the police and fire departments.

He hurried to Home Depot, where he purchased a pair of rubber gloves and a gallon of acetone solvent, the fastest and least traceable accelerant he knew of.

Popeson's "L"-shaped two-story building, with retail shops on the ground floor and office space above, took up nearly a half block in either direction, but it had long since lost its retail appeal to the new strip malls out on the east end. The building was empty, save for his second story offices, a ground-floor pawn shop at one end of the "L" and a small drapery maker on the other. A shoe repair shop occupied the small single-story building at that end that separated Popeson's building from the rear of a large store that fronted on Main Street.

The rear of the building was a weed-choked lot cut off by the surrounding commercial buildings. The lot was accessible by a narrow, dirty alley that ran its grimy length between Popeson's building and an abandoned service station on the corner.

The space directly beneath Popeson's upstairs office had once been a popular furniture store. But today, a heavy patina of accumulated dust on the windows obscured any outside view of the interior.

Blackthorn pried open one of the double rear-entry doors to the storage room behind the defunct furniture store with ease. The dark, cobweb-filled space was full of old cardboard boxes, and musty, unsold overstuffed chairs. The smell of mildewed upholstery roiled his stomach.

Blackthorn lit his way forward with a small metal flashlight, batting cobwebs aside as he went. He found a dust-covered sofa near the front wall of the storage room that was perfect for his purpose. Gathering everything flammable he could get his hands on, he stacked it on top of the sofa until the moldering mound nearly reached the ceiling. An old broom handle aided him in knocking several of the drop-down ceiling panels aside, exposing the dry wooden sub-floor of the second story.

He took a quick look outside to make sure no one was in the area, then returned and doused the mound with acetone, trailing the last of the volatile liquid to the door. He had to work fast. The acetone on the floor was already evaporating. He lit a match and ignited the flammable liquid trail. A lick of flame raced to the incendiary heap and exploded it into an instant inferno. He closed the door and in less than a minute was on his way back to his office. The empty acetone can ended up in a dumpster behind a grocery store over a mile away from Popeson's office.

As he pulled into his parking space at the Gannon Building, he heard the fire sirens cranking up in the city below. *Don't hurry. Please let that building burn to the ground.*

Chapter 82

Jason and Whittington stood in front of the first file cabinet, conducting their review of documents Jason had already copied. Chaco was seated beside the door while Popeson nervously observed from his desk. Suddenly, one of Popeson's workers rushed in with a frightened look.

"Get out of here," Popeson scolded. "I told you I was not to be disturbed."

"But Mr. Popeson, we have a problem. I think there's a fire!"

"What?" Popeson leaped from his chair. "Show me!" he commanded as he rushed out of the room.

Jason caught a distinct whiff of smoke. He looked at Chaco and said, "Better go check it out."

With the room empty of all save the two attorneys, Jason addressed Whittington. "This is a fine mess you've gotten yourself into, Counselor. How'd you manage to let them drag you in?"

"Not by choice, believe me." Whittington chuckled. "I've never heard of this place. Blackthorn called me in a panic and said one of their vendors was in trouble. I have no idea what the relationship between Gannon and Popeson is."

"You're about to get the education of your life."

Whittington grinned. "That's why we get paid the big . . ."

Chaco burst into the room, cutting the man off. "Jason, we've got to get out of here. The whole place is on fire!"

"Seriously?"

"Seriously, man. We've got to move!"

Jason heard screams of fright from the women exiting the outer office. A huge plume of smoke wafted into the room. "Let's go, Counselor," he shouted at Whittington.

Blinding black smoke choked the hallway. Jason thought the floor spongy. How could a fire accelerate so quickly? Chaco led the way to the stairs. Just as they began their descent, flames broke through the wall about half-way down, turning the stairwell into a chimney that funneled hot gasses and smoke up toward them.

"Follow me," Chaco shouted. He dashed up the north hallway. Jason and Whittington followed, holding their shirtsleeves to their faces to try to filter some of the smoke.

Visibility was zero. At the end of the hall, Jason hit the wall hard. An instant later, Whittington plowed into his back, slamming him into the wall again. Chaco must have turned off somewhere.

"Jason!" Chaco's voice called from behind and to their left. Jason felt his way along the wall until he came to a doorway. A hand reached out and pulled him into the room. Whittington was close behind.

Chaco pulled the door to an empty office closed, then opened the window to clear some of the smoke. He looked down on Animas street and saw passers-by staring up at the smoke and flames pouring from the building

"Where are we?" Jason choked out.

"Last office to the north."

"How are we going to get out?" Whittington asked just as a fit of coughing took him.

"Got any parachutes?" Chaco asked.

Jason laughed, but the laugh turned into his own gut-wrenching cough. "Hey, it's only one story to the street. What can that cost? A broken leg—maybe two?"

"Maybe not." Whittington responded. "As I recall, the building next door is only one story."

Chaco stuck his head out the window and confirmed, "You're right. But how we going to get there?"

"We're going to kick our way out. This is one of those old, unreinforced masonry buildings. If we get through the drywall, we can probably kick through the bricks to the outside. It's worth a try. Besides, we can always jump if we have to."

"Makes sense. Where do we start?" Chaco asked.

"Right here." Whittington put his foot through the wallboard in the middle of the north wall. In a matter of seconds, they tore through the drywall and insulation and found that, just as Whittington had predicted, they were looking at the back side of a bare brick wall.

They cleared away the rest of the sheetrock and insulation between a couple of wall studs then Chaco and Whittington kicked at the bricks as Jason watched.

At first, they kicked separately in a staccato rhythm that gave them no progress. Whittington stopped Chaco and said, "We have to kick at the same time, and close together."

The carpet beneath the door started to smolder. "Whatever you do, do it fast," Jason shouted.

The third concerted kick made the bricks bulge outward—not much, but enough to loosen some of the mortar. The next kick bowed the wall considerably. "This time!" Chaco shouted. Their feet hit the wall at the same time with tremendous force. The bricks bowed and several collapsed onto the roof of the building next door. Soon there was a hole large enough to crawl through.

The room was filling with acrid, poisonous smoke. "Come on, Jason," Whittington shouted as he disappeared through the hole.

"Go, Chaco!" Jason yelled. The man didn't argue. Then Jason dove through himself. The bricks ripped and tore at his skin and clothing, but he felt nothing. Two sets of hands grabbed him and pulled him the rest of the way through.

"Over here," they heard a man's voice call. He stood on an aluminum extension ladder, peering over the edge. The three men scrambled to the ladder and climbed to the safety of the sidewalk below.

"Thanks," Jason said to their rescuer.

"I couldn't figure out what was going on," the man said. "I was working in the back when stuff started dropping on my roof."

The conversation was drowned out by horns and sirens as the first of several Farmington fire trucks came screaming down Animas Street. The three men shook hands with their rescuer then moved across the street and down to the corner where Popeson and his four office workers were huddled. Jason thought Popeson seemed disappointed when he saw that that he and the others had survived.

In a matter of minutes fire poured from all the upstairs windows. The first part of the building to go was the south-facing wall, which collapsed outward onto Broad-way. The east side fell into the inferno shortly thereafter.

There was little the fire department could do. A half-hour later, the northwest corner was all that remained standing. Sadly, the small shoe repair building owned by their rescuer was not spared. The fire department had to sacrifice it in order to keep the fire from spreading all the way to Main Street.

Jason felt someone brush his shoulder. He turned and found Kathy silently embracing Chaco, tears streaming down her cheeks. Then she broke her embrace and wrapped her arms tightly around Jason's neck. "I leave you two alone for ten seconds and look what happens," she choked out." Are both of you all right?"

"We're fine," he said, "but now we know what a hot dog would do if it had legs. Where are you parked?"

"Over on Orchard Street. They've got traffic blocked off."

"I'll walk back to the car with you. We need to give Whittington back the original of the ledger. Chaco, keep an eye out here. Don't let Whittington leave."

Jason retrieved the ledger sheets and left Kathy to keep watch over the certified copy. When he returned, the fire department was mopping up the remaining hot spots. Whittington and Chaco were standing side-by-side behind Popeson and his shell-shocked office staff. "Well, Counselor," Jason said to Whittington, "I don't know about you, but I count this as one of my more unusual endings to an examination order. I told you the water ran real deep in this case."

"That's an understatement," Whittington said. "Unless I miss my guess, someone is very determined that you not see those records. As fast as that building went up, I don't see any way this fire could have come from natural causes."

"Fortunately, there's something left." Jason tapped Popeson on the shoulder and addressed the man who had just watched his life's work go up in flames. "Mr. Popeson, you will witness that I am returning the contents of the ledger that you left lying on your desk. We've copied it and filed a certified copy with the court."

"Wha—what?"

Popeson appeared dazed, like he didn't quite comprehend what Jason said. Jason handed Whittington the ledger pages. "This is a ledger we discovered in Popeson's office that confirms the participation of both of your clients and several others in the fraud conspiracy we've alleged in our lawsuit. Talk to your client, Mr. Whittington. He'll give you the bad news about the ledger's contents."

Jason nodded to Chaco, indicating it was time for them to go. He turned and took a couple of steps before turning back. "By the way, Mr. Whittington, thanks for what you did in that building. Without you we might not have made it out. You watch yourself, Counselor, you're swimming with some very dangerous sharks. I think one of them just tried to kill you."

Chapter 83

Chaco's Wagoneer followed Jason's Escalade closely all the way back to Bondad. When they arrived, Chaco asked Jason to join him and Kathy in the Wagoneer rather than going into the office. Jason climbed into the back seat.

"Jason, how far are you from being able to go to trial?" Chaco asked.

"We're there. We could go to trial today."

Chaco looked at Kathy and said, "It's time. Someone's going to get killed."

Kathy nodded.

"I need to talk to Mr. Stewart,"Chaco said, turning back to Jason. "Can you give me his number please?" Chaco took out his cell phone.

"You want it now?"

"Right now."

"What are you going to do?"

"I'm going to solve his case for him. I want him to come up here — tonight."

Jason was confused. "We have a lot of good evidence for the civil lawsuit, Chaco, but nothing that moves Danny's murder case forward."

"Do you trust me?" Jason could hear irritation in Chaco's voice.

"Of course I do. It's not a matter of ..."

"Then stop arguing and give me the number." Jason did so.

Then Chaco asked Jason to step out of the car. Confused and perplexed by the man's unexpected request, Jason complied, pacing outside as he watched rather than listened to Chaco's conversation with his friend.

When finished, Chaco stepped out of his car and said, "I'll let you brief the others about what happened today. Kathy and I are leaving. Mr. Stewart will be here around ten o'clock. Could you have everyone in the office then?"

"Sure, Chaco. What's going on."

"Like I said, you're going to have to trust me on this one. I mean no disrespect. Please, just do as I ask."

Without other options, Jason simply nodded.

Chapter 84

The conspirators were gathered for a late-night emergency meeting at Gannon's ranch. "So how bad is it?" Gannon scowled.

"It's gone. Everything's gone," Popeson lamented, hanging his head.

"I'm not talking about the fire," Gannon snarled. "I'm talking about what that attorney got."

Popeson sank even lower in his chair. "They know about The Sunshine Group. They found the SR-30's. They copied the bank records and the ledger where I kept all the Cayman Island accounting."

"In other words, they got everything."

"Yes."

"Was my name in any of that stuff?" Marlin Webster asked.

"The ledger had a complete breakdown of all our shares in the Cayman account."

"How could you be so stupid as to keep paper records of everything right in your office?" Blackthorn asked angrily.

"My office was perfectly safe until you lost control of that lawsuit," Popeson snapped back. "Nobody told me there was going to be a proceeding that could open my office records like a can of tuna fish. I've got a couple of questions of my own, Mr. Blackthorn. How'd that attorney know about The Sunshine Group? How'd he know the SR-30s were being shipped to my office? Where'd he get his hands on a list of the wells? That information didn't come from my office. The only people who knew about my involvement in all this are sitting in this room right now."

Blackthorn had no answer.

"I'll tell you where," Red Gannon said quietly. "We've got a spy. It's the only explanation. Someone outside this group knows about Stan and the wells. Any ideas?"

"Maybe," Blackthorn said. "The accounts receivable manager has a new assistant. A few days ago, she plugged an unauthorized USB drive into her computer. Parsons let her off with a warning, but he suspects she copied our master production file. I put her on close surveillance and assigned one of our security agents to follow her. I'm supposed to get my first report from him in the morning."

"Not soon enough," Gannon said. "Wake your man up and see what he's got."

"I just wonder if it's all too late," Jim Parker said, shaking his head.

"As do I," Webster echoed. "Thanks to Popeson here, they've got my name. They even know how much we've taken. We have a lot bigger problem than just losing that lawsuit. We could all go to prison."

Webster's statement hung in the air until Gannon broke the silence. "So how do we contain the damage?"

"We've got to find out how far the information's been spread," Blackthorn responded. "Hopefully it's still containable. The key may be this Sanders woman. If we can somehow connect her with this new attorney, the Stevens guy, we can grab her and sweat her until she gives up the information. If it looks like we have a containable group, we have to take them out, and fast."

"Is that always your solution?" Webster shouted. "We're all still holding our breath hoping we've covered up our connection to the Whitehorse killing. How the hell do you propose to massacre several people all at once and make it look like an accident?"

"You got a better idea?" Red Gannon growled.

Webster had been out on this dangerous limb before. He dropped his eyes to the floor and said, "I don't, Red."

"We have to close the lid on this right now," Gannon said. "Get back to Farmington, Blackthorn, and see what your man has on this Sanders woman. If she's connected to Stevens we drop the hammer on her — hard."

Chapter 85

As Chaco requested, Jason gathered Bri, Vic, and Angie into the office. "Jason, they tried to kill you," Bri cried as he revealed the events of the day. Tears streamed down her cheeks. "When is this all going to end?"

"So what's going on with Chaco and Kathy?" Angie asked.

"I don't know. Chaco made a call to Doyle Stewart. He's supposed to be here around ten o'clock. We need to go through the information we copied today before he gets here so I can lay it all out for him."

"Well, there goes supper," Angie chuckled. "Why should this night be any different?"

*

Chaco and Kathy were still absent when Stewart arrived at nine fifty. Jason briefed him on the events of the day.

"I'm glad you didn't end up roasted," Doyle said. "Any idea about the origin of the fire?"

"My first guess would be Blackthorn. He was in the building briefly and saw us there. He certainly didn't want us to see those records."

"Let's see what you've found."

For more than two hours, Jason laid out the evidence trail, taking Stewart from the notice of cessation each family had received at the beginning right up to the records they'd copied at Popeson's office that documented production numbers of all the wells. He showed him the transfer dates of all the Sunshine wells and the huge jumps in production at each terminal well as the clandestine pipelines were connected. The coup-de-grâce was the summary of the money transfers and the breakdown of credits to each of the conspirators contained in the damning ledger pages.

"Chaco thought this might be enough for you to issue arrest warrants maybe as early as tomorrow," Jason said. "I'm assuming that's why he wanted you up here on such short notice."

"It's more than enough evidence to get arrest warrants for criminal fraud. But on this kind of thing, we usually go to a federal grand jury for indictments unless there's an imminent danger of physical harm or probable cause in a capital crime. I'll have to take this back to Albuquerque to the grand jury. The best I can promise is that I'll be back within ten days or so to serve at least five arrest warrants."

Without announcing themselves, Chaco and Kathy quietly entered the room. They'd obviously been listening "If you can issue immediate warrants for a capital crime, your trip won't be wasted," Chaco said.

"Chaco, Kathy, where have you two been?" Angie scolded. "We've been worried sick."

"Believe me, it's been important. Vic, Kathy and I need to use your office in the house. Doyle, Jason, we'll need you in there as well. I'm sorry, but I need to ask the rest of you to remain out here. This may take a while."

*

Once in Vic's office, Chaco invited Jason and Doyle to take seats. Kathy stood beside the door. Sitting cock-legged on a corner of Vic's desk, Chaco said, "Jason, in the next few minutes, you're probably going to be very angry with me, but I want you to know that what I've done has been absolutely necessary. You've become a great friend. I hope you can forgive me."

"There's nothing to forgive. I couldn't have accomplished half the stuff we've been able to do without you."

"There is something to forgive," Chaco said, looking toward the door.

Jason caught a flicker of movement in the hall just before a person stepped from the darkened hallway into the light of the office. Suddenly it seemed as if the air had been sucked from the room. Jason rose from his chair in disbelief. "Danny?" he stammered, afraid to believe his eyes.

"Hello, Jason."

Tears blurred Jason's vision, as two great arms encircled him in a tremendous bear hug. He knew he was blubbering something or another, but later could never remember what. Finally he stepped back and said, "I've got about a million questions to ask you." Then he turned to Stewart. "Doyle, this is my best friend and current law partner, the late Danny Whitehorse."

Looking confused, Stewart tentatively extended his hand. "I've got to say that meeting you is one of the bigger surprises of my life. I've been working on your murder case."

"Glad to meet you, Mr. Stewart. Chaco tells me good things about you."

"Speaking of Chaco," Jason said, turning his eyes to the man who sat grinning broadly from the corner of the desk. "Danny, I'm going to have to talk to you about this employee. He's never to be trusted again. If I weren't so glad to see you, we'd have to fire him."

"I've threatened that for years, but he just keeps hanging around."

"And as for *you!*" Jason turned to Kathy, who was dabbing away tears. "I suppose you've been in on this all along?"

"Almost. We've wanted to tell you a thousand times."

"I know you don't do handshakes, but I have at least one hug left. May I?"

She stepped forward and gave Jason her second long, heartfelt hug of the day.

"Okay, okay," Danny said. "Let's breakup this love fest. There's someone else I want you two to meet. Max, come on in here."

A round, bespectacled man stepped into the room and cast a wary eye at Jason and Doyle.

"Gentlemen, this is Max Schultz, one of the men Gannon Oil sent to murder me. He has a lot to tell, but he's going to need an immunity agreement from you, Mr. Stewart, before he does. When I tell you why, I'm sure you'll have no problem granting his request."

Chapter 86

An hour and a half later, the group made their way back to the studio-cum-office. Chaco had shuffled back and forth between the house and the studio to assure the others that their wait would be over soon. On his last trip, he retrieved Vic.

"What's going on?" the man asked.

"You're about to have the shock of your life. I want you to know about it so you can be near your wife when we tell the girls."

Vic's reaction was even more ebullient than Jason's. "You son of a bitch. You son of a bitch," he said as he repeatedly clapped Danny on the back.

*

Danny remained out of sight just outside the studio door while Chaco settled everyone and said, "Angie, Brianna, we're sorry to keep you in the dark for so long. I'm going to tell you the same thing I told Jason almost two hours ago. You're going to learn something in a few minutes that may make you both very angry with me." He went on to give the girls the same speech he'd given Jason, then said, "Okay Kathy, it's your turn."

"I'm not much of one for words," she said softly. "Chaco and I have a secret we've had to keep from you for a very long time. We feel bad, but it was the only way we could keep you safe. You're going to learn just how much danger every person associated with Danny Whitehorse has actually been in. It's a danger that still exists, as we saw by that fire this afternoon. But things have come together and we can reveal that Danny Whitehorse is actually alive, and he's here right now."

"What?" Bri and Angie cried out as their hands flew to their mouths to cover their shock. Bri turned to Jason in bewilderment as tears streamed down her face. Jason took her in his arms and felt the sting of his own tears for the second time that night. "Is it true?" she asked.

"It's true Bri. He's here. And he can't wait to see you."

Jason heard a great wailing cry coming from Angie and saw Vic trying to attend her, as he was Bri.

"Where is he?" Bri swiped at her tears.

"I'm right here, little sister," Danny said, stepping from the doorway.

Bri broke from Jason's embrace, flew across the room, and leaped at Danny, nearly knocked him off his feet. She hugged his neck so hard, Jason feared she would choke him. "Oh, Danny, Danny," she sobbed as she took his face in her hands and kissed his cheeks and forehead over and over.

Angie arose from her chair so shakily that Vic had to help her up. She walked to where Bri was folded around her Diné brother and waited patiently, dabbing at tears as they came. Bri finally loosened her grip and saw Angie waiting her turn. She stepped aside and embraced Jason almost as hard as she had Danny.

Angie brought another kind of greeting. She stepped squarely in front of Danny, hesitated a moment as she looked hard into his eyes, then slapped him hard across the face. The sound reverberated across the room. "How dare you?" she spat. "We love you! How dare you break our hearts? How could you let us mourn you at your funeral while you're off somewhere laughing at our foolishness?" She raised her hand to strike again, but Vic caught her arm and spun her around. She jerked out of his grip and turned back to Danny. "Danny Whitehorse, I hate…" She never finished her sentence as she wobbled ominously on her feet and dissolved into great, wrenching sobs. Danny and Vic both stepped forward to steady her.

Once she regained a bit of composure, Danny said, "Angie, I'm so sorry, but like Chaco said, this was the only way to keep you and everyone else safe. Please forgive me You'll understand when we tell you why it had to be done this way."

Angie softened and, encircled his neck with her long arms. She

309

whispered, "I'm so glad you're alive."

Once Bri and Angie settled themselves, Danny asked everyone to sit down, then excused himself for a moment. When he returned, he stood just inside the open door of the studio. He gave Bri an impish look, winked and said, "You're going to love this, little sister." He looked at Jason and said, "There's someone here you've never met. He extended his hand back through the doorway and looked to take someone's hand. To Jason's surprise, a petite, long-haired Native American woman stepped in.

"Amanda," Bri squealed with delight.

"Well I'll be damned," Vic muttered, giving Angie a questioning look.

"Jason," Danny said, "I'd like to introduce you to my wife, Amanda Lujan Whitehorse."

"What?" Bri and Angie cried out for the second time that night.

"It's true," Amanda said with a smile. We were married two weeks ago." She held out her left hand so everyone could see the ring.

What began as a reunion turned into a celebration. The girls surrounded Amanda, oohing and aweing and firing dozens of questions, while Jason extended Danny a congratulatory hand and asked a few questions of his own. Once a bit of calm settled over the group, Danny said, "Why don't we all sit down so that Chaco and I can tell you why I had to vanish."

Chapter 87

three months earlier

As Chaco walked to his vehicle from the well site they called Red-22, his mind wrestled with what Danny had said about the wild chase across the alkali flats and his near encounter with a fiery death at the hands of Lucas Blackthorn. It was more than just a simple assassination attempt, it was a sophisticated, coordinated attack using many people and significant resources.

Chaco watched Danny's retreating dust trail. Danny's attempt to return unaccompanied to Farmington last Saturday morning had been a failure on his part. It was a mistake he would not repeat.

Suddenly another vehicle's dust trail appeared a short distance north of where he and Danny had been talking. There were no roads there, only a deep, sandy wash. This vehicle too appeared to be headed toward the road.

Danny's pickup turned north toward Farmington and accelerated up the broad gravel highway, raising a great cloud of dust for Chaco to see. When the other vehicle reached the road, rather than leaving immediately, it stopped for a minute or so, then raised its own cloud of dust as it headed north in Danny's wake.

That guy's really moving, Chaco powered his Wagoneer onto the road, trying to catch up. At least two miles separated him and Danny, and a mile or so from the second vehicle. He pressed his accelerator hard.

Whoa, that doesn't make any sense! Chaco braked to a sliding stop where highway barricades blocked the road. The barricades hadn't been there when Danny passed or he would have stopped. That left only one possible source, and it was barreling after Danny at break-neck speed.

Chaco steered around the barriers and mashed down on his accelerator. At the same time, he reached into the glove box and retrieved his Glock 940 9mm semi-automatic pistol. He soon flew along at nearly seventy miles per hour on a road designed for forty-five.

The road took a wide swing around a set of low hills. Already, the two dust trails ahead had combined into one. Suddenly they disappeared altogether. The vehicles had stopped. Chaco cursed. He was still a minute or more behind.

Chaco halted behind the low hill where he calculated the two vehicles had stopped. The instant he opened his door, he heard gunfire. Crouching in a combat stance, he ran up the hill.

He'd halved the distance to the vehicles when the firing stopped. He heard another vehicle approach from the north which came to a sliding stop on the graveled surface. A voice boomed out, "Stop, Whitehorse!" The command was followed by the roar of a powerful handgun.

The thirty seconds it took him to crest the top of the hill felt like forever. He was about seventy yards from Danny's truck. A gray Dodge van was parked a short distance behind. Across the road and two hundred yards out into the shallow valley, three men stood around an inert body lying in a sagebrush clearing.

Please, God, don't let me be too late.

With the men's attention focused away from him, Chaco made his way to the side of the van and peered down.

The oldest man stood apart from the other two, a large-frame automatic held in his hand. The taller of the other two was dark-headed and lanky, carrying what looked like an oversized shotgun. But the proportions of the weapon didn't seem quite right. The third man was short and round, and appeared to be unarmed.

The older man kicked Danny in the ribs. It took all the control Chaco could muster to keep from stepping around the van door and opening fire. But at this range, the men would make difficult targets for a handgun. They might also simply shoot Danny in response.

Though the men were still one hundred and fifty yards away, Chaco could hear them quite clearly in the still desert air. "So, is he dead?" he heard the older man ask.

"No," the tall man answered, "just unconscious."

Maybe he wasn't too late. Chaco listened carefully as the men made plans to dispose of Danny. Presently, the older man turned and walked back to his vehicle. The taller man began making his way back to the van. As he got closer, Chaco recognized the weapon he carried was an M-203 40mm grenade launcher.

The white car left. *Good.* Now the odds were two to one. If he could take out the man coming up the hill without destroying the element of surprise, he would have a better-than-even chance of rescuing Danny. He concealed himself in a thick clump of sagebrush near the rear of the van.

The tall man opened the van's cargo doors, stuck his head inside and began rummaging around. Chaco slipped up beside him, taking care that the man in the valley couldn't see. The tall man was gathering items into a small canvas bag. Chaco audibly cocked his handgun and said in a quiet voice, "If you move I'll . . ."

The startled man reared straight up and crashed the back of his head into the van's doorframe, knocking himself out cold. His knees buckled and he went down, but as he fell, his temple struck hard on the steel ball of the van's trailer hitch. Chaco heard a sickening crunch, and in the next instant, the man lay at Chaco's feet in the throes of death spasms.

Chaco couldn't believe it. He'd never touched the guy. Now he had an utterly unexpected problem — a body to conceal. It would be only a matter of time until the man's partner came searching for him.

Chaco dragged the body into the barrow pit where it would be less noticeable, then squatted on his haunches, trying to figure out what to do next.

"Tony — where are you?" the shorter man shouted up at the van. A couple of minutes later, he came puffing up the hill and stepped around the open rear door — right into Chaco's Glock, pointed squarely between his eyes. "On your knees, now!" Chaco barked. The man froze for a moment, his eyes staring cross-eyed down the sides of the barrel. His mouth worked, but no sound came. Then he slowly sank to his knees.

"Lay down," Chaco commanded. "Extend your arms straight out. Do anything else and I'll blow your head off. Understand?"

The man nodded and pitched himself forward as commanded, his head only inches from the pool of fresh blood left by his partner.

Chaco placed a knee in the middle of the man's back, shoved the

Glock hard against his head, and asked, "What's your name?"

"Ma—Max Schultz," the man stuttered. Eyeing the pool of blood, Max asked, "Where's Tony?"

"He's dead."

Max appeared to think about that for a moment, then asked, "Are you going to kill me?"

"Depends on what you've done to my friend down there.?"

Shultz's voice quavered as he replied. "He's okay. Really, he is. He's just asleep."

"What do you mean, 'asleep'?"

"It's the gas. It doesn't kill you. Just knocks you out. You'll see. He'll be waking up soon."

Chaco had to get to Danny, but first, he had to secure this man. His eye fell on a bin in the van door containing a number of zip ties. He shoved the gun barrel harder into the man's head. "I'm going to stand up. Don't you move, understand?"

He grabbed three of the ties. "Give me your hands." The man's girth made it difficult for him to put his hands completely behind his back, so Chaco helped, painfully he hoped. He secured two ties around the man's wrists. The third one went between the wrists and looped around the man's belt, arresting all but the most limited arm movement. Then he rolled the rotund man over.

Max's glasses were half off his head. The lenses were so thick, Chaco was sure Max was functionally blind without them. He stuffed the glasses into his shirt pocket and said, "Get up."

Max tried, but with his hands trussed, couldn't make it. Chaco grabbed an arm and assisted him to his feet. "We're going to walk down the hill and find out what you've done to my friend. You'd better pray he's all right."

*

A wave of vertigo washed over Danny as he struggled for consciousness. A sharp stab of pain flashed through his head as he opened his eyes. He closed them again.

Then he heard footsteps approaching. Rolling his head, he chanced opening his eyes again. Though he had a terrible headache, this time there was no flash of pain. He saw the fuzzy outline of two people.

"Sit down," he heard a deep voice command.

"Who's there?" Danny asked. "What are you doing?"

Chaco placed a comforting hand on Danny's shoulder. "*Ya' at' eehii* cousin. It's me, Chaco. Just take it easy. They knocked you out. This guy says you'll be fine in a few minutes."

"That's right, Mr. Whitehorse," an unfamiliar voice said. "You're still suffering the effects of that sleep gas. It will wear off shortly."

"Who's that?" Danny asked groggily.

"Says his name is Max. I've got him tied up. He's one of the men who attacked you."

Danny lay still for a moment, eyes closed, remembering the van that chased him. He remembered running for his life—remembered seeing Blackthorn—the puffs of white smoke and feeling as if he were falling into a deep tunnel. Then it was now, with no memory of anything between.

When he opened his eyes again, his vision was nearly normal. He looked up at Chaco. "I don't know who threw that left hook, but it was a doozy. I need to get up."

"Ouch," he cried as he turned and tried to raise himself. "Feels like I broke a rib."

"You took a pretty good kick from another guy who was here. You think you're okay?"

"I think so. Still a little woozy, but considering the alternative, I'm great. Help me up, would you?"

"So what's the story with this guy?" Danny asked when back on his feet.

"He and his buddy were going to kill you. They were going to put you in your truck and make it look like an accident . . . the old drunk Indian routine."

Danny looked up the hill and saw that the van was still there, right behind his truck. "Where are the others?"

"One left. I think it was that Blackthorn guy. This guy's partner had a little accident. He's dead."

"You killed him?"

"I never touched him. Like I said, he had an accident."

"Show me."

Chaco escorted Danny and the prisoner back to the van, where they put Max on the floor and tied his feet. Then Chaco showed Danny the body.

"That's bizarre," Danny said when Chaco described what happened.

"It is. But now we've either got to either get rid of this body or call the cops. If we call the cops, we'll probably be accused of murder."

"Tell me again what you overheard them planning."

"They were going to put you in your truck, shoot you up with something pretty nasty, pour some whiskey all over you then crash your truck. They said something about a fire."

"Blackthorn likes fire," Danny said with a shudder. "Chaco, take a look at that body. He could almost pass for an Indian."

Chaco looked. "He's got black hair and a dark complexion, but that's about as far as it goes. Why?"

"I told you that my original plan was to disappear for a while, maybe the best thing for me to do is die."

"Are you kidding? I just saved your sorry ass."

"Think about what would happen if I died. I've got Jason Stevens coming in. He can take over the case. I doubt Gannon would dare touch him. If everyone thought I was dead, it would take the heat off Kathy, you, and everybody else. It would give Jason a chance to move the case far enough along that there's nothing Gannon could do to stop it. You and I can concentrate on getting the mapping done and furnish the groundwork for Jason to build the case on.

"I've survived two assassination attempts in less than a week, and they're not going to stop. Why not let Blackthorn and Gannon think they succeeded? They won't find me if they stop looking. What do you think?"

"Who do we tell?"

"Nobody."

"Not your family? Not Bri or the Capalettis? Do you understand what you'd be putting them through?"

"I know, I know. But if Gannon suspects he didn't get me, his next move will be to try to get to me through the people I love. I couldn't live with it if one of you got hurt because of me."

Chaco pondered the thought for a moment, then said, "So how do you propose that we pull this off?"

"We give them a body—exactly as Blackthorn expects. This guy's about my size. We put my clothes on him, put him in my truck, and plant my ID. We have a little crash, a big fire and *voilà,* Danny Whitehorse is dead. You know Gannon's not going to allow an investigation. I doubt there'd even be an autopsy. The only remaining problem is, what do we do with this guy?" Danny jerked a thumb toward Max.

"The CIA gave a few of us some very interesting and highly classified military intelligence training while I was in Afghanistan. We might be able to turn him into an asset. But you have to have the stomach for it. It gets real intense and has to be done exactly right. So how do we know when it's time for your resurrection?"

"I have absolutely no idea. I've never been dead before."

"We have to include Kathy. She knows the case inside and out, and you know she'll only work for you. You'll need to convince her to work for this Stevens guy. Besides, she can report back to you on what Stevens is doing. But more important, if we don't include her, you'll make her your enemy for life."

"You're right," Danny said. "But no others."

"Where are you going to stay?"

"For now, your place. Long-term—I don't know. I need to get away from the reservation and away from Farmington. I'm thinking about something, but it probably won't work out."

In the back of his mind, Danny again pondered a long-put-off call to Albuquerque.

Chapter 88

present

"So that's why we did what we did," Danny said. "I chose to come back to life now so Doyle could connect the dots in his criminal case."

Doyle spoke for the first time. "We've been stuck for weeks in our murder investigation. We were sure we had a murder on federal property, but no suspect we could directly connect to it."

Doyle nodded to Chaco, who got up and left the room. He returned a few moments later with a stranger in tow. "This is Max Shultz," Doyle said. "He's the man Chaco captured. Mr. Shultz has been a very bad man, but tells us he's seen the error of his ways. We're giving him immunity in return for his testimony against Red Gannon and Lucas Blackthorn. After that, if he so much as gets caught jaywalking, he'll go to prison for the rest of his life.

"We no longer have our original murder case because Danny's still alive. But we picked up another one with the death of the man killed in the gasoline explosion. In addition, thanks to Danny and Max Shultz's testimony, we've also got two counts of attempted murder against Lucas Blackthorn. And by the way, Mr. Shultz helped us solve the mystery of that stolen, highly classified military ordinance you folks found."

"So where are things going from here?" Vic asked.

"Many things are happening right now. I have an FBI Strike Force on its way to Farmington. We're getting several arrest warrants from a federal judge as we speak. We'll execute them this morning against all five conspirators in your case. With any luck, the whole gang will be in a federal lockup by noon."

"What time do you expect all of this to happen?" Bri asked.

"The warrants against Popeson and Webster will be executed early this morning. We'll move on the Gannon building mid-morning, once our SWAT team agents are in place."

"I have a bunch of personal stuff in my desk I'd like to get out," Bri said. "I can leave the building on my ten o'clock break. Could you do it then?"

"No!" Jason banged his hand down on Kathy's desk, making everyone jump. "There's nothing in that building that's worth putting you in danger for even one more second."

"Hold on, Jason," Doyle responded. "Is there anything to indicate that they suspect her? It might be helpful to have someone on the inside."

"No. I just don't like it, that's all."

"How about this?" Stewart said. "We wire her. That way, she can give us continual real-time updates about what's going on inside. I'll have two agents monitoring her every second she's in there. You and Danny can be in the surveillance van right outside the building. It looks like just an ordinary UPS truck. When she's ready to come out, nearly two dozen FBI agents will be all around the Gannon building ready to help. We can give her a code word. If anything happens, all she has to do is say that word and we'll bust the doors down and get her out."

"I want to do this!" Brianna said resolutely. "It's another chance for me to contribute. With the FBI backing me up, I'll feel safer in there than at any time since I went to work."

Jason looked at Bri and shook his head. "Remember how you felt when you found out about the fire?" Jason asked. "That's what I'll feel all the time you're in there."

"I'm sorry to make you worry, but you guys have done so much and I've done so little. I'll be careful, I promise."

"This is foolish," Jason argued. "Why step back onto the train tracks if you've already jumped out of the way?" But nothing he said dissuaded Brianna's determination.

Chapter 89

"That's him!" Blackthorn exclaimed as he examined the picture on his computer screen. "That guy's the attorney for the Indians!"

It was an hour before dawn and Blackthorn and Ed Rollo were in Blackthorn's office, examining dozens of pictures taken by the investigator. The picture on the screen showed Jason Stevens getting into Brianna Sanders' car at the federal courthouse.

"It gets better," Rollo replied. Scrolling through several more pictures, he stopped at one that showed the couple kissing. "Off hand, I'd say more going on here than just a professional relationship."

Blackthorn seethed. "What else do you have on her?"

"Routine stuff. She lives a pretty quiet life. She was a high school accounting teacher. No one I talked to understands why she's not teaching this year."

"She's working for those damn Indians, that's why. Good job Rollo. Print out these photos then go home and get some sleep."

Despite the hour, Blackthorn dialed Red Gannon.

"Red, it's the woman. I've got pictures of her and Stevens at the courthouse right after that hearing. They're real friendly. We'd better grab her and have a talk—the sooner, the better."

"When?"

"Today. But we can't do what we need to do here in the building— too many people. We've got to get her out to the ranch. Can you bring the helicopter?"

Chapter 90

7:35 a.m.: As soon as they heard Stewart give the go-ahead to execute their arrest warrant, agents Caleb Patterson and Gerald Justesen walked up the long sidewalk. They knocked on the front door of a tasteful English Tudor-style home in the fashionable Navajo Heights area of northwest Farmington. Footsteps sounded from inside, then the door opened to reveal a plump, pleasant-faced, gray-haired woman. "Mrs. Popeson?" Agent Patterson asked.

"Heavens, no," the woman said. "She's been gone for nearly ten years. I'm Margaret, Mr. Popeson's housekeeper."

"Margaret, I'm Agent Patterson with the FBI. This is Agent Justesen." Both men showed their IDs. "May we come in?"

The woman's jovial demeanor disappeared. "Oh, my! Is something wrong?"

"Just routine, ma'am," Patterson said, stepping past her and into the house without invitation. The other agent did the same as Patterson surveyed their surroundings. Handing her the warrant, Patterson asked, "Margaret, where is Mr. Popeson right now?"

"He's in his study, just down the hall. Can I tell him you're here?"

"No, ma'am. We'd prefer to announce ourselves. Is there anyone else in the house?"

"No, just me and him." The kindly looking woman's eyes began to tear-up. She looked at the warrant. Her lip trembled as she said, "Oh, dear. This is serious, isn't it?"

"Yes, ma'am, I'm afraid it is," Patterson said. "Which door is it?"

"The one on the left."

"We'd like you to step outside for a moment. Agent Justesen, would you help Margaret to the door? Have her go stand on the other side of our car."

Justesen did as instructed, then rejoined his partner.

"I'll lead," Patterson whispered as both men drew their weapons. It was a long hall with two doors to the right and one door mid-way down the hall to the left. That door was open and Patterson could hear activity there. He made his way slowly down the hall to the open door and cautiously peered around the doorframe. He instantly drew his head back and looked wide-eyed at Justesen. He placed his index finger to his temple in the manner of a gun. A voice addressed them from inside the room.

"Gentlemen, this home has an intercom system that allows me to listen to any room I want. I've known who you are since you first came through the front door. You needn't worry—I don't intend to shoot either of you."

Patterson peered around the doorway again to see Popeson seated at an ornate antique desk, holding a small .25 caliber automatic against his temple.

"Please, come in," Popeson invited. "I assure you I'm no danger to you. If I move this gun in your direction, which I won't, then you have my permission to shoot me immediately."

Patterson lowered his weapon and stepped into the doorway. Justesen took a shooter's stance behind and to the side of his partner. "Mr. Popeson, could you put down the gun?" Patterson asked. "We don't want to hurt you, but we get feeling real threatened when someone we're talking to has a gun."

"Oh, no need to be nervous, Agent Patterson," Popeson chuckled. "I would never do someone else harm. This gun is strictly for me."

"There's no need for that, sir. Nothing's worth pulling that trigger. Why don't you put the gun down and let's talk things over?"

"If I do that, Agent, can you guarantee that I won't be arrested? Can you guarantee that the story about this won't be spread all over the community? Can you guarantee that I'll die in my own bed and not in a prison bunk?"

"I wish I could guarantee you those things, Mr. Popeson. You know I can't, but I can tell you that everyone's considered innocent until proven guilty. I can guarantee that you'll be treated well and will get a fair trial."

"Oh, but I'm guilty, Agent Patterson. The sad part is that I used to be an honest man. I used to have integrity. Did you know that I'm highly respected here in my neighborhood, down at my church, and in the community? But I've been living a lie for several years now, thanks to a man named Red Gannon."

"I know it's tough to face something like this, Popeson, but think of your family. They don't want to see you die."

Popeson shook his head. "No need to worry, Agent. My wife died nine years ago and I've been lonely ever since. We never had any children. This house and property are going to belong to that dear, devoted woman you just met at the front door." Popeson patted a hand on the left side of his desk. "It's all in my will, right here in my top left-hand drawer. Please make sure someone sees it."

Patterson couldn't think of anything else to say.

"Agent, I'd like you to do two other things for me, if you would." Popeson picked up a thick envelope from the desktop and tossed it to Patterson's feet. "That tells you everything you want to know about Mr. Red Gannon and me. It also tells you where we stashed an awful lot of other people's money. I spent all night writing it down. Please consider it my death-bed confession. The second thing is a promise I'd like you to make to me."

"A promise? I'm sorry, Mr. Popeson, but I can't make you any promises."

"Oh, you can make this one. All I want you to do is to convey to Margaret my sincerest apology for making such an awful mess in her new home."

Thus saying, Stanley Popeson pulled the trigger.

Chapter 91

It was well after midnight when Mayor Marlin Webster finally crawled into bed, taking care to not awaken his sleeping wife.

His body was ready for rest but his mind was not. He tossed and turned as he wrestled with Popeson's revelations, trying to figure a way out.

He finally gave up on sleep as the first light of dawn outlined the hills east of Farmington. He considered staying home but knew he'd be bombarded with questions about where he'd been all night. Then there would be "Honey can you help me with this - can you help me with that?"

No. The early-morning solitude of his office at the city building was a better alternative, a place he could think.

The Cayman Island conspiracy was collapsing. Webster knew how damning the evidence was. He also knew how conspiracy investigations worked. The police pitted the conspirators one against the other until, inevitably, one would break and rat out the rest. When that happened, the entire house of cards came crashing down with amazing rapidity.

The only winner on the losing side was the first one to bail on all the others. That person usually walked, while the others rotted in jail—or worse.

Marlin consulted a contact list on his computer. He glanced at the clock on his desk. Five minutes after six. He dialed the number he wanted. Granted, he wouldn't get his millions in Cayman Island money, but if this worked, neither would he spend the rest of his life in a prison cell.

"This is Baca," a sleepy voice answered.

"Alex, this is Marlin Webster. Sorry to wake you so early, old friend, but there's something urgent I need to talk to you about."

The man on the other end was Marlin's long-time friend and Doyle Stewart's boss, Alejandro Baca, the United States attorney for the northern district of New Mexico.

*

9:01 a.m.: Accompanied by two agents in dark windbreakers with "FBI" written in huge letters across the back, Doyle Stewart burst through Webster's office door. Stewart found it strange that the man didn't appear to even jump at the abrupt intrusion.

"Marlin Webster, you are under arrest for conspiracy to commit murder, conspiracy to criminal fraud, and a number of other federal criminal violations," Stewart said. "Agents, take Mr. Webster into custody. I'll read him his rights."

"Wait," Webster said, holding his hands up. "You'd better read this first." He handed a fax to Stewart.

Doyle's eyes grew wider as he read the document. When finished, he tossed it back on the desk with disgust and said, "It looks like you snagged the brass ring, Mr. Webster. However, I'm still taking you into custody as a material witness for the next few hours. You'll be held incommunicado at a location in Durango, Colorado. When we've rounded up your fellow conspirators, we'll release you in accordance with this agreement. Congratulations, scumbag. Looks like you're going to walk."

"No need to be nasty, Mr. Stewart," Webster said. "If it weren't for people like me, prisons all across the country wouldn't be near as full."

Chapter 92

Despite being tired from staying up all night, Bri arrived at work at her usual time. But no matter how she tried, she could not trick her mind into accepting that this was just another day. It seemed like every person inside the building was watching her.

She said her usual hellos, put her purse in the bottom drawer, just like usual, and sat down. She was terrified. Her palms sweated, her knees shook, and her head spun. A thin patina of perspiration threatened the makeup she'd so carefully applied this morning.

Repeating the code word, "headache," over and over in her mind, she realized that she really did have a monstrous tension headache. Perhaps this wasn't such a good idea after all. She should have listened to Jason.

"Good morning, sweetie!" Suzanne said, sticking her head into Brianna's cubical.

Bri jumped. "What? Suzanne? You're back. I thought you were off until tomorrow."

"Vacation's nice," Suzanne said, "but work seems more like a vacation after being cooped up in the car with Jack and four screaming kids all week. Ooh, you don't look so good."

"Didn't sleep well. My breakfast isn't sitting quite right and my head is pounding." She almost said the code word, but caught herself before it came out. "But don't worry, I'll be fine."

"No problem, sweetie. Why don't you brief me on what happened while I was gone and then you can go home and start that darned old suspension Parsons gave you. Suzanne held up her coffee cup. "I'm on my way to the cafeteria. I know you're not a coffee drinker, but can I bring you back a sweet roll or something?"

"No thanks, I'm good. I appreciate the offer."

Good, Bri watched her boss walk away and decided to check the electronics the FBI had wired her with. The microphone that allowed them to listen in looked like a button on her blouse. She could hear them through a nearly invisible in-the-ear device she could turn off and on by simply pressing on her ear canal. She pressed and said softly, "This is Brianna. Can you hear me?"

No answer.

She spoke a little louder. "This is Brianna Sanders. Can you hear me?"

This time she received an answer she didn't expect. "Miss Sanders? Miss Sanders? Can you hear us?" It was Agent Spriggs, the woman who helped wire her up this morning. She acted as if Bri had not spoken.

"I hear you," Bri said softly. "Can you hear me?"

"I'm not able to reach her. All I'm getting is a weird back-ground hiss," she heard Spriggs say.

Great. So much for code words and Big Brother watching.

*

Special Agent Maxine Spriggs shook her headset again. "I don't understand, Lew," she said. "It was working fine when we put it on her. All I'm getting now is unintelligible garbled noises that sometimes sounds like someone talking, but it's covered up with a constant middle-range hiss."

Special Agent Luther Labianca checked his screens. The one showing Bri's microphone operation confirmed that it was broadcasting normally. They were hearing exactly what the microphone was.

"White-noise generators," he said.

"What's that?" Jason asked.

Labianca's reply was testy. He didn't like having civilians in his monitoring van. "White-noise generators create a background noise that's difficult for electronic surveillance to decipher. Those inside probably don't even know it's there.

"Can you do anything?" Danny asked.

"For now, we just keep listening. As long as we hear what we're hearing, we know she's in there and probably okay. We just won't be able to understand what she says."

"But she can't call for help if she needs it." Jason's concern rose.

"Calm down, Mr. Stevens," Labianca said, letting his irritation show. "We have no reason to believe anything unusual is going on."

"Her earpiece is probably working," Spriggs said. "It won't be affected by the generators. I'm sure that if something happens that she doesn't like, she'll get up and walk out of there, just like we instructed her to do."

Labianca looked at Spriggs. "Let her know we're having trouble hearing her microphone. Tell her that if she's uncomfortable, she should get out. He turned back to Jason. "Mr. Stevens, why don't you step out of the van and watch the front entrance to see if she comes out? Mr. Whitehorse can stay in here in case anything changes.

"I guess I can do that," Jason agreed.

*

Agent Sprigg's message didn't help Bri's nervousness. After giving Suzanne her briefing, she gathered her personal items from her desk and put them in her purse. On her way out, she stuck her head into Suzanne's cubical to tell her she was leaving, but before she could speak, Suzanne spoke to her.

"Bri, honey, before you go, can I get you to do something for me on your way out? They just called from upstairs. They want you to run some stuff up to room 626." Suzanne hoisted a small stack of file folders. They said something about needing these to get ready for an audit."

Bri paused. It would give her a chance to check out the other floors. "I guess I could," she agreed.

"Thanks Sweetie. We'll see you in a couple of days."

*

The sixth floor was heady territory. She'd never been above the fourth. This was where the high and mighty hung out. Her errand would give her a chance to see if anything suspicious was happening.

The first thing she noticed was the deep-pile carpet that contrasted sharply with the tile and commercial carpet floors of lower levels. The elevator was squarely in the middle of the building and exited into a large hallway that led off in either direction. The hallway sported soft, wall-sconce lighting rather than the harsh fluorescents of the first floor. Wood trim and crown molding matched the tall wooden doors. Expensive artwork decorated the walls. It bespoke an opulence that told visitors they had reached the highest echelons of Gannon Oil corporate

328

society.

A polished wooden sign on the wall opposite the elevator door directed people to their destination. Room 626 was down the hall to her right.

Half way down, she passed a set of open double office doors on her left. She looked inside and saw an attractive woman sitting at a reception desk. She looked up as Bri passed, gave her a once-over, then looked down dismissively, as if Bri was of no significance. The mahogany placard on the wall said. "James E. (Red) Gannon, CEO." Just the thought he might be so near gave Bri chills.

Double doors at the end of the hall were labeled, 'Roof/Heliport.' Room 626 was next to them on the right. She discreetly knocked.

"Come in," a voice answered. She opened the door and poked her head inside. The only light came from a lamp on a table at the far corner of the room where a man in a dark suit was seated. "Come in, come in," he said. "I understand you have something for me."

Bri stepped through the door and heard a faint rustle from behind. A powerful arm encircled her neck. She screamed, but it was instantly stifled by the pressure around her throat. Someone placed a strip of duct tape over her mouth, then the arm around her neck lifted her off the floor. Other arms tried to ensnare hers. She tried to fight them off, but her arms were wrestled behind her and handcuffs snapped around her wrists, She tried to scream "Headache. Headache," through the duct tape, but all that came out was a muffled "MMMMFFFFFFF!"

She tried to twist away, but the arm holding her prevented it. Flailing her legs against the shins of her captor, she flung her head backward, connecting solidly with something fleshy, maybe a nose. "Ugh," she heard. She tried it again, but her captor jerked out of the way.

A deep male voice growled in her ear, "Stop it or I'll knock you out." The arm holding her squeezed tight, then tighter, and tighter until she couldn't breathe. On the verge of losing consciousness, she realized that further struggles were useless, so she stopped.

"That's better," the voice said. His grip relaxed and she took a great gulp of air. "We're going to blindfold you and then tape your legs together. If you resist, we'll knock you in the head and tape you up anyway. Don't struggle and you won't get hurt. Understand?"

Terrified, Bri nodded. Surely the sixth floor would be one of the first places the FBI would come to. She knew the building was surrounded. If her captors tried taking her out of the building, they would never get past the SWAT team.

The arm around her throat relaxed. A large man wearing a dark ski mask stepped in front of her and threw a draw-string fabric bag over her head which he cinched loosely around her neck.

"Now put your feet together," the voice commanded. The thought of losing thelast of her mobility was frightening, but had no choice. When the taping was done, a different voice said, "Get her into the chopper."

The words terrorized her. Helicopter? If the FBI agents didn't arrive within moments, she'd be out of their reach and completely at the mercy of her captors. She shook her head violently and tried to shout, "No, No!" but her gag swallowed the sound.

She was picked up roughly and thrown over someone's shoulder. She tried to writhe out of the man's grip and kick with her pinioned feet. Suddenly, a blow to the side of her head sent blinding flashes of pain down her neck and through her torso. She thought she would pass out.

"Quit struggling," yet another voice barked. "If I have to hit you again, you won't wake up for a long time."

Brianna's went limp. She was defeated. Tears of anger and fear welled up. She was carried out of the room and heard a door open — to the roof she presumed. Even from here, she could hear the *whop, whop, whop* of a powerful helicopter engine revving up to speed.

This was an irreversible act. Her captors had to realize that. Would she ever see Jason again? Would she ever see her family? She felt herself carried up the stairs, heard the blast of sound as the door to the outside opened. A few seconds later she was unceremoniously dumped onto the vibrating floor of the helicopter. A fresh bout of panic struck as a needle was thrust into her arm and something injected. Within seconds, her consciousness faded. Her last thought was a plea. *Jason, help me. Help me pleas . . ."*

Chapter 93

"Top Gun, this is Listener. We've lost contact with Lady Bird. Over." Agent Labianca waited for Stewart to respond.

"Listener, confirm last transmission," Doyle's voice came back. "You lost what? Over.

"We no longer have a signal from Lady Bird?" We've been having trouble with her broadcast all morning. But we lost all contact approximately three minutes ago. It does not appear to be an equipment malfunction. Over."

"Ten-four Listener. I'm on my way. Over."

Jason was surprised to see Doyle approach the van on the run just as Danny opened the van's side door. "What's wrong?" Jason asked.

"They've lost Brianna's signal," Danny said.

Doyle rushed past Jason and through the van's side door. Jason spun to follow.

"What do you mean you lost her signal?" Jason shouted.

"Calm down, Jason," Danny said, putting a hand on his friend's shoulder."

"At first we were getting nothing but the white noise," Labianca explained. "Then we started hearing what sounded like some sort of static and occasional garbled words. A few minutes ago, there was a major sound change. We clearly heard male voices just before the signal faded. It sounded like her transmitter moved out of range fairly fast."

"But how?" Danny asked.

"That's what we're working on now. "Agent Spriggs, put the

331

recording up on the speaker."

The van's interior filled with a throbbing roar. The rhythmical noise accelerated faster and faster until it blended into a single blast. Then it sounded as if someone closed a door against the noise, dulling, but not stopping it. A clearly discernible male voice said, "Okay, Red, take her up!" The thrumming sound increased for several seconds, then faded lower and lower until it was gone.

"What happened?" Jason asked in panic.

"First impression—the equipment was working fine. She finally got out of range of the white-noise generators. I'm pretty sure she was outside the building when we heard whoever it was speak."

"Then why didn't we see her?" Jason asked..

Labianca shook his head. "We're not exactly sure, but a helicopter took off from the roof of the building at the same time this was going on. Ms. Sanders may have been on it. It's the only explanation we have for how the signal faded so quickly."

"We think Gannon was on that helicopter, too," Doyle said. But outside of shooting it down, there was nothing we could do. I'm getting this operation rolling right now." He bolted for the door and spoke into his radio at the same time. "Go! Go! Go!" he shouted.

Danny and Jason exited behind him and saw more than a dozen agents wearing full SWAT gear rush the front door of the Gannon building. Others fanned out around the building to cover all the outside entrances. Jason started toward the front door, but Doyle grabbed him. "Let the professionals do their job, Jason," he said. "If we're going to find Brianna, we need to go somewhere else."

*

Doyle drove them to the airport control tower building. At the reception desk, he flashed his ID and asked, "Where's your radar officer?"

"Third door on the right, sir."

As he walked down the hall, Doyle checked with the FBI strike team leader. "Delaney, what's your status? Have you found the Sanders woman? Over."

"Negative, Mr. Stewart. None of the principal targets seem to be here, either."

The trio entered the darkened radar room that contained six large, round, radar screens arranged back to back in two rows. Only three were occupied. A middle-aged man seated at a desk in the back corner stood and walked toward them. "May I help you, Gentlemen?"

Doyle flashed his ID. "We're interested in what you can tell us about a helicopter that took off from the Gannon Building a few minutes ago."

"That's a local traffic object. It would be on console three.

"Yeah, I remember that bird," the operator said.

"How far did you track it?" Doyle asked.

"We transfer local traffic to regional about 25 miles out. That's the best I can tell you. With choppers, you never know where they're going. Unless they're 2500 feet above mean altitude, regional doesn't even bother with them."

"How about this guy? Were you able to track him?"

"Yeah, he was pretty easy. He climbed to about fifteen hundred feet and headed straight east."

"They're headed for Gannon's ranch." Danny said.

"Let's go!" Jason cried.

"Hold on, cowboy, It's not that easy," Stewart responded. "We don't know anything about that ranch. We don't know the building layout, and we don't know the best entry routes or what kind of force we may be facing once we get there. If we go about this wrong, all we'll do is get her – and maybe some of my men – killed. There's someone we need to talk to."

"Who?" Jason asked.

"The only person I know of who's actually been to that ranch. He's on his way to Durango right now."

*

The forty-minute wait for Webster seemed interminable. Jack Delaney, the FBI Strike Team leader, along with Stewart, Jason, and Danny waited for him at an office at the Federal Courthouse. The terms of Webster's immunity agreement required full cooperation with federal officials.

Before the group was a big-screen TV showing a Google Earth image of Gannon's ranch. "This entry building is usually manned by a single guard." Webster pointed to a structure just off Highway 64, sitting astride the driveway to Gannon's property. "Both lanes have tire spikes that can be activated from inside the guard shack. In addition, two guards patrol the perimeter of the house." Webster pointed at the mansion. There are two guards that patrol the airport, and three or four two-man teams in the woods surrounding the rest of the property.

"What about the house layout?" Stewart asked.

"It's a single-story, designed like an old Spanish hacienda. The whole place is built around a big open-air plaza. You can see the fountain at the center here." Webster pointed. "A wide glassed-in hallway goes all the way around the plaza. Every interior room door opens into the hallway. "The front doors open into a large foyer. There's a huge living room and dining area off the foyer to the left as you go in. All the bedrooms are down the hall on this side." Webster traced his finger down the left side.

"The back is where the kitchen and utility rooms are. In the front, there's a large waiting area and library to the right off the foyer. The right hall has offices and conference rooms all the way down. The first room is Gannon's office. It's huge. He has all kinds of communications gear in there. The next room is a conference room. Then there are three or four smaller rooms going down the hall all the way to the back. I've never been down to any of them."

Delaney scratched his chin. "So what's in the plaza?"

"It's like a jungle. There's a big fountain and pool in the center where he keeps those fancy colored carp from China."

Delaney shook his head. "There's layered protection starting at the highway and leading all the way to the house. We'll need to neutralize the outside guards without alerting anyone inside. The house is a nightmare—lots of places for people to hide. We're looking at a strike force of thirty or more and I don't have that many people here. I don't see us going in there until sunrise tomorrow at the earliest."

"Tomorrow!" Jason exclaimed. "By then Gannon will know we raided his building—if he doesn't already. What's to prevent him from throwing Bri into one of his airplanes and flying her out to God knows where?"

"Don't worry about Gannon knowing about the raid, Doyle said. We've got communications in and out of his building locked down and under our control. I think we can keep this out of the newspapers and off television for the next twenty-four-hours. But if we're going to rescue Bri without getting her killed, this thing has to go down right."

Danny asked a question no one expected. "What if all you had to worry about was the house?"

Delaney eyed him, looked at Stewart and shrugged. "If that's all I had to worry about, I could probably do it with just the men I've got. But that's like saying, 'What if we could have Peter Pan sprinkle some magic fairy dust and fly ourselves in?'"

"Maybe not," Danny said. "How long will it take you to plan a raid on the house?"

Delaney took another look at the aerial photo and asked, "How far is it out there?"

"About sixty miles."

"If Webster would help me brief the strike team, we should be able to get there and be ready to go in about four hours."

"I don't understand how you think you can get rid of those guards and secure the rest of the property," Stewart said.

"Doyle, you're just going to have to trust me on this one," Danny replied. "I have access to one of the largest, best-trained police forces in the Four Corners area, and we don't have to jump through all the jurisdictional BS you guys do. If you'll authorize this, I can walk you and your people right up to the front door of that house. Remember, gentlemen. I'm an Indian. We owned those woods long before you white men ever showed up."

Doyle gave Danny a cockeyed look. "Do I want to know the details?"

"I wouldn't tell you if you asked," Danny said. "We'll be in there and gone like it never even happened. However, I need at least five sets of night vision gear, and I need them by five o'clock."

Stewart looked at Delaney.

"Yeahhh, we can do that," Delaney said with hesitation.

"All right, you got it," Stewart said, "but no bloodshed, understand? If there is, I'll have to come after you just like we're going after Gannon."

"Understood and agreed. But what if they open fire on us first?"

"Then you pull back and let us handle it. I'm signing off on this on one condition. If you haven't neutralized the guards—legally I might add—and not secured the rest of the property by the time we get out there, I'll kill this whole operation until we get a full FBI strike team."

Chapter 94

"Danny, how can you promise those kinds of things?" Jason asked as they sprinted toward his Escalade.

"I'll tell you on the way. Just get us to Shiprock as fast as you can."

The instant they were in the vehicle, Danny dialed Chaco's cell phone. "Chaco, Gannon's kidnapped Bri. Meet us at the Navajo Café in a half hour. Send word to Robert to call up thirty of our best and have them ready to deploy in full battle dress in an hour. This is a hot weapons operation, not an exercise."

Jason was baffled. "Thirty men? It sounds like you're raising an army."

"That's exactly what I'm doing, Jason, and you've got some decisions to make. You're an officer of the court, just like I am, but some things transcend those strict ethical duties. You need to decide right now whether I can reveal some secret information to you that's in direct conflict with your duty as a court officer."

"Are you asking me to break the law?"

"I'm not asking you to do anything. I'm telling you that before I tell you anything, you're going to have to make a decision. I have resources on the reservation that will help free Brianna. Unless you promise you'll never reveal what you're about to hear, even if it means going to jail, I'll just have you drop me off and you can go on back to the ranch."

"You know that's not going to happen. You have my promise."

Jason spent the rest of the trip listening as Danny told him the story of the NALM, the well fires, and he and Chaco's involvement. He was stunned. "Is this little Navajo army good enough to help us?" he asked.

"The best of our people are very well up to the task. Chaco has given them excellent military training, including me. It's all we've got, Jason. Every hour that passes puts Bri in greater danger. The FBI doesn't have an army in place, but we do."

"I'm an ex-Navy SEAL. I've had combat command experience and know a lot more about penetration and capture techniques than anyone you've got. I'm going in with you."

"I never thought for a minute otherwise." Danny grinned. "Welcome aboard, Lieutenant Stevens."

Chapter 95

With the bag still over her head, Bri had no idea where she was when consciousness returned. From time to time, she could hear muffled sounds of activity somewhere, but nothing she could identify. After what felt like hours, she turned her head toward the sound of someone opening a door.

"Yeah, she's awake," she heard someone say, then the duct tape around her legs was slit and pulled roughly from her ruined hose. At last she could freely move her legs.

"Stand up," the voice commanded. Two pairs of hands grabbed her arms and wrestled her upright, then someone stepped behind and unlocked the handcuffs from around her wrists.

The bag's tie string was loosened and the bag removed. The flood of light nearly blinded her. She blinked rapidly as her eyes adjusted to the bright light.

She was in a low-ceilinged, rectangular room, some kind of storage room it appeared, with shelves along one wall and floor-to-ceiling cabinets along another. When she turned around, she was facing two men she didn't recognize. One appeared to be late-fiftyish, with a graying, nearly bald head. The other was a tall, slender old man who had odd-colored hair—snowy white where it came out of his head, but tipped with a hint of reddish orange at the ends. Could this be the fabled Red Gannon?

Anger overcame her fear. "How dare you?" she shouted indignantly. "I demand that you release me right now. This is kidnapping and you'll never get away with it."

"You're in no position to be making demands, Ms. Sanders," the older man said. "You're doing some very naughty things. I'm going to give you five minutes to get yourself together. There's a bathroom next door. You're welcome to use the facilities. Then you'll be escorted to my office, where we're going to have a little chat. And just for your information, if you choose to be uncooperative, this will be the worst day of your life, not to mention, the last."

A heavily muscled man entered. "This way," he commanded as he grabbed Bri by the upper arm. He shoved her through the door into a hallway that fronted on a lushly planted plaza. The man pushed her into the bathroom next door and said, "Five minutes," then closed the door.

The bathroom was austere—a toilet, a freestanding cabinet and sink, and a small medicine cabinet. Someone had laid out a comb and a brush and provided a bar of soap and washcloth. When Bri opened the medicine cabinet, it was bare.

She used the toilet not just because of a strong need, but also from a fear that she might not see another in a long while. She did her best to straighten her wildly mussed hair. Thanks to the duct tape, her panty-hose were hopelessly snagged and baggy. She futilely tried to smooth and straighten them, but finally gave up and simply took them off. She stashed them in one of the cabinets.

She exited the room without being called, hoping against hope that the big man was gone, but there he stood. He took her arm again and propelled her up the hall.

The wide hallway ended at a large foyer, but before they reached it, she was thrust into a large office on the left. A quarter of the floor space was taken up by a huge antique Spanish-style desk and an imposing communications console arising immediately behind. She was startled to see a clock on the console that said 7:35 p.m. She'd been captive for over nine hours.

The man she assumed was Gannon was seated behind the desk. Her escort pushed her into a chair. To her left was the other man, sneering at her from an identical chair.

The old man appeared surprisingly fit and vigorous for someone of an advanced age. He had ice-blue eyes that seemed to penetrate right through her, leaving a sense of violation. "Ms. Sanders, my name is Red Gannon," he said in a deep, oily-smooth voice. "This is my security chief,

Lucas Blackthorn. We're very disappointed in you. We like to trust our employees, but I'm afraid you've bitten the hand that feeds you."

Bri tried to keep her voice from trembling. "I don't know what you're talking about, Mr. Gannon. If this is how you define disciplinary action at your company, I'd say you've gone far over the top."

"Oh, we haven't even begun, Ms. Sanders. As for you not knowing what we're talking about, you might want to take a look at these." Gannon reached into his center drawer and removed a stack of photos. He threw them across the desk in her direction. The top one showed her and Jason kissing in the parking lot of the courthouse.

"You seem to have a very short memory. These pictures were taken yesterday morning. Your gentleman friend is an attorney looking to take millions of dollars away from my company. You obviously know him well—that is unless you go around letting strange men in courthouse parking lots kiss you as a matter of habit."

"So I know this man," Bri responded defiantly. "That's my business, not yours."

Gannon slammed his fist down with a bang, causing her to recoil. He half arose, leaned over the desk and roared, "You made it my business when you joined forces with my enemies by stealing confidential information and giving it to them."

Bri could not constrain her tongue. "No, Mr. Gannon, you chose it when you decided to cheat over six hundred families out of what little they had so you could have more of what you don't need. It's your greed that led Jason Stevens into that courtroom yesterday and it's your greed that's going to bring you down. I'd advise you to release me immediately. You have to know that people are looking for me at this very moment, and this is probably one of the first places they'll look."

"Please forgive me if I decline your advice," Gannon said. "I assure you, no one has any idea that you're here. We need some information from you. You can choose to give it to us or not. If you don't, you're going to suffer pain and humiliation like you've never imagined. And in the end, you'll give us the information anyway. Cooperate, and you may get out of here in as good or better shape than you are now. Otherwise, you may not get out of here at all. I'm going to ask you three questions. Answer them satisfactorily, and this interrogation is over. Do you understand?"

Bri refused to respond, choosing instead to stare defiantly into the man's disconcerting eyes.

"Ms. Sanders, who else besides yourself is working for Jason Stevens?"

Bri didn't acknowledge the question.

"Okay," Gannon said. "Question two: Where does Jason Stevens live, and who are the other people working with him?"

Her response was the same.

"Last chance," Gannon said darkly. "Who is Jason Stevens working with? Is he working with the FBI? Is he working with the U.S. attorney's office, the state police or other police or regulatory agency?"

Bri finally spoke. "Three out of three, Mr. Gannon. You're going to have to figure all of that out for yourself because you'll get nothing from me."

"No," Gannon replied coldly. "Three strikes and *you're* out." He looked at Blackthorn. "I release this lovely young woman to your tender mercies, Lucas. If she's still alive, have her back here in two hours. Try to convince her that it's in her best interest to talk to me." Gannon stood and walked out of the room.

Bri screamed as Blackthorn jerked her from her chair by the hair, walked her to the door, and half-dragged her down the hallway toward the back of the house. At the end, he turned left.

The floor here was commercial ceramic tile, not the plush carpeting where they'd been. Blackthorn turned right at the second door into a large commercial-type kitchen. He stopped in front of a large sink. "On your knees" he growled, forcing her down. He grabbed the dish sprayer and began hosing her down. The shocking cold water took Bri's breath away. What in the world was he doing?

Once she was completely soaked, he let go of the spray head, jerked her to her feet, and pushed her toward the far side of the room in the direction of a large metal door with a small window at eye-level. Bri panicked as she recognized that it was a walk-in freezer.

"No!" she cried, clawing at Blackthorn's hand and trying to pull back.

"Stop that, you little bitch," Blackthorn bellowed. He slapped her hard across the face. The blow sent her sprawling and brought a trickle of blood from her lip. He jerked her up by the hair again and forced her toward the freezer. "Pull a stunt like that again and I'll beat you senseless."

Blackthorn opened the freezer door and shoved her inside. "If any part of your skin touches anything in here, you'll freeze to it. If you sit down, you'll freeze yourself to whatever you sit on. When you're ready to talk, knock on the window. You talk, you live. You don't, you die. We won't even have to worry about you starting to stink." He closed the door.

Chapter 96

Jason and Danny led the rag-tag convoy of a dozen pickup trucks and cars driven by NALM members east up State Highway 64, in Jason's Escalade. The vehicle was loaded with gear and weapons commandeered from the van once used by Max and his dead partner. The van itself, loaded with NALM soldiers, followed Chaco's Wagoneer four vehicles back.

As twilight deepened, one by one, vehicles dropped out of the convoy at their assigned debarkation points. Dark-clad men scrambled out of the vehicles and retrieved their equipment packs and weapons, their faces hidden behind black and green camouflage face paint.

The team leaders donned the night vision goggles the FBI had supplied, then all quickly disappeared northward into the trees. Each group leader had a small walkie-talkie and a hand-held GPS locator. They carried a print-out of the aerial view of Gannon's ranch with their respective targets clearly delineated.

The highway carved a path across the face of a broad hill above Gannon's ranch, providing Jason and Danny a perfect elevated view of the Gannon compound. Perimeter lights lit the grounds surrounding Gannon's residence. Jason saw a black helicopter sitting on a helipad next to the house. He shuddered to think what Bri might have been subjected to for the past ten hours. A half mile to the northeast of the huge house lay the airfield hanger whose bright lights lit the tarmac.

The last three vehicles pulled off at a graveled highway maintenance area a half mile past the driveway entrance. Danny would take nine men with him, Jason just two.

Jason's job was to secure the front gate. Chaco and his group, coming from the west, would provide backup once they cleared any guards from the woods on that side of the property. Danny and his group would secure the airfield and make sure no one made an airborne escape.

Once they checked their weapons and slung their backpacks over their shoulders, Jason said to Danny, "You watch yourself. I've already lost your sorry butt once this year—I don't want to do it again."

"Not to worry." Danny chuckled. "Blackthorn's had his last chance at me. How long have we got?"

The scheduled arrival time for the FBI strike team was ten p.m. Jason checked his watch and asked, "Will thirty-five minutes give you enough time to get into position?"

"Should be plenty. How are your night vision goggles?"

Jason lowered the electronic goggles and switched on the display. It took a few seconds for the green-hued picture to stabilize, but when it did, it revealed their surroundings in surprising detail for more than one hundred and fifty yards out. "I'm a go! How about you?"

"These things are amazing," Danny said. It was the first time he had ever used such a device.

"Watch them around bright lights. They can flare and really mess up your vision for a few minutes. If that happens, take them off and let your eyes adjust to your normal night vision for a minute or two."

"I'll be careful. Thanks. Good luck, my friend. See you in an hour or so."

"Danny, one other thing," Jason said. "Don't forget to duck."

Both teams trotted across the highway and disappeared into the darkness.

Chapter 97

Already cold from the drenching, the effects were multiplied by the frigid, circulating air of the freezer. Bri looked around at stacked boxes of baking ingredients, amorphous masses of unidentifiable material wrapped in plastic, and various types of frozen meats and vegetables. The only sound was a fan at the back of the freezer. The dial-type thermometer at the top of the door read -10°.

She began to shiver uncontrollably. She tried pulling her wet blouse away only to discover that it had already begun to freeze.

She knew body heat was being sucked out of her at a prodigious rate. If she were dry, she might hold out in here perhaps hours, but in her soaked condition, she might make it only an hour. Two hours was out of the question.

After a time, frost circled the edges of her fingernails. Her feet hurt horribly. She tried stomping them and beating her arms around her body to generate heat, but the frozen water in her blouse was so stiff her arms couldn't bend.

Shivering came in spasms, wave after wave. Her teeth chattered so violently she feared they might break. She knew she should be planning how to get out of here, but all her energy was consumed by the overwhelming need to somehow find warmth.

How long had it been? Thirty minutes? An hour? She'd quit shivering and her teeth no longer chattered. Slowly, a feeling of warmth seemed to suffuse her body. Had someone turned on a heater? She looked at the temperature dial. It still read -10°. She realized that she actually was freezing to death.

She knew that one way or another, her life was ending. She knew who her captors were. She'd seen their faces. It defied logic that they would let her go and risk facing kidnapping charges. And if they were willing to kill her, they would have no hesitation about doing the same to the others. *Should I knock on the window? No! I will not hand over the precious lives of my dear ones to these evil men.*

Almost an hour passed. She actually felt fairly comfortable, except that she was becoming sleepy — very sleepy. She knew what that meant, and it didn't upset her. *If only I could leave Jason a message.* She looked around but found no way to do that.

Maybe if I just sit down. As she attempted to sit on a stack of boxes, her solidly frozen skirt swung out and knocked her feet completely out from under her. She tumbled to the frozen floor. In her mind, she knew it should have hurt, but she felt nothing. She suddenly found it hysterically comical the way her skirt stuck up like an ice cream cone lying on a sidewalk. Then a great wave of drowsiness washed over her. She let her head relax and roll to the side. *I'll just rest a bit and then try to get up.* She closed her eyes, and in a moment of clarity realized these were the last conscious moments of her life. *At least the others will be safe. Good-bye, Jason. I truly do love you. How much I wish I had told you that. I'm sorry we will never be . . .*

Chapter 98

"Team one is go," came the whispered radio message. Then came another, "Team two is go," and another, "Team three is go." Chaco acknowledged each with a whispered, "Ten-four."

Twilight out on the road was pitch darkness in the trees. Chaco's team would work closer to the house than any of the rest, where there was a much higher probability of early contact with Gannon's guards. His men quickly spread into a skirmish line spaced about twenty-five yards apart, then began making their way as quietly as possible toward the Gannon compound.

He had trained them well. His men moved silently and stealthily through the nighttime forest, able to maintain formation and contact by simple sound commands that would seem like the natural sounds of the night forest to an ordinary person.

By Chaco's reckoning, his group had traveled a little over a quarter mile when they made first contact. Dead ahead, at the limits of the goggles, Chaco detected movement—just a flare of heat signature that stood out in a lighter green hue than the darker forest background. Chaco gave two distinct clicks of his tongue and heard the signal repeated on both sides of him. The sound cascaded away as each man passed it on.

Chaco moved forward. Each step he took clarified his vision and coalesced the blob of heat image into a distinctly human shape. He had taken only a few steps when he faintly detected a second target at the edge of his vision. He moved closer.

What's the guy doing? The first man was standing a little oddly. Then the purpose revealed itself as the heat signature of a warm liquid stream erupted from the middle of the image. Chaco grinned. The man was not doing his business quietly. He could hear the sound from where he crouched.

As the man finished, a second startling event happened. A bright flare of white light erupted that completely obscured the second man's face. *What the...?* Then the flare extinguished, and left in its place a single pinpoint of white-hot light that burned for a second then died down, but didn't go out.

Stupid man. Doesn't he know that a cigarette lighter destroys his night vision for two minutes or more, and that the smell of the drifting cigarette smoke acts like a beacon for hundreds of yards? These men are not trained for night fighting.

Chaco selected four of his men to assist in the capture. He noted that the two Gannon guards would sometimes glance outward into the darkened woods, but for the most part, they spent their time looking inward toward the compound, talking and laughing as they watched what they were guarding rather than where danger was likely to come from.

The approach was easy, as the men's voices covered Chaco's team's quiet approach. One man's rifle leaned against a nearby tree. The other had his dangling loosely from the crook of his arm. It was a total shock to them when Chaco and Nelson Littlehand simultaneously arose from the forest underbrush, locked an arm around each man's throat, and shoved the tip of a knife under their ears. At the same instant, two other NALM members came from nowhere and pointed pistols directly into each guard's face. "Not a sound or a move," Chaco hissed

Both guards' eyes popped wide in fear, but neither attempted to fight. The bushes rustled as the rest of Chaco's men entered the small clearing. "On your knees," Chaco commanded in a loud whisper. "Put your hands behind your heads and don't make a sound."

Once the men were secured with their own handcuffs, Chaco said in a quiet but menacing voice, "There are two things you need to know. The first is that we're not the police so we don't have to read you your rights or any of that crap. The second is that if you don't do exactly what we say, we'll simply slit your throats and leave you here to rot. No second chances. Understand?" Both men glanced at each other and nodded.

One of the men whimpered in fear. "Shut up," Chaco hissed. He took a menacing step toward the man and brandished his knife. The man recoiled and went silent. "I'm going to ask you some questions. I already know the answer to most of them, so if you lie to me, I'll know. You lie, you die. Answer me in whispers, understand?" Both men nodded.

"Which of you normally responds to your radio calls?"

"I do," choked out the man on the right.

"You will answer every radio call exactly as you normally do. We've been out here listening long enough to know your routine. If you deviate in the slightest, neither of you will live long enough to finish the call. What's your call name?"

"Delta Two," the man whispered.

"For your information, the FBI is coming in less than an hour to arrest your employer and his friends. What you do right now could mean the difference between you going to prison for a very long time as an accessory to their crimes, or going free. Do you understand?"

The guards gave vigorous nods.

"How many other teams are there like you, and where are they?" Chaco looked at the man on the left. "Start talking."

The guard looked at the eight fearsome-looking men surrounding him, swallowed hard, and said, "We don't know anything about what they do in that house. We're just security guards."

Chaco stepped forward and placed his knife under the man's chin, pricking his throat. "I'm not here to argue the merits of your position. I asked you about the security arrangements. Say anything else, and this forest will drink your blood."

"Whoa, sorry, man. Please don't cut me again. We're a Delta team. Deltas patrol the property outside the immediate area of the house and airfield perimeter."

"How many Delta teams?"

"Three others. We normally range all over the ranch, but we were ordered to be in close tonight. They usually do that when some big wig visits."

"Where are the other Delta teams?"

"Delta One is to the east on the other side of the driveway. We cover the front from the west property line to the driveway. Delta three covers the right flank and rear of the house, and Delta Four covers the woods behind the airfield."

"What about the entrance?"

"One guard in the gate house. He controls all the vehicle traffic."

"Where do the radio checks come from?" Chaco asked.

"From the dispatch guy down at the hanger. There should be a radio check coming in about five minutes."

Chaco looked at Nelson. "Better uncuff him." Once the man's hands were free, Chaco said, "Better not try anything cute. What about security units at the airport?"

"That's one of the Alpha units, two guards who patrol the hanger area."

"What about the house?"

"They're the other Alpha unit. Two guards on the outside. One guy walks the sidewalk next to the house, the other guy patrols the perimeter further out, just inside the stone fence."

"Alarms and cameras?"

"The house has a front door camera and alarms on all the entry doors and windows. There's a door alarm on the hanger and a camera inside pointed at the planes. There's also a camera on the front gate. That's all of them I know about."

"Where's the camera on the front gate located?"

"It hangs off the eve of the building on the entry side. Gannon likes to see who shows up before he gives authorization to open the gate."

At that moment, the man's radio crackled to life. "Radio Check." a voice said. "Alpha One?"

"Alpha One." a voice said in return.

"Alpha Two?"

"Alpha Two."

"Delta One?"

"Delta One," came the reply

When Delta Two came up, Chaco pointed his pistol at the man's face and said, "Nothing cute."

"Delta Two," the man responded.

"Delta Three?"

"Delta Three."

"Delta Four?"

No answer. "Delta Four, this is base. Over?"

Again there was no response. Chaco began to worry.

"Delta Four, this is base. Kenny, where the hell are you?"

After another prolonged pause, a voice finally responded. "Delta Four. Sorry, I was a little indisposed."

"What the hell do you mean *indisposed*, Kenny? I damn near reported you to the house." Even over the radio, one could hear the tension in the man's voice.

"Uh, nothing serious, Mike. I was taking a dump, okay? Got a little touch of the trots tonight."

" You need to come in?"

"No, no! I'm fine. We're fine. If it gets any worse, I'll come in."

"Ten-four, Delta Four. Kenny, don't scare me like that again. Gannon's watching us like a hawk tonight. Must be some kind of big doings going on."

"Ten-four base. Delta Four out."

Chaco assumed that Delta Four was securely in the hands of his men. He used his own radio to verify that fact, then relayed the information he'd learned to the other teams. Then he dispatched two men to stay with his captives, and sent five of his remaining troops to surround and observe the routine of the house guards. Chaco and Jonathan Longhand continued eastward through the woods toward the guard house at the entry.

Chapter 99

Bri came back to consciousness in a crescendo of pain, as if thousands of tiny daggers were piercing her hands and feet. She didn't understand the feeling of water washing over her naked body. As the coldness seeped from her bones, the water that at first felt warm, turned icy-cold. She opened her eyes and found that she was lying on the floor of a large marble shower, being pelted with a cold, stinging spray.

Someone had seen her naked. Was it Blackthorn? The thought of that filthy man's eyes on her filled her with loathing. She had to move. She could not allow that to happen again.

Excruciating pins and needles seized her feet as she stood. She found the water handle and tried to move it to warm. Her red, swollen fingers made her cry out as fiery stabs of pain went all the way to her elbows. She moved the handle with her wrist instead.

The flood of warmer water was glorious, but redoubled the pain in her hands and feet. She slowly sank to the floor to let the pain subside. She was alive, but was that a blessing or a curse? She was not free, not in control of anything except the water handle. An overwhelming sense of helplessness washed over her and great, wracking sobs blended her tears with the rivulets of cascading water.

As the pain lessened, she regained a measure of control and reason. She had to get out of here. Suddenly, the shower door swung open and Blackthorn leered down. She screamed, using her hands and arms to give what precious little modesty they could provide.

"Get your bony ass up and out of here," he said. "You're seeing Gannon in ten minutes. There's towels and a robe out here." He gave her a long, lingering look then closed the shower door.

Bri forced herself to stand the instant she heard the outside door close. Leaving the water running to cover her sounds, she stepped out of the shower and found herself in a spacious bathroom with mirrored walls. Her clothes were nowhere in sight, but as promised, two large, fluffy towels hung from a glass towel hanger, and a thick, white, terrycloth robe hung from a hook beside them. She dried herself, then wrapped the towel protectively around her in case Blackthorn reappeared. She used the other towel to dry her hair just enough that it no longer dripped, then put on the robe and tied it securely with a knot rather than a bow.

She started opening cabinet drawers. looking for anything that might be an aid. To her disappointment, all the drawers were empty. She looked around for a medicine cabinet. It took a few seconds to figure out that the end sections of the long mirror above the counter were actually doors. She pressed the edge of the one on the right and it sprang open. Nothing. She went to the other end and did the same.

Laying on the bottom glass shelf was a shiny, six-inch-long metal fingernail file. It wasn't much, but at least it was something. She dropped it into the pocket of the robe.

Taking a chance, she cracked open the bathroom door and peered outside. She found herself looking into the same kind of glass enclosed hallway she'd been in before, this time on the other side of the plaza. To her utter astonishment, no one was standing guard.

Bri knew there was only seconds to act. Despite the lingering pain in her feet, she sprinted toward the back of the building, looking for a way out. Near the end of the hall, she heard voices approaching from around the corner. She ducked left into the last doorway and closed the door as quietly as she could.

The room looked like an 1890s Bordello. Had she stumbled into Red Gannon's bedroom? She rushed to the window and peeked through the heavy, scarlet brocade drapes just in time to see a man wearing a security guard uniform and carrying a gun stride into view. She closed the curtain. There would be no escape that way.

Did the room have any other entrances? She hurried to a set of ornate double-doors in the center of the wall to the left. They opened into a huge bathroom similar in design to the one she'd just left, but this one had a huge oval bathtub in addition to the shower. Atop the counters were toiletries and shavers that showed this bathroom, unlike the other, was used regularly, but no door led out the other side.

She ran back into the bedroom and found an archway on the other side that matched the doorway she'd just come through. *Might as well look there too.*

The darkened archway led into a short hallway with lights that came on the instant she stepped in. A series of three louvered doors opened to either side. Opening them revealed large walk-in closets—male on the right, female on the left, but to her great disappointment, there was no exit

She was trapped. To step back into the main hallway would mean certain capture. "You'll not get another chance at me," she swore.

She decided to make a stand in the last closet on the right. Once inside, she looked for something, anything that could create some sort of defensive barrier, but the closet contained only a few pairs of old, western style boots strewn about the floor and some worn-looking winter coats and sweaters hanging on hangers. This looked to be the sparsely populated graveyard of a few of Gannon's discarded items.

As she scrambled about the room, she felt a slight movement in the floor. She looked down and saw a three-foot-square cut into the carpet. She recognized what it was. The house she grew up in had a similar thing in one of its closets. Bri snatched the fingernail file from the robe pocket and ran it down the seam, then she carefully pried and lifted. If the nail file were a screwdriver, she wouldn't have been so careful, but if the thin instrument broke, it could seal her doom.

Slowly the carpeted square began to lift. As soon as her fingernails found purchase on the side, she put greater strength to the task. With a whoosh, the tight-fitting square lifted clear. She looked down and smiled. Three feet below was bare earth. The trapdoor opened to the house's crawl space.

It would be almost totally dark down there, and probably home to all sorts of creepy-crawly things. She feared scorpions, hated spiders and didn't even want to think about snakes or rats. But the dank space was her only chance.

Chapter 100

Danny and his men moved single-file as they carefully and silently hurried toward where the forest trees came to a point just ten yards from one of the buildings adjacent to the hanger. The route would provide cover all the way and give them a close-in concealed vantage point from which they could observe the routine of the guards.

Chaco's radio call slowed progress. The information that one of the Delta teams was operating on this side of the driveway dramatically elevated the level of caution they would have to use. Danny redeployed his men into a skirmish line. They would have to move much slower now.

They'd gone about three hundred yards when Danny heard the signal from the left side of the line that told him someone on his team had made contact. He moved to the left flank where Thomas Chee anchored the position. The ambient light had steadily grown brighter, telling him they were getting closer to where the wash of lights from the hanger compound provided a degree of illumination.

Danny touched Chee's shoulder. The man didn't turn his head, but acknowledged Danny's presence by holding up two fingers, indicating the number of targets he was observing. He pointed.

Danny had spotted the two flares of heat source some yards before. They were less than twenty-five-yards away, moving slowly and deliberately. One would look inward toward the compound while the other watched outward into the woods. Each held his rifle at the ready, sweeping it in coordination with where his eyes were directed.

The pair, obviously with military training, were employing classic small-team low observability perimeter patrol tactics. Had they been using night vision gear, they would have already detected one or more of Danny's team. Danny tapped Chee on the shoulder and indicated a retreat. The two slipped away, gathering other members of the team as they went.

Danny crouched in a small clearing well away from the route of the two Gannon guards and instructed his men. "The graveled path doesn't show up on our map," he said. "It runs about fifty yards inside the trees. It's probably a trail for quad-runners. These guards are good, and being very careful, but the gravel path they're walking on makes them noisy. We'll have to get ahead and set up an ambush. Here's what we're going to do . . ."

*

Danny's night vision goggles enabled him to see the men as they approached where he and Edward T'so were concealed in the thick underbrush. The rest of the squad were concealed nearby. The two Gannon guards were only ten feet away from Danny when the sound of boots crunching on gravel some distance behind stopped the guards cold. They raised their rifles and turned in the direction of the sound.

"Hello?" called a voice out of the darkness. "Anyone there?" The footsteps came closer.

One of the men retrieved a flashlight from his belt and shined it down the trail. "Show yourself," he bellowed.

"Ouch," the voice came back. "I tripped. Hang on a minute, I'll be right there."

With the Guards' attention diverted, Danny and Edward crept to within touching distance.

"Crap, I busted up my knee," the voice called out.

That was the signal. Danny and Edward erupted from the brush and tackled both guards, felling them face-first to the gravel. Before they had time to react, handguns pressed into the backs of their heads. "Don't move!" Danny growled, as other hands disarmed the pair. "There are at least four weapons pointed at each of you. If you resist, you'll be dead instantly. Understand?"

"Yeah, we understand," growled the man under Danny's knee.

"Put your hands behind your backs. Do it now!"

"Who the hell are you?" the same man asked.

"There'll be time for introductions later. Shut up and do what I said."

Both men did as instructed. With their hands secured by white plastic zip ties, the guards were rolled onto their backs. "What the hell?" one of them choked as he took in the military-style uniforms and camo-painted faces.

"I'm your worst nightmare," Danny said. "I'm not a cop, and I've got lots of friends. You give us one second's worth of trouble, you die. That's the only rule. We don't have time for arguments or second chances. Understand?"

Both heads nodded.

"Good work, my brothers," Danny said in Navajo. "Stand them up and let's get moving." He radioed his success to the others and set out for the airfield.

*

The lights of the airfield were bright enough that they rendered Danny's night vision goggles useless. He stopped his men a few yards short of where the trees ended. A small tool shed stood just a few yards away and beyond that, asphalt ran all the way to the hanger building more than a hundred yards away. He spotted someone walking slowly on the tarmac in the bright lights of the hanger building. Danny used his field binoculars to get a closer look.

The man, a security guard, carried what appeared to be an AR-type assault rifle. He scanned the area as he worked his way across the front of the building. Every few steps, he turned and walked backward, making sure nothing approached from the rear.

As he disappeared around the far side of the hanger, Danny spotted movement at the other end. Another guard appeared, dressed and armed identical to the first. This one walked some distance farther out from the building than the first. This man appeared to take his job far less seriously. He was merely wandering, carrying his weapon absently slung over his shoulder more as a bother than a protection. He smoked a cigarette and gave the forest only an occasional sideward glance.

Danny pulled back and rejoined his companions to explain how they would use the vigilance of the first guard and the casualness of the second to their advantage.

*

Les Faden's hatred of night patrol went back over forty years to when he was in the beautiful garden city of Hue on a balmy February night in

1968. The huge bells of the Buddhist temple rang out wildly as the Vietnamese welcomed in Tet, the Chinese New Year.

He had just taken the first drag on a cigarette when something slammed into his neck and threw him to the ground. A platoon of North Vietnamese regulars overran his outpost, wounded him, and killed a lot of his buddies. He carried the scars with him to this day. It was a memory he could do without.

At sixty-five, he was getting far too old for this. Even though he was in the high-plateau country of Northern New Mexico and perfectly safe, he still could never relax on night patrol. Not for a second.

What's that? A strange flash of light caught his attention when he came around the south side of the hanger building. It came from the woods just behind the tool shed. *That's strange.* He walked in that direction.

A few seconds later, a second flash appeared a few yards to the left of the first. It wasn't bright—just a kind of spark and a lingering yellow light that lasted only a second or two, almost like a firefly. But New Mexico didn't have fireflies. He unclipped his radio and said, "Dispatch, this is Alpha Two, over."

"Go ahead Alpha Two, over."

"I've got some kind of weird flashing light in the woods behind the tool shed. I'm checking it out. Over."

"What kind of light?"

"Don't know, Over."

"Ten-four Les, you want Jerry to help?"

"Not yet. If it turns out to be anything, I'll give him a shout."

Faden moved quickly, but cautiously. He was out of breath when he reached the shed. "I really am getting too old for this," he muttered. He paused for a moment to catch his breath, then peered around the corner of the shed. He saw nothing unusual. After watching for several minutes, he stepped out from behind the shed, leveled his rifle toward the woods, and slowly made his way toward the tree line.

A new light sparked into existence farther back in the forest. *What the hell?* Then another lit behind and to the right of the first. Was it kids messing around? Wouldn't be the first time. During hunting season, they regularly had to chase people off the property.

If those were flames, he had to find their source. It was dry out here.

A spark in the wrong place, and the entire forest could go up in no time at all. He stepped softly past the tree line.

Something erupted from the forest floor on each side of him. He yelled, but the sound was cut off by a hand covering his mouth. In an instant, his weapon was snatched away and he was thrown face-first to the ground. Two large men painfully wrestled his arms behind him and snapped handcuffs around his wrists, then they turned him over. The cold steel of a knife pressed against his neck silenced any protest.

A man appeared at his feet, lit a cigarette lighter and waived it around, solving the mystery of the strange lights. "I'm going to give you some instructions, he said. You will only speak in a whisper unless told otherwise. You will follow my instructions precisely and instantly, otherwise, you die. Is that clear?"

"Yes," Les choked out in a whisper, his heart pounding as his mind flashed back to the jungles of Vietnam.

*

Danny was surprised at the man's advanced age and feared he might have a stroke or heart attack. "You have nothing to fear," he reassured him. "The FBI will be here in a few minutes. We're rounding up Gannon's security people and putting them where they won't get hurt."

"You guys cops?" Les asked, his eyes casting back and forth between Danny and his other captors.

"No, but we're working with them. There's a kidnapping going on up at that house. The FBI will be all over this ranch in less than an hour. When they get here, you'll be very thankful you cooperated with us — unless you'd prefer to be charged as an accessory."

"Hell, no," Les whispered back.

"Then here's what I want you to do." Danny gave the man his instructions.

*

Les got up, walked out of the trees, and lay down on the ground behind the tool shed, fully aware that a number of deadly weapons were pointed at him. He pulled out his radio, aware that he had to do the best acting job he had ever done. "Alpha Two leader to Alpha Two, Jerry, this is Les. I need your help. I fell down. I think I broke my leg. I'm behind the tool shed. Over."

"Alpha Two. Holy Hell Les, how'd you do that?"

359

"Stepped on a damn rock that turned. Get over here quick, will ya? It hurts like a mother. Over."

"You copy this, Dispatch? Jerry asked."

"I copy, Alpha Two. Let me know if you need a hand."

Jerry came huffing around the corner of the shed to find Les lying on the ground, holding his leg as if in pain. "Ah, sweet Jesus, Les," he said with concern. "Let me take a look." He leaned his rifle against the shed and bent to look at the man's leg.

"Don't move," Danny spoke loudly as he stepped from the trees. Five other men stepped out with him, their weapons leveled directly at Jerry's chest. He rocked back in fear, raised his hands and plead, "Don't shoot. Please don't shoot. I have kids."

Danny commanded the man to sit on the ground beside his companion and place his hands behind his head. Then he gave him the same speech he'd given Les. "Better do what they say, Jerry," Les advised. "There's no arguing with all these guns, and if what they're saying is true, you don't want anything to do with what's going on up at that house."

"Okay, okay." The younger man said, "I'll do what you want. Just don't hurt us."

"No one gets hurt as long as you cooperate. How many people are inside that hanger?"

"Just one."

Danny looked at Les for confirmation. Les nodded.

"Is he armed?"

"He has a sidearm in there, but he never wears it. Mostly he handles the radio and keeps track of the air traffic when somebody lands or takes off."

"Would he come out if one of you asked him?"

"Sure. Why not?"

"Tell him you need help with Les' broken leg. And you better make it convincing."

Jerry unhooked his radio. "Dispatch, this is Alpha Two. Hey Marv, I need a hand out here. Les' leg looks pretty bad. I need you to help me get him back to the hanger. Over."

"You want me to bring down the truck? Over." A voice came back.

"Naw. I just need another shoulder he can lean on. Over."

"Ten-four, Alpha Two. I'm on my way."

Less than five minutes later, Danny radioed the NALM teams that the airfield was secure, and instructed the teams to deliver their prisoners to the hanger. Danny left three men to guard his captives and took the rest of his men to take up positions around the house. Once the FBI arrived, the NALM would slip away. Danny could only imagine the FBI's surprise when they unlocked the hanger and discovered a dozen Gannon security guards stashed safely inside.

One task remained — dealing with the guards protecting Gannon's house without giving those inside any warning. He and Edward T'so would join up with Jason and Chaco to help with that task.

Chapter 101

I'm going to need light down there, and maybe I can snag some clothes from the women's closet. Though it was taking a chance, Bri dashed back into the bedroom and took a hurried looked around. She spotted what she wanted on the dresser. A cigarette lighter. She snatched it just as she heard running steps and raised voices in the hallway. *So much for clothes.*

She dashed back to the closet, pulled two dark-colored coats from their hangers, threw them down the hole ahead of her, and jumped in. She grabbed the carpeted door, slid it over the opening, and pulled down. It didn't fit! She thought for a second then spun it a half turn and tried again. This time the slightly irregular door settled easily into place just as she heard loud voices enter the bedroom. She scooted away from the opening as the sound of clomping feet entered the closet area above. A male voice shouted, "Nothing here!"

Whoever it was hurried back to the bedroom. Bri heard muffled curses and conversation from above, then heard the footsteps retreat. Only then did she feel safe enough to flick on the lighter and survey her surroundings. It was exactly as she expected, thick with cobwebs. Heating ducts and plumbing pipes hung from the floor joists. She thought she heard some kind of animal scurrying away from the light toward the front of the house. Thankfully, she saw no snakes or scorpions, but spiders? Cobwebs seemed to be everywhere.

No matter—she had to get away from the trap door and find a place to hide. She uttered a silent prayer, and with the lighter clutched in one hand and the coats in the other, she crawled on hands and knees away from what might be the crawl space's only opening.

Chapter 102

The gateway guard shack was a small but ornate Spanish-style stone structure set in a landscaped island between the entry and exit lanes of Gannon's wide driveway. Windowed doors on each side allowed a guard to approach any vehicle entering or exiting the compound. French windows provided a clear field of vision to the front and each side. Attached to the building were sturdy, electronically operated metal gates that let cars in or out.

Jason crouched in thick undergrowth forty feet away from the right side of the building. He glanced at his watch. Delaney and his team were due to show up in less than fifteen minutes. The diversion had to start now. From down the road, he heard a loud voice singing the slurred words of a Willie Nelson song. "Ma'massss don let chur babiess grow up to be cowboysssss." He had to cover a laugh. A second voice joined in more enthusiastically than the first.

Jason watched the guard peer intently up the driveway as two Indian men, shirts unbuttoned and camo pants hanging dangerously low on their hips, staggered into view. One carried a bottle wrapped in a brown paper sack. The other held an open beer can. Jason couldn't imagine where the bottle or the can came from. *Must have found them on the side of the road.*

The singing was as bad as it was loud. Danny and Chaco, arms draped across each other's shoulders, staggered off the highway and down the driveway. By all appearances, they could barely walk.

Through the open window, Jason heard the guard mumble, "Oh, shit, just what I need." The door of the entry building opened. The irritated guard stepped out and strode up the driveway toward the drunken pair. "Hey. You two just get on out of here." He pointed his nightstick toward the highway.

Danny stopped in mid-verse, leaned precariously to one side, and looked cockeyed at the guard, still some fifty feet away. He smiled broadly and slurred, "Oh. Hello there Ossifer. I'm glad you foun' me becausss ma car got losssst." He staggered toward the guard, appeared to trip, and fall forward several steps, barely able to keep his feet. Chaco looked to be trying to catch up with him. They better than halved the distance between themselves and the guard before Danny came to a wobbly stop. He upended the bottle in the sack. "Whoa," he moaned. "I 'bout didn't move fas nuf to catch up ta ma feet." Then he started to laugh as if he'd just told the funniest joke in the world. Chaco nearly laughed out loud, but covered it by upending his beer can and pretended to guzzle it down.

"You boys are drunk as skunks," the guard said. "You get on out of here before I call the sheriff."

Ray Dixon, the guard, a thin, hollow-cheeked man with a bulbous red nose and rummy, blood-shot eyes, was an alcoholic. It was all he could do to keep himself off the bottle while at work. What he really wanted was to ask one of the men for a shot. But Gannon paid well, and he wasn't about to jeopardize his job — not when he lived clear out here.

Though the men appeared harmless enough, Dixon didn't want to bite off more than he could chew. He pressed the talk key on the radio microphone dangling from his lapel and said, "Alpha One, this is Alpha One leader. Come in. Over."

His call was immediately answered. Alpha One leader. What's going on Ray?"

"Got a couple of drunk Indians up here trying to come through the gate. Can you and Geraldo give me some backup? Over"

"They in a car?"

"Naw, they came walking down off the highway."

"Ten-four. We're on our way."

*

Danny and Chaco once more broke out in song, throwing an arm around each other's shoulders and lighting into it. The harmony was ear-wrenching. "Cowboyyys ain't easy ta love and they're harder ta holdddd. They'd rather give ya a song than'. . . Danny said 'Rubies' while Chaco said 'Diamonds' or golddd."

"Hey dumb-ass," Chaco slurred, giving Danny a shove, "it's diamonsss, not rubies."

"Is not," Danny shot back.

"Look, I been singin' this song a lot longer than you. It's diamonds!"

"Is not."

"Is too."

"Is not." Danny gave Chaco a little shove.

"Is too." Chaco returned the shove, harder.

By the time the two house guards pulled up in a side-by-side 4-wheeler, the apparently inebriated pair were in the midst of a full-fledged wrestling match, shouting and pushing and shoving while apparently barely able to stand. The gate guard was giving them plenty of room.

"Hey, hey, hey," the first house guard to climb out shouted. "You two cut that out!"

The two men seemed not to hear and continued fighting.

The guard looked at his companion and said, "Drunk as skunks. We better break this up." The second guard exited the vehicle and both strode into the fray, each of them taking hold of one of the antagonists.

In an instant, the Indians were no longer drunk. They spun on the two guards, pulled pistols from out of nowhere and pressed them to the necks of the startled men. "On the ground," Danny and Chaco shouted. At the same instant, Jason and his companions leaped from the underbrush, pointing their assault rifles directly at the surprised gate guard. "You too mister. On the ground," Jason commanded. "Hands on your head!"

It was over. In no time, the two house guards had zip ties around arms and legs and were seated on the floor against the wall inside the guard house. The gate guard was confined at his station, one arm and both legs zip-tied to his chair. The other arm was left free in case he had to answer a radio call.

Chaco explained to all three that the FBI would soon be here. "Believe me, this is for your own good," he concluded.

Danny radioed his teams and confirmed that all were in place. Other than the house, the entire complex was in NALM hands.

Jason had just started to walk up the road to call Doyle when the radio inside the guard shack squawked to life. "All units, all units, we have a security breach," someone said. "We have a female houseguest with a mental problem. She may be on the grounds. Repeat, she is having a mental breakdown and may be on the grounds. She's blonde, slender, about five foot five or six, approximately thirty years old. She may be wearing a white robe. If you see her, detain her and report to us immediately. All units acknowledge!"

Had Brianna escaped? Jason ran back to the guard house.

The older house guard looked at Chaco and said, "That's Gannon. He's going to expect us to respond."

"One cute word and I'll cut your throat," Jason hissed. He cut the zip ties from around the man's wrists. The man keyed his lapel mic and said. "Ten-four, Mr. Gannon. We've seen nothing out here. We'll keep our eyes peeled."

"Front gate, nobody comes in or out. Understand?"

The man in the chair keyed the desk mic and in as normal a voice as he could muster said, "Ten-four, Mr. Gannon. I'll lock the place down."

It took all Jason's restraint to keep from running straight to the house to find Bri. Instead, he turned and ran up the driveway toward the highway, stabbing out Doyle Stewart's number as he ran. "Doyle, this is Jason," he said when the man answered. "This place is secure. Get here as fast as you can. We just overheard a radio transmission that sounded like Bri may have escaped.

Chapter 103

Gannon was conversing with Parker outside of Gannon's office when Blackthorn ran up to them, shouting, "She's gone!"

"What do you mean she's gone?" Gannon growled.

"We threw her in the shower of the guest bathroom just up from your bedroom to thaw her out. Last I saw her she was lying naked on the floor looking half-dead. She couldn't even stand up. I went to take a piss and when I came back she was gone. Swear to God, Red, I wasn't gone two minutes."

"If she gets off this ranch, you're a dead man," Gannon thundered. "You and Parker take Gus and start searching. "I'll alert the outside guards and watch for her up here."

Blackthorn beat a retreat to the back of the house with Parker in tow. Halfway down the hallway he yelled out, "Gus, get your ass up here. We've got an escaped prisoner!"

As he watched the men disappear toward the back of the house, Gannon shook his head and made a fateful decision. When they got their hands on her again, he'd do the interrogation himself. Beautiful women know they're beautiful and want to stay that way. He'd start by taking a fingertip or two. If that didn't work, he'd go for the face. Women would do anything to save their face.

With that decided, he made another fateful decision. Friend or not, it was time for Blackthorn to go.

Chapter 104

Bri crawled for some distance, using all her willpower to ignore the cobwebs she encountered. Then her left knee landed on a sharp rock. She yelped softly and paused. She lit the lighter and inspected her knee. Bruised, but the skin was barely broken. Only a small droplet of blood welled up.

She raised the lighter and looked around, amazed at how well the little Bic illuminated the dark space. She reckoned she had crawled about forty feet toward the front of the house. Twenty feet farther on, a large, round HVAC distribution pipe hung nearly to the ground, blocking her path. If she could somehow find a way around it, she'd be out of sight from the access hole.

She crawled toward the pipe, dragging the dark-colored coats with her. If she wrapped herself in them they would hide the white robe and provide at least some protection from the vile creatures that undoubtedly inhabited this dark, foreboding place.

Again she heard footsteps back toward Gannon's bedroom. If they were looking there a second time, they'd probably be much more thorough, increasing the likelihood they'd discover the crawl space access.

There wasn't much time. She reached the pipe and flicked the lighter on. The pipe was too close to the ground for her to crawl under. Her only option was to crawl beside it and put as much distance between her and the trap-door as possible.

She only traveled a few feet before encountering a depression in the ground. She flicked the lighter and discovered that someone working down here in the past had found the pipe to be the same obstacle. Whoever it was had dug a trench under the pipe just wide and deep enough for someone to wiggle under. She dove in without hesitation and shinnied through to the other side, dragging the coats behind her. She flicked the lighter on and found herself in a square formed by the junction of two other pipes of similar size. It was a room-like space where she could hide. Bri wrapped one winter coat in front of her and the other behind, covering all she could of the soiled but still highly visible white robe.

She acted not a second too soon. Someone above found the crawl space. A light from a flashlight probed along the underside of the pipe, pausing for a moment not far from where she huddled. But then it resumed its probing path until she could see it no more. Hopefully, the person using the flashlight was hanging over the edge of the hole in the floor, merely poking his head into the crawl space. She prayed whoever it was wouldn't actually come down here.

Trembling, Bri remained absolutely still. She again heard scurrying feet most likely an animal trying to escape the flashlight beam and looking for a darker place to hide. A place like this. She was resolved that if something touched her, she would not scream.

Then she felt something on the back of her neck. Was it just another cobweb, or was it alive? It took all the control she could muster to not swat at her neck, but she steeled herself and remained absolutely still.

A few moments later the light vanished and she heard the trap door thud back into place. The sound of footsteps left the closet area. Only then did she flail at her neck and hair, trying to dislodge or kill whatever might be there.

Chapter 105

To Jason, it seemed like hours, but was actually only a few minutes before Doyle and the FBI strike team rolled up without lights. Jason led Stewart and Delaney to the guard shack. Stewart was surprised to find Jason, Danny, and Chaco dressed in desert camo, and even more surprised to find the three trussed-up guards. "Do I want to know where those uniforms came from and how you captured these men?" Doyle asked.

"Found these guys strolling down the road and decided to invite them in," Danny said.

"That's what I thought."

"Someone give me a situation report," Delaney demanded.

"The area's completely secure," Chaco responded. "There are several Gannon employees locked in a room down at Gannon's hanger. No aircraft have attempted to leave. A few minutes ago, Gannon made a radio call that indicated that Bri may have gotten away from them. We don't know if she's inside the house or out."

"How many people inside the house?" Delaney asked.

"No idea." Chaco said. "Maybe one of the guards knows."

Delaney turned to the man shackled to the chair. "FBI. I need information—fast. If you lie we'll consider you an accessory to kidnapping. You'll go to prison for the rest of your life. Do you understand?"

"Yes, sir," the man said. "I got nothin' to do with what's happening down there."

"How many people are inside the house?"

370

"Far as I know, there's Mr. Gannon and his muscle-man, Gus, plus whoever came off that helicopter. Mr. Gannon had me call the cook and housekeeper and tell them not to come in today."

"Any other guards around?"

"Just the three of us around the house. It sounds like whoever these guys are took care of the field guards."

Delaney turned to the others. "We've got to move fast. If that woman did escape, they're focusing on finding her, and that's good for us."

He spun on his heel, rushed up to the roadway where his men were gathered, and began barking orders.

*

The strike team positioned itself. Four agents moved to the rear of the house, while a dozen more deployed to the front, careful to avoid being seen through the windows. One carried a heavy two-handled battering ram designed to take down locked doors.

Delaney moved to the front door and carefully tried the latch. To his astonishment, it worked. The instant he confirmed that the team at the rear of the house was in place, he radioed a single command. "Now!"

In moments, a dozen bright flashes of light, accompanied by the resounding sound of multiple explosions came from the rear of the house. It was a diversion intended to make anyone inside believe the threat was coming from back there. Delaney held up his fingers and counted down so all his men could see—five, four, three, two, one. Glass shattered as the agents tossed flashbangs through the front windows. Delaney pushed the front door open and threw in three of his own, then closed it against the effects.

"Go, go, go!" Delaney commanded as the last of them exploded. A dozen helmeted agents with automatic weapons slammed through the front door and poured inside.

Chapter 106

Blackthorn and Parker completed their search on the bedroom side of the house and were working their way forward on the office side when bright flashes of light and loud explosions went off in the utility area. Although protected from the flashes, the explosions painfully assaulted their ears.

"What was that?" Blackthorn screamed at Parker, who had covered his ears with his hands. Blackthorn swatted them away and shouted, "Come on. We've got to find out what blew up."

Then booming explosions came from the front of the house, followed by loud shouts from unfamiliar voices. Gus, a former Denver policeman, was working in the utility area, much closer to the blasts. He stumbled up the hall toward Blackthorn and Parker, shouting, "Cops! Those are flashbangs!"

Blackthorn's heart leaped to his throat and he abandoned any thought of finding the woman. He ran past Gus to the back of the house, sprinted through the short hallway that led to the back door, threw it open, and bolted headlong into four combat-equipped FBI agents pointing deadly M-16 assault rifles directly at his chest. He stopped in his tracks. Parker, coming up behind, crashed into his back. Together they tumbled down the three steps to the ground, landing in a tangled heap at the feet of the agents.

"FBI! On your stomachs. Hands on your head!" an agent shouted. As Lucas complied, he realized that he had likely seen his last moments of freedom. A mortal fear overtook him. His courage drained away and he began to tremble.

*

Red Gannon, furious at yet another failing from his security chief, stood outside the doorway to his office watching the foyer and living room. Suddenly, bright flashes of light and the sound of explosions ripped up the hallway from the rear of the house. "What the hell?" He set out at a run toward where the commotion had come from.

Then the sound of breaking glass from the front windows stopped him. Suddenly the world seemed to tear itself apart as blinding flashes robbed him of vision and concussive explosions assaulted his ears. He stumbled and fell, cracking his shoulder painfully into the floor. Rolling on his back he covered his ears. He knew he was screaming, but couldn't hear the sound.

Then horrible black apparitions appeared. Men in black combat dress pointed assault rifles at him. One appeared to be talking to him but he heard nothing. Large letters on the man's body armor said, "FBI." With terrible comprehension, Red Gannon understood. The fight went out of him. He seemed to shrivel before the agents' eyes and turn into nothing more than a defeated, fearful old man. The light of his once fearsome eyes dulled to a watery, pale-blue, stare as he curled into a fetal ball and wailed, "Don't hurt me! Don't hurt me! Please don't hurt me."

Chapter 107

Despite the FBI's search of the house and grounds, Bri was nowhere to be found. Danny worried, but Jason was frantic.

"Tell us where she is right now," Jason screamed into the faces of the three oil men standing with hands shackled. "If you've hurt her, I'll kill you myself!"

Doyle stepped between his distraught friend and the three hand-cuffed figures. "Jason, go over there and sit down before these agents have to put you in handcuffs, too."

Chaco grabbed Jason and pulled him away. "Come on, buddy. Let's let the professionals do this." Jason allowed himself to be moved farther away, but refused to sit. He didn't take his eyes off the trio for a second.

"I'm going to read each of you your rights," Jack Delaney informed the prisoners. Addressing Gannon, he said, "You have the right to remain silent. Anything you say can and will be held against you in a court of law . . ."

When the Miranda recitation was finished for each of the prisoners, Doyle stepped forward and said, "Gentlemen, you're under arrest for kidnapping and conspiracy to commit kidnapping in the unlawful abduction of one Brianna Sanders. You're also charged with conspiracy to defraud, criminal fraud, conspiracy to murder, racketeering and the attempted murder of Daniel Whitehorse, a Navajo Indian. Other murder charges against you are pending. Do you understand?"

Gannon numbly nodded his head, but Blackthorn reacted with surprise. He stared at Stewart, then cast his gaze about as if confused.

"Looking for me?" Danny asked as he stepped from behind the knot of gathered agents.

Blackthorn's eyes widened. "B—but you're dead! I was there! You're dead!"

"I'm afraid you're mistaken, Mr. Blackthorn, but we'll take that as your confession. You should have shot me while you had the chance. Now I'm going to see to it that you and Gannon go to prison until a needle ends your worthless lives."

Chapter 108

The sound of multiple explosions from above caused Bri to cry out. What in the world was happening up there. Then she heard the thunder of many boots, accompanied by muffled shouting voices. What were they saying? Then she caught it. Someone right above her shouted, "FBI. Do not move!" Relief was so overwhelming that she buried her head into one of the coats and sobbed.

It took her some moments for her to move. Then one of the voices coming from above sounded like the one voice she wanted to hear more than any other. *Jason.*

Abandoning the coats, she began to crawl. She retraced the route she had taken a short time ago. Without the adrenalin that accompanied her first journey, the task seemed to take forever. It took all her strength to push the trap door open and stand up. She tried to lift herself up to where she could roll out onto the floor, but her arms wouldn't hold. She collapsed back into the hole, exhausted and angry that what should have been such a simple thing was now a herculean task. She steeled herself for another try. When she stood this time, she saw a helmeted, black-clad man standing in the closet doorway pointing an assault rifle at her head.

"Miss Sanders?" the man asked.

"That's me," Bri said, feeling her strength return. Would you mind giving me a hand out of here?"

*

Jason heard the sounds of a commotion coming from far down the left hallway. "Get your hands off me. I'm just fine. Leave me alone. Get out of my way!" a female voice said. A few seconds later, Bri appeared, trying to fend off the concerned solicitude of two FBI agents. She was having none of their help.

She wore a filthy white robe. Her face was smeared with dirt and her hair was covered in cobwebs. Jason had never seen anyone so beautiful. He swept her up in his arms, twirled her around and covering her face with kisses, saying over and over, "Thank God. Thank God."

Brianna clasped his cheeks in her hands and kissed him deeply, then pushed back and said, "Put me down, Jason." He immediately complied.

She took a bead on Blackthorn and Gannon and strode straight toward them. As she passed Danny, she looked his way, winked and said, "Great day, isn't it big brother."

She stood squarely in front of Blackthorn. One of the FBI agents made a move to intervene, but Doyle's gesture restrained him. She glared into the man's eyes for several long seconds without speaking, then, without warning, slammed her knee into his groin. As he fell to the floor, writhing in agony, she stepped left, doubled her fist, and delivered a hard right cross to Red Gannon's jaw. Whether by surprise or by force, the man went down like a sack of rocks.

It happened so fast, the agents attending had no time to react. Brianna stood over her antagonists and screamed, "Think you're big men, don't you. You're not. You're nothing but scumbags. Bring it on, both of you. You gonna let a little ol' woman beat you?" The tirade continued even as strong hands reached out and dragged her away, delivering her into Jason's restraining arms. Danny and Chaco couldn't help but laugh. It was a contagion that quickly spread to the rest of the tough-as-nails FBI agents.

Chapter 109

Exhaustion was the order of the day following Bri's rescue — as well as the day after. Three days later, Doyle rang the Capaletti doorbell precisely at nine a.m. with a long list of follow-up questions.

"How in the world did you round up those guards?" Doyle asked the group assembled in the living room. "The agents who freed them told us strange tales about Army troops and painted faces and stuff that just doesn't make any sense."

"Let's just say we hired a pied piper," Danny said.

"Okay, okay," Doyle chuckled. "As long as no one was hurt, I know when to stop asking questions."

"I guess you've heard the latest on Gannon Oil," Danny said.

"No. I've been too busy with the criminal issues."

"There was an emergency meeting of the board of directors yesterday. They put Benjamin Whittington in as the interim CEO. He's asked the State to come in and temporarily oversee all financial operations. The Court has restrained Red Gannon from having any active role in the corporation and has frozen all his stock. Whittington called me last night to open negotiations toward a settlement, and he got real serious right away. We agreed that all of Gannon's ill-gotten gain should be in the settlement basket. That's over six hundred and fifty million, most of which will go to the tribe, but our clients will divide up somewhere north of sixty-seven million.

"They certainly deserve it," Stewart said. "How are you doing, Brianna?" Doyle asked.

"I had to spend a night in the hospital while they checked out my frostbite. There was minimal tissue loss, but my fingers and toes still ache a little. Other than that, nothing's hurt but my dignity. Thanks for asking."

Jason gave her hand a squeeze. "No more Mata Hari for her. She's going to settle down into her boring but safe life as a high school teacher."

"So where do things go on your side of the table?" Danny asked Stewart.

"Our case is rock solid. We have Popeson's written death-bed confession, and Webster is singing like a bird. Max Shultz is tying everything up and handing it to us with a pretty ribbon on top. Blackthorn's already begging for a plea bargain, trying to avoid the death penalty. Gannon isn't doing well in jail. He's already been transported to the hospital twice—heart rhythm problems.

"Couldn't happen to a nicer guy," Angie quipped.

"What about you, Chaco?" Doyle asked.

Kathy answered for him. "He's going to be real busy. Besides working for Danny, the tribal police want him to do some consulting— something about training a bunch of volunteers for a new auxiliary police force."

"He's going to have to do that on the side," Danny interjected. "Jason and I are now formally law partners, and Chaco is coming in as a full partner to run our investigation arm."

"Danny's going to be doing some business of another kind," Brianna said, giving Amanda a wink. "He's got to get his house ready for two."

"That's going to be real easy," Danny chuckled. All I've got to do is kick out my ratty, old double bed and move in a king-size."

"And the Capalettis?" Doyle asked.

Vic smiled and rubbed Angie's belly, just starting to show hints of a baby bump. "Our plans are pretty much in the oven."

Epilogue #1   **12 Months Later**

Danny handed the judge a file-stamped copy of the settlement agreement signed by each party. The judge glanced through it and said, "Mr. Whitehorse, does this synopsis page accurately summarize the contents of this settlement?"

"It does, Your Honor."

"Mr. Whittington, do you concur that the synopsis accurately reflects the contents of the settlement between your client and Mr. Whitehorse's clients?"

Whittington stood. "We so stipulate, Your Honor."

"Thank you, gentlemen. I assume each of you will stipulate that the reading of the synopsis will be adequate for the verbal record of the order and that we may incorporate the written copy in its entirety by reference in the written order that shall become the order of the court?"

"We so stipulate," Danny and Whittington said simultaneously.

"Let the record show that the court is reading a synopsis of the settlement entered into by the parties in the class-action lawsuit of Robert Begay and Plaintiffs two through six hundred and forty eight, et. al. versus Gannon Oil Incorporated:

"Gannon Oil Incorporated shall pay each and every plaintiff herein in equal shares, the aggregate sum of sixty-eight million, six hundred and seventy-two thousand dollars, a sum stipulated to be the amount of royalties illegally diverted from them by the conspiracy of certain officers of Gannon Oil Incorporated. Payment shall be in four equal payments made in six-month increments until paid in full.

"The balance of monies earned from the illegal diversion of natural gas from wells drilled on the property of the Navajo Nation and recovered from the Caribbean Atlantic Banking Corporation S.A. of Grand Cayman in the amount of six hundred and eighteen million, forty-eight thousand dollars, is hereby awarded to the Navajo Nation. Said monies to be administered by the Navajo Nation Education Authority under the supervision of the Whitehorse/Stevens Charitable Foundation, and shall be used for the sole purpose of enhancing public education and providing scholarships to higher education institutions for students residing on the Navajo reservation.

"Gannon Oil shall endow in perpetuity twenty annual scholarships, including tuition and books, to the University of New Mexico for Navajo students electing to seek advanced degrees in the fields of law, civil engineering, economics, electronic or software engineering, law enforcement and/or public administration.

Plaintiffs' attorneys shall be entitled to recovery for reasonable attorney's fees in the amount of twenty five percent of the aggregate amount awarded to the tribe and to the individual plaintiffs. Said attorneys' fees shall be paid by Defendant directly to Plaintiff's attorneys and shall be in addition to all other sums awarded herein.

Should Defendant fail to pay all sums awarded herein within two years, Plaintiffs' shall be entitled to judgment for treble damages as provided in law.

This stipulation acknowledges that Defendant, in good faith, has restored production of all natural gas wells at issue in Plaintiff's lawsuit and has resumed monthly payment of all royalties thereby owed.

The judge set aside the voluminous copy of the signed stipulation, rapped his gavel, and said, "This is the order of the court, to be effective upon publication by the Clerk at the end of this day. Court dismissed!"

Epilogue #2   **22 Months Later**

Federal District Court, in and for the Northern District of New Mexico, Farmington Branch.

"We, the jury, find the defendants guilty of count one — aggravated kidnapping."

"We, the jury, find the defendants guilty of count two, aggravated assault upon the person of Brianna Sanders."

"We, the jury, find the defendants guilty of count three, attempted murder."

"We, the jury . . ." The litany of guilty charges continued on through twenty-one counts, including criminal conspiracy to defraud six hundred and forty-eight Navajo Indian families out of over sixty-eight million dollars in royalty payments by way of operation of the secret pipelines.

*

The judge's sentencing order was explicit, succinct, and harsh. "Never in all my years on this bench have I encountered a more diabolical, heartless, evil, or extensive conspiracy to engage in criminal activity. If I were to sentence Mr. Gannon and Mr. Blackthorn, to one thousand years, it would not be enough to redress the misery and suffering they willfully, intentionally, and maliciously caused to hundreds of people, some of whom took their own lives as direct consequence of their evil conspiracy.

"Mr. Gannon, Mr. Blackthorn, I hereby sentence you, each of you, to the maximum allowable sentence on each and every count for which you stand convicted, the sentences to be served consecutively. I've counted them up, gentlemen. They total seven hundred and sixty-one years each. You will both be eligible for parole in just under three hundred and ninety years.

"The defendants are hereby remanded to the jurisdiction of the state of New Mexico for adjudication of the charges of murder and various other state charges."

AUTHOR'S COMMENTS

The underlying story of this book has actually come true. Even the creation of the NALM has an equivalent in truth that I was unaware of when I began writing. The Aneth Oil Field is a large oil and gas reserve that sits largely on reservation land near the communities of Aneth and Montezuma Creek in southeastern Utah. On March 30, 1978, nearly a thousand Diné physically took over the main Texaco pumping station in Aneth, and stopped all production throughout the entire region. The group, known as the Utah Chapter of the Council for Navajo Liberation, aka 'The Coalition,' occupied the facility for thirteen days and made thirteen demands that were ultimately agreed to. The State of Utah was appointed trustee to receive and disburse the multi-million dollar settlement proceeds and future royalty payments. Utah later breached their trusteeship by shorting the Navajos millions of dollars in trust payments. When the Navajo's filed a claim against the State, it took 18 years to reach a settlement that, even then, resulted in the tribe getting less than the full amount to which they were entitled.

On September 14, 2014, just as I was putting the final touches to this book, yet another such settlement was announced. The culprit this time - the U.S. Government. The Interior Department's Bureau of Indian Affairs (BIA), is the administrative agency who issues oil and gas leases, pipeline right-of-way leases, grazing leases, timber and mining leases, etc. in behalf of the Navajo Nation and other tribes. Payments for such tribal resources are not sent directly to the tribe, but, rather, are sent to Washington D.C. and placed in a trust fund administered by the BIA. The largest single income component of the Navajo trust fund is oil and gas royalties.

For years, the money poured in, but much of it never made it back to the tribe. The amount owed to the Diné eventually reached over $900 million. Only after a decades-long legal battle over alleged mismanagement of the trust fund did the feds finally agree to a $554 million settlement, meaning that the government has been unjustly enriched by some $360 million at the expense of some of the poorest, people living within our nation's boundaries.

It is this author's opinion that the very agency charged with protecting and preserving the rights of Native Americans, has become the greatest exploiter of the precious few resources these people have. In my opinion, our government will never be worthy of our trust until they act in good faith in regard to the promises they made to the first Americans.

If you liked this book, please do me a favor.

One of the most valuable assets any author can have is fans who tell others about his writing. One of the best ways to tell others about *Wages of Greed* is by submitting a review to Amazon.com, Goodreads.com, Smashwords.com and other sites that accept reader feedback. Thanks.

What's next?

Wages of Greed is the first in the Danny Whitehorse/Jason Stevens series. The second book in the series is entitled, *Fountains of Fire* and will be published in the summer of 2016.

The first book in Mr. Clark's Cass Rosier/Sam Martin mystery/ thriller series, *All The Pretty Dresses*, published Feb. 9th, 2014, was awarded a top ten finish in the 2014 international Critique My Novel book competition. The second book in that series, entitled 'Scimitar, ' will be published in summer/fall of 2015. It is an action-packed, nail-biting tale of intrigue that stretches from the mountains of West Virginia all the way to the steps of the White House. The first chapter of Scimitar is included below for your enjoyment.

(Name subject to change at the author's whim)

Chapter One - In The Water

Wow, that guy's traveling fast! An older yellow Mercedes sedan appeared from nowhere in Sam's rearview mirror and was rapidly closing the distance between them. It was traveling far too fast for this twisting highway through the Blue Ridge Mountains.

Sam rarely traveled state road 39 out of Summersville, also called Turnpike Road. It first led north to Gilboa, where the giant Consolidated Mine her father once owned was located, then turned west toward the village of Drennen before cutting a path southwest between steep canyon walls for miles until it intersected the Gauley River gorge at the tiny hamlet of Swiss. There the road turned west and paralleled the river and a set of railroad tracks all the way to her destination, the town of Belva.

What a memorable day it was. Consolidated Mining had thrown a luncheon honoring Daddy as the mine's founder. They presented Sam with a plaque and a large picture of Daddy shaking hands with Consolidated's president the day the mine sale was complete.

God, I miss him. Her heart was warmed and her eyes were still a bit misty at the deluge of kind words spoken by company officials and Daddy's old friends.

She was now on her way to interview a witness in a drug bust case. She welcomed this leisurely forty-five mile per hour drive through twenty miles of some of Nicholas County's most scenic country.

As she drove she couldn't help but contemplate the momentous changes in her life during the past eighteen months. Her divorce, leaving her lucrative law practice in New York, Cass' recruitment of her to help solve the evening gown murder case, and her decision to run for county office. She could scarcely believe she'd pulled that one off.

In the wake of her high-powered New York practice, it still surprised Sam how busy her little prosecutor's office stayed. Drug and alcohol cases, petty theft and burglaries, even an embezzlement case—a school administrator caught dipping into school trust accounts.

It was a welcome respite to honor dad and enjoy a leisurely drive, even though a work connection waited at the other end.

Something's wrong, Sam thought as she watched her rearview mirror. The car was weaving erratically. *Is he drunk? Is he going to crash into me?* With steep canyon walls on each side and trees right down to the shoulder of the road, there was nowhere for her to go.

The car filled her rearview mirror. She gripped the wheel and braced for what appeared would be an inevitable crash, but at the last second, the Mercedes swung sharply left and swept past her—directly into the path of the Consolidated Mining coal truck laboring up the canyon in the opposite lane.

Sam perceived that the driver was a woman, not a man, but she had no time to speculate. On the way by, the car clipped Sam's rear bumper, just a tap, but it was enough to send her car fishtailing wildly. Her hands flew as she steered to counter the skid to the right. Then the back end fishtailed sharply left, carrying her directly into the path of the semi. Just as it seemed the truck would surely rip off the back half of her car, the rear wheels swung right again out of the truck's way. She countered swing after violent swing, trying to keep the car on the road – praying that it wouldn't roll over.

The sound of screaming tires seemed to go on for an eternity, but Sam finally brought her car under control and slid to a stop, half on the road and half in the right side barrow pit, her front bumper only inches from the trunk of a large oak tree.

Stunned and trembling, her white knuckles gripped the steering wheel in a strangle-hold. As white smoke and the smell of burning rubber caught up with her, she realized the tires weren't the only thing screaming through the ordeal. It was as close she had come to dying as she could remember.

Then her fear turned to anger. The woman had nearly killed her. How the Mercedes missed the truck she couldn't fathom, but she didn't care. "You're not going to get away with this!" she shouted at the retreating vehicle as it disappeared around the next curve. She wheeled her car back onto the road and tromped on the accelerator, raising a trail of gravel and dust. "Nobody's going to run the Nicholas County Prosecutor off the road and get away with it," she vowed. She had to at least get a license plate number she could pass on to sheriff's deputies.

Her speedometer nudged sixty, but try as she might, she couldn't catch the Mercedes.

She finally spotted the car on a long straight-away as it swept through the village of Swiss, where the highway turned west to parallel the railroad tracks that lay beside Gauley River and its world-famous whitewater rapids.

Even a half-mile behind, Sam could tell the Mercedes was traveling far too fast to make the curve. She caught her breath as she saw the rear end of the Mercedes break loose and swing toward the river. The driver corrected, causing the car's rear end to swung back the other way. The right wheels caught the gravel just off the paved surface as the rear end swung left again. This time the driver over-corrected. Sam held her hand to her mouth and watched in horror as the car veered across the eastbound lane and crashed through the guard rail, then sailed across the railroad cut and disappeared into the thick brush and trees that covered the steep riverbank.

Sam screeched to a stop where the car had crashed through the railing, her car blocking traffic in both directions. She leapt out, ran to the top of the railroad cut to look for the Mercedes. More than a hundred feet down the forty-five-degree river embankment, the car was perched precariously atop a large rock that projected into the dark, swirling river, the front end half-submerged, while the back clung tenuously to dry land. Even as she watched, the front end of the car sloughed to the right, threatening to tumble the vehicle into the treacherous water.

There wasn't a second to loose. A semi-truck coming the other direction braked to a stop as Sam stepped off the brush-covered cut and half-ran, half-fell twenty feet to the railroad bed below. Somehow keeping her feet, she sprinted across the tracks and did it again, this time following the path cleared through the tall weeds, brush and brambles by the car as it careened down the steep riverbank, somehow missing at least three large trees.

There was no shore at the bottom, only a rocky, two-foot shelf at the waterline. The protruding rock on which the car landed on was surrounded by water on three sides. Had the car's path varied mere feet in either direction, it would have plunged straight down into a watery grave.

The vehicle's airbags were deployed. Sam could see the driver, apparently unconscious, leaning forward against her seat belt. When Sam placed her hand on the trunk she could feel the vehicle vibrating with the force of the water. It might be only a matter of moments before the car was torn from the rock and swallowed by the river. She had to get the woman out—now!

Someone behind her said, "I saw the whole thing." Sam looked up the bank and saw a dark-haired, heavy-set man dressed in a dark blue tee shirt and jeans, struggling to keep his footing as he made his way down to her. "That idiot must have been going seventy miles an hour." he said.

"You the truck driver?" Sam asked.

"Yeah," he puffed.

"You got a cell phone?"

"There's no service here. Phones don't work in this canyon until you get nearly into Belva."

"The car's going into the river. We've got to get the driver out. You with me?"

"Yeah, sept' I don't swim so good." The man eyed the dark, swift-moving water.

"Don't worry, I'll go in," she said, moving to the passenger side. It'll have to be from over here, I'll never be able to open the driver's door against the current. Can you steady the car for me and try to keep it from slipping off the rock?"

"Sure. But what should I do if it does?"

"Let it go and pray for us."

Sam looked up to see several people making their way down to the crash site. Then she heard metal screech as the river turned the car on the rock. There was no time left..

"Have them help you," she shouted, pointing toward the descending rescuers, then she kicked off her shoes, thought about ditching her skirt, but decided that once she hit the water, it would be up around her waist or higher anyway. This was no time to worry about modesty.

She thought briefly about what would happen if the car came off the rock while she was inside—well—it would be a nice funeral. Willing such thoughts aside, she stepped into the cold, water and immediately went to her armpits. She thought about trying to reach the front passenger-side door but another step and the water would be over her head, making it impossible to kick herself up and unlatch the front door. It was the rear passenger door or nothing.

She could barely reach the latch but caught enough to lift it up. To her relief the car was old enough that the doors didn't automatically lock. The downward angle of the car caused the door to swing open of its own volition.

Here we go! She reached up and grabbed the seatbelt strap with her left hand and lunged for the door rest with her right, then pulled herself up. As she sought a toehold on the door frame she felt the car move again and heard metal screech. The car sloughed a little more to the right and listed more heavily toward the river.

As she pulled herself fully into the car, a dark object blocked her path. She saw movement; a tiny hand. It was a baby seat. She pulled a brightly colored baby blanket back to find a pudgy-cheeked, dark-headed infant staring up at her, smiling and cooing.

"Baby!" Sam shouted out the door. "Someone needs to take this car seat." The baby responded to her shout with a frown and a loud wail.

Sam heard a flurry of voices from the shore but couldn't understand over the noise of the rushing water. Suddenly a man's head, bald and bespectacled, appeared in the water below the open door. He was tall and thin and had taken a step further into the river than she had. Water was nearly to his neck. "Hand the baby to me," he shouted. He raised his long arms toward her.

Sam unbuckled the car seat. "Sorry Baby," she said to the crying infant as she wrestled the seat up and pivoted to hand it over to the stranger in the water. "You got it?" she shouted. The man nodded as he took a firm grip then turned to hand the baby seat off to someone behind him.

"I'm going for the driver!" Sam shouted. "Have them hold the car as steady as possible."

Moving swiftly but delicately so as to not disturb the car's precarious balance, Sam leaned forward and peered over the seat to assess the driver's situation. She was a pretty woman, medium build, with long, dark hair. A colorful scarf had slipped off her head, and now partially covered her neck. A nasty gash on her forehead spilled a rivulet of blood over her left eye, down the side of her nose and over her mouth. She appeared to be in danger of drowning in her own blood.

The intruding water was nearly to the woman's chest. Sam couldn't see her feet to tell if they were entangled in anything. She shouted at the woman. "Miss! Miss! Can you hear me?"

No response.

She felt the woman's neck and detected a pulse, albeit a weak one. Alive! Good! Now how to get her out of the car? With the car pointing downward, the minute she released the belt the unconscious woman would likely collapse forward, straight into the water. She had to think this out.

Again metal screeched as the current pushed the car. The water level inside rose. Sam heard voices shouting for her to get out. The people trying to keep the car from slipping into the river were losing the battle.

There was no way Sam could drag the woman over the top of the seat back and out the rear door. She found the passenger side door latch and pulled. To her relief, the water vortexing on the downstream side pulled the door open. She and the woman were going into the river where their chances of survival were much better than being trapped inside this car.

Sam scrambled over the top of the seat. Hopefully her buoyancy in the rising water on the passenger side would reduce the overall weight load and not upset the car's precarious balance. She positioned herself and put her right arm across to take the woman's weight when she released the belt. She found the belt latch and pushed it. The woman indeed slumped forward. Sam had to fight to keep her upright. Now to maneuver her to the door. She put her arms under the woman's armpits and pulled.

Thank God this old car had bench seats. If there had been a console, it would have been far more difficult to slide her to the passenger side. But taking the woman's weight meant Sam could no longer float. She had to plant her feet against the car's firewall, adding more weight to the front of the car. The the car shuddered and begin to move. They had only seconds.

Good. The woman was half-way out. Then for some reason, she stopped. Sam repositioned herself in the doorway, got a new grip, braced her feet against the doorframe and pulled. But the woman wouldn't budge.

The car was moving and people were shouting. She could feel the car's inexorable roll as the river pushed it further to the right and down. Water spilled over into the back seat. Men standing on the bank trying to hold the car shouted more urgently. But she would not abandon this woman.

Sam practically climbed over the woman, trying to determine what was holding her. She never saw what it was but could see that the right side of her slacks were pulled down practically to her thigh. Something had snagged her pant leg. Without hesitation Sam unzipped the woman's pants and slid them down as far down as she could. Then she again hooked her arms under the woman's armpits and gave a mighty push against the doorframe just as the car began a final roll. There was no stopping it now. The car slid down the side of the rock and fully into the water.

The woman was nearly out of the door, but her pants, slowly peeling away, inhibited their progress. The car submerged and moved with the current, dragging Sam and the woman with it. Sam took a deep breath as water closed over her head, reached forward and grasp the woman's underwear by the waistband and pushed harder against the door frame than she had ever pushed in her life. She felt the car turning in the strong current. If the passenger door closed—she couldn't think about that. All she could think about was pushing.

Sam's strength, and her air, were nearly gone when the woman suddenly pulled free. Sam grasped her blouse, pushed away from the car and kicked for the surface, struggling to keep her hold as the current tried to pull the woman away.

Sam's breath was gone. A dark tunnel seemed to close around her vision. She desperately fought off the instinct to open her mouth and try to breathe. Suddenly her head broke the surface and she gulped a huge, blessed breath of air. She kicked to stay afloat as she pulled the woman's head above the surface. Had she already drowned? Sam prayed she wasn't rescuing a dead person.

The current clawed at them, trying to snatch the woman out of Sam's grasp. She released her grip on the woman's blouse and flung her arm across her chest, then put her hip under the limp, body and began side-stroking toward shore. She looked and saw people running along the steep riverbank, trying to keep pace with her drift. They shouted and pointed downstream, but she could hear nothing of their words. She looked to where they were pointing and saw that the river was rapidly carrying them toward a couple of large rocks at the head of one of the dangerous rapids for which the Gauley River Gorge was famous. She gathered her waning strength, took a fresh grip across the woman's front and began kicking toward shore.

Exhaustion drained her. Each stroke was weaker and slower than the last. As she tried to gulp air, the river sometimes delivered water instead, leaving her choking and coughing, wasting what precious breath s. had left.

The water moved faster. She made it past the first rock but was about to smash into the second. *So close!* Only a dozen more strokes would put them on shore. But the rock would take her first.

Suddenly a man was in the water beside her. He took the woman in his grasp and shouted for Sam to let go. Something splashed into the water directly in front of her, the end whipped across her shoulder. A rope! She wrapped her hand around it twice and hung on as the man who had taken the woman from her sought a handhold just ahead. Then they were dragged through the water toward shore by people pulling on the rope.

Her feet bumped the face of the second rock as she swept past. Her legs were dragged downstream toward the whitewater. In her exhaustion she had but one thought, *Hold on, hold on!* Then she felt hands grasp her and lift her from the water. Only then did she let a wave of darkness and delirium take her.

ABOUT THE AUTHOR

Award-winning author, Steven Clark, is the former Publisher and Editor-in-Chief of a national trade newspaper for the Manufactured Housing industry and has written extensively for local and regional newspapers. After being raised in Utah, he spent most of his adult life in California, Texas and Tennessee. Steve and his wife, Lauri, now reside in a tiny town in a high mountain valley in central Utah. Mr. Clark's debut novel, *All The Pretty Dresses,* a mystery/thriller set in the mountains of West Virginia, was recently awarded a top ten finish in the international Critique My Novel book competition. He loves to hear from his fans and welcomes your email contacts at sjc@cut.net. He also invites you to visit his website at www.stevenjclark.com. You can like/follow him on Facebook and Linked-In, and can tweet him on Twitter @stevenjclark1.

Made in the USA
Charleston, SC
01 August 2015